# NO
# ROOM
# FOR
# ERROR

# NO ROOM FOR ERROR

## JULIE MOFFETT

**W🌐RLDWIDE®**

TORONTO • NEW YORK • LONDON
AMSTERDAM • PARIS • SYDNEY • HAMBURG
STOCKHOLM • ATHENS • TOKYO • MILAN
MADRID • WARSAW • BUDAPEST • AUCKLAND

Recycling programs
for this product may
not exist in your area,

No Room for Error

A Worldwide Mystery/March 2017

First published by Carina Press

ISBN-13: 978-0-373-28400-9

**Printed in U.S.A.**

To my brother, Brad, my sister, Sandy, and my mom, Donna. Without your support, this book wouldn't have been written! Love you guys!

# Acknowledgments

There comes a time in every author's life when things get hectic, deadlines loom too largely, and treading water turns to sinking under. I owe an immense debt of gratitude to my brother, Brad Moffett, my sister, Sandy Parks, my mom, Donna Moffett, and my stellar editor, Alissa Davis, for keeping me on track, encouraging me, extending the deadlines, and helping me cross the finish line on this one. Lexi and I are quite grateful for your support! I also want to give a shout-out to my nephew's girlfriend, Gina Ridolfo, who just happened to be in Papua New Guinea when I wrote this book and sent me the coolest gifts to keep me inspired. Thank you all!

# ONE

NEARLY FIVE HOURS into fighting off a multipronged and well-organized cyberattack, my back hurt, the muscles in my neck were knotted tight and my fingers were cramped and aching. Plus I had to go to the bathroom.

But the fate of the city's electric grid was at stake and I wasn't going to let it fall to a bunch of hacker thugs because I had to pee. Stopping was not an option. If I stopped, or took a break—even for two minutes—it was game over. That was unacceptable, so my bladder would just have to wait. Protecting the grid was critical to the city's overall security since so many other sectors depended on it to deliver essential services. No way would it fall.

Not on my watch.

Not ever.

I crossed my legs, considered my next move, and then took a series of steps to thwart the hackers.

I was having the time of my life.

My breath came in hitches as my fingers flew across the keyboard. The hackers were fast, clever and smart, but I was better.

*Gotcha!*

I laughed—okay, cackled—as the hackers encountered an unexpected layer of security I'd hidden. They had to stop to rethink their approach for a second or two, and that put me ahead. Just the way I liked it.

I'm Lexi Carmichael, and technology has been my life ever since I was old enough to reach a computer keyboard. Some kids carried around security blankets and stuffed animals to feel safe. When I was two years old, I had to know where the family laptop was at all times. Twenty-three years later, my computer is a lot fancier, but not much else has changed. I was exactly where I was supposed to be—in the heated throes of a virtual battle, fending off a full-frontal hack on my system while figuring out ways to make the crackers—hackers with malicious intent—who'd started it sorry they'd ever picked my system to hack.

I took advantage of the nano-pause to lift my hand from the keyboard for a quick stretch and flex. Jeez, my fingers ached.

I began running another complicated trace on one of the hackers, searching for a weakness and determining the best way to strike back. Cybersecurity wasn't only about protection. It was also about deception, exploiting the vulnerabilities of your opponent and strategizing effective counterattacks. A complex orchestration of data, numbers, code. My heart beat in time with my fingers as they tapped on the keyboard in perfect tempo with my brain.

"Five minutes," a voice called out. "That's all we've got left."

*Buffer, buffer, buffer.*

They were splitting up and campaigning against me on three fronts. I reversed my setup, pivoting to confuse them as my opponents threw everything they had at me in a last-ditch effort. They were close to breaking in. Damn, I hadn't expected it to be this hard.

*Focus. Hold the course.*

I did a quick check on one of my traces and realized I was close to nailing one of the hackers. Someone had gotten careless in the past few minutes. They were getting tired, too, and had stopped working as a team. I could exploit that.

I feinted an attack on one of my opponents' soft spots, a back-end administrative support device. As one of the hackers abandoned the attack to protect it, I struck at the careless opponent, tagging their position and causing a complete upheaval in the group dynamic as they scrambled to retreat and regroup.

"Time's up."

Blowing out a breath, I pushed back from the keyboard and leaned back in my chair, stretching my arms over my head. "Holy freaking crack. That was close."

Wally Harris, one of my high school interns at X-Corp—the Washington, DC-based cyberintelligence firm I worked for—bounded into the room, pushing his glasses up on his nose. "Close? Did you even break a sweat, Lexi? You freaking slayed us."

"*Slayed* is *not* the word I would use."

"You totally shut us down. I'd never seen half of those moves. You were prime, boss. Wow. I've never had sex before, but I think that was the closest I've ever come to an orgasm in the presence of a woman. No kidding. Those were five of the hottest hours of my life."

I winced, then held up a hand. "Jeez, Wally. TMI."

"Can't help it. The program was ace and you were a spectacular opponent." His voice squeaked with excitement. He shoved his fingers through his hair and the strands stood straight up. "What a blast. My brain is completely fried."

A teenage girl strolled into the room. Her brown hair

was in a ponytail like mine, and her eyes were lit up with excitement. "Holy cow, Lexi. That was amazing." Piper O'Neill, the second of my trio of interns, leaned over my chair and peered at my monitor. "I had no idea what you were doing half the time, but it kept me so busy I was mostly in retreat instead of attack, which I suppose was your plan all along."

"Of course that was her plan." That comment came from my third intern, Brandon Steppe, who was also Piper's boyfriend. He entered the room swinging his arms around, presumably to increase circulation. "Three against one and we went down in flames." He stood next to Piper, his hand on the back of her chair. "So, we really sucked, right, Lexi?"

I rolled my neck to ease the tension in my shoulders. "Actually, you guys have no idea how close you were to breaking in."

Piper perked up. "Really? How close were we?" She was the brightest and the most competitive of the group. A girl after my own geek heart.

"Too close. That unusual twist on the SQL injection was clever. Was that you, Piper? I thought I recognized your signature move in the code."

Her cheeks pinked in delight. "Yes. It was a bit unorthodox, but I thought it might take you off guard."

"It did. It was a good call. Don't hesitate to embrace the unexpected. While it was a good technique, I have a few suggestions to make it even more powerful." I leaned forward, glancing at my screen. "Okay, who was using the code name Yorick?"

Brandon raised a hand. "Yo. That would be me."

"Well, I nailed you at the end. You left yourself vulnerable after the last round of cross-site scripting."

He leaned against the wall, crossing his arms over his chest. I saw the defensive look in his eyes and posture and was sure I'd had that same look at some point in my past when receiving a critique. Good. That meant I'd made an impression. Whether he liked it or not, he'd remember this lesson.

"Sue me, I got tired," he said, frowning. "Five freaking hours."

I kept my voice neutral but firm. "You're lucky we capped it at that. I've been on hacks that lasted days. Luckily, I had help on those, unlike today where I operated alone. But you three were a team and should have better distributed the work to stave off fatigue. You each got way too compartmentalized. Not a good strategy. Teamwork, communication and coordination are all critical, whether you're hacking or protecting against a hack. Even when you're tired, you have to stay in sync."

"It was totally an eye-opening experience," Piper said, flexing her fingers. "Wow. What a fantastic way to spend a Saturday. The programming was totally brilliant."

A voice came from the doorway. "Good to know."

My boyfriend and said programmer strode in. Dressed in a short-sleeved white T-shirt and blue jeans with his dark hair loose and tucked behind his ears, Slash looked more like a sexy movie star than one of the most brilliant cyberwizards in the United States.

"I'm happy to report that all remains safe in the virtual town of Byteville," Slash said, smiling at me. He turned toward my interns. "However, there were several points in the game where you guys actually had the advantage but didn't capitalize on it." He lifted an eyebrow at me. "You do know how close your interns came to besting you on a few occasions?"

"I know. Don't rub it in."

"But it was three against one," Wally argued. "In the full scope of things, that's not really fair odds."

I shrugged, though it *was* sweet he was trying to defend me. "It is if you count my experience. Look, you guys didn't crack in, but you performed well. I'm proud of you."

Wally leaned back against a table, resting his hands on the tabletop. "All I can say is the whole setup was extraordinary. Seriously cool. Slash, how did you come up with it?"

"Design and redesign." Slash stood behind me, putting his hands on my shoulders and kneading the tight muscles in my neck. "I discovered several more flaws that need adjusting today, so I appreciate you all flying here to New York to help me test it out."

"Anytime, dude. This office, the equipment, the private plane… Man, it's a geek's wet dream."

I grimaced. "Wally, TMI. Again."

"Well, at least I understand why you left me for this guy." He jerked a thumb at Slash before swiping a bottle of water from the table and taking a long slug.

"I didn't leave you." I rolled my eyes. "That implies we were dating, which we definitely were not."

I'd met Wally at his high school, where I'd gone undercover on a case. I'd faced off against a ruthless international cybermercenary, but with the help of Wally, Piper and Brandon, we'd beat him. However, Wally had somehow got it in his head during the situation that he wanted to date me, which was a complete surprise, seeing as how I had never once been asked on a date for the entirety of my *actual* high school years. It was also totally inappropriate, which I'd made sure he understood on numerous occasions.

Wally smirked. "Sure, Lexi, if that's your story, I'll back you up."

Everyone laughed and even Slash's smile widened.

"So, what's next, guys?" Piper asked. "Can we do it again? Please?"

I understood exactly where she was coming from. After a little break, I would definitely be up for another round.

Slash shook his head. "Not today. I'll take everyone to dinner and then I'll have my driver take you to the airport to head home."

I glanced at him. "What about me?"

He took my hand, lifting it to his mouth and kissing it. "I have other plans for you."

All three of my interns gazed curiously at us. A kiss on a hand was hardly overt PDA, but the way Slash looked at me made my cheeks heat nonetheless.

"Great. I'm starving," Wally said, stretching. "But give me a minute to drain the vein."

Brandon snorted. "Yeah, I need to make my bladder gladder."

The two guys dissolved into laughter, high-fiving each other. It reminded me that despite their prowess at the keyboard, they were still teenage boys.

I covered my ears. "I'm going to pretend I didn't hear that."

"Neanderthals," Piper sniffed.

Slash held up a finger, pointing down the hallway. "Go use the facilities—all of you. You're coming off an adrenaline rush. If you don't eat soon, you'll get the shakes. I'll shut the simulation down and we'll go."

We strolled—okay, ran—down the hall.

"Last one done picks up the check," Wally shouted as we disappeared into our respective bathrooms.

# TWO

It was official. Slash had ruined me for any other pizza.

The gooey, loaded slices at Antonio's New York Pizza Pies were spectacular.

It had taken us exactly thirteen minutes and twenty-seven seconds to demolish four extra-large pizzas...except for one final delectable piece that sat in the pan looking as appealing as ever. Even though I'd already had five large pieces I eyed it, wondering if I should go for it.

Piper snatched it before I made up my mind. Sighing, I leaned back in the chair and picked up my wine, sipping it. Not only was the pizza incredible, I was enjoying the discussion about bypass protocols and zero-day exploits. For the first time in recent memory, I felt relaxed at a dinner that involved multiple people in an external social setting.

I peeked sideways at Slash and caught him smiling at me. I liked having him nearby. As if he could read my mind, he reached across the table, took my hand and threaded his fingers with mine. I smiled back, my hand and heart comfortable with him.

Piper stopped midsentence. "Oh, that is so sweet. You two are the cutest couple. You know, if you ever decide to have a family, I'll bet your kids would be the best hackers ever."

Suddenly every eye at the table was on our joined

hands and then me. My face heated from the attention, my comfortable feeling vaporizing. I tried to gently extract my hand from Slash's, but instead I jerked it, knocking over my wine. Showing an amazing reflex, Slash caught the glass one-handed as it started to topple off the table. I reached over to retrieve the glass from him and bumped his plate with a half-eaten piece of pizza directly onto his lap.

When he scooted his chair back in surprise, I snatched the plate and pizza off his lap and began trying to clean the tomato sauce off his jeans with a napkin.

"Oh, jeez." I scrubbed harder, then peered up at my interns, who were watching me with wide eyes. "I'm such a klutz. I trip over my own feet, bump into anything stationary, and knock things over with amazing consistency. Once, during a math test, I managed to flip my pencil all the way to the other side of the room while writing. You can't take me anywhere."

I'd now done a fantastic job of smearing the pizza sauce all the way across Slash's crotch. I dabbed the napkin in water and rubbed at it some more, hoping to remove the residue before a stain set in. After a minute I looked up from his lap. Slash was watching me intently. It suddenly occurred to me that people might be getting the wrong idea about what was going on, seeing as how I was bent over Slash's lap rubbing with vigorous abandon.

Another look around the restaurant indicated that pretty much everyone in the place was staring.

I jumped up and dropped the napkin on the table, my face flaming. "Ah, I'll just wait out there."

Piper ran out after me, watching as I pressed my back

against the rough brick wall outside the restaurant. People streamed by and I took deep breaths.

"I'm *so* sorry, Lexi," she said after a moment. "I didn't mean to embarrass you. It's just that you and Slash are so cute together the words just popped out of my mouth. I do that a lot—you know, say things without thinking. But you guys are so perfect for each other, I couldn't help myself."

I waved her off. "It's okay. I know you didn't mean to embarrass me. You didn't have to. I did a good job of doing that to myself."

She bit her lip. "Not to rub it in, but it was kind of funny when you knocked the pizza into his lap. That's a sneaky way to cop a feel. From my angle I couldn't tell exactly what you were doing to him, but the expression on his face…"

"Not helping, Piper."

She laughed. "The way you get all klutzy around Slash is adorable. You guys are so lucky to have each other."

This girl talk wasn't easing my embarrassment. I shoved my hands into my jean pockets. "Can we change the subject?"

"Of course."

Piper mostly chatted with herself until Slash, Wally and Brandon exited the restaurant. By that time I'd decided to pretend the entire incident had never happened. Thankfully everyone seemed on board with that plan. We stood around talking about safe topics like what to do in New York until Slash's driver arrived to pick up the teens and take them to the airport.

Piper gave me a big hug before getting into the car.

"Sorry again," she whispered in my ear. "See you at X-Corp next Tuesday after school, okay?"

"Okay. Forget about the restaurant. Thanks for coming and for helping us out with the simulation."

"No, thank *you*. I mean it. I'm so lucky you're my friend. In fact, I think you're the best friend I've ever had."

I smiled, more flattered than she knew. "Well, see you Tuesday, Piper."

I waved as the car pulled out of sight. Slash slid an arm around my waist, seemingly unconcerned about the restaurant fiasco—which was exactly one of the reasons we got along so well.

"So, what shall we do?" he said, pressing a kiss on my hair. "We have an hour and a half until the concert."

"Concert? What concert?" I was stuffed and my brain was exhausted. I had been hoping for a nap, but I didn't want to disappoint him.

"Pianist Hai Tsang. His music is exquisite. I think you'll enjoy it."

The last time Slash and I had listened to music together was at the opera. It had been a less than satisfying experience, especially when the lead soprano made fun of my small breasts and then attacked me for stealing Slash's affections. But I had nothing against the piano, and I was still on a mission to expand my horizons outside of the computer, so I agreed.

"Sounds good. Are we staying in New York tonight? Do you have an apartment here?"

He shifted his gaze away from me for just a moment. It probably would have been unnoticeable to someone who didn't know Slash well, but I'd made a point of studying his facial expressions to help me gauge his moods.

He took my elbow, steering me down the sidewalk. "*Si*, I have an apartment in New York, but I got us a room tonight at the Peninsula Hotel instead."

I stopped in my tracks. He wasn't going to show me his apartment? Why?

Slash took a step without me, then turned, lifting an eyebrow. "*Cara?*"

Uncertainty flooded through me. Slash was my boyfriend. I loved him. I'd slept with him and told him things I'd never told anyone else before. We'd been to hell and back together...and I had no clue where he lived.

"I'd really like to see your place, Slash. Either here or in DC." The words came out sounding way more anxious than I'd intended.

I might as well have said a group of Chinese cyber-terrorists had hacked into the White House mainframe. The expression on his face said it all—total shock.

"You want to see my...place?"

I tried to act cavalier, like I invited myself to guys' apartments all the time. "I've never been to any of your places before. I don't even know your address. I'm just curious."

"Oh, *cara*, you'd be sorely disappointed. They're nothing more than a space to sleep and shower. They aren't really homes. They lack warmth, like your place. Besides, the hotel is much nicer."

"But if there's a bed at your place, we could sleep there, right?"

There was a long pause as he studied me. "It isn't that I don't ever want to show you where I live. But the truth is, I've already got us a room at the Peninsula. Maybe another time?"

I swallowed my disappointment. "Sure, okay."

"It's important to you." He pressed his palm against my cheek. "Why?"

I searched for the right words. "Why shouldn't it be? You're my boyfriend and I don't even know where you live. You've never invited me. I understand there are security concerns and all, but…"

"But what?"

"Well, it seems logical to assume that if you're keeping your place a secret, there might be other things you're keeping from me."

He hooked a finger under my chin. "My apartments hide no secrets from you, and you know me better than anyone ever has."

This coming from the man—my boyfriend—who'd never brought me home *once* in the several months we'd been dating.

Still, perhaps foolishly, I forged ahead. "Maybe. But in many ways you're still a mystery to me, Slash. I don't want to invade your privacy. I just think seeing your place would bring me one step closer to understanding you better. That's all."

"I've nothing to hide from you."

"Perhaps. But that's different from wanting to share yourself with me." I sighed. "Look, I'm about as far away from an expert in relationships as a person can get, so I don't know if I'm explaining myself right. I'm not rushing you. I just want to put it on the table. When you're ready, you'll invite me. Okay?"

"Fine. Let's go, then."

I took the arm he offered. I'd made him uncomfortable, but I wasn't sure why. Even though I understood the value and necessity of boundaries—especially in our line of work—did that mean he would always remain so mysterious to me? Dating was far more complicated than I had ever anticipated.

"So, where is this Peninsula Hotel?" I asked.

"It's just a block from here. We can change there."

"Change?" I looked down at my jeans and green sweater. My hair was in a ponytail and my shirt had a smear of tomato sauce on it. I didn't want to look, but I assumed his jeans still bore the evidence of my clumsiness. "I didn't know a pianist was on the agenda. I didn't bring a change of clothes."

"It's okay. I got you something to wear."

"You did?"

"I did." He tucked my arm tighter inside his. "Come on. I'll show you."

As we started to walk, I noticed a black sedan trailing us. I tilted my head toward the car. "The FBI?"

He nodded. Slash was considered so integral to national security that he had his own special detail 24/7, much like the Secret Service agents that protected the President. It was weird, but I was getting used to it.

I stepped over the curb, tapping on the sedan window. It rolled down slowly. I leaned in and saw two guys in the front seat. The agent in the passenger seat was drinking coffee from a to-go cup.

"Hey, guys," I said. "How's it going?"

The agent with the coffee lifted his cup in greeting. "Good evening, Miss Carmichael. How are you liking New York?"

"I like it, which is strange because it's way too many people for me. I just wanted to tell you to try the pizza at Antonio's. It's down that alley over there. It's amazing. Best. Pizza. Ever."

"Thanks, we'll keep it in mind. Where are you guys going?"

"To the Peninsula Hotel to change clothes. Then we're going to a piano concert."

The two agents looked like they were having a silent conversation. Then, the driver spoke. "You guys want a lift?"

Slash leaned down next to me, peering into the car. "It's okay. We'll take a cab."

"You sure?" The driver turned down the radio. "We don't mind. It'll give us something to do."

Slash considered and then shrugged. "If you wish. We'll be out in front of the hotel at seven forty-five."

It was a quick walk to the hotel after that. The doorman let us in without even asking who we were. Slash led me to the elevator and pushed the button for the seventh floor. We arrived at Room 707 and he pressed a card to the door unit, pushing it open for me.

I walked in and looked around. It was a suite with a sitting area and a spectacular view of the city in the fading dusk.

I stood by the window, looking down at the busy streets. "New York. The city that never sleeps. Nice view."

"I like the view, too." I glanced over at him. He wasn't looking out the window, but at me. "Come here."

I walked toward Slash, who was leaning against the bedroom doorjamb. He drew me into the room. On the bed lay a knee-length blue velvet dress. A pair of blue shoes with a medium heel were next to the bed. A tuxedo lay on the bed next to the dress.

Slash picked up the dress and handed it to me. "So, what do you think?"

"Wow." I ran my fingers across the soft material. "It's beautiful. You clearly have better taste in clothes than I do. I hope it fits."

"Hold it up against yourself."

I did and Slash walked around me, nodding. "It's perfect. The color and cut. The size looks right. You'll be stunning."

"I'm encouraged by your confidence in my ability to transform so thoroughly in an hour and a half."

He laughed, taking the dress from me and pulling me into his arms. "I'm planning on it taking less time than that. We've time for a shower, if you're game." He nuzzled my neck.

"Depends. What's the game?"

He leaned back to look at me, his eyes narrowing. "Best use of soap in a shower."

The gauntlet was thrown. I quickly went through a mental list of what I could do with a bar of soap and then nodded confidently. "You're on. I've got some pretty good ideas. You're going to lose, you know."

He pulled off his coat, tossing it onto the bed. The earlier tension between us faded. "I assure you, this will be a win-win situation."

# THREE

FORTY MINUTES LATER we were both clean and thoroughly satisfied. We had declared ourselves dual winners in our little shower game, although secretly I thought he'd won in terms of creativity. Either way, I'd never be able to look at a bar of soap in the same way again.

We took turns laughing and blow-drying our hair while completely naked. At some point we left the bathroom. However, instead of getting dressed, we ended up making out on the couch, then in a chair. One thing led to another, which meant we left ourselves with only ten actual minutes to get ready.

Totally worth it.

I brushed my teeth with a spare toothbrush the hotel had provided while Slash shaved. Afterward I slipped into my dress. It was a perfect fit. The shoes fit just right, too. I borrowed his brush and combed my hair until it shone.

I stared at my reflection in the mirror. "I don't have any makeup, Slash." My face was pale, but my hazel eyes were bright and surprisingly happy.

He came up behind me, putting his hands on my shoulders. "You don't need any. I was right. You look stunning."

"You're just saying that so you get some more nooky later."

He brushed my hair aside and kissed the side of my

neck. "Guilty as charged. But I mean what I said. You're beautiful."

I stared at my reflection and didn't see anything special. "I'm not sure how, but you make me feel that way."

"Good."

I turned around in his arms. He hadn't fastened his bow tie and it dangled on one side. "So, what do you like about him?"

He blinked. "Him?"

"Hai Tsang. What's it about his music that you like?"

"Ah, Tsang." He scooted me to the side and gazed into the mirror as he fastened his tie. "Well, his interpretation of the music is spiritual, for lack of a better word."

"In what way?"

"In the way he plays. He uses the music to appeal to both the intellect and emotion, engaging both on a masterful level. His creative techniques permit him to rise above the challenges of interpreting the complex demands of the music."

"Sounds interesting."

"It is. I think you'll like it."

He gave my bottom a pat and steered me to the bedroom. I picked up my gray coat and started to put it on, when he held up a hand. "Wait. I forgot."

He walked over to the closet and opened it, pulling out a long, wool coat. He strode over to me and slid it over my arms and onto my shoulders. "Perfect."

Slash steered me toward the mirror, standing behind me with his hands on my shoulders as I examined my reflection. "You bought me a coat, too?"

"*Si.* Do you like it?"

"It's white."

"And that's bad?"

Did he know me at all? "It's only a matter of time before I spill something on it."

He laughed while pulling on his own coat and fastening the buttons. "That's what dry cleaners are for." He held out a hand. "Come on."

I stood where I was. "Slash, why are you buying me all these things?"

He paused, his gaze steady on mine. "What else would I spend my money on?"

"Oh, I don't know. Computer equipment, travel, important technical and cyber research, more concert tickets." Well, that's what I'd spend mine on, minus the concert tickets, but adding in a boatload of chocolate éclairs.

He closed the gap between us, brushing his fingers across my cheek. "None of those things are worth anything if I'm alone, okay?"

It didn't escape my notice that Slash knew me far better than I knew him. Or if I were being technically correct, Slash knew me far better than he *allowed* me to know him. There was a significant difference and I wasn't sure if there was anything I could do about it if he refused to open up to me.

We just stared at each other until I nodded. He took my hand and we headed out. The spring night was cool, but I felt warm and safe in the big city, holding hands with my mysterious boyfriend.

The FBI sedan was waiting for us in front of the hotel. The two guys waved as we approached. Slash opened the door for me, so I climbed in. It smelled like pizza.

I fastened my seat belt, leaning forward. A pizza box sat on the center console. "Hey, you guys took my advice."

"Guilty as charged. We made a small detour for dinner. You planted the seed." He licked his lips. "And you were right. Best damn pizza ever."

Slash smiled as he came around the other side and got in.

"So," the driver asked him. "Where to?"

"Carnegie Hall."

I lifted an eyebrow. "*The* Carnegie Hall?"

Slash leaned back against the seat and took my hand. It was almost as if he couldn't bear for us not to be touching. I suspected our earlier conversation about his apartments had made him uncharacteristically concerned. That hadn't been my intention, but I had no idea how to fix things on that front. Especially since I wasn't sure it was something I could fix anyway. "*Si.* Have you ever been?"

"No." I shook my head. "But I've read about it in books."

"You'll like it. Trust me."

"I do or I wouldn't be here."

We pulled up to the front of the building and Slash and I exited the car. The agent in the passenger seat got out as well. He stretched and I saw his shoulder holster under his jacket.

"So, what time is the concert finished?" he asked Slash.

"Eleven."

"We'll be waiting."

The sedan drove away, leaving the other agent at the curb.

I stared at him. "What are you going to do?"

The agent grinned. "Be invisible." He walked into the building.

I pushed away all thoughts of FBI surveillance and marveled at the sight of Carnegie Hall. It was lit up like a jewel against the night sky. Slash held my hand as we walked into the building. We left our coats at the coat check and wandered into a dazzling hall where dozens of impeccably dressed people milled about chatting.

I stared in amazement at the glittering lights. "It's magnificent, Slash."

"We're in the Isaac Stern Auditorium. There are five levels of seating." He pointed to the left side of the stage. "We're on the next level up—the balcony seats near the stage."

"Looks like we'll have a great view."

When we got to our seats, he sat next to me, resting his arm on the seat behind me. "Here." He handed me the program for the performance.

I opened it and read about Hai Tsang and his upbringing in China. Apparently he'd been abandoned at birth because of a cleft foot, which was considered a sign of evil in the small village where he'd been born. Hai had been taken to an orphanage in Beijing, where he'd taken to playing on the piano in the children's recreation room. He had an extraordinary natural talent and had caught the ear of famous Chinese pianist Wen Leung, who took the boy under his wing and began to train him. By six years of age, Hai had performed his first formal recital at the Beijing Concert Hall.

The lights dimmed and Hai Tsang entered the stage. I estimated him to be maybe sixty years old, quite handsome and distinguished. He pushed back his tuxedo tail with a flourish and sat at the piano. He started playing and music filled the hall. After a few minutes I looked at Slash. He had closed his eyes as if to better concentrate on every note.

I'd never seen Slash look like this before—open, blissful and genuinely peaceful. Something in Tsang's music had transformed him. I'd caught him, my mysterious man, in a truly unguarded moment. This was the part of him I wanted to know, the part he seemed intent on keeping from me.

I returned my attention to Tsang. He played softly at first, before rising to powerful passion that nearly took my breath away. He'd made me a fan by the end of the first arrangement. Rhythm was something I lacked in spades, so I appreciated his subtle flow. This time when I looked at Slash, his eyes were open and his concentration was on the man behind the piano.

The first half of the recital seemed to pass quickly. During intermission, Slash brought me champagne and we sipped it while watching patrons wander about the hall.

Once Tsang resumed playing, I lost track of time. The music seemed to merge into one masterful performance conducted with fluid transition and breathtaking finesse. As the last note faded through the hall, I was the first to leap to my feet clapping.

Tsang glanced up to the balcony and seemed to smile right at me before leaving the piano to bow before the audience. The crowd, myself included, cheered wildly. Someone threw a couple of bouquets of flowers onto the stage, which Tsang picked up with another appreciative bow.

Slash stood to leave. This time I slipped my hand into his as we filed out.

"So, your evaluation of the entire performance, *cara*?" He put an arm around my shoulders.

"Well, I think it was clear that I loved it." I took a minute to collect my thoughts. "It surprised me because I didn't expect to connect so completely with piano music, but I did. It's hard for me to say how good Tsang is in comparison to other pianists, because this is the first formal piano concert I've ever attended. However, given that caveat, my opinion is that his technique seemed flawless and the patterns within the music flowed effortlessly. But…"

I paused and Slash leaned forward. "But what?"

"Even though I have an untrained ear, it seems to me that the mathematical cadence and rhythm of his music seemed to transcend the ordinary."

"How?"

I sensed that my answer was important to Slash, but I couldn't figure out why. I fiddled with a button on my new coat. "Well, I'm not certain. I once read that scientists believe there is an actual physiological relationship between the brain and music. Some experts believe that children who are exposed to music at a very early age can actually forge an emotional, biological and physiological connection to music. The notes, cadence and patterns become imprinted on the brain. The findings don't mean that every child exposed to music at an early age will become a virtuoso, but it does seem to suggest that many of these children are able to go on to not only produce extraordinary music, but *understand* it. I think Tsang may have been one of those children. He has somehow transcended the understanding of the notes and melody to make an emotional connection to music, perhaps as a result of the trauma and abandonment he suffered at an early age. Even more important, he can translate and share that experience with the average person who may not have that kind of access or understanding of the music. Someone like me."

I paused, expecting Slash to respond, but he didn't. Instead a thoughtful expression crossed his face. I had no idea if I'd said something that made sense or if he thought I was a babbling idiot.

We stepped outside and I spotted the FBI sedan. We walked to the car and Slash opened the back door for me. I climbed in and Slash shut the door before going around the back to get in.

I noticed there was only the driver, so I leaned forward. "Hey, is your partner still inside?"

"He's off duty."

"Off duty? But I thought—"

I stopped. It was a different voice. A different guy. And the car didn't smell like pizza.

Before I could say anything else Slash yanked opened the door, leaned inside and grabbed a fistful of my coat.

"Get out," he shouted, yanking me hard.

# FOUR

THE DRIVER GUNNED the engine. Slash fell backward out of the car and my coat ripped with a sickening sound.

"Slash!" I yelled as the sedan shot forward and screeched around a corner. The door swung shut. A glass divider automatically rose between the front and the backseat. I pounded on it and tugged on the door handle, but to no avail. I was locked inside.

"Stop," I shouted at the driver as if he would magically listen to me. "Stop the car right now."

"You'd better buckle in," the driver advised.

I leaned forward, staring at his face in the rearview mirror. I'd never seen him before. He looked to be in his mid-twenties, dark hair, Asian. The driver swerved around a corner and my face slammed against the window, nearly breaking my nose. I fumbled for the seat belt, glancing behind us. To my astonishment, Slash was right behind us on a motorcycle.

The driver saw him, too, because he floored it, the engine whining with the sudden speed. It was late, but this was the city that never sleeps, so there were plenty of people and cars. We swerved across lanes, cutting off drivers and flying over sidewalks. I was barely able to fasten my seat belt while I was sliding and bumping all over the backseat.

I heard the wail of a police car and moments later

Slash flanked us on the left. The driver rolled down his window and a gun emerged.

"Slash!" I screamed, pounding the window with my fists. "Gun!"

I had no idea if he could hear me. All his focus was on the road and the driver.

The driver fired just as Slash swerved. The first bullet ricocheted off the aluminum rim of the front tire. Another shot hit the composite frame.

The gunfire didn't deter Slash. He continued to flank us and didn't draw his own weapon, even though I knew he had one. Was it because he had to keep all his focus on handling the motorcycle, or because he was worried about hitting the driver and crashing the car? Either way, I hoped he had a plan in mind, because right now I was coming up blank.

The driver yanked the wheel hard to the left, trying to use the car as a weapon and sideswipe Slash. Slash anticipated it and maneuvered away just in time to avoid the front bumper.

My driver stopped shooting. Apparently he needed both hands on the wheel. He pulled hard to the right and the car rocketed down an alley, almost losing Slash. Slash accelerated as he leaned into the turn, nearly scraping his knee on the asphalt, and followed us in.

The alley narrowed until the side doors screeched as they grated against the brick, sending sparks flying. We left the narrow alley and shot out into a parking lot. The driver suddenly slammed on the brakes. The tires squealed and the smell of burning rubber flooded the car.

Dead end.

The car skidded sideways until it hit a brick wall. The right rear passenger side took the force of the hit. Metal crunched as we came to a bone-jarring stop. If not for the seatbelt I would have pitched headfirst into the window.

My driver threw open the door, jumping out. The chatter of gunfire sounded. I unbuckled my seatbelt and threw myself to the floor. A car window shattered, so I put my hands over my head. I heard a lot of shouting and the scream of a police siren, but I had no idea what was going on.

After another volley of shots, there was silence. I lifted my head just as the door lock clicked and the door was yanked open.

*"Cara!"*

Slash stood there in his rumpled tuxedo.

I'd never seen a more welcome sight. "Slash!" He was alive and seemingly unhurt. Thank God.

Relief crossed his face. Stretching out a hand, he helped me out of the car. *"Madre di Dio.* Are you okay?"

"I'm fine." I looked down at my ruined coat. "I told you it was a mistake to buy me anything white."

He tugged me into him, kissing the top of my head. "Now I can breathe."

I looked over his shoulder. Police filled the alleyway and stood over a guy, presumably the driver, who lay on the asphalt. "Is he dead?"

*"Si."*

"Who is he? What happened? Where's your FBI detail?"

Slash held me tighter. "I don't know yet."

"Why did he want to kidnap me? Or us?"

"I'm going to find out."

Slash rubbed his hands up and down my arms. He was shaking. Adjacent to the car, the motorcycle lay on its side, bullet holes evident.

"Whose motorcycle is that?"

"I have no idea. Some poor bystander. He abdicated without a word when I showed him my gun."

"I bet. So, does this mean we are spending the rest of the night at the police station?"

Slash sighed. "I'm afraid so."

# FIVE

It was nearly four o'clock in the morning before we got back to the hotel. A new FBI team accompanied us to the hotel and cleared our room before they let us in. They weren't nearly as friendly as the other guys and left without saying a word. I shrugged out of the remains of my coat, trying to hang it up in the closet. It kept sliding off the hanger.

"Don't bother." Slash took off his jacket. "It's a complete loss. I'll get you a new one."

I laid it over the back of a chair and unzipped my dress. "So, at this point we know exactly squat about what happened."

Slash and I had been questioned separately by both the police and the FBI and had only been allowed to reunite just prior to our departure from the police station.

"All I know is the man had no identification on him. The sedan was stolen. They are running his fingerprints now and an autopsy is scheduled in two days."

"How did they know the FBI was going to pick us up from the concert?"

Slash pushed his fingers through his hair. "They had to be observing us. Perhaps they saw them drop us off, so they extrapolated they would pick us up."

"Why were they watching us in the first place? Who are they?"

"I don't know."

I put a hand on his arm. "Why didn't you get in the car, Slash? How did you know?"

He sighed. "I should have noticed at once, but I was too preoccupied thinking about Tsang and what you'd said. The car was different. I realized it when I was going around. I should have checked out the driver before I let you in. This is on me."

"What happened to the real FBI tail?"

"Apparently the driver was circling the hotel when he encountered a so-called accident." He removed his cuff links and set them on the dresser. "He was delayed just long enough to miss us."

"That's convenient."

"Nothing convenient about it. Smells more like a well-laid plan to me."

I sat on a corner of the bed. "What about the agent who was inside with us?"

"He was right behind me when we exited the hall. He didn't want to shoot at the car for fear of hitting you. The agents are under investigation as well."

"They didn't have anything to do with this, Slash."

"We'll see." His voice was hard. I had a feeling most of his anger was directed at himself.

We got undressed without talking. I missed the laughter and intimacy of the pre-concert time, but the kidnapping attempt had taken its toll. Since I didn't have any pajamas, not even my usual oversize T-shirt, I slid naked into the bed, pulling the covers to my chin. Slash joined me shortly and pulled me into his arms. I rested my head on his bare chest, listening to the steady thump of his heart.

He stroked my hair for a long time, but said nothing.

Then, without warning, he squeezed me so tightly that for a moment I couldn't breathe.

"I don't want you to leave me, *cara*." There was something fierce in his tone.

I was so astonished I didn't know how to answer. I wanted to ask him why he would think that and what was the matter—maybe that's what he was waiting for—but while I pondered what to say and *how* to say it, I heard him breathing deeply. He'd fallen asleep and I'd missed my opportunity.

I kept my head on his chest, listening to his heart and breathing. Soon my own eyes grew heavy and I began to slip into slumber as well. My last thought before I fell asleep was that in many ways Slash remained as much a mystery to me now as on the day I'd first met him.

# SIX

It was business as usual after we woke up, making me think I had imagined Slash's odd mood right before we'd fallen asleep. After breakfast in our suite, we took a quick flight home to DC.

Slash was quiet as we drove to my small apartment in Jessup, Maryland, in his SUV, so I started when he abruptly spoke.

"I'm arranging private security for you."

"What?"

"When I'm not with you, you'll have private security. I'm not risking you again."

"Don't you think this is overkill? This isn't Broodryk. He's dead."

Johannes Broodryk was a psychotic cybermercenary with whom I'd matched wits for the past few months. Slash and I, along with some help from the Navy SEALs, had finally brought him down, but not before he'd taken a toll on my friends and me with his sick games.

Slash didn't answer.

I tried again. "Look, this could have been just a robbery attempt or something. I don't think I need extra security. You don't even know that this is about me."

"It doesn't matter what it was about. He almost got away with you. I'm not taking that risk again. Just humor me a while."

"How long is 'a while'?"

"Until I figure out who this guy is."

His jaw was clenched tight. I thought about protesting but I knew he'd put the security on me even if I didn't agree.

"Fine. If it gives you peace of mind."

"It does. There will be an FBI agent following you until my guy is in place. The FBI agreed to do this as a courtesy for me. So, don't be surprised to see someone as soon as we get home."

"Great. They'll probably be bored to death with my schedule."

"As long as you're safe. Be aware of your surroundings, okay? I've got some things to do, but I'll be back tonight, if that's okay with you."

"Sure."

When we got to my apartment, a black sedan was already idling in the parking lot.

"That was fast," I observed. "By the way, doesn't the FBI like any color other than black for cars?"

A small smile touched his lips. "Black is a largely indistinguishable color and it's good for night surveillance."

He walked me to my door and checked inside my apartment to make sure it was clear. As we stood in my doorway, he gave me a lingering kiss goodbye.

"Be back soon. Stay safe."

I went to the window and watched him climb into the SUV. As he left, another dark sedan followed him. The agent in my parking lot turned off the engine and sat staring up at me. I waved and after a moment he waved back.

I let the curtain fall into place with a sigh. Whether

I liked it or not, I'd started to get a firsthand glimpse of the fishbowl Slash lived in on a daily basis. And I didn't like it one bit.

"Lexi?"

My thoughts were so preoccupied with car chases, gunfire and explosions I didn't even hear my name being called. This wasn't good because as the Director of Information Technology for X-Corp, I should have been thinking about firewalls, penetration testing and system back doors.

"Lexi!"

This time the voice was insistent enough it broke me from my thoughts. Unfortunately, it also startled me so when I looked up, I almost knocked the coffee mug off my desk.

"Lexi, are you alright?"

I caught the mug before it toppled. "Hey, Basia. Sorry, I was just thinking. It's really great to have you back in the office."

She'd been in Hollywood for the past several months taking my place—thank God—on a reality television show about geeks. The series had wrapped a couple of days ago. I had spent three days back in California two weeks ago filming my part in the finale. While I'd been glad to see my geeky contestant friends again, I couldn't wait to hightail it home to my computers and real job.

She slid into my visitor chair. "I'm getting reacquainted with things. It's been so long since I've been here, I've forgotten where everything is."

"I really missed you."

"I missed you, too. Believe it or not, I even missed this place. I've got a boatload of work to catch up on."

"I bet."

Basia was X-Corp's resident translator and had been helping Finn reach out to international markets with our cyberintelligence business before she'd gotten sidetracked into the work in Hollywood on my behalf.

"So, what's new?"

I took a sip of my coffee and tried not to look too worried. "Well, I was in New York this weekend and survived either a kidnapping or robbery attempt."

*"What?"*

Okay, maybe I could have eased into that better.

I quickly brought her up to speed. Not surprisingly, her first thought was of Johannes Broodryk.

Her face paled. "It has to be related to Broodryk."

Broodryk had badly injured her boyfriend, Xavier Zimmerman. Xavier's twin brother and one of my closest friends, Elvis, had been kidnapped and nearly killed by Broodryk before we shut him down. I felt sick just remembering it. We were all recovering the best we could.

"Look, Basia, don't worry. I sincerely don't think it's Broodryk. But Slash will look at every angle."

"He's investigating?"

"Of course, along with the NYPD and the FBI. I've now got private security on me 24/7. That's how seriously Slash is taking it."

That solicited a small smile from her. "Well, that makes me feel better."

"In my opinion, Slash is overreacting, but better safe than sorry."

"Absolutely."

I leaned back in my chair, making a conscious effort to change the subject. "So, how are you and Xavier doing?"

Basia had been dating Xavier for a couple of months on an exclusive basis, and it seemed to be getting more and more serious between them. It was a big step for a free spirit like her.

"Good. His recovery is going really well." Her expression softened. "It's been quite a process, but he's been a good sport. He goes to every physical therapy session and he listens to me when I boss him around and tell him to take it easy."

"He probably loves that. He's lucky to have you."

"Yes, he is." She ran her fingers through her dark bob. "And I'm lucky to have him. In fact, we're damn lucky we have a second chance at things."

"I'm happy for you guys. Really." I truly was. I'd never imagined in my wildest dreams—not that I had many of those—that she would date, let alone get serious, with a geek like Xavier.

"Speaking of happy, why were you and Slash in New York in the first place?" she asked.

"We were working on a training program at his office in New York." I picked up a pencil and fiddled with it. "It's a cyberwarfare frontier simulation. It's wicked prime."

"You guys are such geeks." She rolled her eyes, then smiled at me. "You do know that most people go to the city for a swanky dinner and a Broadway show?"

"Well, there was pizza and a concert, both of which were awesome, before the unfortunate ending to the evening."

She sighed. "You know, I think you and Slash may be far more compatible than I ever suspected."

Before I could respond, my phone rang. I picked it up. "Lexi Carmichael."

"Hey, Lexi, it's Finn."

Finn was the co-owner of X-Corp and a onetime romantic interest before I'd realized I couldn't handle the complicated nuances of dating my boss.

I peered at the number he'd dialed me from. "You're calling me from a conference room?"

"Yes, can you join me for a client meeting?"

"Of course. I'll be right there."

Basia raised an eyebrow, clearly curious to know where I was headed. Before I could mouth the words *client meeting*, Finn spoke again.

"See if you can find Basia and bring her with you, would you?"

"What a coincidence. She happens to be sitting right here."

"Excellent. See you both in a few."

I hung up and unplugged my laptop, sliding it under my arm. "Our presence is requested in Conference Room 3 for a client meeting."

"Mine, too?"

"Apparently so."

Basia rose from the chair, smoothing down her skirt. "And so the day begins."

# SEVEN

WE MADE A quick stop in the company kitchen for coffee, then headed to the conference room. I entered the room and almost tripped when I saw Elvis and Xavier sitting at the table along with a couple of guys in suits I didn't know.

I kept my eyes on Elvis as I slid into a vacant chair next to Finn. I hadn't seen him for several days, but I was encouraged to see the bruises on his face were healing and his color was healthier. I knew he was still recovering from internal injuries, but he was alive and alert, and I couldn't have been more thankful for that.

He gave me a smile but said nothing. Basia sat at the other end of the table and she looked as surprised as I was to see the twins.

Finn spread out his hands. "Lexi, Basia, thanks for joining us. Let me introduce our guests. You already know Elvis and Xavier, of course. Joining them are Mr. Andrew Garrington and Mr. Fox Cutler, Chief Operating Officer and Director of Research at ComQuest Technologies in Baltimore."

There was no handshaking, just a nodding of heads around the table as acknowledgment. Elvis and Xavier both worked for ComQuest, so my curiosity was piqued as to why they were all here at X-Corp. When I looked at Basia she lifted an eyebrow as if to say she had no idea what was going on either.

Finn shuffled some papers and then folded his hands on top of them. "I'm going to turn this meeting over to Andrew to bring Lexi and Basia up to speed."

Andrew looked between Basia and me. "Elvis and Xavier have been working on a special project for Com-Quest for the past year. It's an extremely confidential project and one that has great promise, not only for our company, but worldwide."

Interesting. I observed Elvis again, but he was watching his boss speak.

"The project involves a proprietary invention they've created. We're ready to begin a limited trial manufacturing of the device."

Fascinating, but I still couldn't figure out why they had come to us. X-Corp was a cyberintelligence and cybersecurity company, not a manufacturer. But I kept my mouth shut and let Andrew get to the point.

"The problem is that, due to the extreme circumstances of the past few months, neither Elvis nor Xavier feel they are physically capable of making the trip to Indonesia, where the device will be manufactured."

Finn jotted something on a piece of paper. "Okay, but if the prototype is finished, why would either of the Zimmermans have to accompany the device to the manufacturers anyway?"

Elvis answered. "The nature of the prototype makes it highly likely adjustments will have to be made on-site, especially since properties can change during a manufacturing process. If even the slightest calculation is wrong, it will have to be adjusted on the spot or it won't work. This is very precise and delicate work. Nothing like it has ever been created before."

"Understood." Finn stopped taking notes and rested

his pen against the paper. "So, gentlemen, how exactly can X-Corp help ComQuest in this matter?"

Andrew leaned back and crossed his arms against his chest. "This prototype is of exceptional value to Com-Quest. We've invested a lot of money into the project and have fended off multiple attempts at industrial espionage and theft. When I say this is a revolutionary product, I assure you I am understating the matter at hand. The information we are about to share is extremely privileged."

My gaze locked onto Elvis's and I saw a spark in his eyes. Pride. Satisfaction. Intense excitement. My heart kicked up a notch.

Finn looked at Basia, then me. "I assure you all of us at X-Corp will keep any information spoken here completely confidential."

We nodded, and Andrew continued, apparently reassured by Finn's promise. "ComQuest needs someone to accompany the prototype to Indonesia—someone who can fill in for Xavier and Elvis and adjust the device as necessary during the process. A person who could understand and act upon the instructions that either Elvis or Xavier would provide remotely. A person they trust implicitly that could do the work."

Every head in the room turned to me.

"Of course, I'll help." I addressed Finn. "If X-Corp is on board with it, of course."

Finn picked up his pen, poised to write. "What would Lexi be required to do?"

Fox, the research director, said, "We'd need her to meet this week with Xavier and Elvis to learn about the prototype and any potential issues that could arise as a result of the manufacturing process. We're scheduled to be in Indonesia early next week."

Finn turned his head to me. "Lexi, can you clear your plate?"

"Absolutely. But first I want to know more about this device. What is it?"

Elvis exchanged a glance with his boss, Andrew, who gave a small nod. "It's pretty prime, Lexi. We've created a special microplate that can be bonded to microchips to allow computers to operate at faster speeds and still remain cool."

"Wow. How much faster?"

He leaned forward, his hands flat on the table. The flexible cast on his arm peeked out from beneath the sleeve of his shirt. "Faster than anything operating today. We're talking totally game-changing. Imagine quantum computers becoming a hundred times faster than they are now. A thousand times faster. That's the level we're talking about."

It took me a minute to absorb that concept. Game-changing would be an understatement. The technical world would explode.

"Extraordinary," I breathed. I wanted to add *impossible*, but I knew better than anyone that with the Zimmermans, nothing was impossible.

"It will be our first manufacturing test," Elvis explained. "The prototype must be able to withstand the process or we're back to square one."

"How long will you need to bring Lexi up to speed on the prototype?" Finn asked Elvis.

"Just a week should do it. She's good and won't require much more than an overview. She'll need to work with Xavier and me in the lab outside Baltimore for some demonstrations. Once the manufacturing process is under way in Indonesia, we can assist her remotely.

But we need a hands-on observer, and I can't think of anyone I trust more than Lexi."

I was touched by his faith in my abilities. "Thanks, Elvis. I'd be honored to do it."

"What about me?" Basia asked. "How can I help the effort?"

"We need a translator," Fox explained. "I understand from Xavier that you speak French."

She nodded. "I do."

"Good. Our project manager at the factory, Antoine Paquet, speaks decent English, but French is his first language. Given a project of this importance, every nuance matters. You'll need to come to the lab, too, to learn the vocabulary and precise definitions."

"Understood."

"Most important, we want to keep this as tightly contained as possible. The fact that we are able to have all of you from the same company under a binding nondisclosure agreement makes it much more secure for us." He regarded both twins. "They trust you implicitly, and by extension, so do we."

"Excellent." Finn stood. "Ladies and gentlemen, it looks like we have a deal."

It looked like my life had just gotten a lot more interesting.

# EIGHT

I SPENT THE rest of the day at X-Corp clearing my desk for the next two weeks before heading home to my small apartment. A dark blue Toyota followed me. Stan, my new guard, had showed his identification and explained that, thanks to Slash, he'd be keeping a close eye on me. I thanked him and pretended it wasn't going to be weird having someone watching my every move.

I had several chores to do once I got home. I'd just changed into sweats and an old T-shirt and gathered all my laundry when my cell phone rang.

I picked it up. "Hello."

"Hey, Lexi, it's Elvis. Any chance you can swing by the house? There's something I want to give you."

Sounded interesting. I quickly changed back into a pair of jeans and a T-shirt and drove over to the Zimmermans' house with Stan trailing behind.

I pulled into the driveway next to Xavier's blue pickup truck while Stan parked across the street. I rang the bell and Elvis answered, ushering me inside. He moved a lot slower and stiffer due to his injuries, but I was encouraged by the fact he was determined not to let the pain slow him down.

"Wait here for a sec, okay?"

He'd disappeared toward his bedroom, so I wandered into the room affectionately known as the Command Room. The twins had transformed their dining room and living room into a high-tech operating center. Long tables crowded with a mixture of desktops and laptops ringed the room. The Linux cluster of thirty-four computers they used to break encryption and do serious number crunching took up an entire corner of the room. Cables, wires and routers snaked across the floor and draped over tables. The room was freezing and I shivered, looking for the blanket they always left for me. I found it slung over one of the chairs, so I grabbed it and wrapped it around my shoulders.

Xavier sat at his laptop in a short-sleeved T-shirt, typing away, oblivious to the cold. He swiveled his chair toward me. "Hey, Lexi. How are you?"

"Good. Even better now that we'll be working together."

"It's going to be prime." He made some calculations on a sheet of paper and then stuck the pencil behind his ear. "Can't wait to show you."

"I can't wait to see." I wanted to ask him more about it, but due to the highly secret nature of their work, we couldn't speak about it outside secure areas.

Elvis walked into the room and motioned me to follow him. "To the kitchen."

I followed him and we stood at the counter while he took something out of his pocket. "Close your eyes and hold out your hand."

"Why?"

"It's a surprise."

I did as instructed and felt Elvis press something hard and cool in the palm of my hand and then close my fingers around it.

"Open your eyes."

I looked down at my hand. He'd given me a necklace. I pulled it up by a gold chain and inspected it. On closer examination I saw it wasn't a pendant, but a delicate locket with an exquisite jade and gold inlay cover. It looked oriental.

I carefully slid my fingernail into the crack and popped it open. Inside was a grainy photo of a woman standing next a young girl in pigtails who looked about eight or nine years old.

I raised my eyes to meet Elvis's. "Who are they?"

"The older woman is my grandmother. She was a nurse during World War II. She was sent to Japan during the Pacific campaign and saved that little girl's life. The girl's mother gave her this locket as a way to thank her. My grandmother put their picture inside to remember. Now, I'm giving it to you for saving my life in Somalia. I guess you could say that I'm paying it forward."

My breath caught in my throat. "Elvis, it's beautiful." I closed my fingers around it and handed it back at him. "But I can't possibly take this. It's a precious heirloom. You need to save it and give it to your wife, daughters or granddaughters someday. It should stay in the family."

He took my hand and closed it around the locket. "You *are* family, Lexi. Please take it. It would mean a lot to my mom, my grandmother and especially to me."

A lump formed in my throat as I put my arms around him, hugging him tightly. "In that case, I'd be honored to have it."

We wandered out into the living room. I stayed a bit longer, drinking a beer with the twins before leaving to finish my laundry. Elvis was walking me to my car when a silver car pulled into the driveway, blocking my exit.

Elvis looked at the car and said, "Uh-oh."

"Uh-oh, what?" I looked between Elvis and the car. "Whose car is that?"

Before he could answer, the car door opened and a girl with a platinum pixie haircut, dressed in a tight pink and white sweater, black tights and knee-high boots, walked up to us.

Elvis didn't even have a chance to open his mouth before she spoke. "Elvis, baby. What's up?"

"Hey, Ginger. You're an hour early."

"I couldn't wait to see you." She planted a long, wet one on his lips. Then she looked over at me. "Who's that?"

Elvis cleared his throat and turned to me. "Lexi, this is Ginger. Ginger, meet Lexi."

Ginger examined me, her eyes narrowing. "She's your sister or something?"

"No, she's a…friend. Ah, Ginger, why don't you move your car behind Xavier's and go in the house for a minute. Xavier is inside. I'll just say goodbye to Lexi and then I'll be in, okay?"

Ginger looked between Elvis and me and then shrugged. "Fine. Can I have a beer?"

"Help yourself."

Ginger moved her car and then disappeared into the house.

"Well, this is awkward," Elvis said, studying the driveway.

"You think?" I hesitated and then decided to just ask. Elvis was my best friend after all. "So, what happened with Bonnie?"

Bonnie was the headmistress of an exclusive high school for technologically gifted students where he and I had been on a case together—the same school I'd obtained all three of my totally excellent interns. Elvis and Bonnie had started dating shortly after that case and, until now, I thought they were still together.

"Nothing happened with Bonnie. We're still seeing each other."

"Does she know about Ginger?"

"Bonnie and I aren't exclusive."

His words surprised me, as did the matter-of-fact tone he used. I wondered if his torture at the hands of Broodryk had anything to do with this sudden change of heart.

"Are you okay, Elvis? This doesn't sound like you." Elvis had always been almost as averse to social interaction as I was. Why in the world would he choose to juggle more than one relationship at a time?

"Why not?" He tilted his head, studying me. "I'm finally sticking my feet in the dating waters."

His love life wasn't any of my business, but this felt like an important milestone in our friendship evolution, so I decided to speak my mind.

"The serial dating thing… It's just not you."

He shrugged. "I'm fully aware of what I'm doing."

Maybe he was, but I wasn't sure. Either way, there wasn't much I could do about it. "Elvis?"

"Hmm?"

"See you tomorrow at the lab."

"Okay. Looking forward to it." He started to turn away.

I didn't want to leave things on an uncomfortable note, so I racked my brain for the words I needed. "Wait, Elvis. There's one more thing. Good luck with Bonnie and Ginger and whomever else you intend to date.

I mean it. No matter what happens, you know you can count on me as a friend, right?"

I wasn't positive, but I thought I saw a flash of relief cross his face. "Thanks, Lexi. You don't know how much that means to me."

I touched the locket at my throat. "Yes, I do. Because that's the kind of friends we are."

# NINE

SLASH HAD TEXTED me earlier in the day to let me know that he would pick me up at eight o'clock for dinner. While I waited for him, I did a little gaming. I expected to see Elvis playing as usual, but he didn't show. I did end up playing a couple of games with Xavier, but I didn't ask where Elvis was. Xavier didn't offer the information either, so I remained clueless.

Exactly at eight, Slash arrived, kissed me on the cheek and stepped inside while I got my coat.

"How are you so punctual all the time?" I asked. "You make it seem effortless."

"I assure you, it's not effortless. I have at least three technological items reminding me at any given time."

"Still, punctuality is a nice quality to have. I like that about you."

"Good. I'm storing that in my Ways to Impress You file."

"You have a Ways to Impress Me file?"

"Of course."

He stepped back into my kitchen to get out of my way while I set the alarm. We left my apartment and stepped out into the cool night, heading toward the parking lot. Slash slid an arm around me as we approached his SUV.

"Any preference as to where we go tonight?" he asked.

"How about Japanese food? It's on me. I'm celebrating a new adventure."

He reached down and took my hand in his as we walked to his car. "Japanese sounds perfect. You'll tell me all about this new adventure?"

"As much as I'm able. I won't be able to provide specific details, but I can say a trip to Indonesia is in my future."

He opened the SUV door and I climbed in. "Indonesia? Why does that make me extremely nervous?"

"Nothing to be nervous about other than the flying part. Not my favorite activity. But I'll manage."

He came around to the driver's side and slid in. "I can't wait to hear all about it. When do you leave and how long will you be gone?"

"I leave next Monday. We're scheduled to be there for five days. Basia is coming, too, as a translator backup. There's a chance it may go a bit longer, but I doubt it. Either what I'm going for works or it doesn't. I don't believe it will take more than five days to figure it out if they got it right."

"You have me totally intrigued."

I looked over his shoulder and saw the lights turn on from a dark sedan parked alongside the nearby curb.

"Where's my guy in the blue Toyota?"

"He's off duty when I'm around."

That was a relief. One fewer set of eyes on me.

I rattled off the address for the restaurant. Slash plugged the address into his GPS and put the SUV in Reverse.

"So, what in cybersecurity has you traveling to Indonesia?"

"Well, it's not exactly cybersecurity. I'm doing a favor

for ComQuest—Elvis and Xavier's company—by traveling in their place to Indonesia. Neither of them felt up to world traveling, given their recent injuries. Anyway, the twins invented something totally prime and I'm going to personally oversee the manufacturing process for them."

He slid a sideways look at me. I'd piqued his curiosity. "Any chance you can spill about the invention?"

"I totally wish I could tell you more, but you know how that goes."

"Unfortunately, I do."

That was one of the nice things about our relationship. We both worked in industries where secrets were the norm. We understood that about each other. However, it made me wonder if his choice of occupation had turned him into an extremely private person or whether his personality had lent itself to that kind of career. I wondered about that myself. I wasn't sure, but here we were—two private people trying to figure out the best way to get to know each other on a deeper level. It wouldn't be easy, but I was confident it'd be worth it…if we could ever figure it out.

I leaned back in the seat. "I'll be spending the rest of the week at ComQuest's headquarters in Baltimore working with Elvis and Xavier. I need to learn as much as I can before Basia and I head out bright and early Monday morning."

I could tell Slash really, really wanted to know more, but he didn't ask, understanding why I couldn't answer.

When we got to the restaurant, the maître d' led us to a booth. I ordered a glass of plum wine and Slash got a Japanese beer. Slash convinced me to try sushi. Although I'd never had it before and the thought of eating

anything raw scared me, I figured I could live danger-
ously at least this once.

After he ordered, I took a sip of my wine and leaned
back in the chair. "So, any new developments on the
Asian guy who tried to take off with me?"

Slash leaned forward. "We have a name. Jian Lum.
We ran his fingerprints and they pulled up a visa docu-
ment. Lum was twenty-nine years old and from Tianjin,
China. He came to the US on a graduate student visa
six months ago to study computer science at Columbia
University in New York City."

"Computer science? Now that is interesting."

"I did a little investigating and it turns out Lum has
quite an interesting past."

"How interesting?"

"Very interesting." Slash took a drink of his beer.
"Seems he may be connected to the Red Guest."

I set my wineglass down. "Whoa. Seriously?"

The Red Guest was a group of dedicated hackers and
a significant threat to US national security. They'd been
relentless in their attacks on the NSA, the Department of
Defense and defense contractors' networks. They were
a clever, talented and well-funded group, almost certainly supported by the Chinese government. I worked
peripherally on the defense against some of their attacks
while at the NSA. I knew their style and methods. They
were very, very good.

"*Si.* Turns out that Lum just happens to be the nephew
of Jiang Shi, who just happens to be the leader of Red
Guest."

"That's a pretty significant coincidence."

"My thoughts exactly."

"But what would they want with me?"

"Maybe the new project you're working on for the Zimmermans?"

"I don't see how. The attack happened *before* I even knew about the job."

"Maybe Elvis or Xavier told someone they were considering you for it?"

I ran my finger along the stem of the wineglass. "Maybe, but it still doesn't make sense. Why snatch me before I know anything?"

Slash sighed. "I don't know."

The waiter brought our food. It hadn't taken long to fix it, I guess because they didn't have to cook it. Slash left to use the restroom, so I stared at my plate, trying to figure out what was on it. I didn't recognize anything but the rice. A couple of small dishes with sauces had been arranged next to our plates. I took another sip of my wine and tried not to be nervous. Sushi was considered popular and trendy. Millions of people ate this stuff every day around the world, and, as far as I knew, no one had ever died. I assumed it was safe for me to eat, especially because I was hungry.

The waiter hadn't given us any forks. Slash was a pro, but I'd never used chopsticks before. Still, I was pretty sure I could figure it out. How hard could it be? Two wooden sticks. It shouldn't be too difficult to calculate the size and thickness of each piece of food in relation to how much pressure I needed to use to squeeze the chopsticks together and bring them successfully to my mouth.

I chose a large wrapped up rice ball with something squished in the middle. The piece was too big, so I shook it to get it down to a more manageable size. Unfortunately, a large chunk fell off and landed with a plop in the small dish with what looked like green toothpaste.

Embarrassed, I scooped it out with my fingers, taking most of the paste with me. I couldn't figure out how to get it off the rice and my fingers, so I just popped the whole thing in my mouth. After a furtive peek to make sure no one was watching, I licked my fingers, too.

I swallowed. A nanosecond later, the heat rose in my throat, burning my nostrils. I gasped in horror. Grabbing my water goblet, I gulped the entire glass. I then chugged my wine. My throat still burned as if it were on fire and my eyes watered madly. I wasn't even sure I was breathing.

I reached across the table and grabbed Slash's beer. I glugged it, then drank his water, too, tears streaming down my face.

Slash returned to the table and looked at me in alarm. "*Cara?* What's the matter?"

Before I could say anything, our waiter, who was carrying two beers to another table, saw me gasping for breath. He abruptly stopped, set the beers down on the ledge between the booths, and peered over Slash's shoulder.

"Is everything okay, ma'am?"

I shook my head, pointed to my throat and the two empty water glasses. Slash's eyes did a quick sweep of the table, including my plate, and understanding dawned in his eyes. He grabbed a water pitcher and glass from the waiter's table near the bar and began pouring me another glass.

I stood to move toward Slash when my elbow knocked the two beers from the ledge behind me, tipping them down the back of a male customer sitting at the booth adjoining ours. The man yelped and jumped up. Given his rather wide girth, the tablecloth had become wound between his legs. Everything on his table—the food, the glasses, chopsticks and even a candle—went flying, landing on the floor with a huge crash.

I stood there in disbelief, wishing a hole would open up in the floor and swallow me. Tears streamed down my cheeks and my throat and nose were still on fire. Slash pressed a water glass into my hand and I drank it and then closed my eyes.

"This would be the exact moment that teleportation would come in handy," I said.

For the longest moment of my life, the entire restaurant was silent. Then the man whose dinner and clothes I'd just ruined collapsed with laughter. Our waiter, who had been joined by other waiters and the manager, joined him. Soon everyone—including the customers—were howling as if they'd just witnessed the funniest thing. Maybe they had, but it was a joke at my expense.

I profusely apologized to the man and offered to buy his dinner and foot his dry cleaning bill while the busboys cleaned up the mess. He waved me off with a hearty laugh and a punch on the arm.

"Forget it, my dear." He swiped at the back of his neck with a napkin. "I'm fine."

I would have helped him mop up but I remembered what happened last time I got busy with a napkin.

"Are you sure?" I tried again.

"I'm sure." He dumped a few soggy napkins on the table. "I swear I haven't laughed this hard in a long time. Accidents happen. It's no problem."

Wanting to show my appreciation, I punched him back. "Well, uh, thanks for being such a good sport. I appreciate your kindness."

After he left, I sunk into our booth and covered my

face. "Someone shoot me. Please, I beg you. Can we go now?" I asked Slash.

Slash slid into his seat across from me. When I peeked out between my fingers I could see the amusement twinkling in his eyes. "Tried the wasabi, did you?"

I sniffled. "Holy hot sauce. What the heck was that?"

"A complimentary sauce to be used with the food in moderation, especially if you've never tried it before."

I poured myself some more water, but the burn was subsiding at last. I wiped the back of my hand across my eyes. "I tried using the chopsticks, but I didn't apply enough pressure to hold the food tightly. It dropped into the toothpaste stuff. I couldn't get it out with the chopsticks, so I used my fingers. Ate the whole thing, sauce attached, in one big bite. Epic fail."

He chuckled. "It will pass."

"I'm not sure about that. There is a distinct possibility I have permanently burned my taste buds for all of eternity."

"Not at all." He signaled the waiter to bring him another beer. "We're just getting warmed up. Come on, try a couple of other things."

"Are you serious? You want to stay after that?"

Slash picked up his chopsticks, his grin widening. "Certainly. You've single-handedly provided the most excitement this restaurant has ever seen. Customers will be talking about it for months. It will likely bring them more business than actual advertising."

I eyed him with mistrust. "Are you just saying that to make me feel better?"

"No." He sipped his beer. "I speak the truth. Now, come on, let's see how the sushi really tastes."

"I didn't think sushi could kill you, but now I'm not so sure."

"It won't kill you. Trust me. Besides, I'll be here to perform CPR as needed."

I was pretty sure he was laughing behind his glass. He was enjoying this, the cad.

"Fine." I picked up my chopsticks. "Are you going to show me how to properly use these?"

"Of course. This time, however, I suggest you go light on the paste."

# TEN

SLASH WAS RIGHT. I didn't die. I even ate most of what was on my plate. Once I figured out how to use the chopsticks and use the proper amount of soy sauce on the food, I discovered I actually liked sushi. I was going to forgo the wasabi, possibly for the rest of my life, but I would definitely eat sushi again. I only had to go to the bathroom six times after all the liquid I'd drank, but I enjoyed the meal and, as always, the company.

After I paid for dinner and Slash left a *really* big tip, we headed back to my place. I shrugged out of my coat and then peered over my shoulder at Slash. He stood in the doorway and didn't remove his jacket.

I stared at him with a question in my eyes. "Aren't you staying?"

"Do you want me to?"

I considered the question, what it meant and where it was coming from. He'd been staying at my place on and off for the past several weeks and he knew he didn't need to ask. There was something else going on.

"Yes, I want you to stay, Slash. Have I given you any reason to doubt that?"

He abruptly crossed the room, his hands cupping my face. His mouth covered mine with surprising possessiveness, his hands sliding down my arms and moving around to my lower back, pulling me against him.

"No, you haven't," he murmured against my lips. "It's just… I don't want to go. I'm tired of being alone."

"You're not alone. Slash? What's wrong?" I sensed there was a deeper current to this conversation I wasn't getting. But unless he'd talk to me, I didn't know what I could do to help him.

I closed my eyes and waited. His body was warm against mine. My hands touched his shoulders, biceps, and finally rested on his hips. I realized his body—all of the hard angles, planes and curves—was completely familiar to me now. I could feel the steady beat of his heart against my mine. He was struggling with something, but what was it? Would he tell me?

He lifted his mouth from mine and brushed his lips over my hair. "Never mind. Let's go to bed."

"If that's what you want." I tried not to sound disappointed. When he was ready, he'd talk to me. I hoped.

"*You're* what I want," he said softly. He kept an arm around me as we walked toward the bedroom and added, "You're what I've always wanted."

SLASH AND I were up early to head to the ComQuest lab on the outskirts of Baltimore. We planned to leave at seven o'clock. I'd told him where I had to report and he insisted on driving me. It was out of his way, but he wouldn't let me argue, so I agreed.

After a quick breakfast of scrambled eggs and coffee, I grabbed my purse. "Give me a sec to find the address to ComQuest's laboratory."

"I don't need it. I already know where it's located."

"You do?"

"I do. Everyone knows where the fabs are."

I frowned, puzzled. "Fabs? Don't you mean labs?"

"No, I mean fabs. That's what they call the factories that create microchips. There are only five fabs in the United States. ComQuest has one of them. Those in the business know the location of each of the fabs, much like NASA geeks know the location of the launch sites."

"How come you know all this?"

"I may have a peripheral interest."

"Really? Are you going to tell me more about it?"

"Ah, *cara*, I adore you. You might be the only woman in the world whose eyes light up at the thought of hearing about my interest in a fab. Of course I'll tell you. I don't know what you'll be doing there, but I suspect you're going to have to brush up on your microchip knowledge."

"I know," I grumbled. "Microchip and circuit design is *not* my strength." I was more than a tiny bit embarrassed he'd uncovered a major weakness in my tech knowledge.

He grinned. "Looks like you're going to get a crash lesson."

"Yep." Truthfully, I was looking forward to it. While my first love was hacking and cybersecurity, the thought of branching out and learning something new about technology excited me, especially if my teachers would be the Zimmerman twins. He must have sensed my excitement, because when we stopped at a red light, he leaned over and gave me a lingering kiss.

"Don't get so caught up in circuits and chips you forget about me."

"Don't worry," I assured him. "I'm sure the microchip won't kiss nearly as well as you."

He smiled as we pulled up to a guardhouse. Slash rolled down the window and I passed my driver's license to the security guard. The guard checked an electronic tablet for my name and then nodded.

"Lexi Carmichael. You're on the list, so you're cleared to enter. I'm sorry, but your driver won't be able to accompany you through the gate. He's not cleared. I'll call a ride for you, so please exit the vehicle and wait here."

I slid my purse over my shoulder. "Looks like I have to dismiss my driver. Thanks for the ride. I'll catch a ride home with Elvis and Xavier. Can I leave my bag in your car?"

"Of course. I'll bring it over later. Hopefully we can catch dinner together."

"Great."

After Slash disappeared from view, I turned and looked at the ComQuest building. It was impressive— sleek, modern and rectangular, shaped in a long *L* with specially curved windows. There was a large parking lot. Even though it was only about seven-thirty in the morning, the lot was full.

"Lot of early risers," I observed to the guard.

"The building is in operation 24/7."

Before I could comment further, another security guard in a golf cart pulled up to the guardhouse. He hopped out, took my driver's license from the other guard and examined it and then me closely. They were not messing around with security.

"Okay, Ms. Carmichael," he said, handing me my license. "Get in. You're expected."

"Thanks." I climbed into the golf cart and we sped toward an entrance. He pulled up to the front and indicated I should get out.

"Go straight through this door. They're inside waiting for you." I wasn't sure who *they* were, but I went through a revolving glass door and was immediately greeted by three more armed security guards. All three had their hands hovering over their weapons.

Jeez.

"Can I help you?" one of them asked me in a gruff voice.

Hadn't the guard who just brought me already called ahead? "Um, I'm Lexi Carmichael. I have an appointment. I'm here to meet with Elvis and Xavier Zimmerman."

The big one in front motioned me to follow him to a receptionist, who sat behind a big marble desk.

"This is Lexi Carmichael," the guard explained. "She's here to see the Zimmermans."

The receptionist smiled at me. "Driver's license, please."

What the heck? I dug out my license, again. I wasn't sure what the point of this check, recheck, and reconfirmation was, but it was bordering on paranoia. Apparently no one was taking any chances that I had somehow morphed from Lexi Carmichael into someone else in the time it had taken me to go through the revolving door.

The receptionist studied my license, then me. He, like all of the guards, was dressed in a security uniform with a badge and patch that read Markmaster Security. Apparently he was satisfied with what he saw, because he scanned my license and printed out a badge with the picture of my driver's license on it.

"We'll hold your license here until you check out," he said.

Since I could hardly argue with him about it, I nodded.

"Please follow me this way, ma'am," one of the

smaller guards said. We walked through a lovely lobby with a soft rust-colored carpet, two glass coffee tables and plush armchairs. Modern art decorated the walls. It looked more like a hotel lobby than the waiting area for a microchip factory...fab.

I followed him down a hallway where we had to stop twice and pass through two glass doors with a biometric reader. It didn't escape my notice that there were security cameras mounted along the wall at every door, tracking our progress. After the second door, the hallway veered sharply to the left and we started down what appeared to be a corridor of offices. At the third door to the right, the guard abruptly stopped. He rapped three times and I heard a familiar voice. "Come in."

The guard opened the door and motioned for me to enter, closing the door behind me. Elvis sat behind a desk, typing something on a laptop.

"Hey, Lexi. Give me a sec, okay?" he said without looking up.

"Okay."

While he was busy I took a moment to look around. I counted seven laptops, including the one he was typing on, and two desktop machines, all of which were whirring away at some kind of calculations. I took a couple of steps around the office, looking at the various displays on the monitors.

Elvis finished typing and stood. "Glad you're here. Let's get started."

That's what I liked best about the twins. No extraneous chitchat or niceties. No offer of coffee or water. No asking me how I was feeling or what I thought about the weather. Just straight to the important stuff, which was exactly the way I liked it.

"Sure. Where's Xavier?"

"He's already suited up and in the lab."

"You mean the fab."

"No, I mean the lab. There is a lab in the fab, just in case you were wondering."

"I was wondering. Thanks for clearing that up."

He handed me a badge and told me to hang it around my neck. He already had one, but I hadn't seen it because he'd tucked it beneath his T-shirt. He pulled it out as we went back into the corridor and continued along the hallway.

"Can I say I'm surprised you've been working on this invention?" I said as Elvis stopped at yet another glass door and pressed his palm print to it after typing in a code. "I never knew you had an interest in microchip design."

"I didn't really. Not at first, anyway. And it's not a microchip design. Not exactly. We were misleading in the meeting with Finn. It's a security issue. Our invention is actually a solution to keep the chip from overheating. Xavier and I hit a brick wall about a year ago with some computations we were doing during our programming. We couldn't get the speed we needed with the chips that are out there. The problem was we needed the speed, but the higher we stacked the microchips, the hotter they got. We had a series of meltdowns until it brought our work to a screeching halt. I wanted to tell you about it, but proprietary information and all that."

"I understand. So just like that, you started studying microchip design?"

"More or less. It was pretty simple. If we wanted to continue our work, we had to solve this problem. So we turned our attention to doing just that. ComQuest supported the effort from the beginning, mostly because they already had a few scientists working on a similar project here at the fab, but they hadn't made much progress. Still, it was useful to have them available to us because they've been a great source of information as Xavier and I determined the best way to address the problem."

"Lucky you. So, what did you guys come up with?"

He smiled. "Can't wait to show you."

I couldn't wait to see it either. Whatever it was going to be, I had a feeling it was going to be spectacular because that's how the twins rolled when it came to technology.

Elvis stopped at another door and this time keyed in a code and endured an eye scan. When the door opened, he ushered me through first.

We walked into a lab that held unusual-looking microscopes and more computers. Through a glass window, I saw someone dressed head to foot in what looked like a white biohazard suit with a little plastic visor where the eyes were located.

"Wave to Xavier," Elvis said.

I held up a hand and waved. Xavier waved back.

Elvis motioned to two more white suits hanging along one wall. "We have to suit up and go in. You okay with that?"

"Of course."

Elvis handed me one of the suits and showed me how to climb in. He helped me zip up and added the gloves before suiting up himself.

I waddled toward him feeling like something between a storm trooper and a giant marshmallow.

"This is seriously ace," I said.

He reached to the side of my head and pushed something. "Can you hear me?"

"Yes." He sounded like he was speaking through a tunnel. I figured it was similar to how astronauts must feel talking to each other.

"Man, this is great, Elvis. I can't wait to see what you've done."

He grinned and gave me a thumbs-up with his glove.

He punched in a code on a keypad near a door and when it slid open, we walked into a chilly room. The suits were insulated in part to protect us from the cold temperatures required to keep the chips cool.

We walked over to Xavier, who was looking at something through a totally funky microscope. I'd never seen anything like it.

Xavier gave me a high five. "Hey, Lexi. Welcome to our humble abode."

I looked around at all of the million-dollar equipment. "Wow. Hardly humble."

"Yeah, I guess not."

"Is it ready?" Elvis asked his brother.

Xavier stepped aside. "All yours."

"Take a look at it, Lexi," Elvis said, taking my elbow and guiding me to the microscope. "Tell me what you see."

"What am I looking for?"

"You'll know when you see it."

It wasn't easy pressing my eye against the plastic to get a look, but after a couple of tries a microchip came into view.

I studied it for a moment. "Okay, what are those odd lines? I thought you guys had developed a pad to attach to the microchip to keep it from overheating. But it looks like you did something right on the microchip."

"We didn't create a pad, Lexi. We just said that in the meeting because the fewer people who know what's truly here, the better. Only a few people at the very top of ComQuest and a couple of their scientists actually know what we've created."

"Okay, you win. The anticipation is killing me. Tell me already."

I felt a weird tingle in my stomach, as if I were teetering on the edge of a vast cliff, waiting to hear something so amazing, so earth-shattering, I would fall and never be the same.

"Brace yourself."

"Braced. Look, if you guys didn't create a pad to cool the chip, what *did* you create?"

Although there was no way anyone could have heard us, Elvis lowered his voice and spoke in a hushed tone.

"Microfluid."

# ELEVEN

WHATEVER I'D BEEN expecting to hear, that wasn't it. I stared at him for a full minute as my brain processed and discarded all possible theories until I came up empty.

"Huh?" I finally said. "What's that?"

Elvis tapped the microscope. "Microfluid is tiny liquid droplets that will cool the chip. It's designed to flow through specially carved mini-canals built right on top of the chip."

I had no idea what he was talking about. "How could that possibly work? How does it cool them? Water would just run through the canals and off the top chip if they were stacked."

"It won't if there are gaps."

"But there are no gaps between the capacitors on a microchip."

"There are if you stack the chips."

I still wasn't getting it. "How?"

"This way. Look again, Lexi." Xavier nudged me toward the microscope again. "Let me change the view."

He made some adjustments to the slide and I bent over the lenspiece again.

"See?"

This time I did. I lifted my head, looking at Elvis in wonder. "Wait—what? 3-D stacking? Okay, I totally didn't see that coming. But it makes sense and it's really, really clever."

Elvis shook his head. "No, not so clever. 3-D stacking is not the new part. It's been around for a year or two. The real revolution is adding the canals and the micro-fluid to the stack. Our unique cooling system will work only in this format."

I looked again into the microscope. "How on earth did you come up with this configuration? I see where you're going with this. Once the capacitors are stacked in 3-D, the gaps will occur naturally. But the cooling fluid is totally out there. How did you reduce the liquid to such a microscopic level that it will run through the canals?"

"Very carefully."

"I bet. And how did you stop the fluid from interfer-ing with the electrical connectivity of the chips? How and where is the heat transferred? How much liquid do you have to add, and at what intervals, to keep the chips from burning up?"

A million more questions threatened to tumble out, but Elvis grinned and held up a hand.

"All in good time, Lexi. I promise you. First, what you need to know is that the system works. It really works. The most important test for us is whether it can be mass-produced. Otherwise, we have a great design without practical application."

I took another look at the chip and then looked be-tween Elvis and Xavier. "I don't know what to say, you guys. You do realize the significance of this invention *if* the production works on a mass scale—the impact it could have on the entire world, right?"

"Yes." Elvis spoke simply, without arrogance or supe-riority, to which he and Xavier were certainly entitled.

Elvis leaned back against the counter, and a flash of pain crossed his face. I pulled out stools for both him and Xavier, motioning for them to sit. Neither of them had fully recovered yet. They sat as best they could in the biohazard suits.

I preferred to pace. I could barely process the magnitude of what they'd done for the future of technology and how close we had all come to losing one half of that genius.

Xavier pushed a few glass slides over and leaned forward. "We had a lot of setbacks, but we finally got it to work. We've been testing the stack using our cooling system and have, at this time, reached maximum capacity."

"So, just how fast is maximum capacity?" I pulled out a stool and joined them at the counter. "How fast were you able to make the microprocessor work?"

Elvis smiled behind his visor. "Hold on to your hat, Lexi. We improved the speed by two thousand times the maximum they are capable of doing now."

*"What?"* My breathing sounded harsh in my helmet. "Two thousand times? Are you freaking serious? Elvis, that's just impossible. No way."

"Way."

It boggled my mind. The twins had somehow invented the impossible. Beyond impossible. The implications were staggering. The tech world was about to be presented with the most important discovery since the microchip in 1958, and I had a front-row seat.

# TWELVE

Slash texted me he was running late and wouldn't be by my place until after ten o'clock. That worked well for me because it gave me plenty of time to unwind. I had just started a new level in "Hollow Realm" and was seriously kicking butt against an army of ogres. Neither Elvis nor Xavier were online, but Wally had recently gotten hooked, so he and I were merging our armies to face the threat.

It was past ten when I heard the door open and the beep of my alarm signaling someone had entered. I sent a message to Wally that I was signing off.

I stretched and walked into the foyer. Slash had set down his briefcase but hadn't removed his coat. He just stood there staring out my window, not saying anything.

"Hey," I said quietly.

He came to me, ran a hand lightly over my hair and leaned in for a kiss. "Hey, back. How was your day?"

"Amazing. Incredible. One for the history books."

He raised an eyebrow. "That good?"

"That good."

"I suppose you can't tell me a thing about it."

It was harder than I expected to keep it from him, because he was one of the few people in the entire world who would totally understand and appreciate the importance of what the twins had invented. I wondered if he'd ever felt that way about his work and wanting to talk it over with me.

"I'm sorry. I wish. I really wish I could, Slash."

"I know."

The fact that he knew, and understood, didn't ease my desire to tell him.

He tucked a strand of hair behind my ear. "Go pack an overnight bag."

I hadn't seen that coming. "An overnight bag? I have to work tomorrow."

"I know. At the fab in Baltimore?"

"Yes."

"Then bring whatever you want to wear to work."

"Why?" I stepped back, regarded him thoughtfully. "Where are we going?"

His eyes met mine, held. "It's a surprise."

I stared at him for a beat more, then went to my bedroom and put some clothes, shoes and a toiletry kit into my backpack. My curiosity was on overdrive. I walked back to the living room where Slash was pacing. He always did that when he was nervous, which wasn't very often. My curiosity was turning into concern.

"Ready?" he asked me.

"Yes. When do I get to know where we are going?"

"When we get there. Come on."

Once we headed out, the FBI pulled in behind us. Slash took the interstate north toward Baltimore, but remained silent. I shifted in my seat, folding my hands on my lap and trying not to be anxious. I failed miserably.

Slash punched a button on the stereo and soft piano music filled the SUV.

I listened for a minute. "Tsang?"

"Did you guess or did you know?"

"A little of both. I haven't heard this piece before, but something in the rhythm seems familiar."

We listened for a few more minutes. As a song was ending, I turned in my seat to look at him.

"You're nervous."

He took his gaze off the road for a moment. "Why do you say that?"

"When I came out of the bedroom, you were pacing. You always do that when you're nervous. You're also drumming your fingers on the steering wheel."

"To the beat of the music."

"We're between songs."

He paused, listened to the silence, and then stopped drumming his fingers.

"Slash, where are we going?"

He took my hand, lifted it to his lips and pressed a warm kiss against my skin. "You'll see."

I sat back in my seat as a piano riff filled the air. If he insisted on being mysterious, there was nothing I could do about it.

I watched out the window, noting which exits he took. He was headed directly downtown toward the Inner Harbor, the nicest part of the city. We drove past the expensive restaurants and glittering lights of the city, until he drove up to a closed garage at the base of a high-rise. He rolled down the window and pressed his wallet to a metal stand. As the garage door opened, I observed the FBI tail pull over to the curb and park. Slash drove the SUV inside, parking it at a spot near the elevator. He hopped out and grabbed my bag.

"Come on," he said, taking my hand.

Our footsteps sounded loud against the concrete floor. There were a few cars in the garage, but otherwise it was eerily empty. We reached an elevator and Slash pushed the button. After a moment it dinged and we got on. Slash pushed his wallet against a pad on the elevator control panel and the elevator began to rise.

"Are you going to tell me where we are?"

"Soon."

When the elevator opened, we walked off onto a nicely carpeted hallway. Slash stopped in front of a door with a gold knocker. The door number was 1202. He withdrew his wallet and pulled out a key card. He slipped it into the opening and pulled it out quickly. The door blinked green and beeped. He opened the door and motioned for me to enter first.

I stepped into a dark room. Slash followed me in, reached over my shoulder and tapped out a code on an alarm system. He flicked on the light and I blinked in the sudden brightness. After my eyes adjusted, I saw we stood in a small foyer. Ahead of me was a living room and to the right, a kitchen. A hallway stretched into the darkness on my left.

I looked at Slash. "Is this your apartment?"

"One of three. I have one in New York and one in Italy."

Emotion swamped me, taking me off guard. Affection, surprise and love. I didn't understand why it was so hard for him to show me his apartment and open this part of his life to me, but I suspected there was far more significance to the gesture than met the eye.

I took a couple of steps forward on the hardwood floor. The living room had a magnificent row of floor-to-ceiling glass windows, void of window coverings of any kind. The lights of the city twinkled and glowed. I crossed the room and looked out the window.

"You have a nice view of the harbor."

"It reminds me of my home in Sperlonga. It's no co-incidence I'm within walking distance of Baltimore's Little Italy."

I turned away from the view and looked about the living room. He switched on the lamp and set my bag down. The room had a black leather couch, two side tables, one lamp and a black coffee table. That was it. No books or bookshelves, no rugs, no television and no stereo equipment. The walls were bare. No artwork or mirrors hung on the wall. Calling Slash a minimalist would be an understatement even for me.

"No television?" I asked.

He shook his head. "No time. Even if I did, I'd stream."

"What about football?"

"American or European?"

"I think that answered my question."

A smile touched his lips. "There's a sports bar on the corner. If I want a large screen, I go there." He held out a hand. "Come, *cara*. I'll show you the rest of the place."

I took it and he led me into the kitchen, which was modern with clean lines and stainless-steel appliances. There was an espresso machine and a bowl of red apples on the countertop. He opened the refrigerator. It was empty except for a dozen water bottles, one carton of milk, a half dozen eggs and a block of cheese wrapped in clear plastic.

"Wow," I said. "You've got even less food than me, which I thought was a near impossibility."

He grinned and, still holding my hand, drew me down the hallway. He stopped at the first room on the right, turning on the light. It was a home gym with a multifunction bench, weight rack, curl pad, T-bar row handle on a barbell and leg developer. A treadmill stood in the corner in front of a wall-to-floor mirror and next to a small refrigerator and water cooler. A stack of clean towels sat on top of the refrigerator and several discarded ones were in a basket on the floor in the corner.

"Well, at least I know how you keep in such good shape."

He grinned and turned off the light. We passed a bathroom and then stopped at another room. The door was closed and alarmed by a biometric keypad. He pressed a finger to it and it opened. I felt a blast of cold air and knew where I was before he turned on the light.

His office. A large desk stood in the middle of the room flanked by a variety of printers and scanners. There were three desktop computers and two laptops, all linked, on the desk alone. The soft whir of the computer equipment was like a siren's call to me.

I couldn't keep the excitement out of my voice. "May I?"

"You may."

I wandered in and looked around, then had to stop myself from drooling. The equipment was expensive and at least half of it I'd never seen before. My fingers twitched. I wanted to sit down and touch it all.

"Holy cow," I breathed. "I could spend all night in here. Maybe all my life."

He smiled. "Not tonight, you won't. I've got other plans for you." He crooked his finger at me, so I left the room and followed him down the hall to the next room, which was clearly the master bedroom.

A king-size bed had been positioned in the middle of the room. At the foot of the bed was a black bench with a white cushion. Other than a low dresser with six drawers, there was no more furniture. The huge walk-in closet was tidy, perfectly arranged and less than half-full with his clothes, jackets, belts, ties and shoes.

"The bathroom is in here." He led me into a large room. To my immediate left was an enormous standing shower with glass doors.

I peeked in. "There are three showerheads in here, Slash." I couldn't imagine why anyone would need three showerheads to get clean.

"One is a full-body spray, one is a kinetic body massage and the other is soft rain." Slash explained, leaning closer. "It feels great when all three are on you at the same time."

"They all rinse you, right?"

"Right, but in significantly different ways." His mouth curved into a smile. "I think you'll like how they feel."

"You want me to shower here?" Suddenly he'd gone from showing me his place to inviting me to shower in it.

"If you wish."

Of course I wished for it, but even more, I wanted to know what had changed his mind about showing me this previously secret part of his life. I just didn't know how to ask in a way that didn't seem intrusive.

I walked over to a spa bathtub with jets and turned around in a circle. "My entire apartment might just be the size of this bathroom."

"It's a lot for one person, but it's comfortable."

"I bet."

He took my hand, pulling me against him, then tilted my face up. Emotion churned in his eyes. "Would you like to stay the night?"

"You asked me to pack an overnight bag, so I assume that was your intention."

"It was. But I'm asking you formally."

"Why?" I studied his face. "You could have just shown me your apartment, Slash. You didn't have to invite me to stay the night, too."

"I *want* you to stay. It was important to you to see where I live, and therefore, it's important to me."

"Then why are you so nervous?"

He hesitated. "I've never had anyone here before."

"Why not?"

He stepped up beside me. "Because I don't typically share this part of my life with many people. Actually, with *any* people. Until you." He put his hands on my shoulders, coaxing me closer. "It's a big step for me."

"What made you change your mind about showing me?"

"You." There was a huskiness to his voice. "I never wanted to share this part of my life with anyone before I met you. Part of it was the nature of my work—it doesn't lend itself to long-term personal relationships—and part of it was my reluctance to open up the way I knew I'd need to in order to sustain such a relationship. I simply wasn't prepared for the way I feel about you."

I wasn't sure what to say to that. "I never wanted to make you uncomfortable, Slash."

"I know." He laughed hoarsely. "But for the first time I've met someone who can force me out of my comfort zone. I'm still figuring it out." He tugged on my hand. "Come on, let's get ready for bed."

It was an abrupt end to the conversation, but we had a lot to think about. For now I took off my clothes and left them folded on top of the dresser. I slipped on an oversize T-shirt while Slash stood shirtless at one of the sinks washing his face.

"Come." He motioned at me from the bathroom doorway, a toothbrush in one hand.

I joined him at the counter. We brushed our teeth, smiling at each other in the mirror. I don't know what I'd expected when I asked to see his place, but it wasn't this contented sense of familiarity.

I brushed and spat. "Slash?"

"Hmm?"

"You were wrong."

"About what?"

"About your place. It does have warmth."

He leaned against the countertop and shook his head. "No it doesn't."

"Really? Why do you say that?"

"Because until tonight this was just an apartment, a place to shower and sleep."

"And tonight?"

"Tonight, with you here, it's home."

# THIRTEEN

SOMETHING SHIFTED IN our relationship. It's hard to explain, but there was a new, intangible component to our lovemaking. Somehow, by allowing me access to his personal space, Slash had opened a part of himself. Frankly, I was astonished I even recognized the change. Either I had become surprisingly intuitive or Slash had become easier for me to read.

After a while of lying in silent contentment in each other's arms, Slash got up to go to the bathroom.

I sat up, too. "I'm going to the kitchen to get a drink of water."

"Okay. Bring a big glass and we'll share."

I fumbled around in the dark for my T-shirt. When I got close to the dresser I turned on a small lamp. I slipped the shirt over my head and padded out into the hallway. There was a room directly across from the bedroom—one Slash hadn't shown me.

I wondered why.

The door was closed. There wasn't a keypad on the door like there was with his office, so curiosity won out. I pressed down on the handle intending to take a quick peek, but the door was locked. I wondered why Slash hadn't shown me what was in the room and, if he lived alone, why he kept it locked.

I went to the kitchen, looked around until I found a glass and drank from it while standing in front of the refrigerator. I filled the glass again and brought it back to Slash, who finished it off. When I climbed back into bed, Slash slid his arms around me and kissed my head. I pressed my ice-cold feet against his legs and heard him catch his breath.

"*Mio Dio*, how can you possibly have such cold feet all the time?"

"In return I might ask why you are so hot all the time. And I'm not talking about looks, although if the shoe fits…"

He chuckled and tightened his arms around me. "These are my favorite moments—when it's just the two of us. I like having you to myself."

"I've kind of become partial to it myself."

He stroked my hair. "Tell me something about yourself I may not know."

"You already know everything of interest. I'm a pretty boring person."

"Not true." He wound his fingers in my hair. "I discover something new and intriguing about you every day."

I lifted my head. "You do? Like what?"

"Like you've been wondering where I lived, but you were nervous to ask me about it."

"That's calling the kettle black. You were nervous to show me."

He traced my lower lip with his thumb. "And yet here we are."

"Yes, here we are. You know, we're not so different, Slash."

"I never thought we were."

"You didn't? Why not?"

He rolled me over on top of him, tightening his arms

around my waist. I was effectively pinned against him. I couldn't see his eyes in the dark, but his voice deepened with emotion. "I knew from that first moment I met you in your bedroom. You were dressed in that ridiculous T-shirt and you challenged me to a hack."

I remembered waking up and seeing him sitting on my bed. I'd had no idea who he was or how he'd gotten into my bedroom and past my security alarm. "You do know you scared the heck out of me."

He chuckled. "Which is why you decided to test my skills?"

"Well, I figured since you were already there..." Although I'd been terrified at the time, the memory made me smile now.

"And yet, I still wish to know more about you. Come, tell me one of your dreams."

The question surprised me. "Why?"

"Because I wish to know your heart. We Italians are funny like that."

His request fascinated me. "A dream?"

"*Si*, a dream, a goal, a desire of the heart. Something you've always thought about doing. It could be a place you always wanted to visit, something you wish you could own, or lifetime goal you'd like to achieve. It can be anything...or everything."

"That's an intriguing question." I considered. "It can be anything?"

"Anything."

I've had a lot of goals in my life, almost all of them involving breaking through the glass ceiling of the tech world and ruling it through my keyboard. But now that I thought about it, that wasn't what really drove me...at least not anymore.

I placed my elbows on the bed on either side of Slash, my hair spilling onto his shoulders. "Well, there is this one thing, but I don't want you to laugh."

"Ah, *cara*, dreams are no laughing matter."

Still I hesitated. It was one thing to dream, but it was something entirely different to share that dream with someone else. I'd never told anyone about this, but now that he'd asked, it hovered on the tip of my tongue. I wanted to share it with him.

He waited patiently. Not rushing me or insisting—just waiting to see what I would say, if anything.

I plunged ahead before I lost my nerve. "Well, all this work with Piper, Wally and Brandon has made me realize how much I like working with kids. There's something deeply rewarding about showing them the ins and outs of cybersecurity."

"And?"

"And I like the thought of instructing them and kids like them."

"A teacher?"

"Yes and no. I like the idea of hands-on teaching, much like what we did in New York, but not just that. I'm thinking from the top down—crafting an entire program, a special academy of high school students dedicated solely to the study of cybersecurity. The academy would teach all the subjects—math, science, English, physics—but tying them into a full understanding of cybersecurity. I think that's their future—our future. Lexi Carmichael, Headmistress. What do you think?"

He lifted his head and kissed my nose. "I think it sounds magnificent."

"Can I say I'm surprised you *don't* sound surprised?"

He rolled me over, so that this time he was on top. He

kissed my chin, my neck. I shifted my head so he could have better access and sighed in pleasure as his mouth grazed the sensitive skin behind my ear.

"Actually I cannot think of a better use of your talents than to shape the minds of young people."

His confidence warmed me. I touched his cheek with the pads of my fingers. "Okay. Your turn."

"Me?"

"No, the other guy kissing my neck. Of course, you. Fair is fair."

He rolled off me onto his back, putting his arm across his forehead.

I sat up. "Okay. That was awkward. Did I say something wrong?"

"No."

"You pulled away. I've made you uncomfortable."

He paused and then sighed. "This kind of intimacy is unusual for me."

"You started it."

"I know. It's just I don't know what to say."

"Why? Because you already have everything?"

"No. Because I don't."

I hugged my legs to my chest, resting my chin on my knees. "Really, Slash? You're the most accomplished person I've ever met. What could possibly be left for you to achieve other than total world domination?"

I could hear the smile in his voice. "I'm certainly encouraged by your high opinion of me."

"I'm not the only one who thinks that."

"Perhaps. I…I have a hard time trusting people."

"Why?"

He was silent for so long, I wasn't sure he'd answer.

Finally he spoke, but it was not to answer my question. "Do you know what I dream about, aside from you?"

"You dream about me?"

"All the time. But I also dream about having deep and lasting friendships—the kind you have with Basia and…with Elvis. I envy you that."

Wow. I totally hadn't seen that one coming. Friendships? Everyone liked Slash, admired him and wanted to be like him.

"That's not true. You have lots of friends. Finn, Basia, Elvis, Xavier, even my interns—they all like you. Plus, I consider you an excellent friend and lover."

"*Si*, I have you. Thank God for that." He kissed the gold cross around his neck. "The others…they like me, perhaps. I agree there is potential for deeper friendships. But they are not truly my friends. Not yet. Now they accept me because of you."

I started to protest and then I considered. Was Slash right? Elvis, Basia, Xavier. They liked him—right? But were they really his friends in the same way they were mine?

The truth hit me harder than I expected.

"You have Tito," I said quietly.

I'd met Tito Blickensderfer when Slash and I had gone to Rome to help his uncle clear his name after falling under suspicion for stealing euros from the Vatican Bank. Tito worked for the Swiss Guard protecting the Pope and had helped us clear Slash's uncle's name. He was a great guy and I would have said that even if he hadn't almost been killed trying to help us.

Slash squeezed my hand. "Tito is perhaps the closest I have to a friend after you. But even he is more like a comrade than a friend. Friendships do not come easy to me."

"Me either," I admitted. "But I've been lucky."

"No, you've worked hard at it. You've been genuine, open and truthful in your dealings with people. It's rarer than you may realize. Your openness and honesty inspires a special kind of dedication within others, myself included. You're unguarded in your attempts at friendship, whereas I seem unable to do that."

I struggled for the right words. "I didn't know you felt this way, Slash. I've felt alone most of my life, so I understand where you're coming from. Forging friendships has been a pretty bumpy journey for me. You seem so capable at everything, the friends thing never even crossed my mind. I guess everyone has their secrets, even someone as successful as you."

"*Si*, we all have our secrets…and our demons. The trick is finding someone whose demons can play well with our own. For me, that's no easy task."

I wanted to ask him for further clarification, but I sensed he was done with the topic. The emotional intimacy we were veering into seemed to have made him uncomfortable. Honestly, it had made me a little uncomfortable, too. We needed time to process. All of this deep emotional bonding was new territory for both of us.

We lay there in each other's arms, drifting off to sleep. But something was still bothering me. Now that Slash had praised my honesty and openness, I felt guilty for trying to look into the locked room.

Shifting in his arms, I decided to be direct. "Slash, why didn't you show me what's in that other bedroom?"

He stroked my hair, his mouth warm against my cheek. "Ah, you noticed, did you?"

"I not only noticed, I tried to peek. I'm sorry."

"No need to be sorry. But neither of us is ready for what's in that room yet. Okay?"

His voice didn't sound angry or sleepy. I wondered if he'd been lying there that whole time thinking.

"Okay, Slash. I trust you."

And I did. Implicitly. He'd already revealed a part of himself I'd never seen before. I understood all too well the emotional risk he'd taken in doing it. If he wasn't ready to reveal any more of himself to me at this time, I wasn't going to push. He'd been patient for me, and now it was my turn.

He pulled me close and murmured something in Italian against my hair.

"What did you say?"

"I said, 'A candle loses nothing by lighting another candle.' It's an old Italian proverb. I'm just talking to myself."

"Why?"

"Because sometimes I need to remind myself not to mess this up."

I wasn't sure why he would be worried about messing up, but I was too tired to figure it out. Tomorrow I'd replay the conversation and see if I could determine the significance. For tonight it was enough to simply lie in his arms.

"Good night, Slash."

He leaned his chin against my forehead. *"Buonanotte, cara."*

As I slipped into sleep, I felt hopeful that maybe a bit of the mystery that was Slash had finally started to unravel.

# FOURTEEN

THE NEXT MORNING I ran into Basia in the bathroom at the fab. She looked both beautiful and professional in a soft pink blouse and black skirt. Her dark bob looked sleek and shiny.

I stared at my reflection. My ponytail was stuck to my head after several hours in the hazmat helmet and my blouse was wrinkled. But my eyes were happy and a permanent smile seemed stuck to my lips. I hummed as I washed my hands.

"So, how's it going in the lab?" she asked me, smoothing down a stray hair.

"Great. We're making a lot of progress." I snagged a paper towel and wiped my hands dry. "It's amazing."

"Yes, it is. So, how does Slash feel about you leaving for Indonesia?"

"He's okay with it." I aimed and shot the paper towel at the wastebasket. I missed. "He's good like that."

"He's good at a lot of things." Her eyes softened as she met my gaze in the mirror. "So, how are you two doing?"

I picked up the paper towel and threw it at the wastebasket again. This time it went in. "We're great, surprisingly. I don't know how significant it is, but Slash showed me his apartment in Baltimore for the first time last night. I stayed overnight at his place. He said he'd never brought anyone there before."

Basia's eyes widened. "He did? Really? Do you know what this means?"

I thought, but came up empty. "No, what does it mean?"

"It means Slash has moved things to the next level."

Holy cow. Levels hadn't been mentioned in *Twelve Steps to Keep Your Relationship Alive and Healthy*, which I'd just finished reading last week. Panic caused a small hitch in my throat. "Wait. There are levels? No one told me anything about levels."

"Yes, there are levels. Did anything else change between you?"

Wow. Where to start? "Like what kind of change exactly?" I asked cautiously.

"Emotionally."

I hesitated for too long. "Look, Basia, I just spent the night with him at his place. One night. That's it."

"But something changed between you two. Something significant."

I sighed. "Okay, yes. Something changed. It seems more serious now."

"It's because Slash is opening up to you emotionally. That's a whole new level."

"I'm not clear about this level thing. Can you write it down and mark exactly where I am, where I need to be going, and provide a short summary of each level? Then I'll be more prepared as we advance. Look, should I be nervous about this new level?"

"Are you?"

"Strangely, no. I liked being with him at his place. It felt normal."

"Oh, God." She started pacing back and forth in front of the stalls. Thank goodness no other woman in the building needed to pee, because it would have been awkward having to conclude our heart-to-heart just when it was getting to the part where I'd start understanding what was going on. Hopefully. "It really is getting serious between the two of you."

"So, normal is serious?" I wished I had my laptop so I could take notes.

"Yes. Lexi, think about it. You're falling for him."

"Thank you, Captain Obvious. I've *already* fallen for him, Basia. His apartment. Spent the night. Remember?"

"I know *that*." She threw up her hands. "What I mean is you're forging a deeper, lasting connection with Slash. He's letting you in. I'm beyond surprised. I didn't expect it."

I thought about her words, realizing I was a little surprised myself. I'd never imagined myself capable of it, but here I was in brand-new emotional territory. It was a bit scary.

"So, what's his apartment like?" Basia gave a little squeal. "Spill. Inquiring minds want to know."

"Well, it's nice, but he doesn't have much furniture. He does have a cool home gym, three shower heads in a bathroom the size of my apartment, an office with super expensive tech equipment I sincerely hope he'll let me explore in greater detail. Oh, and there's a locked room."

"A locked room?"

"Yes. He showed me everything else in the apartment, but one room stayed locked. It didn't have a biometric lock on it like his office, but it was definitely locked. I tried to peek in. Later I asked him what was in that room."

"What did he say?"

"He said neither of us was ready for what was in that room."

Silence. Then Basia gave a quick small gasp before saying, "Oh. God."

She didn't elaborate. "Oh, God, what?" A flicker of panic shot through me. "Basia, you can't say 'Oh, God' without an explanation."

"You do know what's in that locked room, right?"

Was she kidding? I didn't even know what color underwear I had on. "Of course I don't know. I just told you I tried to peek and it was locked."

"For crying out loud, Lexi. Have you been living in a cave for the past year? Wait—don't answer that. Of course I can tell you what's in that locked room."

"You can? Then tell me."

"BDSM."

I waited for more information, but she remained silent. My cranky meter went up another notch. "You'd better have a good explanation why those letters have entered this conversation."

"Bondage and discipline, sadism and masochism. I bet Slash has his very own Red Room."

"What the heck is a Red Room?"

"It's a special room with sex toys and costumes. I'm talking handcuffs, blindfolds, collars, crops, whips. It's quite popular these days. Erotic literature and movies have moved into the mainstream."

I wasn't getting her leap of logic. "How can you possibly extrapolate a Red Room from a locked door?"

"Because it makes perfect sense. This is Slash we are talking about. Don't you get it? That's why he said you weren't ready. He has to break you in more."

"Break me in? I am *not* a horse." I glared at her.

She laughed again. "I told you Slash was the adventurous type."

"I can be adventurous, too, if I plan ahead. How hard can BDSM be? It's just sex, right? I'm a quick study. I'll research a bit and get up to speed."

She giggled. "You do that. I'm here if you have any questions."

We left the bathroom and I took a breath to calm myself. Priorities. I would simply balance work with pleasure.

A little BDSM and a little microchip design.

I could do this.

Later I'd grab my laptop and take a quick tutorial on BDSM. I figured YouTube would certainly have at least a half dozen videos I could study for visual aid.

Feeling better about my plan, I headed back to the lab and got to work.

# FIFTEEN

WHEN SLASH ARRIVED at my place about ten o'clock, I was sitting on the couch with my laptop reading about micro capacitors. He dropped his briefcase by the door, hung his jacket in my coat closet, then walked over and kissed me on the cheek.

"Hey," I said, closing the laptop and setting it aside. "How was your day?"

"Better now that I'm here."

"Did you already have dinner?"

"*Si.* I had a dinner meeting. I was thinking about going for a short run, followed by some wine and conversation. I'd like to hear as much as you can tell me about your day. You want to join me?"

"Yes to all three. I'll just change into a sweatshirt and some shorts."

"Great. I'll grab my bag from the car and let the FBI know what we're up to."

"Okay." I paused in the hallway. "Wait. Do they have to run with us?" That seemed creepy to me. Plus I didn't want them to see me huffing and puffing.

"I'm afraid so. I'll give them our intended path and ask them to stay back a bit. We're not going far and we won't be long."

"Okay."

Slash disappeared outside and then returned with his

bag. When we were both ready, we sat side-by-side on the couch tying our tennis shoes.

"You won't run too fast, right?" I asked. "I'm not in as good shape as you."

"I'll let you set the pace."

"Thanks. Appreciate that."

We went out into the cool spring night. The moon was full and bright, and I was glad for my sweatshirt. Slash didn't have anything on but a muscle T-shirt and running shorts. As he bent over to stretch his legs, he provided a nice view of his back end. He glanced over his shoulder and I immediately became fascinated with the pavement.

"Aren't you cold?" I tightened the scrunchie on my ponytail and shook out my legs.

He shook his head. "No. Besides I'll get hotter as we run."

The two agents, one male and one female, were out of the car, tying on tennis shoes. They were dressed in slacks and shirts, their guns in holsters beneath jackets.

"You're going running in that?" I asked them.

The woman tightened her shoulder holster. "Jogging only. We only run in case of deadly peril or a jelly donut. Don't worry. We'll stay back just enough to keep you in our sights, okay?"

"Okay, thanks." I thought about them behind us, laughing at my pace.

Slash and I took off. Regardless of my embarrassment about my fitness, it felt good. I wasn't much for regular exercise, and I was a klutz at most sports, but running was the one thing I could do without causing anyone else bodily harm. Well, at least most of the time.

We didn't need to talk while we ran, which worked

for me in two ways. One, it meant I didn't have to worry about casual conversation while engaged in a physical activity. That was good because since I'm clumsy, I need to keep all my focus on the physical part. Two, it meant I could save my breath for running, which was really good because I was getting winded a lot faster than I'd thought I would.

We'd been running for about fifteen minutes when we entered a park. Slash moved a little closer to me. "Don't look back, but the FBI is no longer behind us."

"Jeez. If they were going to stop for a donut, I wished they would've asked me if I wanted one. Wait. Why can't I look?"

"Because someone else has taken their place and they don't look friendly."

*"What?"*

"I said don't look."

I kept my gaze focused in front of me. "Who is it?" My breath was coming in hitches. Maybe it was out of fear or maybe he was just trying to stay ahead of them, but Slash had picked up the pace, and I was struggling. "What if they're out for a late evening run, just like we are, and they just got in between us and the FBI agents by accident?"

"They aren't in running clothes."

"The FBI weren't in running clothes either."

"Exactly."

"Wait. How do you know they are behind us? I haven't seen you turn around."

He touched my elbow lightly. "I peeked over my shoulder a while ago when we went around a curve. Let's veer off to the right to see if they follow us. Stay close."

I followed him as he turned down the street toward

a strip mall. It was harder to see where we were going, because this stretch of road didn't have streetlights, but the moon was bright.

I held my breath. Now I heard the slap of their feet on the pavement behind us. They'd given up any pretense of being stealthy.

"They're definitely following," Slash said.

"Who is *they*?" Anxiety clogged my throat. It occurred to me that if whoever was following us wished us harm there wouldn't be a lot we could do to stop them. Slash didn't have his gun and I wasn't going to be able to outrun them.

"Listen carefully to me." His voice remained completely calm. "We're going to run as fast as we can toward the strip mall ahead. I'm going to stay slightly behind you. When you reach the first building, run around the back as fast as you can. Don't stop running even if I do."

"What? You're going to stop?"

"As soon as we get around the building. But you must keep running for as long as you can. Find a place to hide or keep safe until either I find you or you're certain it's safe to head somewhere and call for help. Do you understand?"

Panic gripped me. I needed more information. A plan. "Yes, but—"

"No time for buts, okay? Just do as I say. Let's pick up the speed even more. Go."

Adrenaline and fear propelled me forward. We ran in a full-out sprint. My lungs and legs were burning as someone starting yelling at us to stop. I reached the building first and tore around the corner just as he instructed. I didn't stop running even when I heard shouting behind me. I had no idea how Slash was going to take them on by himself.

My preoccupation with Slash caused me to lose concentration and stumble. I tripped…just as a gunshot sounded.

# SIXTEEN

I THRUST MY hands out to break the fall, so my palms and knees took the brunt of my weight. My chin bounced off the pavement and the breath was knocked out of me with a huge *whoosh*. I slid into the side of a Dumpster, banging my right shoulder.

I rolled to my side, gasping until I could breathe. As I pushed myself up to my knees, I heard more noise and shouting. Oh, God. Slash was in trouble, possibly shot. I could hear footsteps running my way. Someone was coming after me.

I staggered to my feet, ducking behind the Dumpster. Blood dripped from my knees, sliding down my shins and into my socks. I looked around for something, anything, I could use to protect myself. I spotted the glint of a metal pipe leaning against the side of the Dumpster. Snatching it, I crouched down, holding it like a baseball bat.

Seconds later a dark shape ran past the Dumpster. The shape had long pants on, which meant it wasn't Slash. Even though I hadn't moved, the shape must have sensed me, because it stopped and turned around slowly.

It was a man. I didn't see a gun in his hand, but even in the dim moonlight, I could tell his expression was not a friendly one. I couldn't recall ever meeting him before. He was Asian, probably in his mid-thirties, and looked like he lifted weights for fun.

He held out his hands to show me he was unarmed. "Well, hello there. Calm down. You're Lexi Carmichael, right?" He didn't have an accent.

"Who are you?"

"Just someone who wants to talk to you. Okay? No one is going to get hurt. Put the pipe down before you hurt yourself."

I gripped it harder. "Where's my boyfriend?"

"He's been, ah, detained."

I narrowed my eyes. "Don't come any closer. I mean it."

He didn't answer. Instead, in a series of motions I didn't see coming, he knocked the pipe out of my hand, twisted my arm behind my back and shoved me up against the Dumpster.

"I told you to calm down," he growled. "Now I'm going to have to get rough." He leaned his head back and yelled something in a foreign language.

When no one answered, he looked concerned. He yanked me toward him, putting me in front of him in a headlock. "Let's go. Nice and easy."

Slash's approach was so silent that when my attacker was suddenly yanked backward, it was a complete surprise to both of us. The maneuver freed me, however. When I whirled around, Slash had the man in some kind of body-lock.

Slash kicked at the back of the guy's knee. Unfortunately, the guy didn't go down and instead shifted his weight, swinging a fist at Slash. Slash leaned into the punch, twisting sideways at the last moment so his bicep took the brunt of the punch. At the same time, he delivered a hard jab of his elbow to the guy's sternum.

A crack sounded and the guy took a step away, clutching his chest and reaching under his jacket.

"Gun!" I shouted.

To my surprise, Slash moved toward the gun, not away from it, delivering a sharp chop to the guy's inner wrist with his left hand while punching the guy's left temple with his right fist. The attacker staggered once and went down face-first.

Slash knelt next to him, fishing in his pockets, but came up empty. He picked up the gun and approached me, pulling me toward him hard. "Are you okay, *cara*?"

I stared at him. He wasn't even breathing hard. "Am I okay? Are *you* okay?"

He kissed me, keeping an arm around me. "Didn't I tell you to run?"

"I got distracted and tripped. Are you hit? I heard a shot."

"I'm fine. I surprised them. I knocked the first one out as he ran around the corner. They didn't expect me to be waiting there to confront them. He was holding a gun and it went off when he went down. The second one didn't have time to get his weapon, so we quickly got acquainted. He was well trained, so it took me a bit longer than expected. The third one came after you, which really pissed me off."

"Who are they?"

"I don't know, but I don't think it's a coincidence that all three of them are Asian and this one, at least, has no identification on him. Again."

Before he could answer, someone said, "Are you okay?"

I turned around. The two FBI agents stood there, looking around worriedly.

"What the hell is going on?" the female agent asked Slash. "Where did you go?"

"I was going to ask you the same thing." He tipped my chin up and examined the scrape. "Looks like it hurts. You okay?"

"I'll live." I touched my chin and winced.

"Sorry." The female agent rubbed the back of her neck. "Someone hit us from behind but didn't take the time to cuff or restrain us. They must have been in a hurry."

"That's probably because they were busy chasing us," I offered.

Slash motioned behind the agents. "Did you find those two?"

"Yes. We just cuffed them. Did you take them out?"

"*Si*. There's one more over here."

The male agent walked over and bent over the guy. "Damn. What the hell were they after?"

Slash shrugged. "I'm not sure, but it was a calculated attack." He put an arm around my waist. "I think they wanted her."

I looked at him in surprise. "Me? How can you be sure they wanted me?"

"Because after I took one of them out, they didn't double team me. It was more important to go after you."

I considered. "You could be right. He did call me by name."

"He did?"

"Yep. Then he said he just wanted to talk to me. Of course, I didn't get that vibe at all, especially after he knocked me around and said I wasn't playing nice."

Slash's jaw tightened and he hugged me tighter.

The female agent stared at me. "So, what do they want from you?"

It could have been any number of things, but the twins' invention topped my list. "I'm not sure. Our chat didn't last long. Slash, what do you think?"

He shook his head. "I don't know. None of them have identification on them, which smacks of a professional job. Other than the fact that they are all Asian, and trained in a paramilitary style, I don't know why they were chasing us. I don't think they expected us to fight back, especially unarmed. We'll have to question them."

I heard the wail of a siren. The police were on the way.

I leaned my head against Slash's shoulder. "Oh, no. Does this mean I have to spend the rest of the night in the police station answering questions again?"

"At least an hour or so."

"You got any quarters for the vending machine? Those processed peanut butter crackers always taste better after midnight."

He sighed. "I had a feeling you were going to say that."

# SEVENTEEN

IT TOOK THE police a couple of hours to question us. Seeing as how the FBI was involved due to Slash's presence, there was a lot of cross-examination between the two agencies. Whatever the case, I'm pretty sure my file at the FBI was getting thicker as Slash kept getting assigned new sets of agents. I wondered if there was a running bet at the FBI as to who would be assigned to Slash next and how long they would last. I could picture them sitting around a conference table and marking all the times my involvement with Slash had put him in some kind of mortal danger. I was surprised they hadn't put a hit out on me themselves.

*"Cara?"* Slash handed me a cup of water. "You okay?"

"Yes. Just thinking. I'm tired and my chin and knees hurt, but I'm thankful it's not worse." The police had given me alcohol pads and a few bandages to patch myself up. "How much longer do we have to stay?"

"We're done. Let's go home."

I glanced down at his hands, which were scraped and bloodied. He'd also taken a hit to the jaw. A purple bruise was forming there. "You got hurt, too."

"The other guys look worse."

"I know. I saw. Are they awake and talking yet?"

"Two of the three are conscious. The second one I

took out hasn't come around yet. No one is saying anything and they have lawyered up."

"Aren't you going to stay and question them?"

"No. The police are handling it with FBI assistance. We'll see what they get out of them."

We headed to the police parking lot holding hands. I glanced at my watch. "Jeez, I have to be at the fab at nine. That's in about five hours."

"I'll drive you."

"No, it's okay. You've got to work, too."

"I don't mind."

"I know you don't and I appreciate that. But I've got it. I'm only sorry we never got that wine or conversation."

"We've always got the car ride home."

"That we do."

We climbed into Slash's SUV and started the drive to my apartment. I peered behind me. The FBI was on our tail again.

"I guess this means no more runs alone."

"I'm afraid not."

I sighed. "It's not easy to be you, Slash. I'm sorry I'm not making it a walk in the park either."

"*Au contraire*, you have no idea how much better you make it."

"But I keep putting you in danger."

"*You* do nothing of the sort. It's the business we are in. We both know that."

I didn't exactly agree with that, but I didn't say so. "So, what do you think those guys wanted from me?"

"Only one thing comes to mind. The twins' invention."

I thought of the revolutionary invention—the microfluid and the tiny canals built onto the microchips. If the manufacturing process were a success, it would completely change the landscape of the technical world. Elvis had warned me.

*There are people who would kill for it.*

I still wasn't sure how that would make me a target. "But why me? Why not Elvis or Xavier?"

"The twins have had security on them since they came back from Broodryk."

"Well, we've both had security on us and that didn't stop them from trying."

"True." He tapped his fingers on the steering wheel. "Just how much do you know about the invention?"

I considered. I wasn't an expert by any stretch of the imagination, but I certainly knew enough to compromise the project. "You think they wanted to question me about it?"

"*Question* is a loose term. It wouldn't have been a friendly exchange."

I shuddered. "What? So you are saying this is some kind of industrial spying? Kidnapping? Torture?"

"Unfortunately those techniques are not new to industrial spying. But, *si*, that's what comes to mind. This invention, truthfully, how significant is it?"

I threaded my fingers in my lap. "Truthfully? Game-changing. World-changing."

His gaze lingered on me a bit longer before turning back to the road. I didn't have to explain further. He understood the Zimmerman twins as well as I did. He was fully aware of what they were capable of producing.

"The police have already informed the ComQuest executives," he said. "Apparently they've arranged private security for you until you leave for Jakarta. That includes a driver to and from the fab."

"How do you know this?"

"I was in the room when the police spoke to the CEO. He was quite distressed."

Probably not as distressed as me, but I considered it a moot point. I rubbed my knee. I didn't want to be the weak link in this situation, but it was looking like exactly that.

I must have been silent longer than I thought, because Slash reached across the seat and patted my knee. "Don't worry. Between the private security, the FBI and me, we'll keep you safe."

"I know. Truthfully, I feel the safest with you. But I'm sure things will be fine in Jakarta."

"I'm not sure it's a good idea for you to go. Can you cancel?"

"I have to go. It's that important, Slash."

"Can't someone else do it?"

"Xavier and Elvis won't trust anyone else with their invention."

"Okay, then I'm going, too. Actually, I've been thinking I'm due for a vacation."

"What?" I turned in my seat.

He kept his gaze on the road. "I've only been to Jakarta once, a long time ago. I'd like to see the city again."

I held up a hand. "Whoa—wait. You want to go to Jakarta?"

"Never hurts to be nearby. Just in case."

"Just in case…what?"

He sighed. "Honestly, I'd rather not speculate. Would it bother you if I came along?"

"Why *wouldn't* I want you to go? As long as it doesn't interfere with your work and you *want* to go, I'm fine with it. Besides, if you didn't go, you'd still worry about me, right?"

"You already know the answer to that."

"I guess I do."

A rumble of thunder sounded when we pulled into my apartment parking lot. Slash came around to help me out of the car, even though I was completely capable of doing it with two banged-up knees and a hurt chin. There were definitely perks to this boyfriend/girlfriend thing.

Slash held my hand as we walked to my apartment. "Slash, will the US government allow you to go to Jakarta?"

"I'd have to request it. Jakarta is considered a relatively safe location. If I agree to follow certain protocols and agree to be accompanied by a team, they might let me go."

"Even after all of this?"

"Even after all of this. As long as I'm not making a request to go into direct combat or enemy territory, the leash can only be so tight." A scowl crossed his face.

I squeezed his hand. "Are you sure about Jakarta? I don't want to put a crimp in your schedule."

"I'm sure. It's been a while since I've had some time off. I'm due."

"But if you're watching me, it wouldn't really be a vacation."

"Says who?" He flashed a grin at me. "Jakarta is a beautiful city. I can look around while you are safely ensconced in the factory. I might even invite some friends to go with me."

"Friends?" I looked at him in astonishment.

His grin widened. "It's time I got to work on that."

# EIGHTEEN

WHEN I WOKE UP at seven-thirty, Slash was already in the shower and I had a text on my phone letting me know that my new company driver and two armed security guards were in the parking lot ready to take me to the ComQuest fab at my convenience. To confirm that, Andrew Garrington, the COO of ComQuest, called me personally at eight o'clock.

"Good morning, Miss Carmichael. I apologize for bothering you so early. I understand you had a scare last night."

"I did."

"Do you think it might be connected to your work at ComQuest?"

"I don't know for certain. It's a possibility."

"We are taking this very seriously. We've arranged for a driver and guards to accompany you to and from work and watch you until you leave for Jakarta. I'm sorry if that feels intrusive, but we are committed to keeping you safe."

Wow. How many security guards could one girl have?

"Okay, thank you, I guess."

"We've also arranged a meeting with you this morning at one of our conference rooms at the fab to go over in greater detail our plans for your security now and in Indonesia. My secretary will send you the security and meeting info. See you at nine."

"Okay. I'll be there."

After we hung up, I looked out into my parking lot and saw the guards were already there waiting for me. I ate a spoonful of Cheerios and waved my spoon at Slash when he came into the kitchen. "You can cancel your security. I now have my own personal driver and two armed guards. Ugh. I don't think I'll ever get used to this."

"You will." He kissed the top of my head. "Trust me, I speak from experience."

I pointed to the box of Cheerios. "You want some?"

He reached into his jacket pocket and pulled out an energy bar. "No. I'm set for now. But thanks. Finish up and I'll walk you out to meet your new detail."

I quickly ate the rest of my cereal and grabbed a sweater and my purse. True to Andrew's word, a tan SUV sat idling in the parking lot, along with the blue Toyota and Slash's FBI detail in a black sedan.

It was a freaking circus. It was a wonder my neighbors had any place to park.

Slash walked me to the car, his hand resting beneath his jacket. The guy in the blue Toyota got out to accompany him, which made the FBI get out of their car, too.

Slash held up a hand and everyone stayed back while he did a thorough check of the driver's and the two security guards' identification. When he appeared satisfied, he gave me a kiss on the cheek.

"See you later," he murmured against my cheek. "Be safe, okay?"

"I've got my own personal army. I'll be fine."

We headed off to the fab. Other than initial pleasantries about how I felt this morning, there was no conversation with my security detail, which was just fine with me. It felt freaky to be chauffeured around, anyway.

Once we'd arrived at the fab and the receptionist had checked me and given me a badge, I was escorted to a conference room.

There were several people already seated around the table including, to my surprise, Finn. Elvis stood when I entered the room and came over to greet me. "Lexi, are you okay? We were just told what happened."

"I'm fine, Elvis. Thankfully Slash was with me."

"Is it connected to that attack on you in New York City?"

"I don't know."

"What did those guys want last night?"

"I don't know that either. One of them knew me by name and said he just wanted to talk to me. That was right before he attacked me. It might not have anything to do with your invention. The problem is they didn't have any identification on them and they aren't talking at the moment, so it's hard to confirm either way."

"Who else knows you are involved with us and the invention?" Elvis asked.

"No one except Slash and Basia. Slash knows nothing specific about the invention, only that I'm working with you and ComQuest on something and headed to Indonesia to help you out."

He nodded, then motioned for me to sit next to him. As I sat down, I met Finn's eyes. He nodded at me without a word. What was he miffed about?

Oops. I probably should have called him first thing this morning. There was probably some kind of protocol that required you to call your boss after being attacked, possibly while on assignment for said boss's company.

But everything had happened so fast. I'd spent half the night at the police station and this morning, the driver and security stuff had thrown me for a loop. Still, I felt like I'd committed a professional faux pas, so I gave him an apologetic smile.

Andrew Garrington, the COO, sat next to Finn. Beside him was Fox Cutler, the Director of Research. Xavier was to my left and two men I hadn't met sat next to him farther down the table.

Andrew spoke first. "Thanks for meeting with us this morning, Miss Carmichael. We are deeply concerned about the events of last night, even if you are unable to confirm they had anything to do with your assistance here on the project. As I mentioned to you this morning, in an attempt to ensure your safety and the integrity of this project, we are implementing specific security measures."

He motioned at the two men who sat further down the table. "I'd like you to meet Oliver DeWitt, Director of Security at ComQuest, and his deputy, Cezar Alcantaro. Both men are highly trained security professionals who will lead a special security detail assigned to you and Miss Kowalski while you are in Jakarta."

Both men lifted a hand in greeting. It seemed like a little overkill to send both of them with me, but better safe than sorry.

Andrew continued, "Mr. Shaughnessy will also be accompanying you."

I blinked. "What? He will? I mean, you will, Finn?"

He met my gaze. "I will. Your security is of the upmost importance to X-Corp."

Elvis held up a hand. "Wait. Can I just say I'm having second thoughts about sending Lexi? I had no idea she might be put in physical danger."

"I agree," Xavier chimed in. "Maybe we should just try and do this remotely."

I saw the alarm that crossed Andrew's face and I shook my head. "Look, guys, doing this remotely is not a good solution and we all know it. The work is way too delicate to risk it in that way. Besides, we have no idea if those thugs were even after me for information on the invention. It could be something else entirely."

"Like what?" Elvis asked.

"Like... I don't know. Anything. It's not like I have a shortage of enemies."

"But the timing is statistically significant." Elvis covered his hand with mine and squeezed. "You do know that you and Basia are far more important to us than the invention."

Xavier nodded. "I totally agree."

I squeezed Elvis's hand, but said nothing.

Andrew leaned forward on the table. "Ladies and gentlemen, please. I assure you that every possible precaution will be taken to keep Miss Carmichael, Miss Kowalski and the invention safe. We have already secured two private jets to fly you and a security detail to Jakarta. We have two teams of security working around the clock both inside and out of the factory. You have my word that everyone will be completely and utterly safe."

I looked at Elvis. "See? Private and dedicated security team inside and out. It's okay, Elvis. Honestly, it's an honor for me to do this, to be a part of making history. I *want* to do it. As long as Finn is on board with it, that is."

Everyone in the room turned to look at Finn, but he only had eyes for me. "Are you sure about this, Lexi?"

"Unequivocally." It was the truth. There was no place I'd rather be. The technology was that important.

He didn't look convinced, but he didn't argue either. "Fine, if you're sure, then we'll proceed. I'll admit I feel better knowing I'll be there in person to keep an eye on things."

After another half hour of discussing more security issues, the twins and I were released to continue our work in the lab. The ComQuest bigwigs and Finn would finish hammering out the rest of the security details without us.

Elvis, Xavier and I returned to the lab, where I worked on understanding the complicated intricacies of the chip and the precision calculations of when to add the microfluid to ensure it would work properly. It was such exacting, exhausting work that none of us realized we'd worked through lunch until it was three o'clock."

We left the lab and peeled off our suits.

"No wonder I'm hungry," I said, hanging my suit on the wall. "And I seriously have to go to the bathroom."

"I'm starving, too. Let's have a late lunch at the cafeteria."

After the bathroom, we headed down to the cafeteria. While we munched on club sandwiches and fries, Elvis told me about the special titanium briefcase that would be carrying the microchip prototype and microfluid.

Xavier scooted his plate to the side and leaned forward. "The briefcase is made of a special titanium that can resist bullets, crowbars, drills, fire, water—anything you can think of that could be used to force it open. It's got a GPS locator on it so we can track it. Even better, we've programmed it with a special trigger to blow if someone attempts to break in without completing the very specific protocol. Wouldn't do much more than scare the person trying to open it, but would totally ruin the chip."

"You'd blow the chip?"

Elvis swiped a French fry through a glob of catsup. "Better that than have it fall into the wrong hands. By the way, the briefcase was Xavier's design. It's seriously brilliant."

"I have no doubt of that."

Xavier grinned. "No false modesty on my part. A freaking nuclear bomb couldn't open that thing."

I wiped my fingers with a napkin. "So what's the protocol to open it?"

"Biometric palm print. Yours. Plus a special code. Other than Xavier and me, you'll be the only person who will know it. As an added measure, I'm not going to tell you the code until you arrive in Jakarta and are safely ensconced in the factory. It's an extra layer of security that no one else knows about, not even our bosses. We feel uncomfortable with all the things happening to you, so we decided to keep a few things just to ourselves. Too many people already know too many details about this."

"Makes sense to me. Personally, I think getting it to Jakarta is going to be the easy part. Figuring out the manufacturing procedure is going to be a lot harder."

Elvis patted me on the back. "No way. You're a quick study, Lexi. I can't think of anyone else we could have caught up so quickly."

"No one you trust, you mean."

The twins exchanged glances, but Elvis spoke. "Yes. No one we trust more. You're it, Lexi."

I smiled. "Appreciate the vote of confidence. But we've still got more ground to cover before I feel ready."

Just then Finn strolled into the cafeteria accompanied by a security guard. My boss looked completely out of place in his expensive steel-gray suit. He made a bee-line directly for me.

"You're still here?" I said in surprise, standing up.

He took me by the elbow. "All day. A lot of details to work out. Can I talk to you privately for a moment?"

"Of course."

We walked over to a seating area with a bench and sat down. He shifted so that he faced me.

"I need to know for sure, Lexi. Are you positive you want to do this? I wanted to ask you privately, outside of the pressure of the twins and everyone else. Convince me this is the right thing to do."

I studied him. His Irish accent was pronounced, which told me he was a lot more concerned than he might have wanted to let on in the meeting.

"I'm sorry I didn't call you last night, Finn. It was just another really long night at the police station. You seem really worried."

"Of course I'm bloody worried. There's been a lot going on in your life over the past few months. Serious stress and trauma. I care about you and I don't want to see you injured, exhausted or otherwise burnt out, especially not while on another case for X-Corp."

"You don't have to worry, Finn. I'll be fine. It sounds like security will be so tight I won't even be able to go to the bathroom alone. Plus, you'll be there in person to hold my hand and make sure I don't get too exhausted." I nudged him with my elbow. "Don't worry. I've got this."

My attempt to use humor to lighten his mood didn't work. "There's a big difference between a challenge and fighting off some well-financed thugs."

"I know. Look, Finn, the twins need me to do this."

"I need you, too."

"I really appreciate that. You probably don't know how much. You were the first person to trust me enough to give me a job of significant importance. You've always believed in my abilities, and I'm really grateful. But what the twins have invented, what they've created, is something extraordinary. I assure you, it will change the landscape of the technological world. What we are doing here—you and me—it's more than a job. It's making history. It will put X-Corp on the map forever in terms of playing a role in the transformation of the tech world. It's that important."

He searched my face, then sighed. "Fine. If it's that important, I'm in. But I'm not letting you out of my sight the entire time we are in Jakarta. Understood?"

"Understood. You know, Finn, you're the best boss ever and a pretty good friend to boot."

I leaned over and gave him a hug before realizing how impulsively I'd acted. "Oops. Sorry about the hug. Hope I didn't wrinkle the suit or break the number one rule of boss-employee etiquette." I patted his expensive suit.

He laughed. "We're friends first, and that's what friends do." He put an arm around my shoulders. "Besides, it's not like you were checking out my bum or anything."

My cheeks heated. "Right. Ah…well, not today anyway."

# NINETEEN

AFTER A LONG DAY, the ComQuest driver let me off at my apartment and two security guards escorted me to the door. After I'd disarmed the alarm, they checked out the apartment before declaring it clear.

One of the guys handed me his card. "If you need anything, ma'am, we'll be in the parking lot. Are you expecting any visitors?"

"Just my boyfriend."

"The one we met this morning?"

"Yes." Jeez. How many boyfriends did they expect me to have?

They left and I sighed, tossing the card on my kitchen table. I opened the fridge to see what I had to offer Slash for dinner. Nothing but bologna and bread. I made two sandwiches, adding a little lettuce and tomato for garnish, and brewed some decaf coffee. I was just pouring the first cup when Slash let himself in.

"*Ciao*, honey, I'm home."

"Ha, ha. In the kitchen."

I smelled something good as he walked in. He held up a bag and waved it back and forth. "I brought dinner."

"Holy chopsticks." I put down the coffeepot with a thump. "Is that Chinese food?"

"It is."

"Wow. It's *so* sexy when you bring food over."

He chuckled. "I happen to love when your eyes light

up like that, which happens a lot when I bring food around." He waved the bag again and I stared at it hungrily.

Laughing, he set the bag on the table. I came up behind him, putting my arms around his waist from behind, resting my cheek against his back. It surprised me how easy it had become to touch him. I hardly even thought about doing it anymore—it seemed to come naturally.

"I think I may be too transparent in the food department." I sighed. "Maybe I need to work on that. But whatever is in that bag will be infinitely better than the bologna sandwiches I just made us for dinner."

"You made me a bologna sandwich?"

"Of course."

He turned in my embrace and pressed a kiss on the top of my head. "Ah, it must be love."

"Must be. I don't make bologna sandwiches for just anyone."

When I released him, he shrugged out of his jacket, hanging it over the back of one of the kitchen chairs. He left his shoulder holster with his gun on. I got out a couple of plates and forks, while he found a bottle of wine in my cupboard. Grabbing two wine glasses and a corkscrew, he carried them to the table as I added the napkins.

"You're in a good mood," I observed as he pulled the cork from the wine.

"My vacation has been approved."

"That's great."

"Yes it is." Slash poured the wine and we lifted our glasses to each other's. "To a memorable time in Indonesia, then." We clinked glasses and drank.

I set down my glass and passed him the rice. "So, how was work?"

"I was going to ask you the same question."

"Yes, but I asked first."

He set down the rice, his expression turning serious. "I don't want to ruin the mood, but I think you should know. The men who attacked us have been released from police custody."

*"What?"*

"They claimed they were out jogging and we attacked them first. The FBI agents didn't see who hit them, so they couldn't pin it on them. The first guy claimed he pulled the gun on me in self-defense. Anyway, they called someone who brought them identification and proof that they had legal permits for the weapons. The police couldn't hold them."

"That totally stinks. At least we know who they are, right?"

"Right. Turns out they work for Sinam Tech in Silicon Valley. Computer technicians who were in the area for a conference and went out for a run."

I paused with a forkful of sweet and sour pork at my mouth. "In jackets and dress pants?"

"Apparently so."

"What is Sinam Tech?"

"A Chinese technology company. Their official portfolio states they work in standard interfaces, communications and data architecture."

"And the unofficial portfolio?"

"Certain peeks into their network indicate they serve as a front."

I wasn't going to ask for his definition of *certain peeks*. "A front for what?"

"Cyberattacks. Cyberintelligence. Hacking. You name it."

"Hmmm...Silicon Valley. That would be a pretty convenient location. You know, I'm seeing a lot of avenues going back to China. Any connection to the Red Guest hacking group?"

"Funny you ask. Remember I told you about Jiang Shi, the head of Red Guest? His nephew was the one who tried to kidnap you in New York. Turns out Jiang Shi's uncle happens to own Sinam Tech."

"Wow. Talk about keeping it all in the family." I set down my fork without eating the bite on it. "I think you may be on to something, Slash. But my role in all of this is unclear."

"Maybe not as unclear as you think. I still think it has to do with whatever you're working on with the Zimmermans. But they won't get close to you again. They may be good hackers, but they're amateurs at capture and deception."

"Well, that certainly makes me feel better."

He reached over and took my hand, looking directly at me. "They aren't going to get you. I mean it."

"I believe you."

"Good. So, let's eat." He released my hand and picked up his fork.

I pushed my food around for a moment, trying to steady my nerves. "So, what's on the agenda after dinner?"

He took a bite, chewed and regarded me thoughtfully. "You up for some gaming?"

"Really?" I perked up. "I don't think we've ever gamed together before."

"We haven't."

I took a slow sip of wine. "I should warn you, I'm pretty advanced."

"Excellent. I was afraid I might be bored."

I narrowed my eyes. "Just so we're clear, I'm *not* going to go easy on you."

He touched my cheek with his fingertip. His eyes shone back with interest and something else…a sexy, competitive edge. My pulse kicked up a beat. Wow, who knew that gaming with him would be such a turn on?

"Trust me, *cara*. I wouldn't have it any other way."

THE REST OF the week passed with the twins walking me through the precise steps of the manufacturing process and teaching me how to calculate various calibrations while spotting dangerous deviations. Slash stayed every night at my apartment, which meant a double dose of security on both of us.

The twins and I finally finished up my training on Sunday afternoon. I was exhausted, but confident I could oversee the process with at least some predicted measure of success.

"You're going to do great," Elvis said, patting me on the shoulder.

"I agree," Xavier said. "You've got this."

I rubbed the knot at the back of my neck. "You guys are just saying that to make me feel better for screwing up that last round of calculations."

"Not true." Elvis unzipped his suit and carefully stepped out of it, leaning on the counter. "I made a series of errors in that exact same place. It set us back three weeks. I couldn't figure out what I was doing wrong. Xavier spotted it finally, thank goodness. Otherwise we would have been sunk for good. I let you make the same mistake so you'd remember it."

I shuddered to think what the world would have missed out on if Xavier hadn't caught the error. Then again, I wondered how many scientific discoveries were lost because of mistakes…or found because of them.

"So, what are you guys doing tonight?" I asked the twins.

"I'm going to Basia's." Xavier hung his suit on the hook. "We're going to have a quiet night in and watch some television before you guys leave for Indonesia in the morning."

"Great." I bumped elbows with Elvis. "How about you?"

"Bonnie and I are going out."

"Really? That's great. Is everything okay?"

"Maybe. I'm figuring it out."

Xavier punched his brother lightly on the arm. "Come on, guys, let's get out of here."

Xavier put an arm around each of us as we headed to the elevator, laughing and jostling.

"So, what are you doing tonight, Lexi?" Elvis asked.

"Going to my parents' house. I promised to stop by and see them before I left. My mom is completely freaking out about the trip. All the incidents that have happened to me lately have her convinced that I've got one foot in the grave and the other on a banana peel."

Elvis shook his head. "Wow. I don't envy you that conversation with your mother. Good luck."

I thought about how my mother's voice had sounded on the phone. I had a feeling it was going to be a long evening.

"Thanks, Elvis. I'm going to need it."

# TWENTY

SLASH PICKED ME UP at my apartment after nine o'clock.
He'd been running late trying to finish up some last minute work before heading out. To my surprise, he suggested we stay overnight at his place since it was closer
to the airport. I agreed and was waiting in my kitchen,
my suitcase by the door when he arrived.

He kissed me on the cheek. "There's a convoy of security vehicles in the parking lot."

"Ugh. My neighbors are beginning to wonder what's
going on."

"How was your visit with your parents?"

"You don't want to know." I rolled my eyes.

"*Si*, I do." He brushed his arm against mine. "Tell
me."

"Painful. They're worried about me."

"*I'm* worried about you, so I totally get it." He tousled
my hair. "You ready for tomorrow?"

"Strangely, yes. I'm actually getting kind of excited.
How about you?"

"I packed this morning, figuring it would be a late
evening at work tonight."

He took my suitcase while I grabbed my purse and set
my alarm. We walked down to the parking lot. I stopped
by my security detail.

The driver rolled down his window. "Where are you
going?"

"To my boyfriend's. You can follow us there."

"We already know where it is."

Of course he did. "Okay. What time do you want me to be ready for the airport tomorrow?"

The driver consulted with the guy in the passenger seat. "We leave at ten-thirty. Meet us out in front of the building."

"Okay. Have a good night."

"You, too."

Slash had already loaded my suitcase, so I climbed into the car. He pulled out of the parking lot, with the FBI and my security detail in tow. I watched them over my shoulder, then turned around in my seat.

"This is so annoying."

Slash fiddled with his sound system. "Welcome to my world." He pushed a button and the piano music of Hai Tsang filled the car.

I sighed, immediately relaxing. "His music is so soothing."

"*Si*, it is."

I listened for a few minutes before I spoke. "I wish we were traveling together, but I have to be on the company plane. I don't like flying."

"I know." He put his hand on my knee and patted. "But you'll be fine, flying in luxury, or so I understand, on a Gulfstream plane."

"You researched my plane?"

"Of course."

He always seemed one step ahead of me. "What time does yours take off?"

"Seven-thirty in the morning. I've got to leave at four o'clock to make it. I've got a layover in Tokyo, but I should be in Jakarta before you land. Your layover is in

Hawaii but you should be right behind us. I'll be at the airport watching for your arrival, but I'll meet you at the hotel later. I made sure we're staying at the same one."

When we got to Slash's place, we headed right for the bedroom. Slash pulled me in for a kiss and then touched the earrings he'd bought me.

"They need cleaning," he said.

"I thought you said never to take them off."

"Except to clean them." He reached behind my earlobes and slid them out. "Don't worry about it, I'll take care of them. You go hop in the shower and I'll join you there shortly."

I undressed and stepped into the shower. "Which showerhead do I turn on?" I asked.

"Turn on all three and see which one you like."

I did as he said and stood underneath each of them, before stopping at the vortex of all three. It was an amazing feeling, like a rinse and a massage at the same time.

"Wow." I slicked back my hair with my hands. "They all feel great, Slash, but I like the kinetic spray best."

Slash stepped in and stood under the massage one, letting the water beat on his neck and shoulders. "I choose depending on my mood."

"It's entirely possible I could live my entire life in here. All I'd need is computer access."

He grinned. "I'm working on it."

We soaped each other up, laughing and enjoying ourselves. I didn't understand how we weren't sick of each other after spending so much time together. There was so little logic to relationships, and yet for mystifying reasons, this one was working for me.

After we dried off, Slash stood at the sink shaving and I went to the bedroom to get my pajamas. I opened my suitcase and carefully pulled out the royal blue lace teddy I'd ordered online and received yesterday. It was really soft, but in terms of material, there wasn't a lot there. I slipped it over my head and it slid down my stomach, reaching just past my hips. It wasn't as racy as some of the others I'd seen, but it showed an awful lot of leg. The front was mostly see-through lace with some cross-stitching and the girls were on full display. I didn't quite understand the rationality of wearing anything that was see-through. I mean, if you can see everything anyway, why even bother covering it? But my research had indicated this style was popular among males, so I'd bought it.

I stood nervously near the bed, shifting on my feet and trying different poses in an attempt to appear sexy. What I really wanted to do was crawl under the covers and hide.

When his hand touched my hip from behind, I jumped and whirled around. "Wow, Slash. You about gave me a heart attack. Are you finished in the bathroom?"

He didn't say a word, just let his gaze slide over the length of me all the way down to my toes and back. Sliding a finger under the strap on my shoulder, he nudged me closer.

"Is this new?"

I tried to relax and act like I bought lingerie all the time. "Sort of. I thought I would spice up the wardrobe, you know. Women do that all the time. Spice things up."

"Basia suggested it?"

My cheeks burned. "No. I just thought it was time for a change. You know, to indicate that I'm open to trying new things. Not that I think there is something new."

Aaack. This was *not* coming out as casual and sophisticated as I'd hoped.

His brown eyes assessed me thoughtfully. "You do know I love you no matter what you wear, right? Remember the first night we met? You were dressed in that ridiculous T-shirt and nothing else. I was captivated from that moment."

"You were?" His confession made me smile. How far we'd come from that first moment. "Well, in that case, I'll go change into my T-shirt."

He put a hand on my shoulder, holding me to the spot. "No, you don't. Stay right here. I like it. You did this for me?"

I touched the lace on the front. "Yes. I researched the different kinds of lingerie and cross-referenced it with popularity with males based on culture and preferences. I purchased it online. I wasn't sure about the color, so that was a guess, but teddies were the most popular choice among European males, so I went with that. Was it a good choice?"

He turned to assess me, sliding both his palms down my sides and securing them on my hips. "I assure you, it's an excellent choice. You're bringing it with you to Jakarta?"

"Yes."

"Even better. We'll break it in tonight and have plenty of time to explore it more while in Jakarta."

I wasn't sure exactly how we'd go about exploring lingerie, but knowing Slash and his inventive mind, I was pretty sure I'd enjoy it.

My pulse jumped. "Count me in."

# TWENTY-ONE

SLASH WOKE ME UP to give me a lingering kiss before he headed out. It was still dark outside. As I yawned, he gave me the key and the alarm code to make sure I locked up tight.

"See you in Jakarta in about twenty-four hours," he murmured against my cheek.

I slid my arms around his neck. "I wish we had more time to say goodbye."

He was already dressed with his leather jacket on. "Don't tempt me." He cupped my cheek. "Be good, *cara*, okay?"

"Okay."

"I put your earrings on the dresser. Don't forget them." He kissed me and stood to leave.

"Hey, Slash."

*"Si?"*

"Have a good flight."

"You, too. See you soon."

After he left, I went back to sleep for another few hours. I got up at nine, brushed my teeth and got dressed. I was about to head downstairs when I got a call from Finn.

"ComQuest security called and it looks like an airplane mechanical problem has delayed pick-up until about three this afternoon."

"Great." I tried not to sound disappointed. After all I

was going to Jakarta to make hardware history. It's just I was losing all those hours with Slash in paradise where I could be sharpening my womanly prowess.

After a dull day of reviewing my upcoming duties at the production plant and taking on another level of Hollow Realm, at two fifty-five sharp I locked up Slash's apartment and met my security detail in front of the building as planned. My driver told me we were headed to the executive side of the airport where a private chartered Gulfstream waited for us. Sounded like a cool plane, but traveling on anything smaller than a giant airliner left me feeling a bit queasy. I'm not a big fan of flying, but I sucked it up in the name of technological revolution.

"Do any of you know how many hours it takes to get to Hawaii?" I asked the security guard next to me. "It's our first stop before heading on to Jakarta."

The driver met my eyes in the mirror. "My wife and I took a trip to Hawaii for our fifteenth anniversary. It was hotter than the devil and expensive as hell, but she loved it. Took us about thirteen hours from here, I'd say. In your fancy jet, you might get there faster."

The other guy typed something on his cell phone and looked up. "Yep, and that's the short leg. You'll have thirteen more hours from Hawaii to Jakarta. It's going to be a heck of a long ride."

I sighed. It was going to be a freaking flying marathon. Ugh. At least I'd dressed for the occasion. Jeans, T-shirt, my gray comfy sweatshirt and tennis shoes. My hair was in a ponytail and no makeup. Not exactly corporate dress, but I'd rather be comfortable. I'd brought more businesslike clothes for working, even though I'd spend most of my time in a hazmat suit in the factory.

The airport soon came into sight. The driver skirted the main airport and drove along a fringe road ringing the runways. I started to worry something weird was up until we made a turn and headed toward a small, swanky terminal with tall glass windows and a roof that swept up like a wave. Maybe this executive travel wasn't so bad. No busy public terminals and long security lines.

Glass double doors swung open and a woman in a neat suit and colorful scarf welcomed us in. My suitcase was plopped onto a cart and disappeared before I had time to scrounge in my purse and dig out a tip for the handler. At least I wouldn't have to wait in line to check my bag.

Inside, our group mingled, munching cookies and drinking coffee. I could use some of each to jump-start the long flights ahead. Others in the group stood attentive, ignoring the food and monitoring the people and their surroundings. More security, I presumed.

Finn and Basia chatted with each other. Finn wore a suit, likely a casual one by his standards. Basia had on navy pants and a comfortable top in Xavier's favorite color, keyboard white. Her oversized red purse hung on a shoulder and matched her shoes. I didn't envy her the heels, but she made them look as comfortable as my tennis shoes.

To my surprise, Xavier and Elvis were there, too. Elvis's blue eyes lit up as he walked over to me. "Lexi, glad to see you made it. I was afraid the flight delay gave you time to reconsider the dangers involved."

"Are you kidding? I wouldn't miss this for the world. This is going to be better than beta testing Dragon Kingdom VI. You came to see us off?"

"Of course. That's our baby you're bringing to life."

A funny look swept across his face and then he laughed. "Seriously, Xavier and I really appreciate this. I appreciate it."

I shoved my hands into my jeans. "I'm honored to do it. Honored you considered me capable. History, here we come."

"I wish I could be there to oversee it, too." He hesitated for just a beat too long and I saw something flash in his eyes. "But I'm just not ready to travel yet."

"Look, Elvis, it's okay." I put a hand on his arm. "Broodryk totally screwed with our minds and bodies. You took the worst of it, and you're going to need time to recover from it. We all will. That you've been able to focus on your work to the degree you have impresses me. Give me a chance to impress you."

His expression relaxed. "You're right. I've had a lot on my mind lately. It helps that Xavier and I were essentially finished with the prototype before we left for Greece." He reached out, touched the locket around my neck. "You wore it."

I looked down at it. "I thought it should be saved for special occasions. I figured this qualified. So, in a way, it's as if a part of you will be there, too."

He met my gaze for a long time, then looked away. "I appreciate that more than you know. Be careful, Lexi, okay. Call me as soon as you arrive."

"I will."

We looked up as Basia and Xavier came to greet us. They were holding hands and beaming. Basia's cheeks were flushed. "Hey, Lexi, did you notice? We're flying in a Gulfstream. That means we'll be traveling in total style. God, I love my job."

"Only the best for my girl," Xavier said, kissing her on the cheek.

Basia threw her arms around him and kissed him back. I would have never guessed in a million years that guy would be Xavier, but I guess that's what kept the universe interesting. Basia was transforming in front of my eyes.

We chatted for a bit more until Finn waved us over. "Everyone have their passports?"

We nodded and security hustled us out the door to the tarmac and into a luxury van that drove us to the plane. Fox, Andrew, Oliver and Cezar were standing at the bottom of the airplane steps talking to two men in uniform, presumably the pilot and copilot.

Andrew handed me the titanium briefcase. I'd expected something like an oversized briefcase, but this sleek little thing wasn't much bigger than a large notebook. Could it really rain doom and destruction on anyone tampering with the lock?

"Remember it can pack a punch to the wrong people trying to open it," Andrew said, noting my curiosity. "Only you know the process, right?"

"Right." I took the case from him. "Do I have to chain it to myself or something?" Like the military guy who carried the nuclear football around.

Andrew shook his head. "Not necessary. It won't be going anywhere. Oliver and Cezar, ComQuest's security directors who you met earlier in the week, are flying with you and will accompany you at all times. They are both armed for your protection."

Oliver, with his muscular neck and thighs, looked more like a football linebacker than an executive. I felt sure he could tackle any bad guy that might try to overtake us, even without a gun. His eyes were hidden behind a pair of dark sunglasses as he lifted his jacket to show me his weapon.

"They're allowed to take a gun on the airplane?"

"It's our plane."

"Okay."

"Don't worry, Miss Carmichael," Cezar said. He was smaller than Oliver in terms of build, but he appeared quite fit and serious. He crossed his arms and his suit jacket pulled tight across the bulge at his waist where I presumed his gun was located. "Once we land in Jakarta, the rest of the team will be there to greet us. You'll always have someone looking out for you."

Andrew patted my shoulder. "In fact, your security team is already en route so they are ready and in place when you land. I want to assure you that we're taking your safety very seriously."

"Good to know."

We talked for a few more minutes before we were instructed to board the plane. I gave Xavier and Elvis one last hug before climbing on board. A blonde flight attendant dressed in a light blue shirt and navy skirt greeted us with a smile.

"Welcome aboard. My name is Amanda and I'll be your flight attendant for the trip to Hawaii. Please sit wherever you'd like and let me know if I can get you anything before takeoff."

One look at the interior, and I froze with indecision. This Gulfstream wasn't like any airliner I'd flown. Basia pushed me along from behind. I passed four leather recliner-type seats facing each other, each against a window.

"Keep going," Basia encouraged.

I passed another two seats on one side and a long couch that promised an ultra-comfy place for a snooze should I need one. Large oval windows ran down both sides and through them I could still see the twins watching us board.

The last grouping of four leather seats faced a foldable worktable. Across the aisle ran a long credenza with a flat screen television. A galley with sparkling crystal glasses, microwave and tiny oven finished off the back before ending in a polished wood door that I guessed went to a glorified bathroom.

Basia tugged on my arm. "Look at this."

On the table were two of those sparkling glasses. Between them was an ice bucket with a champagne bottle and a quart of juice. Freshly squeezed orange juice, strained, no pulp. Rather like Bond's shaken not stirred. Maybe I had more in common with Bond than I thought.

Basia snatched up the chilled bottle. "Rosé Champagne. How did they know?"

The twins had struck again. Basia must have figured it out, too, because she scooted into a seat on one side of the table and waved out the window. I didn't have to guess her grin was meant for Xavier. She blew him a kiss.

I leaned onto a chair across the table from her and glanced out my own window. Elvis gave me a casual salute and I waved back.

As the engines started up, I slid my purse and the titanium case in a cubbyhole in the credenza adjacent to our seats. Basia tossed her red purse into a cubby next to it. I sunk into total luxury of the comfy seats and buckled my belt.

I grinned over at Basia. "Wow. You are right. This plane might even change my mind about flying."

While we taxied, the flight attendant gave a safety spiel and then explained all the electronic functions of the plane at our fingertips. I could raise and lower any of the window shades, choose what movies to watch on the flat screen, use the internet, make phone calls and do more with this multifunction seat than I thought possible on an aircraft.

The pilots wasted no time getting airborne and Baltimore grew smaller before disappearing beneath clouds.

Amanda served the champagne, and Basia and I toasted the start of a new adventure—her with the champagne and me with my orange juice. We chased the setting sun for a bit of the trip, but in between the movies Basia and I watched, I managed to check in with Elvis and discovered a message from Slash, sent on one of his layovers.

Finn, Oliver and Cezar played cards until Finn broke away to get work done. Amanda brought us drinks and food so often I had to turn her away. I felt a little sick from eating too much and sipping some of Basia's champagne.

The pilot and copilot each visited the cabin and stopped to chat. I noticed the flight attendant was careful to sit with whomever was flying the plane so no one was alone in the cockpit.

After a while, I dozed. When I woke up, Basia and Finn were sleeping, their seats reclined way back and footrests deployed. Neither Cezar nor Oliver seemed inclined to sleep on this leg of the trip, and I caught them staring at me on more than one occasion. It was a bit creepy.

It seemed to take forever, but finally the pilot told us we were about twenty minutes out of Hawaii. Basia woke up and went to the bathroom to freshen up. She came out smelling like toothpaste and looking as if she'd just visited a spa. My ponytail was plastered to my head and my teeth were fuzzy. I felt a zit forming on my chin. Even with all the luxury, I felt cranky.

"I wish we could have a day or two in Hawaii. It's my first time here." Basia peered out the window. "Look at the lights of Honolulu. That big shadow over there must be Diamond Head." She pointed it out for me as I leaned over her to get a glimpse. "I'd love to check out the beaches in the daytime."

"I don't care for the beach," I grumbled. Our last beach vacation had ended in disaster. Then, I smiled in spite of myself, because it was also when I'd first met the Zimmerman twins. Now we'd gone from Ocean City, Maryland to Jakarta, Indonesia. Who knew where our friendship would take me next?

We landed outside of Honolulu a few minutes later and were instructed to stay on the plane while we had a crew change, refueled and got more food supplies. Wendy, a pretty Asian girl with long black hair, replaced perky blonde Amanda. She stowed her gear and immediately insisted on serving us champagne and hot washcloths to steam us awake or make us go back to sleep again. Either way, I just wanted to get the heck on with it and get to our destination already. I needed people to quit plying me with food and asking me if I needed anything. My grouchy level was rising exponentially with each mile we travelled.

My mood must have rubbed off on our new pilot. He came back for a personal announcement to us after we'd been on the ground for an hour, and informed us we had a bit of a delay.

As soon as we took off I played a couple of games on my phone, and started *Sixty Shadows of Black* on my electronic reader. A few hours later, with night fully in vogue and the stars shining outside the big windows, I dozed off thinking about paddles and nipple clips. I awoke six hours later after dreaming I'd been chased around a factory by an oversized microchip with a whip.

My neck was stiff and I needed to go to the bathroom. After I returned, I continued reading and must have gasped aloud at some point because Basia gave me a weird look.

"What in the world are you reading?"

I hugged the reader to my chest. "Nothing. Why do you ask?"

She looked at me and tugged at the reader. I released it and she lifted an eyebrow when she saw the title. "Really?"

I peered up the aisle at Finn, but he was asleep. Oliver was reading a magazine and had his chair in massage mode. Cezar was laid out on the couch with eyes closed and earplugs in.

"Keep your voice down," I whispered. "I'm doing research."

"So, you're taking it seriously?"

"Of course I'm taking it seriously. But I'm worried. So far, I don't think I am cut out for this level of sexual experimentation, especially the role-playing part."

"It's just fantasy."

"I know it's fantasy. But there is *real* pain involved."

"Only as much as agreed to ahead of time." She handed my reader back to me.

"And just how do you calculate that? Are there specific metrics I need to be aware of? A mathematical equation of some kind to determine the correct threshold of pain? How is it measured, you know, in the moment? For example, how do I determine the correct velocity at which to snap the whip in order to meet the previously agreed-to level of pain?"

She giggled. "Only you would ask that question."

"Of course I'm asking that question. It's logical to know the exact parameters before the roleplaying starts. What if I hurt Slash?"

"Wait. OMG. You're worried about hurting Slash?"

"Shhhh." I looked around but no one seemed to be paying any attention to us. "Of course I'm worried about hurting him. There are whips and chains involved, in case you didn't know. I'm a total klutz. What if I seriously injure him? I mean, come on. Dating Slash is like dating the President. He's followed around like some freaking national treasure. If I injured or impaired him, I could be locked up in the slammer for life."

The giggles turned into laughter and she had to cover her mouth to keep it quiet. "Oh, dear God, Lexi. I would seriously pay to see you in action. Who needs *Sixty Shadows of Black* when we can have *Geek Girl Dominatrix*." She shook with silent laughter.

"Not helping, Basia."

She pressed one hand to her chest and wiped her eyes with the other. "Oh, honey. You slay me. Totally. Look, you can relax about this whole BDSM thing. The game stops once you use a safe word. If he hurts you or you are hurting him, all you have to do is say the word and the roleplaying stops."

"What if I'm gagged? I read about that, too. It can be part of the game."

She looked like she might start laughing again, but managed to compose herself. "Well, in that case, you'd better have a safe gesture, too."

I threw up my hands. "See, this is exactly what I'm talking about. There are too many variables and rules, all of them weirdly kinky. I'll need a complete spreadsheet to consult, which might take away from the spontaneity of the moment."

"You'll figure out what you want." She patted my arm. "If you don't like it, by all means tell Slash."

My stomach rolled uneasily. "What if I say I don't want to do BDSM at all and it drives a wedge between us?"

She adjusted her seat, then sighed as it reclined. "You are way too worried about this. Slash won't make you do anything you don't want to do, and he certainly won't let it drive a wedge between you. He adores you."

"I know." I started fiddling with the controls on my seat. "But I feel like I owe it to him to at least give this a try. I mean if he has a whole room dedicated to it, it must be really important. He took me to his place because it was important to me. Now I want to reciprocate by doing something in return for him."

She slipped her hands behind her neck, cradling her head. "Lexi, let me give you a word of advice. Don't stress any more about it. I'm sure you guys will work it out."

I wasn't convinced, but returned to the book anyway and kept reading. About ten minutes later the copilot came out of the cockpit to go to the bathroom. Wendy went in to sit with the pilot. When the copilot exited the crew head, he caught my scrutiny and walked back to ask how the flight was going. I made sure to press the reader to my chest so he couldn't see what I was reading.

Just in case.

I gave him a thumbs-up. He smiled at me and headed back toward the cockpit. Finn, who had awoken a minute ago, stopped the copilot and asked a question. Finn pointed to a small flat screen next to his seat. I craned my neck to see him pointing to the view of our flight path.

Whatever conversation he had with the copilot made the guy's face pale.

The copilot hurried to the cockpit door where he knocked firmly. I exchanged a worried look with Finn who stared directly at me, worry etched on his face. While I sat there wishing I could read his mind, the door to the cockpit opened.

Wendy stepped out, but the copilot didn't take her place in the cockpit. Instead, she closed the door behind her. The copilot backed up quickly to the first set of seats. His motion seemed a bit odd and I couldn't figure out what was going on.

It wasn't until the copilot shifted that I could see Wendy's gun.

# TWENTY-TWO

"Whoa." The copilot held up his hands. "What the hell's going on?" He backed up to the first set of seats.

Everything seemed to move in slow motion. Basia must have caught the horror on my face. She turned around and took a quick look toward the cockpit, then screamed. The reader fell from my hands and clattered to the table. Behind Basia, Oliver jumped to his feet with a strangled cry. Finn unbuckled his seatbelt and stood. Cezar, across from Oliver, ripped the headphones from his ears and swung his feet off the couch.

"Everyone put your hands up now." Wendy motioned the copilot to sit.

He obliged by quickly sitting in the first empty seat and keeping his hands in the air.

"What's the meaning of this?" Oliver demanded.

"I urge all of you to sit back down and not make any sudden moves," she said.

She trained the gun on Oliver, standing in front of his seat. "Take your gun out with two fingers and put it on the floor. Now."

Wendy stayed near the front, blocking the aisle past the crew compartment and lavatory to the cockpit. If she came too far forward, she'd put herself between the co-pilot and Finn. Obviously aware of her position, she motioned again at Oliver. He frowned and reached slowly under his jacket, pulling out his gun and placing it on the floor in front of him.

"Kick it toward me."

Oliver hesitated for a long moment, as if assessing his chances of rushing her and surviving. After a few seconds he kicked it to her and she picked it up, tucking it in her waistband.

"Good. Now sit down. Buckle your seatbelt and sit on your hands."

He obliged and she turned the gun on Cezar. "Your turn. Give me your gun. Same process."

His jaw tightened, but he carefully withdrew his gun and kicked it to her. He didn't kick it hard enough, though, so it stopped several steps from her.

Wendy left the gun in place. "Everyone. Buckle your seatbelts and sit on your hands. If everyone remains calm and does exactly what I say, no one will get hurt. We are making a small diversion. That's all. We will land, take what we need and leave in a different plane. We will not hurt you." For a small woman, she looked very much in charge.

"What is it you want?" Finn asked.

As if we all didn't already know. Still Finn never asked dumb questions, so I figured he'd asked for a reason. Maybe it was to disguise the fact that he hadn't buckled his seatbelt. Or maybe he intended it to serve as a distraction. Whatever the reason, I hoped he didn't have a plan that involved trying to grab Wendy's gun and getting shot.

My brain was racing at an alarming speed, imagining potential scenarios and disregarding them. I glanced toward the titanium case in the nearby cubby—certainly the cause of this hijacking.

Wendy looked at me. "We want Lexi Carmichael and the case. That's all."

I froze. Her answer surprised me. Not about the case, but because there would be no reason to want *me* along with the case, unless she *knew* the case was set to my palm print. However, *no one* knew any of that, not even Finn or Basia. Just Elvis, Xavier, me and a few top Com-Quest bigwigs.

So, if Wendy had that piece of knowledge, that meant she had access to information at the top echelon of Com-Quest.

Exactly how did Wendy know about me?

As I pondered that strange turn of developments, Wendy signaled the copilot to use his foot and slide Cezar's gun the rest of the way to her. The pilot slid forward in his seat and stretched out his foot, but instead of kicking the gun, his hand released his belt and he leaped up and charged her.

She managed to get two shots off before the copilot was almost upon her. He kept on moving. Cezar charged into the aisle behind him. The copilot landed against Wendy, slamming her hard into the cockpit door, and then falling to the floor with her. I saw the two struggle with the gun in her hand. Another shot fired off before Cezar joined the pile.

*Holy shots on a plane!*

I pulled Basia under the table, trying to make us as small a target as possible. Finn and Oliver jumped in to help the copilot. Wendy must have hung onto the gun for a few more seconds, because another shot rang out.

A million thoughts ran through my head. First and foremost was that someone was shooting a gun on a plane. *What the heck?* Didn't anyone get the memo about not doing that *ever*? Holes in an airplane fuselage were *not* a good thing at forty-some thousand feet.

When the shooting and yelling had subsided, I heard Finn call for help. I crawled out and headed toward the front. Wendy was pinned to the ground with Cezar on top of her. The copilot had rolled to one side, moaning and clutching his abdomen. Finn knelt beside him. I gave a sigh of relief when I saw Finn appeared uninjured.

The cabin seemed a bit hazy. Oxygen masks dropped above my head and dangled on clear tubing. Jeez, we were losing air. I didn't know how many shots had pierced the hull, but I calculated we had about ten seconds to grab a mask or pass out.

"Get on oxygen fast," I yelled out.

Finn grabbed the copilot under his arms and dragged him back to a seat. Blood covered his white shirt. Finn put a dangling mask over his face before securing one on the copilot. The plane's nose pitched down. My feet felt strangely light and I had trouble keeping them on the floor. We were rapidly descending.

Oliver and Cezar wrestled Wendy out of sight into the private crew seat. Until the captain made it to fourteen thousand feet or so, we wouldn't be able to move freely.

"Lexi, the copilot is wounded," Finn shouted, his voice sounding funny behind the plastic mask. "Find something to help stop the bleeding."

I was able to stretch my length of oxygen tubing enough to reach the galley drawer where I'd seen Amanda, on the leg to Hawaii, grab linen dinner napkins. I grabbed a wad and stretched up to the sofa where I traded for a new oxygen mask. Eventually, I reached the copilot by exchanging masks until I kneeled down next to him.

I pulled his hand away, taking a look at the injury. He groaned and writhed as I pressed the cloths against his bloody abdomen. I swallowed hard. I'm not particularly squeamish, but it didn't look good. He'd been hit on the right side, where the kidney, liver and pancreas were located. There was blood on my hands and on the floor beneath him. He moaned again, then passed out.

Finn patted my hand on top of the linens. "Keep it there. I have to figure out how to get to the cockpit." He secured Cezar's gun from the floor and tucked it in at his waist.

I watched him, feeling a twinge of guilt that he'd come along with me, even if I'd tried to dissuade him. Slash was right. My mom was right. Trouble followed me like a stalker.

I heard a banging on the cockpit door and shifted to look toward the front. Cezar had a portable oxygen unit the crew used and was trying to open the door. Unfortunately for all of us, it was locked and he was making exactly zero headway.

"That's no good." Oliver spoke sharply to Cezar from the crew compartment where he'd secured Wendy. "We can't break down the door. What good would it do anyway?" He looked out of the little compartment back at the rest of us. "No one else can fly the plane. Right?"

We all, in our funny little masks, looked at each other and then the copilot. I kept holding firm pressure to his abdomen, but the cloths I had brought had completely soaked through.

Cezar held up a gun, probably Wendy's. "They were in it together." He pointed to Wendy, tucked away in the crew seat. "The flight crew changed in Hawaii. That's where they came on. But how could that happen? We reviewed their bios in detail."

"No time now to figure out where things went wrong." Oliver tucked his own gun, which he'd retrieved from Wendy, back in his holster and signaled Cezar to hand hers over. Cezar gave it to Oliver, who checked the magazine before shoving it back in place. "Six rounds left." He tucked it behind his waist.

Whether from the shortage of oxygen or the rollercoaster drop, my brain spun into overdrive. Something totally bugged me about this situation. How had our tight level of security been breached?

I wanted to voice my concerns, but events were unfolding too rapidly around me.

"What's the plan?" Finn asked Oliver.

"I'm working on it."

I peered out the window. The pilot was steadily descending. Sunrise must be near, because the sky had lightened enough to dim the stars. Below, I could no longer see whitecaps from the waves reflecting starlight. Instead, it was shadowy and rough. We flew over land. "Do we know where we are?"

Finn shook his head. "All I know for certain is the pilot diverted from our path to Jakarta. That's what I was discussing with the copilot before he was shot."

Cezar, who had moved to check on the copilot, pressed his face against the window. "Looks like we're heading over jungle. Certainly not near a city or town. All I see are mountains and a lot of green."

"Here." Finn handed Cezar his gun.

Cezar tucked it back into his holster. "So, where did the copilot say we're headed?"

"Port Moresby."

"Guys, what's that over there?" Basia interrupted.

I squinted into the sky and saw the flash of navigation lights. "Holy cow. It's another plane. Coming right toward us."

Finn cupped his hand against the window and watched. "No, not coming at us. Coming alongside us."

"OMG! I can see the people inside," Basia said after a minute. "Who are they?"

Finn shook his head. "I don't know, but they're shadowing us."

"Maybe they'll help." She sounded hopeful.

I hated to be the voice of doom, but I didn't think a plane that had appeared out of nowhere, at exactly the time of the hijacking, was there to help us. It wasn't statistically feasible.

"I'm sorry, Basia, but I sincerely doubt that's their intention."

"Are you saying those are bad guys, too?"

"My vote is yes. I presume they're following us to wherever the pilot intends to land this plane."

"Would be nice to know who they were working for." Finn's voice was low and hard.

"It's a Chinese registered aircraft." Cezar pointed out the window. "See that B followed by numbers near the tail? I used to work protection for a guy that repossessed aircraft from around the world, and that's how they were identified"

I considered it significant that there was a Chinese connection again. "That might account for the Asian guys that attacked me twice."

Cezar nodded as rays of morning light made a nice crown on the horizon. "We were warned that the Chinese have been hacking the company's system for the past six months. They couldn't get through. The Zimmerman twins apparently gave the tech guys some solid ways to keep them out."

No surprise there. "I guess they had to find another way to get the knowledge," I said.

"I guess they did." Oliver spoke the words, but his tone was wrong.

We all turned away from the window.

Oliver had released Wendy. This time they both stood, holding weapons pointed at us.

# TWENTY-THREE

THE PIECES FELL into place. The detailed information about our flight plan, the ability to put whomever he wanted on the plane, the knowledge that the case was wired to my biometrics—Oliver had known it all. Only someone at the very top could have pulled this off.

All wasn't lost, however. They could steal the case, but it would be useless without the code. The bad news was that we were all going to bite the dust now that we knew Oliver was a traitor. I was pretty sure he wouldn't let any of us live after learning of his participation in the hijacking, not to mention murder charges if the co-pilot didn't survive.

Oliver motioned at Cezar. "Face down on the couch. Arms out and palms up."

Cezar grumbled but complied. Oliver worked his way toward Cezar, having to ditch one mask and secure another. When he reached Cezar the first thing he did was extract the gun from Cezar's holster. He then zip-tied Cezar's hands together behind his back. Next he pulled an oxygen mask down and switched it with the portable one Cezar wore. Great. Now Oliver had even more mobility.

Wendy kept a close watch on Finn. She looked like someone had clocked her good. Her eyes were still glassy and she had a massive bruise building on her cheek. I didn't feel one bit sorry for her.

Oliver patted Cezar down and came up with another pistol, a switchblade and a set of brass knuckles.

*Holy gangster.* Apparently Cezar had been prepared for every occasion…except a betrayal from his boss.

As an extra precaution, Oliver tied Cezar's feet together and handcuffed him to the couch. I couldn't see how we would get any assistance from him now.

The copilot started to moan and come around.

"We have to help him," Basia said to Oliver. "He's going to die." She rose from her seat.

"Really, half-pint? You a nurse or something?"

"No, simply a lot more human than you are."

"Sass won't get you anywhere. Park that skinny butt back in your seat."

Basia glared at him. She might be petite, but she detested when people underestimated her.

"We'll get him assistance when we land," Oliver said. "No one was supposed to get hurt. He made a stupid decision to rush Wendy."

Cezar grunted. "No. He made a calculated decision to fight for his life." He pulled against his restraints. "How can you do this, Oliver? I thought you were my friend. Now you're selling out to the Chinese? It goes against everything you stand for."

Oliver shrugged. "I stand for making eight million dollars. Shut up."

During Cezar's trussing, Wendy had worked her way well into the cabin area. She pointed her gun at me. "Give me the case. Now."

I didn't have to ask which case she meant. I pointed at the cubby in the credenza. Oliver snatched it and handed it over to her. She tucked the titanium case into a black sports bag with the carry strap slung over her neck and one shoulder.

After she zipped it shut, she motioned at Finn. "You. Join the two ladies and belt in. Now."

Finn tossed aside his mask and moved back to their table. He donned a new mask and then folded up a leaf of the table on the side next to me so he could drop into a seat.

"Wait." She pointed at me. "You sit on the aisle. He goes in the seat by the window."

I rose and played musical seats with a scowling Finn. We buckled in again. A quick peek out the window indicated we'd dropped closer to the jungle. I suspected the pilot was nearing ten thousand feet and we no longer needed the oxygen.

Wendy stood guard while Oliver headed to the cockpit. He gave a series of complicated knocks. It seemed like forever and no one opened up. A sickening fear hit my gut. Was the pilot okay?

The door finally opened. Oliver caught the pilot as he nearly dropped into his arms. *Holy crap.* He'd been shot.

Oliver helped the captain back to the pilot's seat. We sat too far away to hear any discussion, but Oliver returned minus his mask, looking pale and distraught. He did a quick check on the copilot and then approached Wendy. "We've got a problem."

"What's wrong?"

"The pilot has been hit. One of the bullets penetrated the cockpit. We're damn lucky it didn't kill him. He's bleeding badly. He's managed to hold the course so far, but he's pretty sure he's minutes from passing out."

"What?" Wendy looked horrified. "I thought the doors were impenetrable to bullets."

"Are you crazy? A plane couldn't lift off with that kind of weight. They are reinforced, but a bullet will still go through."

"Oh, God."

"The pilot says we have to put down now. He's not going to make it to Port Moresby."

"Isn't Port Moresby in Papua New Guinea?" I whispered to Finn.

"Yes. That's what I asked the copilot about when I noticed our flight path was off. He thought it was a planned stop on our way to Jakarta."

Great. The captain had literally led him astray.

Wendy looked out the window into the dawning new day. "Is there an airport before Port Moresby? I don't see anything out there but jungle and mountains. Not even a road."

"He's looking for something suitable for us to land on."

"How suitable?" For a totally cold-hearted woman, her voice sounded a tad panicked. "Maybe we can get the copilot awake."

Oliver shook his head. "He's near death, thanks to you."

"He attacked me."

"You should have stuck with the plan. We agreed no one would get hurt."

"It happened so fast. I didn't think he'd be that stupid."

"Water under the bridge now. I've got to get back to the cockpit."

"Wait. Did you relay the information to them?" She jerked her head toward the other plane which, as far as I could see, was still matching us in speed and pace."

"Of course." He held up a walkie-talkie. "There's nothing they can do at this point except track us. According to the pilot in the other plane, there may be an abandoned logging road ahead. He has no idea how long or straight the road is, but he says it's our best chance. He's sent over the coordinates and our pilot has programmed them in and is headed that way. He thinks he can make it, but it's going to be a rough landing no matter how you look at it."

Wendy looked at him in incredulous disbelief. "You have got to be kidding me. A logging road?"

Horror swept through me. I was totally with Wendy. Landing a plane on a logging road in the middle of a jungle surely was right at the top of the official pilot's manual of something *never* to do in an airplane. It certainly topped *my* list of things never to do in my lifetime.

"It's better than nothing." Oliver's expression was grim. "The good news is no one else will know where we are. The pilot reported his last position as nowhere near our current position."

"What about radar?"

"There isn't any out over the ocean. Transponders are useless there. So, all we have to do is land. Shi will make note of our coordinates and come back with a helicopter to extract us out of this hellhole."

"This can't be happening." Wendy had paled considerably. "What if the pilot passes out before we land?"

"He won't. I'm going to go help him stay awake."

Short of a blood transfusion, I didn't see what else could possibly keep him from dropping into unconsciousness. No matter which way I looked at it, we were totally screwed.

Wendy still looked at Oliver as if he could get us out of this. "Do you know how to fly a plane?"

"No." Oliver shook his head. "But I'll have him show me the basics, just in case. I'm a quick learner. By the way, we're low enough now you don't need the masks."

Wendy yanked hers off. "You'd better not mess this up, DeWitt. There's a lot of money at stake."

He didn't answer her and returned to the cockpit, slamming the door shut. We removed our oxygen masks, too. Basia started to shake beside me. The copilot moaned louder from his seat. I wanted to check on him, but Wendy's glare indicated that wouldn't be happening soon.

"If we're going to crash land, I need to get this table folded down." Finn eyed Wendy and rose slowly to reach across toward Basia. She helped him get her side of the table released and dropped into place. He gave Basia's hand a squeeze before he sat back in his seat next to mine. He reached over and took my hand. I leaned forward and Basia reached her hand across to me. The three of us sat there holding hands and squeezing hard, as if willing ourselves to stay calm.

Wendy pointed at me. "You. Lexi. Come here."

"No." Finn stretched a protective arm across me.

Wendy took aim at his head. "Back off or I'll shoot. I'll do it."

I unbuckled my seatbelt and stood. "It's okay, Finn. I've got this."

He looked at me for a long moment. I nodded encouragingly at him, so he sat back.

Without taking her eyes off of Finn or me, Wendy unzipped the sports bag and took out the case. She handed it to me. "Open it and press your palm print to the bioscanner."

"It's not that simple."

"Don't argue. Just do it."

Sighing, I sat back down and set it on my knees. I opened a thin metal plate set in the lid. Inside was a palm pad. I turned on the power and waited.

The plane took a sharp dip to the left. I nearly dropped the case. My stomach rolled and Wendy staggered to the side. Worriedly she glanced out the window, but the plane straightened and flew on.

She frowned at me. "What are you doing?"

"You told me to open it, so that's what I'm doing."

"Why is it taking so long?"

"That would be the 'it's not that simple' part."

"Explain." She scowled at me.

"Well, I just turned it on. The case has to power up. When it's ready, it will request my palm print. After that I'll have to enter a series of numbers before it will actually open."

"I wasn't told about the series of numbers. How long will that take?"

"Well, it takes a minute or two to power up before it's ready for my palm print. However, it will be an indefinite wait for the code."

"*What?* Why?"

"Because I don't have it. The twins decided to give it to me when I land in Jakarta. Guess Oliver didn't know about that part. See, the twins are pretty paranoid about security…and obviously for good reason. By the way, it's wired to blow to kingdom come if anyone tries to get in any other way." Ha! Take that, you stewardess shrew.

She narrowed her eyes, but then seemed to come to a

conclusion. "Press your palm print as soon as it warms up. We'll worry about the code later."

I had to give it to her. It was the smartest move under the circumstances. The hack would take some time and might not work, but it wasn't impossible either. I would venture a guess that they had access to hackers of impeccable quality in China who would be willing to spend an inordinate amount of time on it, especially if they were being well paid. Unfortunately, her realization of all of this meant I'd just made myself expendable. After all, she didn't need me alive to get my palm print.

A mechanical screech sounded outside on the wings and the plane dropped like an elevator before leveling off. Basia gasped and Wendy grabbed onto the credenza across from our seats. We all looked out the window.

I could see a stretch of road in the distance. Correction. Road was too strong a word. It looked more like a stretch of rocks and it was barely as wide as the plane's tires. The jungle was cleared on either side of it, but whether it would be wide enough for the plane's wings to fit was debatable.

"Mary, Mother of God," Finn said grimly. "That doesn't look like a good place to land."

I could feel the plane descending. I wasn't a pilot, but if we were supposed to be landing, shouldn't we be slowing down sometime soon?

"Is it ready yet?" Wendy asked, snapping my attention back on the case.

I looked down at it. The light was green, but I needed to stall. "Not yet."

She put the gun closer to me. "Press your hand on that bioscanner now."

Sighing, I pressed my hand to the screen. There was

a pause and then the green light blinked several times. There was a soft whirring noise and a keypad appeared.

"Good. Give it back."

I obliged, closing the case and handing it to her. She stuck it in her black bag just as the plane took a hard dip to the right.

Off balance, I tumbled from my seat directly into Wendy. The two of us fell, rolling around the cabin like bowling pins. Given the opportunity, I fought for control of the gun. She was stronger than she looked, but one of her legs got hooked against a seat, hampering her movement. Finn leaped out of his seat faster than I could blink and knocked her unconscious with one blow to the jaw.

The plane leveled out again. Finn gripped a corner of the seat to brace himself and held out a hand to me. I took it, standing, but my legs almost collapsed beneath me.

I looked up at him. "Wow. That was an impressive right cut."

Finn put an arm around me. "Steady there. You okay?"

"Actually, I've been better."

"Yeah, me, too. I've never hit a girl before. Didn't like it much."

"Well, this girl appreciates it." I rubbed my chin, where Wendy had smashed me with her elbow. "Thanks, Finn."

He looked around on the floor. "Where's her gun?"

"I don't know. I think I knocked it out of her hand. It's probably under one of the seats."

"Look!" Basia pointed out the window. "OMG! We're landing. Now."

We followed her gaze. She was right. The ground

was coming up fast. Too fast. The airplane had started to shudder alarmingly.

Finn grabbed my hand, pushing me back toward our seats. "Forget the gun. Buckle in and assume crash position."

"Wait." Wendy lay still on the floor. "What about her?"

"No time to drag her to a seat and strap her in."

"Okay, but I have to get the case first."

I skidded to a stop next to her and yanked on the black bag, pulling it off over her head. Slipping it over my shoulder, I staggered back to my seat. The airplane was shaking really hard now. It was almost as if it were afraid to land.

Finn slid into the aisle seat I'd occupied moments earlier. My hands were trembling, making it hard to fasten my seatbelt.

"Did I mention I really hate flying?" I said.

I glanced over at Finn, who was fastening his belt. Our eyes met in an instance of understanding that this might be the end.

"Well, it's a bit shorter than expected, but it's been a bloody good ride," he said. "No regrets, Lexi."

I had a feeling he wasn't talking about the plane flight. Still he smiled at me, so I made the effort and smiled back, adding a thumbs-up for good measure.

I bent over and put my head between my knees, closing my eyes. Finn's hand crept into mine. I squeezed it hard. I tried to imagine the road as the pilot would see it. My brain began to calculate the speed and velocity we'd have to meet in order to land safely. I was trying to factor in wind shear when a horrible jolt jarred my teeth together. The seatbelt tightened around my waist so painfully it took my breath away.

Touchdown.

Basia's scream rang in my ears.

*Boom!*

The sound of metal twisting and groaning was followed by a deafening shriek and more cracking sounds. I squeezed my eyes shut tight. I felt a huge dip to my left and then the right, my limbs jerking, my body as floppy as a rag doll. I opened my eyes to see what was happening when my forehead smashed against something hard and the world went black.

# TWENTY-FOUR

AIR. I NEEDED AIR.

I inhaled, then yelped as pain shot through me. I tried to open my eyes, but my eyelids felt like they weighed a hundred pounds. I tried to remember where I was, who I was, but nothing seemed to make sense. Sleep called to me, but for some reason, I fought it. Piercing pain between my eyes. Urgency and panic swept through me although I didn't know why.

I took another breath and then coughed. Ouch, that hurt.

The coughing seemed to signal something important to my brain, but the connection wasn't complete yet. I tried to open my eyes again and was rewarded with weird, blurry images, none of which I recognized. I blinked several times, trying to focus. When I attempted to move, something held me down.

I willed myself to proper consciousness, staying still until my brain caught up with my surroundings. The smell of fuel and burning of leather and roasting wires assaulted my nose. Panicked, I yanked my arms free but I was pinned at the waist.

Arms. Someone's arms were wrapped around me tightly. I pulled at the arms, realizing they had become tangled in my sweatshirt. When I got free, I rolled to my side, screaming as pain exploded again in my head.

I waited a second, breathing hard, until the pain

ebbed to a dull throb again. Tentatively, I reached out and touched the face of whoever had held onto me.

A man.

"Hello? Are you okay? Oh, my God." My voice didn't sound right. It was hoarse, barely audible. I coughed and said again, "Are you okay?"

I shook his shoulders gently a few times, but there was no movement or sound. He looked very familiar. Who was he? Where was I? Why was I having a hard time remembering?

Wisps of smoke swirled toward us. Shafts of lights penetrated the gloom. The large, bright area was probably the best exit from the smoke and wreckage. I scooted around to his head, and groped until I found his armpits. Scooting on my bottom, I pulled him inch by agonizing inch toward the bright light.

Thankfully nothing but his weight held us back. No debris had fallen on him, and as far as I could tell, nothing was on fire. But my strength was ebbing and I was having more trouble breathing than I could attribute just to the smoke. Debris blocked our path and I pushed it out of the way, pulling the man with me. As we got closer to the opening, I could see my surroundings much better, but the fog in my brain still wasn't lifting.

I recognized a seat lying on its side. It had a distinctive armrest.

An airplane.

Or at least what was left of one. As I reached the opening in the fuselage I was trapped in, I could see what was left. The tail had apparently split off and was listing sideways. The smoke wasn't coming from our location, but I could see fire a hundred or so yards ahead in a treed area. A strong breeze blew it in our direction.

A part of my brain registered that the front of the plane must have slid forward after breaking apart from the tail. The smoke was drifting back to us, thick and black.

I didn't need a degree to know I'd been in a plane crash. But the details were still residing in that special compartment of my brain where I typically saved all of my mother's recommendations for my health and happiness.

I knew enough about plane crashes to know that we had to get away from the wreckage. Now. Even if the tail wasn't on fire yet, it might start at any moment. I yanked hard one more time and lifted him up over the jagged edge of the fuselage. We tumbled to the ground. Thankfully, I somehow managed the maneuver without cutting either of us on the metal. I made a mental note to include body dragging in my future exercise routines.

The fall, however, must have shoved the knife in my forehead further into my brain. The impact knocked the breath from my lungs. I lay on my back, once again unable to move, the man equally immobile beside me.

Between the wisps of black smoke, I saw blue sky. A gauzy white cloud drifted by. It looked like a fish swimming past.

I closed my eyes and the world went dark again.

# TWENTY-FIVE

*TAP. TAP.*

Consciousness fluttered around my thoughts like a hyperactive butterfly. I tried to hide in the comforting black, but the butterfly was insistent.

"Lexi? Lexi, wake up."

My body seemed unusually heavy. Was someone sitting on me? I couldn't see.

I wanted to go back to sleep. Surely there were other flowers for the butterfly to pester. I tried to sink back into the black comfort when there was the voice again and another cool tap against my cheek.

My face hurt. A lot.

"Please, oh, God, please wake up. Lexi, I need you."

"Basia," I croaked.

"Oh, my God. My God. You're alive."

My vision swam and then I saw her. Her face was a bloody mess of cuts and swollen bumps, but I recognized it.

"When..."

I wasn't sure if I'd actually spoken. My brain was still trying to catch up. I saw blue sky. I was lying on my back.

"When...did you start buying your makeup...at Frankenstein's of Hollywood?"

She laughed. "Oh, thank God."

Using considerable effort, I wiggled my arms. "Help me up."

Basia sat behind me, maneuvering me into a sitting position.

I focused on what really hurt. Something wet dripped off my face. I tasted blood in my mouth. My nose and cheek were in agony. When I touched my nose and pulled my fingers back, they were covered in blood.

I tried to clear the fog from my thoughts. What else was important?

*Finn.*

I jerked my head to the side, sending a shaft of white pain searing through my brain. I moaned and clutched my head. Still, the thought seemed to wake up my brain and put a goal to my urgency.

"Where's Finn?"

"Right here next to you. He's alive. But he hasn't come to yet."

I needed to clear my head. "Are you...hurt?"

"My left arm. Broken, maybe. I feel nauseated, too. I woke up and saw you and Finn lying there on the ground. I crawled over to you. I don't remember the crash at all."

"Me neither. Is anyone else alive?"

"I don't know. I haven't seen anyone else."

"Can you help me up?"

She extended her right hand and helped shoulder my weight as I braced my feet against the ground and struggled to stand. Once upright, I swayed a bit and then the world steadied. Thank goodness, my legs could hold my weight.

Something heavy hung on my waist. When I looked down, I saw Wendy's black sports bag tangled in my sweatshirt. I still had the titanium case. The bag was intact, but my sweatshirt had been ripped to shreds on one side. I pulled the bag off over my head, dropping it on the ground.

Inhaling a steadying breath, I got a first good look at the entire wreckage of the plane.

I had no idea how we'd landed, but the result wasn't pretty. It reminded me of my one attempt at snow skiing, where I'd left a trail of items behind me on the slope when I cartwheeled to an icy landing.

The tail section, including the two engines mounted to it, had been sheared off near where we must have touched down. Cables and wires hung loose. The engines, hanging askew from the tail, smoldered and provided the source of acrid smoke drifting our direction. A wheel that had been sheared off sat in the middle of a dirt road covered in divots and fresh trenches made from the landing. Off to the side, as though ripped from the fuselage and embedded into a ditch, lay a piece of wing. The main part of the fuselage, from which I had crawled, was crumpled next to us.

Not far ahead, the detached cockpit had broken off. It sat at a funny angle off the road against a treed area. I could only assume low fuel reserves had contributed to the lack of fire in our section of the aircraft.

I held my head. "Wow. I survived a plane crash. I'm pretty sure my survival is conditional, though. Mom, Dad, my brothers or Slash—take your pick—are going to kill me as soon as they learn I didn't stay out of trouble."

Basia laughed, but it was more a sound of desperation than mirth.

I tested my legs, taking one step and then another. While I still felt shaky, nothing seemed broken.

I turned to assess Finn. He still lay on his back. His

face was pale and his eyes were closed. He had a huge knot on the side of his head.

Suddenly he opened his eyes, grabbed the front of my sweatshirt and pulled me down closer to his face.

"Check my buns," he said in a garbled whisper and then he fell back again.

Basia looked at me. "What did he say?"

My brain was slow to catch up. "I'm not sure. I think he said to…check his buns." I started to laugh, partially with relief that he was alive and partially because the first thing we were talking about after a plane crash was Finn's behind.

"Maybe something's hurting him there," Basia offered.

"He's lying on his back. I don't think it's a good idea to roll him over and check. His back might be injured."

"Agreed. It's good he came around, though."

Mosquitoes found us, likely after being attracted by the burning plane's heat. I swatted them away and then gently turned Finn's head to the side. "Finn. Finn. Can you hear me?"

I watched carefully. There was some restless movement, but no sign he could hear me. I pulled my sweatshirt over my head, unable to stop the tortured shriek ripped from my throat as the shirt brushed over my forehead and nose.

"Are you okay?" Basia asked me.

Tears pooled in my eyes at the pain. "I'm okay. It's my nose and possibly my cheekbones or skull. I think something is broken, fractured or all of the above." My fingers went to my throat and I felt Elvis's locket. It had survived, too.

Still shaking from the pain, I folded the sweatshirt

and put it under Finn's head. "We need to find a first aid kit and fast. That fire could spread this way, so we have to be ready to move."

She pressed her lips together and nodded. "Where should I look?"

"I'll go." I took her hand, put it on Finn's arm. "Keep talking to him. Do what you did for me. Try to get him to come around. Promise him anything. But call for me if he stops breathing. We'll have to perform CPR. Do you know how?"

Her hand shook, but her voice was steady. "Yes." She paused and then added, "Wait. Did you just say I'm supposed to promise him *anything* if he comes around?"

"Yes. I learned that from observing you. Promising *anything* to a man without specifying what *anything* is seems certain to get his attention, even if he is half conscious."

"Wow. I may cry I'm so proud of you."

I rolled my eyes, but it hurt. "Ha, ha. Good to see you haven't lost your sense of humor. I'm going to go find something to raise Finn's legs to help prevent shock, then I'll be right back."

I stood, every muscle screaming in protest. My forehead and nose throbbed so badly I could hardly think. My nose still trickled blood. Still, it was a miracle that Basia, Finn and I were still alive. I intended for all of us to stay that way. The next question was, what had happened to everyone else?

I snagged a piece of a seat cushion and lugged it back to Basia. I put his feet on it and raised them higher than his head. "Okay, I'm going to go look around."

I took a few steps away so I could survey the wrecked section. Wow. I would put the odds of negotiating an asteroid belt while being chased by an imperial star cruiser better than surviving this crash. Finn, Basia and I were very lucky it hadn't caught on fire.

Still, given the condition of the rest of the plane and our survival, I'd have my best chance of finding someone or something intact back in there. I staggered forward to crawl inside when I heard moaning nearby.

I changed direction and walked around the large hunk of fuselage to the other side. Wendy lay there, trapped under a long piece of aluminum. Her eyes were closed and blood pooled at one corner of her mouth.

"Oh, no." I bent over the metal and tugged at it, but in my weakened condition it was too heavy. I looked around and saw a sturdy branch broken in the crash. I slid it under the metal piece and levered. My muscles screamed in pain, but I managed to push it off her.

Exhausted, I dropped the branch and knelt at her side. I was breathing so hard I worried I might pass out. I took a minute of deep breaths to calm down before pressing my finger against her neck.

Her pulse was erratic, but she was alive.

"Basia," I shouted.

"Coming. Where are you?"

"On the other side of you. I found Wendy."

# TWENTY-SIX

BASIA JOINED ME. "Oh, God." She pointed at Wendy's left leg. A jagged shard of metal had impaled her shin just below the left knee.

I moved closer to get a better look. I examined the wound and lifted it slightly to see if it had gone all the way through to the ground. It hadn't. The wound looked grisly, but fortunately it wasn't bleeding too badly.

"It's not gushing blood, so that's a good thing, I think," Basia said.

"Agreed. I don't think we should pull it out. It will likely do more damage than help. I also don't think we should try and move her. She's probably in shock."

Basia nodded. "We'll have to cover her up and raise her legs like we did for Finn. Find some painkillers until help arrives."

I nodded. "Okay, I'll do it. Go back and keep an eye on Finn. I'll do my best to help her, but we've got to find some supplies to help or we're all in trouble."

Wendy moaned again. I walked around until I found a piece of small wreckage to lift her feet off the ground. I was thankful she was mostly unconscious, because the pain of moving her legs would have been excruciating.

Since there wasn't much else I could do, I picked my way through the twisted metal on the ground, careful not to step on anything that could puncture my tennis shoes. I picked up two torn but mostly intact blankets along the way and put them in a pile to pick up on the way back out, then I entered the fuselage and crouched down.

After a moment of initial panic passed, I managed to crawl through the wreckage. Several seats were ripped from the floor and oxygen masks, wires and the accumulated smoke from the other wreckage made me cough. I finally reached a spot where I could stand, so I came to my feet by holding on to a seat that was still intact. I stepped over what looked like a chunk of the ceiling and found what remained of the rear galley.

The fancy crystal glass had shattered. The minifridge and a cabinet hung open and packages of gourmet treats lay scattered around. The smell of coffee was strong and I presumed a carafe had taken flight and sprayed the cabin.

I picked up a handful of treat packages. Macadamia nuts, dried fruit mixes and some kind of dark chocolate. The chocolate, not a fan of equatorial heat, drooped in my hand. I tucked in the tail of my shirt and began stuffing in all the packets I could find, except, regrettably, the chocolate. I jammed the last ones in my jeans pockets and felt like a chipmunk with ever-expanding cheeks. Only it was my middle getting bigger.

I found several cans of soda and a couple cans of beer but had to discard all but three because they were punctured. I needed something to carry everything in, so I opened a couple of drawers until I found plastic garbage bags. I pulled out one and started dumping items from the drawers into it. I had no idea what we might need, but nothing would go unused. Coffee filters, crackers, toilet paper, and bottles of water. One drawer warmed my heart. Inside was a copper-colored box tied with a brown ribbon. The lid said Hawaiian Premium Short-bread and Chocolate Chip Macadamia Nut Cookies.

The last drawer left intact in the galley was jammed shut. No matter how hard I pulled, it wouldn't open. I found a real dinner knife and forced it into a crack in the drawer until it opened.

A first-aid kit. Relief swept through me.

After making sure I had everything that might be of any use, I tied up the bag, slinging it over my shoulder like Santa Claus. I crawled to the front of the wreckage. When I couldn't crawl anymore while carrying the bag, I pushed it in front of me until I came to the spot where I'd entered. I slung the bag out and then slipped through the wreckage myself. I stepped down hard and the motion jarred my face. I yelped in pain, doubling over as a wave of nausea swept through me.

I detoured to Wendy first and checked on her. She was still alive and breathing. I knelt down beside her and nearly fell backward when she abruptly opened her eyes and then gave a hoarse scream of pain.

"My leg. What…happened?"

She tried to sit up and claw at her leg, but I pushed her back down.

"Lie still. Wendy. We were in a plane crash. You were injured, but you're going to be okay." I fumbled with the supplies and pulled out a couple of acetaminophen. "Can you take a couple of pills? It's not much, but it's the best we've got."

Tears leaked from her eyes, but she nodded. I lifted her head and dropped the pills in the back of her throat. I handed her a bottle of water. She swallowed, gagged and then managed to swallow. I gently put her head back on the ground.

"My leg," she rasped. "What's wrong with it?"

"It's been impaled by a piece of metal. But the good news is that the metal itself has staunched the bleeding."

"That's good, right?" Her lower lip quivered.

"Sure." It was sort of true. What I *didn't* tell her was that I didn't know how much blood she'd already lost or how close the metal was to a major artery or vein.

"I don't think it's a good idea to move you until help arrives."

Wendy closed her eyes. "They'll be coming soon for you."

"Just who is *they* and why have they done this?"

She looked up at me with desperation and fear in her eyes. "If you promise to help me I will tell you who is behind this."

"I will help you regardless."

She grabbed my wrist. "You promise?"

"I promise."

She closed her eyes. "Jiang Shi and his younger brother, Quon."

"The leaders of the Chinese hacking group the Red Guest? Why? For the microchip?"

"Yes."

Something wasn't adding up for me. Everything I knew about these guys pointed to a serious hacking group, not hijackers, kidnappers or murderers. They would definitely be interested in the microchip, but why were *they* the group trying to get it? It didn't make sense.

I shifted from a kneeling position to a sitting one, taking the weight off my knees. "So, what was the plan? Why were we headed toward Port Moresby?"

"A plane…is waiting there to take you and the briefcase to China. We wouldn't have hurt the others. Really. No one was supposed to get hurt."

I frowned. "Me? Why do they want me to go to China? You already got my palm print."

"They want you—" Wendy's teeth started to chatter and she began shaking violently.

She was having a seizure. I held her firmly by the shoulders, turning her head slightly so she wouldn't swallow her tongue. "Wendy, it's okay. Hang on. It will pass."

After several seconds, she stopped. "Wendy? Are you okay?"

She didn't respond, but when I checked her closely, she was still breathing. I stared at her for a moment and then rose. Basia and Finn were waiting.

I hauled my precious cargo over my shoulder and returned to Basia.

She looked up when I arrived and dumped the garbage bag at her feet. "Did you find anyone else alive?"

"Not yet. But the others are likely to be with the front part of the plane. I'll check there shortly. Wendy just came to. I gave her some painkillers and a blanket, but she's in bad shape. She said the plan was to divert our plane to Port Moresby, where another plane is standing by to take the briefcase and me to China. A hacking group called the Red Guest is behind this."

"They want the microchip, but why do they want you?"

"I don't know. Maybe to walk them through the manufacturing process."

"Is it safe to stay here and wait for a rescue if we're not sure who's going to find us first?"

"No. It's not safe for us to stay with the plane. Leaving the site of the crash goes against all logic, since the rule of thumb is to stay near the site so rescuers can easily find you. The problem is that the people who will likely find us first won't be our rescuers."

She nodded without comment.

I sought to reassure her. "However, on the upside, it will take them time to find a helicopter and return. Another positive is when we don't arrive in Jakarta on time, it will also trigger a search with ComQuest and Slash. It's not clear who will find us first—the good guys or the bad—but our immediate concern is bringing Finn to consciousness. We're going to have to move and soon. If we are able to do that, we'll worry about the rest later."

She took it better than I expected. "They don't want Finn and me. They'll kill us if we're captured, right?"

I didn't sugarcoat it. "Maybe. So, we'd better not be here when they get back."

"What do we do about Wendy?"

"We have to leave her behind. We don't have a choice. We'll stabilize her as much as we can and leave some medicine, food and water. Whoever arrives first will be able to help her."

She thought it over. "I just realized you said medicine. I take it that means you found a first-aid kit?"

"Yes. In the rear galley."

I pulled out the first-aid kit and opened it up. Basia reached over and picked up the bottle of acetaminophen. Snapping open the bottle, she shook out two pills and handed them to me.

"First take care of yourself. Swallow a couple of painkillers and wipe your face a bit." She tossed me an antiseptic wipe. "It won't help much, but we need you to be at your best."

I ripped open a wipe and dabbed at my face, avoiding the nose and high cheek area. After a few swipes the entire wipe was red. It probably hadn't done any good. I cast it aside, popping the pills in my mouth and taking several gulps of water from one of the bottles to wash them down. The first few swallows tasted like blood. I finished more than half the bottle before I stopped myself. We had no idea how long we'd be here and we had to ration our supplies."

"You take a couple of painkillers, too," I said. "That arm has to be killing you. We have to manage our pain to think better."

I poured two tablets into her hand. I passed her what was left of my water and she swallowed them down.

I leaned over Finn, tapping his cheek much as Basia had done to me. "Come on, bud. Wake up."

Basia put a hand on my shoulder. "Lexi, we have to check Finn's buttocks. He may be bleeding out there even if we can't see it. He wouldn't have told us to check if it wasn't for a reason."

I sighed. "Fine, let's take a look."

She took the blankets off him and I removed his feet from the cushion, carefully putting them on the ground and spreading them. I crawled between his legs and squinted.

"I don't see evidence of bleeding from here. I'm going to have to cut his pants open if I'm going to get a decent look at his behind without moving him."

She reached for the first-aid kit. "There are scissors in here. They're small, but might do the trick."

I took the scissors from her. They were really tiny. "I guess these will have to do."

"Good thing he didn't wear jeans. Those wouldn't cut through denim."

"No they wouldn't. You know I'd laugh about the absurdity of this, but it would hurt my nose."

I knelt down at Finn's feet and started cutting through his pant leg. I did the left leg, cutting up the side seam until I reached his crotch.

"Sorry," I murmured.

I pulled the pants apart until his underwear showed and bent my head closer to his crotch, trying to look inside.

"Lexi?"

Gasping, I lifted my head. Finn's eyes were open.

"Are you…playing doctor?"

# TWENTY-SEVEN

FOR A MOMENT Basia and I just stared at him.

Then, I crawled to his side. "Finn, how are you feeling?"

He reached up to touch the knot on his head. "I'm not sure."

"We've been worried sick about you."

"How long was I out?"

"I don't know." I took his hand, squeezed it. "It's hard to say. You woke briefly to give me a message a bit ago and then lapsed back into unconsciousness."

"I remember. Sort of. Did you get the gun?"

"Gun?"

"I told you to get the gun."

I exchanged a worried glance with Basia. "Gun? You told me to get the *gun*? You said, 'Lexi, get the *gun*?' Those were your exact words?"

His brow furrowed "I think so. What did you think I said?"

"Never mind." Nope. I wasn't going there. At least not now. "I didn't see the gun, Finn. I'm sorry."

"Everything is still a bit blurry."

"You hit your head. You're most likely suffering a concussion, if not worse. But you're awake and talking in sentences. You remember things. That's good. Really good."

I looked over at Basia, who had tears in her eyes. I felt rather emotional myself.

He attempted to lift a hand to touch my face. "Lexi, what happened to you?"

I leaned back. I didn't want him to touch my face because I knew it would hurt. A lot. "Plane crash, remember? I think I broke my nose."

"You definitely broke your nose," Basia offered. "You're sporting two shiners now. The left side of your cheek looks smashed in and you have this greenish purple knot on your forehead."

Finn lifted his head. "Basia?"

"Yes, Basia's here, too. We're okay. Alive. Finn, what hurts?"

"Bloody everything. Mostly my head." He wiggled his arms and legs. "I think nothing is broken. But I'm thirsty."

I wiggled in behind him, as Basia had done for me, propping him up with my arms. "Okay, first I'm going to sit you up and then we'll get you something to drink."

His breathing harshened as I moved him. Probably fighting the same dizziness and nausea I had. Basia handed him a bottle of water and he took a few sips.

"Slowly," I cautioned.

He drank a bit more and then waved me away. "Let me sit up on my own."

I scooted to the side and he straightened, rolling his neck. "I've got a hell of a headache. Does anyone have a painkiller?"

I got him a couple of tablets and he swallowed them down.

He pressed a hand to his forehead. "Hope that helps the hammer in my head."

Basia sighed. "Lexi, give it to us straight. What are the odds we are going to die?"

I considered her question. Statistically, the odds were against us. If you factored in that we were injured, located in what appeared to be a remote jungle and the first responders to the crash would likely be people who wanted to kill us, it wasn't looking good at all. But I sensed informing Basia of that wouldn't be the right thing to do at this point in time.

"The odds are actually in our favor," I lied. "We survived, we've got a head start, and we're smart. All we have to do is avoid the bad guys and wait until the cavalry arrives."

She breathed a sigh of relief. "Oh, thank goodness."

Finn didn't say anything, but he was watching me. Even with a head injury, he knew better.

I hated to admit it, but the truth was we'd need a real miracle to survive the next twenty-four hours.

# TWENTY-EIGHT

I'D BEEN AVOIDING IT, but it was time to check the front half of the plane for survivors. I doubted anyone could have survived considering its damaged state, but I had to find out for sure. I'd seen no trace of Cezar, who had been on the couch when we crashed. Someone might have been thrown from the plane and survived, as Wendy had. I needed to know for sure.

I left Basia to watch over Finn while I made the trek toward the cockpit. As I passed what looked like mangled landing gear, probably sheared off from the nose, I came across another dump of debris. Nothing usable except for a ripped blanket. I tied it around my waist anyway. I wasn't going to waste anything that might help our survival.

A hundred feet ahead, the front of the plane had left the road and veered off into jungle. On one side of the road a giant swath had been harvested, on the other the jungle remained untouched. A huge black trail of flattened foliage and grass ran up to the cockpit and tall, canopied trees it had nosed into.

I worked toward the wreckage, giving it a wide perimeter and looking for bodies. I stopped to listen in case someone called for help but heard nothing but strange chattering and cawing from what I assumed were birds. I moved forward carefully, stepping into the jungle undergrowth and stopping at the edge of a sharp incline.

I barely saw it hidden by the thick foliage. When I got closer, I saw half of the cockpit was balanced precariously on the edge of an incline where the trees ended. No wonder this side of the road hadn't been harvested.

"Jeez," I murmured.

To my left I saw a large piece of wreckage, so I detoured toward it. I glanced to my right and saw a man's shoe protruding from beneath it. My heart jumped as I bent down for a closer look. The shoe was still attached to the leg. I recognized the pants.

Cezar.

To the right of him, beneath more wreckage, was another body. I could only see one arm and shoulder, but the insignia on his shirt indicated I'd just found the co-pilot.

My stomach heaved. I leaned against the wreckage and covered my mouth. "Oh, God," I said aloud.

I wasn't sure how much more of this I could take. Still, I had to make sure they were dead. I sucked up more courage than I thought I owned and touched both of the bodies. I wasn't sure what it should feel like, but neither felt normal and I could find no pulse of any kind.

Tears welled in my eyes. Even though I knew intellectually the events that had transpired weren't my fault, I still felt guilty and sickened by their deaths. I wanted to cry, to crawl to a shady spot and take time to grieve, but I didn't have the luxury. Instead, I gave myself a moment to get composed and then pulled myself into a standing position, holding onto a piece of the plane.

I had to focus on the living. On the here and now.

Steeling myself, I walked closer to the cockpit. It had probably smashed into a tree or the ground during its final slide. The nose had crumpled.

I circled around to the left-hand side, away from the incline. On this side, the cockpit was cracked wide open.

The pilot was still sat strapped into his seat, his head hanging sideways. Insects buzzed around.

"Hey," I shouted, swatting at them. "Hello. Are you are okay?"

No answer.

He could be unconscious. He could be dead. There was no way to tell for sure. I couldn't reach him from my angle and I wasn't sure I wanted to try. Any extra weight on the cockpit might cause the whole thing to slide down the incline. I looked around and saw a long branch. I poked it gently at the pilot.

"Hey, are you okay?"

His limbs were limp. I squashed the nausea that roiled in my stomach and forced my feet a little closer.

"Hello? I'm here to help. Can you make a movement of any kind?"

He didn't answer.

Testing the stability of a small piece of wreckage, I stood on it so I could get a better look at him. Using the stick, I carefully turned his head toward me. I dropped the stick and nearly fell down. One side of his head had been crushed in.

I slipped off the wreckage, shaking so hard that I had to steady myself against a piece of the hull.

I forced myself to examine the other side of the cockpit. Surprisingly, the seat was intact, which is where I presumed Oliver would have been sitting. The black seatbelt dangled down. I peered up at the seat and could see blood spatters. But there were no signs of another body.

I crept as close to the cockpit as I could and noticed

a black canvas bag partially wedged under a piece of debris. I yanked on it until it finally came free. The bag was surprisingly heavy and I dropped it to the ground to examine its contents. I knelt beside the bag and unzipped it. I pulled out a hand axe with a strange looking hook on the back. I set it aside and pulled out the rest of the contents. There was a flashlight, a thin silver space blanket, a roll of duct tape, a black tarp, a coil of rope and another small first-aid kit.

Bingo.

I put everything back in the bag and slung it carefully over my shoulder. I did a quick tour of the area, but found no additional bodies or usable supplies. Staggering, I hiked back to Basia and Finn.

I was encouraged to see Finn looking more alert.

"Did you find anyone else?" he asked.

"Everyone except Oliver."

"Do you think he might still be alive?"

"I have no idea. I didn't see his body anywhere, but it's possible he got thrown from the plane. The cockpit was traveling at a pretty high speed when it smashed into the trees."

I dropped the canvas bag next to them. "This was in the cockpit. Looks like an emergency bag. It's got some useful items and another first-aid kit." I unzipped it and pulled out the odd axe with a hook. "This may be our only weapon. Pilots use it to smash the window in case of an emergency."

It wasn't a traditional axe. It looked more like a small pickaxe with a flat, slightly curved blade mounted like a hoe on the end of the handle.

I pulled out the silver blanket. "This will be useful.

It's an emergency space blanket. It retains eighty percent of a person's radiated body heat."

I needed some water to push off the lightheadedness. I squinted at the sun trying to calculate the time. We were supposed to have landed in Jakarta at seven-thirty in the morning. I figured it had to be closer to nine or maybe even ten o'clock by now. My watch had been torn off in the crash and I didn't see one on Basia or Finn either. I had no idea where my purse was and a quick check of Finn's pockets didn't turn up a cell phone either. Guess we'd have to tell time the old-fashioned way.

The first spatters of rain hit my arm.

I stood up and shook out the black tarp. "We need to cover our supplies. Basia, help me stack our supplies on either side of Finn."

I retrieved the titanium briefcase, still inside of Wendy's sports bag, and added that to the pile. As I dropped it next to Finn, I snapped my fingers.

"Wait. The titanium case has a GPS locator. I totally forgot. Xavier and Elvis should be able to track us via the case."

"What?" Basia's eyes lit up. "Really? That may be the best news I've ever heard."

Finn looked stunned as well. "So, that means we just have to stay out of reach of the bad guys until we are able to be rescued."

"Hopefully, yes." I dropped a blanket on his lap. "We can't count on them getting here first, so we have to plan accordingly. But maybe now we have a fighting chance."

Basia and I each took a corner of the tarp and then covered Finn and our supplies. It wasn't an ideal set up, but it was the best I could come up with on short notice. Finn instructed us to funnel the tarp so the water would run off of it and into the bottles. It was a good idea so I did what he suggested. When I finished, the droplets were coming down with a bit more regularity.

"Let's go, Basia," I said. "We need to hurry."

Finn peered at us from under the tarp. "Wait. Where are you going?"

"We've got to check on Wendy. We'll be right back."

We walked as quickly as we could toward Wendy when Basia spotted something red in the bushes. She gave a small cry and held up a red bag. "Look! I found my purse. What a good omen."

She held the strap, letting the purse dangle from one hand. It was red and had a big black gash on one side, but was remarkably intact. She unzipped it and peeked inside. Giving a gasp of triumph, she pulled out her cell phone.

"Please work, please work." She turned on her phone and then beamed when it turned on. "It's working."

I sighed. "I doubt we'll pick up a signal out here, but it's worth a shot."

She waited while it loaded and then walked around trying to find bars. "No service. Well, crap."

I hadn't in my wildest dreams expected her to find bars, but I still felt disappointed. I chalked it up to extreme desperation.

I rubbed the back of my neck. "Turn it off and save the battery. We're on our own for now."

She turned it off and stuck it back in her purse and then rummaged around. "At least I have my wallet, a couple of credit cards and some lipstick."

"Just what you need in the jungle."

She rolled her eyes and put the strap over her good

shoulder. I followed behind her. As she walked, I suddenly noticed something else.

"Basia, stop."

She stopped, turning around. "What? What's wrong?"

"What kind of shoes do you have on?"

She lifted her foot. "A red medium heel from Versace. I got them on sale—a complete steal. They're comfortable, although a little snug. That's probably why I didn't lose them in the crash. Why?"

"Why?" I threw up my hands. "Let me see. Because we are on a freaking mountain and you have heels on."

She straightened. "They're medium heels and I'm walking just fine. In fact, I walk better in heels than flats. They are very versatile."

It wasn't like I could do anything about it at the moment, so I just sighed. "Fine. Let's go."

More raindrops pattered us as Basia reached Wendy. She knelt beside her, then touched her wrist.

"Lexi, she doesn't have a pulse."

I dropped the first-aid kit and squeezed in beside her, pressing my finger against Wendy's neck.

Nothing.

I immediately started CPR and instructed Basia to give her breaths. We worked on Wendy for several minutes until the rain started to fall, softly at first and then in a heavy dump.

"It's no good," Basia finally said, sitting back on her heels and pushing the wet hair off her forehead. "She's gone."

I kept pumping. "We can get her back." I kept frantically pumping on her chest. "I promised I would help her. I promised."

"Stop it, Lexi. Please. She's gone."

"She can't be dead. She was alive when I left her. I shouldn't have left her."

"Please Lexi." Basia's voice was so soft I barely heard it over the rain. But the heartbreak in it stopped me.

"She's cold. She's probably been gone for a while."

I touched Wendy's cheek. Basia was right. It was cold. Maybe not cold as ice, but that's how my heart felt at the moment.

I sank back on the wet ground, staring at the body. It was too late. No matter how hard I pumped, it wouldn't make a difference.

Wendy was dead. And if I didn't do something soon, we'd be dead, too.

# TWENTY-NINE

I SAT THERE in frustration, resting my elbow on my knee. I might have been crying, but it was hard to tell with the rain. Wendy was someone's daughter, sister and maybe even mother. I should have done more to help her. I'd promised. But she'd made a bad choice, helped the wrong people and now she was dead. As much as I wished for a different outcome, it was too late to change that.

Rain fell harder, sluicing down my cheeks. As I looked down, I could see that the water dripping off my nose was tinged with red. The weight of our situation and my helplessness collapsed on me. I wondered how far gone I really was.

"I can't do this, Basia. I just can't."

"Do what?"

"Save us. Figure out what to do next. People are dying, possibly us next, and I don't know how to stop it."

"We'll figure it out. We have to."

"Exactly how are we going to do that? I'm a geek. We're not supposed to figure out how to survive plane crashes in a tropical environment. I don't even do well in the sun. You know that!"

"You're going to do fine."

"How? I've never been in a jungle before. I've never even been camping. I can't search the web to find out what to do. Don't you get it? Without a computer I'm useless. A total fish out of water."

Basia knelt beside me, the rain dripping off her nose and chin. She grabbed my shoulder with her good hand and glared at me. "Haven't you learned a single damn thing since we've been friends? Do you really think you are nothing more than a geek?" She wagged a finger at me. "Now you listen to me. The computer is nothing more than a tool in your hands. It is *not* an extension of you, and it's certainly not what defines you. You may be a geek, but you're a hell of a lot more than that, Lexi Carmichael. You're a good person with a kind heart, a wonderful friend and a strong woman with a smart and resourceful mind. You don't need a computer to survive and you're *not* alone."

I stared at her surprised by her vehemence, so I tried a different approach. "I appreciate your belief in me, Basia, I really do. But I don't think you realize how much trouble we're in. Finn is injured. You're a city girl. You're wearing heels, for crying out loud. Those guys are coming back to get us and soon. I guarantee you they will be trained professionals, probably expert trackers and marksmen. They will be fresh and not hampered by injuries or lack of food or water. If they find us, it's going to get ugly. How are the three of us going to survive against that?"

Her eyes narrowed. "That's your answer—we'll survive because we're *survivors*. We made it out of that plane crash alive. We're *going* to make it out of here. Slash will be frantic looking for you and so will Elvis, Xavier and all the executives at ComQuest. We just have to hold on until someone figures out how to rescue us. I'm not giving up. I don't like wet feet or snakes, but I don't care what I have to do to survive. I will. So will you. Died on some remote jungle mountainside will *not* be our obituaries."

She poked me in the chest. "Now if we are going to survive, we are going to need that unique analytical brain of yours to start analyzing our situation and resources and come up with some practical solutions. That's the Lexi Carmichael I know and love."

I watched her in fascination. Through the curtain of rain, she glared at me. Her chin was set and her eyes ablaze with determination. Basia wasn't giving up. The city girl was game to give survival in the jungle a go. What was wrong with me? If she could accept the challenge, then so could I.

Shame swept through me. Of the three of us, only I had been in a survival situation even remotely like this recently. Yet somehow I'd become the one least convinced we could survive. The more I thought about it, the madder I got at myself.

I wiped the water from my eyes. "You're right, Basia. The pity party is officially over. We just have to put our heads together and think—use our skills to the best of our abilities. The truth is I feel hobbled and vulnerable right now without my digital crutch. That scares me. A lot. It's totally uncharted territory. But you're correct. We don't need technology to survive. We've already got what we need—our brains, our determination and each other. So we need to start using our brains…right now."

"Now you're getting it." She patted my shoulder. "There's nothing else we can do for Wendy, but Finn needs us and we need a plan."

She began to walk away, heels wobbling on the gravel of the road. As she did, I had an idea. Offering a small prayer and an apology to Wendy, I took her wet blanket then slipped off her flight safety-approved flats from her feet, wrapping them up in the blanket. We couldn't overlook anything that could help us survive.

In the short distance it took us to return to Finn, it had stopped raining. A surprisingly bright beam slid out between clouds, blinding us with the transition. I wished for my sunglasses or at least a hat to shade my face, but neither was forthcoming. Unlike Basia, I hadn't found my purse. My wet clothes clung to me and my shoes squished from the downpour.

As we approached, Finn smiled at us from beneath the blanket.

"How's Wendy?" he asked

Basia beat me to a response. "She didn't make it."

"Then it's just the three of us?" he asked

I nodded. "I'm afraid so."

I watched him for a moment. His speech and visual acuity had improved. He was recovering much more quickly than I had hoped.

"Can you ladies help me stand?"

I hesitated. "Are you sure you're ready?"

"No better time than the present to find out."

I didn't want to rush him, but before we could make plans, we needed to know how well he could move. I stretched out a hand and Basia and I got on either side of him, pulling him to his feet. He swayed unsteadily, but we kept him upright. He tested his legs.

"Nothing seems broken or sprained."

"Thank goodness." I'd probably said that with too much enthusiasm, but I was totally in the moment and hoping for the best.

As soon as I said it, he swayed and nearly toppled Basia. I managed to straighten him, but he was darn heavy. He stood there for a few additional minutes, adjusting to the new position, getting his bearings and wiggling his legs.

He looked down at the gaping hole that stretched up to his crotch. "Mary, Mother of God. My pants are nearly ripped off."

I felt my cheeks heat. "Can you walk?"

"I'll give it a go." After a bit of initial unsteadiness, he seemed pretty good on his feet.

Basia stood in front of us, her hands on her hips. "Okay, team, now that we're all vertical we've got to figure out what to do. Lexi, what do you think?"

"Let's start by inventorying our supplies and agreeing on a plan of action."

"Do we know where we are?" Finn asked.

I considered. "Well, if we were diverting to Port Moresby, it's reasonable to assume we are somewhere in the mountains of Papua New Guinea. As I recall, Port Moresby is on the southeastern coast of the island. Since we're in the mountains, then it means we are somewhere in the middle of the island. Unfortunately, that's probably a couple hundred miles from Port Moresby. That's actually good because it buys us some time. I doubt the other airplane will be able to land, get access to transportation like helicopters or all-terrain vehicles and get back here very quickly. However, the bad news is that there are no major towns or cities nearby and no place for us to go for help. So they may be able to take their time, figuring that if we survived, we would just hunker down here and wait for rescue."

Finn bent over to look at the gravel. "We're on a road. I think I heard Oliver say it was an old logging road. It's pretty heavily compacted, but none of the ruts look recent. I doubt it's seeing much traffic. Do we have any ideas about locals? I mean, perhaps there are native villages where we might get assistance to help us to a phone or one of the larger towns."

I considered. "Any chance French is the primary language of Papua New Guinea? They colonized much of this part of the world, didn't they?"

Basia swatted a mosquito on her neck. "Yes, they did. But the primary language is Tok Pisin. And before you ask, no, I don't speak it. It's an English-based creole language, so if I could find someone who spoke it we might be able to share a few common words. But it is unlikely because the only reason I even know about Tok Pisin is because of Papua New Guinea's distinction as the most linguistically diverse country in the world. I think there are over eight hundred different languages spoken on the island. There's no telling what dialect they'll speak *if* we encounter anyone in this godforsaken area."

That didn't seem like a promising development, but it was good to know.

I made some rough calculations of flight distances and times, estimated the time to rent one or more helicopters—assuming they were available—gather supplies and fly back to this location.

"We have to start walking and soon. I estimate that we have somewhere between four and eight hours before the bad guys are likely to return. We may have more time than that if they watched our crash landing and determined that no one was likely to have survived. In that instance, they might try and avoid attracting more attention while they organized a recovery operation."

I squeezed water from my ponytail. "We have to put as much distance between the crash site and us as quickly as possible."

Finn nodded. "I concur. But given our condition and lack of equipment, we are going to have to follow the road for as long as possible if we are going to make any time at all."

"Agreed," I said.

"My suggestion is to head downhill on the road for as long as we can." He checked the position of the sun. "The walking will be easier in that direction. I would guess we have five or more hours of daylight left at least. Even if we walk slowly we can cover a number of miles. Plus I suspect we'll find the larger and more civilized villages and towns in that direction rather than higher up in the mountains. We should be able to hear an approaching airplane or helicopter from a decent enough distance to be able to hide ourselves as needed."

Basia stood up. "Alright, let's do it then."

I held up a hand. "Wait. I'm going to play devil's advocate here. Let's put ourselves in the shoes of our Chinese adversaries and think from their angle. If I were the Chinese mastermind behind this operation, this is what I would do. If I felt the crash was not survivable, then I would only send one helicopter to retrieve the briefcase. However, if I felt it were possible some crew and passengers survived, then I would need enough people to recover or dispose of the survivors. Given the amount of money they've already sunk into this hijacking I think that's a safe assumption that they will play it safe and assume there are survivors. I think they'll return with more than one helicopter if they can get them."

No one said anything, so I continued thinking it through while talking out loud. "I would first land at the crash site to check for survivors. If I couldn't account for everyone, then I would establish a search cordon to contain the survivors until I could find them. They would most likely assume we would head south because it is downhill and more traversable. They will probably set up a roadblock there. Just to be thorough, they will go uphill and do the same. Once we are sealed in, they'd begin searching inward toward the crash. If we are caught within that perimeter, I'd calculate a ninety-four point six percent chance of being caught within forty-eight hours."

Basia and Finn stared at me with mouths open.

I blushed. "Okay, maybe I picked up a little something from my time with the SEALs. Guys, I think if we are going to survive this, we have to outwit them, continuing to do the unexpected and keeping them off balance until the advantages swing our way. It's a sound maneuver in cybersecurity, so why can't we apply it here? We take the road north as far as we can, getting outside of their cordon if we can. Then we find a way to go south by following a stream or river. There are enough trees along the streams to protect us from aerial observation until we move down into the thicker lowland jungle. Still, even if we don't escape their perimeter, if they start searching downhill first, it will give us more time to put a greater distance between them and us despite our injuries. What do you think?"

Finn snapped his mouth shut. "One question. How will we know which helicopter has the good guys and which one has the bad guys?"

"We won't. We'll have to assume all of them are bad unless we can get a safe, secure look to make sure."

After a moment, he nodded. "As much as I dread the thought of trudging uphill, I like your plan. I'm in."

"I'm in, too." Basia cradled her arm to her stomach. "So, now what?"

# THIRTY

I STOOD. "THE NEXT step is to get organized, and fast. First, we need to use duct tape to seal Finn's pants shut or he'll get eaten alive by insects. Next, we rub mud on any exposed skin to protect us from mosquitos and bugs."

Basia gulped. "Mud? On my face?"

"Not just on your face, Basia, but behind your ears, on your feet and around your neck. Everywhere I see skin it's going to get covered. When it dries, the mud will form a crusty barrier against insects. "Since we don't have insect repellent, managed to miss our inoculations and we can't afford to get sick, we have to take precautions."

Better to lay it on the table so it was clear. There was no time for balking. "Then we pack our stuff. I'll divide our supplies into three piles so we can spread the weight. I'll take Wendy's sports bag, Finn can take the pilot's bag and I'll make a pack out of a garbage bag for you, Basia."

Finn nodded. "Good plan. While you're making the packs, I'll make a sling for Basia's arm. We have to immobilize it or she will have agonizing pain for each step she takes. Lexi, are you sure about taking the briefcase with us? Maybe it would be better to bury it somewhere. That way, if we get captured, they won't find it on us. We could come back and retrieve it later."

I considered and then shook my head. "As much as

I'm tempted, the briefcase has to go with us. We have to trust that Xavier and Elvis will be looking for the signal. If they can pinpoint our location, it's our ticket out of here. We just have to stay alive until they can find us."

"Okay, then the case stays with us. Finn stood up and brushed off his hands.

We worked quickly and efficiently—a good team. I figured it had taken us less than twenty minutes to finish all of our tasks except for slipping on the packs and putting Basia's arm in a sling. I had avoided the mud on parts of my face because of my injuries, but finally put it on the best I could. Finn and Basia, however, looked full on ready for military engagement with just the whites of their eyes flashing. I couldn't help but smile.

I crisscrossed Wendy's bag with the titanium case and my share of the supplies over my body. Finn slung the pilot's black canvas bag over his shoulder and kept the crash axe in his hand. He seemed steadier with every passing minute, but I didn't know if it was simply determination or if he was actually feeling stronger. It was hard to tell. Since I wasn't sure I wanted to know the answer, I didn't ask.

Now came the hard part. I stood in front of Basia. "I'm going to have to ask you to lift your arm so I can tie your pack on." It wasn't pretty, as I'd fashioned it out of a garbage bag and duct tape, but it would do the job. "As soon as it's secure Finn will put the sling on your arm. I'm sorry, Basia, but it's going to hurt. A lot. Are you ready?"

She squeezed her eyes shut and lifted her arm. To my surprise, she didn't make a sound as I arranged the pack on her back, although the pain had to be excruciating. I'd underestimated her grit. City girls were apparently a whole lot tougher than I'd expected.

Standing behind her reminded me how petite she was compared to my five foot eleven frame. She wasn't more than five foot two inches on a good day and probably weighed one hundred and ten pounds after a seven-course dinner at a fancy French restaurant. I'd given her the lightest pack, but now I wished I'd taken even more.

"Looks good," I said. "Let's get that sling on her."

She opened her eyes as Finn handed me the long piece of blanket he'd cut off. He'd made a sling out of it, so I looped it around her neck and secured it tightly on top of her shoulder. She clenched her teeth in pain as I arranged her arm in the sling, but otherwise remained silent.

The blanket was thicker than I'd expected and didn't tie very easily. "Does that feel okay?" I asked.

She gave me a tight smile. "Sure, perfect."

I looked at her doubtfully. "Really?"

"Yes, Florence Nightingale. Now let's go, we have a lot of road to cover before dark."

"Wait, take this." Finn handed her a thick walking stick. He tossed another one to me and then took one for himself. He held the axe and a walking stick.

I followed him, grateful for the aid of the stick. "Hey, a walking stick is a really good idea."

"That's why I'm the CEO. I have good ideas. Like hiring you two, for example."

"You know, I'm really glad to hear that," Basia said, falling in behind Finn. "I've been meaning to ask for a raise."

"Don't bloody push it, lass."

I laughed and then winced as pain shot through my nose. Still my spirits were lifted by the banter. We were alive, we weren't giving up, and somehow we'd retained a shred of humor.

At this point, I couldn't ask for more.

# THIRTY-ONE

WE HAD BARELY gotten started along the rock-filled road when I heard a rustle in the bushes to my right. Finn heard it, too.

Lifting the axe, he stepped toward the bushes to investigate and I followed him, circling to the other side. Basia stayed back. When we got closer I realized the road had narrowed and was backed up against the same sharp incline that the cockpit had been balanced over. I looked down the incline, shuddering. If the plane had landed even a few hundred feet earlier, we probably would have gone over it.

Suddenly the rustling got louder. A large rat, or maybe a mountain shrew, darted out of the bushes at my feet and headed straight for Basia. She screamed and scrambled out of the way.

"Oh, my God." She pressed a hand to her chest.

Finn laughed. "That put the heart in me sideways, too."

I opened my mouth to speak when Oliver DeWitt stood from a crouch behind the bushes, holding a gun aimed at us. I lurched backward until I bumped against Finn.

"Oliver?" I stared at him. "You survived?"

"It will take a lot more than a plane crash to keep me away from eight million dollars. I see you all got a lucky break, too. All three of you survived?" He smirked at Basia. "Actually make that two and half."

She glared at him, but didn't say anything.

Now that I had a minute to recover from my initial surprise, I studied him. Oliver didn't look good. He had a gash running from his scalp down the left side of his cheek. A bloody and jagged cut slashed across the side of his neck and both of his hands were scraped raw. He swayed on his feet, but unfortunately the hand holding the gun seemed quite steady.

He motioned at Finn. "Toss the axe in the bushes. Now."

Finn complied without a word.

Oliver looked between us. "I'll take the briefcase. Whoever has it, bring it to me nice and slow."

I started to move from behind Finn when to my astonishment, Basia stepped forward. "I've got it in the pack on my back."

I froze. I had no idea what she was doing as she approached Oliver slowly. He smiled as she got closer. "You know, I'm really surprised you made it this far, princess."

Basia scowled. "What's wrong with you? Why do you have it in for me so bad? I barely know you."

"Maybe because you remind me of my ex-wife." He blinked and swiped at his brow with one hand. He was sweating profusely. "I know your type. She was a high society type, just like you. She had to have designer shoes, purses and clothes. I never made enough money for her, so she dumped me for some other guy."

"How can you compare me to her?" Basia flushed angrily. "You don't even know me."

"I can tell."

"God, you're such an idiot, Oliver. If we were married, I'd have left you, too."

He snorted. "If we were married, I'd give you poison on our first night together."

Basia pretended to gag. "If you were my husband, I would gladly *drink* it on our first night together."

Oliver waved the gun at her. "Shut up and bring me that case before I shoot you on principle."

I held my breath and Finn tensed next to me as Basia approached him. Neither of us had a clue what she was planning.

When Basia finally came within arm's length of Oliver, she turned around, so her back was to him. "I'm sorry, Oliver, but with one arm, I can't get the pack off. You'll have to take the briefcase out of my pack."

As soon as Oliver reached out to tug on her pack, she shot her leg out behind her, the heel of her shoe catching Oliver squarely in the crotch. Oliver shrieked in pain and took a step back, realizing too late he stood at the edge of the precipice. His arms did a windmill once before he disappeared over the side. His scream echoed for three long beats and then all was silent.

Basia turned around, looking a bit freaked out. "Oops." She peered over the side. "I was aiming for the hand with the gun."

Finn and I stood completely flabbergasted.

Finally Finn walked over to the precipice and looked over. He glanced back at me and shook his head. Oliver hadn't made it.

"Bloody hell, Basia," he said. "After seeing you do that, I'm going to think twice before I give you a bad job evaluation."

"That's good to know," she said.

I still couldn't believe what she'd just done. I groped for the right words to say. "You, you…just saved us, Basia. Single-handedly. I didn't know you had that in you."

"Why not?"

"I don't know. I just thought you'd be too afraid."

A smile touched her lips. "I was afraid. A lot. And pissed as well. But I was *more* afraid of dying."

Finn retrieved the axe. "Well, let's get the hell out of here, ladies. We have no idea how much time left we have to get away."

We walked along the road with new determination. After the encounter with Oliver, it reminded us how much danger we were still in.

It was difficult to determine how long we trekked. The last time I'd glanced up, the sun had long passed the midway point in the sky. I knew it had been at least three hours, even if it seemed like all day. My breathing came in short, labored bursts and I was probably in the best shape of the three of us. Our journey was compounded because we were in the mountains. The air was thinner and we were injured and exhausted. So far, we'd had only two short stops to drink, rest and eat some peanuts and crackers.

I wasn't sure how far we'd gone, but at our trudging rate, it wasn't far. I could still see the crash site each time we crested an intermediate ridge as we trudged towards a jagged spine that divided this valley from the next. We needed another break, but I was afraid to call a stop again. It had become increasingly hard to urge them to continue when I didn't want to keep moving either. But we had to keep moving or die.

The sun was starting to slip behind the mountains,

though it was still over an hour until sunset when I first heard the helicopter. I figured it was several miles away, but it was hard to tell exactly where as the hills echoed the sound.

"This way," I shouted to Finn and Basia, motioning them toward the cover of the trees along the edge of the road. As we watched the skies, one helicopter came into view following the road from the south followed closely by another.

"Two helicopters." Basia's voice shook from exhaustion or fear. "You were right, Lexi."

I watched it pass over, my mouth dry. "Let's just hope I'm right about the rest."

The first helicopter circled around the crash site, probably looking for a good place to land, and then lowered from sight. The second one followed.

I exchanged a glance with Finn and Basia. "We have a few minutes while they check out the site for survivors, then they're going to come looking for us. We have only about a half-mile to the top of that main ridge. That's my best guess as to where they are likely to set up a roadblock since they will be able to see anyone coming up the road. If we can get there before they do, we will have time to escape while they search the inside perimeter. Do you think you can make it?"

Finn nodded, his eyes locked on where the helicopters had disappeared from sight. "They'll send one in each direction, so we have to move now."

"Let's go."

We raced for the ridge top. Unfortunately, the harrowing day had almost exhausted our stores of adrenaline. After an initial burst of semi-jogging for a hundred yards or so our pace and gait began to resemble that of drunken zombies. Basia was amazing in her heels, despite almost twisting her ankle several times on the rocks. Finn caught her once, just before she was going to pitch sideways into a bush.

The crash site was strangely silent, but just as we approached the ridge, we heard the sound of a helicopter starting up. That gave us the impetus for a final sprint over the top and down fifty yards on the other side.

Exhausted, we slipped into the trees and hoped the cover and approaching darkness would provide sanctuary.

Over the ridge and out of sight, we could hear the helicopter approaching. I kept my voice even. "It's just checking the entire length of the road in the immediate vicinity of the crash. Stay calm."

We pressed farther back into the trees so that we could barely see the road at the top of the hill. I sincerely doubted anyone on the helicopter could have seen us from their vantage, but better safe than sorry. I still felt chills as the copter crested the ridge and passed directly over us. Suddenly it turned and came back to our direction. To my horror, I heard the whine of the rotors slowing.

Damn! I wondered for a fleeting second if they had somehow spotted us. "It's landing."

"Bloody hell." Finn gripped the axe. "Better be ready."

I put a hand on his arm. "Wait."

We watched as the helicopter passed over us, then began its descent. It landed on the road less than a hundred yards from our hiding place at the top of the ridge. Two figures dressed in black holding automatic weapons jumped out of the helicopter. Basia stiffened beside me, but to my enormous relief they turned away from us, walking deliberately up and over the ridge, heading down the road toward the crash.

As soon as they disappeared from sight, I let out a sigh of relief. "Those don't look like the good guys."

"Agreed," Finn said.

"We barely made it outside their perimeter," I observed. "They're setting a bigger search area than I expected and aren't taking any chances. But fortunately for us, that means it will take them a lot longer to confirm we aren't there. So we have more time to escape."

"The real question is escape to where?" Finn got a bottle of water out of the sports bag, drank, then passed it to Basia and me.

We all took big swallows, preparing ourselves for what came next. Until now, our path had been relatively easy and on a road. Now we were headed into the trees on the slopes of the mountain, down toward lowlands teeming with thick jungle. It was clear from the lay of the land and the rain that the centers of each valley would contain streams that would head downhill, hopefully toward civilization. We just needed to follow one, while avoiding well-armed men who were hunting us, and the swarms of insects who wanted to eat us.

I started to calculate our chance for success and then stopped. For once I didn't want to know.

Finn stood first and whispered quietly, although the sounds of the birds and the insects had picked up as twilight approached, masking most sounds. "First priority is to find a place away from the road to make camp for the night before it gets dark. They're going to be busy checking the crash site and immediate area for the next little bit. I presume they'll stay there for the night. But everyone will be on the move in the morning."

I nodded. I understood his wisdom, but the thought of sleeping in the open with wild animals, snakes and hordes of insects held absolutely no appeal. Basia's eyes widened and I knew she was more worried about it than I was. But it wasn't like we had a choice.

I stood and held out a hand to help Basia up. "Finn's right. Let's see if we can find a four-star resort. I'm even willing to sleep three in a queen bed, if necessary."

Basia rolled her eyes. "Ha ha."

We walked downhill, away from the road and the ridgeline, but the going was rough in the growing gloom. Going farther would be dangerous and we were all way past our limits.

"Let's stop there," I said pointing between two trees. "We need to take inventory and plan for the night."

Basia found a soft spot and sank to the ground. "Thank God."

Finn was already opening his bag. "I'll spread the tarp out. Due to the altitude it will get colder here than we might expect. We'll need to huddle together tonight in order to conserve energy and heat. We'll share the blankets.

As soon as he mentioned the cooler temperature Basia's teeth started to chatter.

I nodded. "Let's eat some crackers and drink a bit more water before taking another round of painkillers. The food will help cushion our stomachs from the medicine. Hopefully the meds will get us through most of the night."

After Finn spread out the tarp, I emptied all of our supplies on it and sorted them out.

"What are you doing?" Basia asked me.

"Dividing our supplies based upon the Rule of Three."

"What's that?"

"The Rule of Three says you can live three minutes without air, three days without water, and three weeks without food."

"No way. There is no way I could live without food for three weeks."

"Fine, we'll make it two weeks for you, Basia."

I resumed surveying our supplies. "Alright, team, my best estimate is that we have two days of food and water."

"Two days?" Basia repeated. "That's it?"

"That's it."

Finn tossed me a water bottle and the acetaminophen. "Actually, make it a day and a half. We have to drink, eat and take some medicine now so we can make it through the night."

"Okay. So revised. Our limit is really going to be water. We can drink some of the juices as replacements, but once we run out of our supplies, we are going to need to drink stream water to survive. But we want to put off the risks of that as long as possible until we have no choice."

After we had eaten and taken our painkillers, we lay on the tarp, huddled beneath the blankets, staring up at the twilight sky. The buzz of mosquitoes and other insects was a constant in our face and ears. It surprised me that I was getting used to it. Clearly, I was not in my right mind.

"Shouldn't one of us stay awake to stand guard?" Basia asked.

"No," Finn said. "Our only weapon is the axe and we

are so exhausted, we couldn't fight them off even if we wanted to. The odds of them coming across us tonight is remote. They're hunkering down at the crash site."

"I agree," I said. "Better for all of us to just get some sleep and regain our strength."

We fell silent for a while before Finn sighed. "You know, it's been a bloody dream of mine to sleep between two amazing women under the stars of the great outdoors, but honestly, this wasn't quite the way I pictured it."

Basia snorted. "Leave it to a guy to think about sex after surviving a plane crash and being chased through the jungle by Chinese hit men."

He chuckled. "If you've got a bloody better topic— I'm all ears."

I threaded my hands behind my neck. "Well, since we are on the topic…Finn, I checked out your buns."

"Likewise."

I could feel myself blushing. "No, I mean seriously. I did it after the plane crash. That's what I was doing when you came to."

"I can't see how it would have been too difficult seeing as how my pants were split open all the way to the crotch."

"That's the thing. They weren't split. I cut your pants to the crotch. Deliberately."

It was quiet for a moment and then he spoke. "Okay. This conversation is moving in an increasingly interesting direction."

"Well, when you woke up for a brief moment after the crash, I thought you said 'check my buns' not 'get the gun.' I didn't want to roll you over in case you had hurt your back, so, I cut your pant leg to the crotch checking for an injury. The pants were collateral damage. I never did find Wendy's gun."

It was silent and then Finn laughed. He stopped, caught his breath and then laughed some more. I thought he might choke he started laughing so hard.

Basia started laughing, too, and after a moment I joined in. Now that I thought about it, it seemed pretty absurd. I laughed so hard I had to wipe my eyes. Exhaustion had made us silly.

"I'm really sorry about the pants, Finn. I'll buy you a new pair when we get home."

"That story is worth a hundred pairs of pants. Forget it. I feel better already. Besides, it will make a good story to tell my grandkids someday."

Thinking about grandkids made me think of my parents. I wondered if they'd been informed that our plane was missing. Holy cow, I'd never hear the end of it from my mother or father if we ever got out of here alive. Thinking of my mom made me think of Slash. He'd know by now we were missing. He'd be marshaling resources, arranging security and God knew what else. If only he or ComQuest's security could pinpoint us from the GPS locator on the briefcase before the bad guys, we had a fighting chance.

It suddenly occurred to me that as the head of ComQuest security, Oliver had also likely known about the GPS locator. If he had told the Chinese, they might be able to use it to track us, too. Guess I should have thought about that part.

Wearily I pressed my hand to my head. We didn't have a choice. We had to take the risk and keep the briefcase with us. Without the GPS locator, the good guys wouldn't have a prayer of finding us.

I touched the locket around my neck and I thought of Elvis, Xavier and their invention. They were working to better mankind with their technology, but so far it had resulted in only death and destruction. Had it been worth it?

I considered. It would be. I understood, perhaps better than most, that technology could be a double-edged sword. You got the internet, instantaneous worldwide information communication and knowledge sharing. But you also got spam and criminal hackers. The microchip and microfluid were so revolutionary we needed the good guys to get a head start with them. That's why our effort was so important.

Sighing, I ran my fingertip against one of the earrings Slash had given me for Christmas. Knowing he was nearby made me feel safe, even in the middle of nowhere. So when I finally fell asleep, I dreamed of him… and the world's biggest mosquito.

# THIRTY-TWO

I WOKE WITH a start, completely disoriented with a pounding headache, a dull ache in my nose and a gnawing hunger in my belly. My mouth was dry, which meant I must have been breathing through it. A weird chattering filled my ears. For a moment I had no idea where I was, why there was an elbow pressing uncomfortably against my ribcage, and who was snoring softly in my ear.

I sat up and blinked a few times to get my bearings. With the sight of the trees and Finn's muddy face right next to mine, everything came flooding back. The crash, the Chinese and the helicopters. I looked around. It was well after dawn, but the ridge we had climbed still shadowed much of the valley. I could now see the tree trunks and bushes. Looking up, the sky was a clear blue through the leaves. The chatter got louder. Even as I watched, the light began filtering in through the trees.

My neck was stiff. Whether that was from the crash or the night on the tarp without a pillow, I didn't know. Finn was asleep, breathing heavily from his nose. Basia lay with her head on his chest, cradling her damaged arm in the sling against her stomach. Their faces were still caked with dry mud although most of the dirt had come off of Finn's lower jaw, most likely due to the beard that was growing in beneath it. He looked like a zombie and I couldn't begin to imagine what I looked like with two black eyes, a knot on my forehead and a smashed nose and cheek. I groaned. We needed to get going soon but it was warm and cozy under the blankets and I didn't want to get up quite yet.

"Lexi?" Basia's voice was barely a whisper.

I turned my head. "Yes?"

"What's that screeching?"

"I don't know. Animals, I guess."

"I have to go to the bathroom."

I rubbed my eyes. "Me, too. It's probably time for us to get moving anyway."

Finn yawned. "Is it time to get up?"

"How are you feeling?"

He touched his head. "Like I was run over by a lorry. Or an airplane. Take your pick. How did you girls sleep? Was it as good for you as it was for me?"

I stood up, pain thrumming through my nose. "I suspect I inhaled a few bugs. Basia, how's your arm?"

"It hurts pretty badly. I think we can all use some more painkillers this morning."

I stood and every muscle screamed in pain. "Ouch." I rolled my neck from side to side and that hurt, too. We weren't going to be moving with great speed and agility today.

Basia had managed to sit up with some help from Finn. I reached out and pulled her to her feet.

"Don't go far to go to the bathroom," I warned.

She took two steps and stopped. "Lexi, our supplies. They're gone."

*"What?"* I rushed over next to her. Our supplies had been rifled and most of the cans of juice and bottles of water were missing.

The screeching sound got louder until it seemed to come from all sides of me in surround sound.

"What's going on?" Basia said, covering her ears.

I looked up, spotting a water bottle in the tree.

"Monkeys," I shouted. "Hey, give our stuff back."

A water bottle whizzed past my ear. I tried to grab it and missed. Another monkey swooped down and caught it, chattering at me as if my inability to get it was the most hilarious thing ever.

I put my hands on my hips and frowned. "Okay, the fact that I'm the monkey in the middle is not lost on me."

Basia and Fin also tried to get the monkeys to return our supplies, but to no avail. After five minutes of trying to get our stuff back, we faced defeat.

"What are we going to do?" Basia looked panicked. "This isn't a game. We're going to die if we don't get that water and food.

She was right, but I had no idea what to do. Outsmarting international hackers and criminals I could handle. Outwitting monkeys in the trees seemed beyond my capabilities at this point.

Frustrated Basia picked up a rock and threw it at one of the monkeys. "You rotten little thief."

Something flew from the tree, hitting her on the back of her shoulder. A water bottle ricocheted off and rolled to my feet.

"That's it, Basia," I shouted. "Throw something at them and they'll throw back. They want to play, so let's make it a game."

For the next few minutes we threw sticks, stones and whatever we could find. Projectiles were flying everywhere through the air. When it was all said and done, we'd retrieved most of our supplies and I'd tucked them safely away in our bags.

Basia rubbed her shoulder. "That will teach them to

steal from us again." She marched off to go to the bathroom. When she came back, she opened her pack and pulled out a tube of lipstick.

I stared at her. "What are you doing?"

"What does it look like?"

Our faces were caked with mud, so I wondered if it were a trick question. "You're going to put on lipstick?"

"My lips are chapped." She smeared it on and then clicked it shut.

Her commitment to normality reminded me of my mother saying that you should always wear clean underwear in the morning, because you never knew if you were going to be in an accident. Of course that reminded me of *my* mother, and *that* made my head hurt more.

I helped Basia get her pack on and we started out, leaning heavily on our walking sticks. Basia was having a hard time walking in her heels, despite her protestations to the contrary.

"Are you sure you're going to be okay walking in those?" I asked.

"I'm fine. Seriously."

"Okay, just asking."

We moved diagonally down across the ridge toward the stream at the bottom. In occasional breaks in the foliage, we could see a sliver of water at the valley floor. By the midday, we were panting and sweating and our knees were getting wobbly from the stress of continually walking on downhill slopes. The slopes were covered in scrub grass, large volcanic boulders and rock formations too steep to be climbed. In the distance, we could see the start of the jungle. We were finally leaving the mountain area and entering completely unfamiliar terrain.

Crossing this region, we would be exposed to view

from the air. We would need to travel carefully and be prepared to hide at a moment's notice. I scanned ahead, trying to plot a path that offered the least exposure.

"Oh, my God," Basia said, fanning herself. "Could it get any hotter?"

"It's the humidity," I said. "It's hard to breathe the air when it's wet."

Finn glanced at Basia's shoes. "You do know it's going to be even tougher walking from here on, especially when we get to the jungle."

"Bring it on."

Finn shrugged. "Okay, don't say I didn't warn you. Let's move. I don't like being in the open."

We picked our way, weaving among the boulders and rocks as much as possible. Some of them had razor-sharp edges of volcanic glass and we had to be careful we didn't trip and fall. We weren't in a position to deal with another serious injury.

We were nearly halfway across the boulder field when we heard a helicopter.

"Damn it," Finn cursed. "We aren't going to make it. We need to hide."

"Where?" Basia asked, looking around.

"Find a hole to crawl in or a big enough boulder and get under it if you can." I pointed to some boulders. "It's our only option. The key is to break up the outline of your body and make it hard to distinguish you from the terrain. Once you're settled, stay there. Motion is easy to detect from the air. Now move!"

I'd just hunkered down underneath the overhang of a big black rock when the helicopter came over the rise behind us. I managed to refrain from peeking out and trying to see the helicopter, and instead hunched up and pressed my shoulders against the boulder. Basia was several boulders over. She had wiggled under a gap between the boulder and the ground. That had to be painful on her sore arm, but we all did what we had to.

I had no idea where Finn was hidden. Hopefully he'd found something suitable.

The helicopter above us seemed overly loud, the rotors making a loud whooping sound. I tried to slide around the boulder, timing my position with the sound of the helicopter to keep myself hidden from sight. Unfortunately, I was caught out of position lying in the shadow of the boulder when the copter suddenly reversed direction and flew right over me. It hovered just past my position for a few seconds and then moved on. After another pass, it suddenly circled back and hovered again at a spot just to my left and not too far from Basia's hiding place. While I was well hidden, I could see into the cockpit through a crack in the rock as it was flying so low. Rocks, dirt and sand were flying around from the helicopter rotors, but I could still see one of the men inside. It was hard to tell for sure, but he looked Asian. Since our lives were at risk, I had to err on the side of caution. I stayed where I was. I hoped everyone else came to the same conclusion and stayed put, too.

The pilot circled our location a third time. I had no idea what he was doing and whether we'd been spotted. No one yelled at us or shot in our direction. The helicopter just seemed to hover above us for an inordinate amount of time before it finally flew away, continuing its search down the valley.

I waited until I couldn't hear the rotor any more before I came out from behind the boulder. "Basia? Finn?"

"Over here," Finn called out. "Everyone okay?"

Basia wiggled out from under the rock. "Oh, God, I thought they'd never leave. My arm is killing me. Do you think they spotted us?"

I saw something dark laying on the ground a little ways away from Basia and right near where the helicopter had been hovering.

My stomach plummeted. "Okay, guys. I've got bad news. You lost your pack, Basia, and I think the helicopter may have spotted it."

## THIRTY-THREE

BASIA PRESSED A hand to her chest. "Oh, no! I didn't even feel it fall off."

I walked over, snatched it up and tied it back on her. "Not your fault. But we've got to move and fast. We have to assume they saw it. They may think we are in the area, but they can't be sure. If they were sure, they would have landed and searched."

No one argued and we navigated the rest of the rocks as quickly as we could.

"Maybe they didn't know it belonged to us," Basia said.

"It's a plastic garbage bag. I'm pretty sure they knew. They'll be back."

We made it the rest of the way across the open area without suffering any major injury. Panting and sweating profusely, we stopped for a moment on the edge of the jungle.

"It's time to enter the jungle proper," Finn asked. "Are you girls ready?"

Basia raised her chin and I nodded. Finn entered first and we followed him. It was darker there and a bit cooler. The sunlight was all but blocked by the heavy canopy of foliage. The smell was different, too. The ground was moist, damp and held rotting undergrowth. It became harder to walk. Vines hung from every tree and distended roots made walking difficult and dangerous.

My ponytail was plastered to my neck and I lifted it up, hoping for a breeze that didn't come. Sighing, I forged ahead, pushing aside a vine only to have it come loose in my hand.

I yelped, tossing it in the air. It landed on Basia's pack. She screamed and danced around until Finn came to her defense, brushing it off her pack and onto the ground where it slithered away.

"If you girls keep making all this noise, we are going to be an easy target," he said, frowning at us.

"Sorry," I said. "It took me by surprise."

Basia pressed a shaking hand to her chest. "Oh, my God. Was it poisonous?"

Finn leaned on his walking stick. "I don't know, but we have to treat all snakes as if they are dangerous. Be hyperaware of your surroundings. Use the walking stick to push vines out of the way. Consider it an extra line of defense."

"Oh, God." Basia was trembling. "I don't know if I can do this."

"You can," Finn assured her. "You're at the top of the food chain, even here. Stay strong and vigilant."

I reached out and tentatively pushed aside another vine with my stick. This was going to be a very long trek.

It was. The more we pressed in, the more treacherous it became, especially for Basia in her heels. I constantly worried about having to carry her if she sprained her ankle. Still, she'd proved herself to be worthy of a worldwide Versace shoe ad. Whereas I would have been in ankle splints within ten minutes of wearing those shoes, she'd climbed down a mountain and run from helicopters without falling once. While defying all logic, it was seriously impressive.

We continued forward, worried about who might be following. Sweat stung my eyes and dripped off my sore nose. I felt lightheaded and thirsty, but we kept going.

Another hour or so passed. I was about to call for a rest when I suddenly spotted a wide stream.

"Water," I exclaimed.

We staggered toward the edge. When we got there, we dropped our bags and sat down at the edge to look at it.

Basia dipped her good hand in and squealed with delight. "It's cold."

"Don't drink it," I warned.

"I won't. I'm not an idiot."

She slipped off her shoes and stuck her feet in the cool water. "Oh, God, I can't tell you how good that feels. My feet are killing me."

I wanted to do the same, but my feet had swollen and I worried about getting my tennis shoes back on, so I resisted the urge. "You can have Wendy's shoes, you know."

"I'm *not* wearing a dead person's shoes."

"She has small feet like you. I bet they'll fit and you'll be much more comfortable."

"No. Discussion closed."

"Fine." I reached into my bag and grabbed a couple of water bottles. "Let's get something to drink, take some acetaminophen, reapply our mud cover and press on."

The rest was shorter than any of us would have liked, but we had to keep moving. Our food supply was dwindling and I remained concerned that the helicopter had spotted us and was either returning with people to drop off to chase us or was directing those on the ground where to find us.

It was significantly easier to follow the stream rather

than trying to hack our way through the underbrush. The insects were worse here, as well, and despite the relief from the direct rays of the sun, the humidity was a killer. It was like being slow cooked in a pot. We stopped several times to splash water on ourselves to keep cool and then reapplied mud.

Eventually we came to a dead stop when our path along the side of the stream was completely blocked by a series of tree trunks and assorted debris that were probably leftovers from a flood.

I wiped my brow. "We'll never get over that. We have to go around."

Finn's face was scarlet, his shirt completely soaked. His chin sported the start of a scraggly beard. "I'll take a look."

"Maybe we can cross the stream," Basia suggested. "It could be deep in the middle, but it's not that wide."

I stared at the water in disbelief. Cross it? I couldn't swim, so this was not an option.

Before I could voice my concern, Basia spoke. "I'll backtrack a bit and see a spot where we could cross." She took off, leaving me no choice but to follow.

She retraced our steps until she saw a potential path across the water. A rotted log stretched halfway across and several mostly flat rocks provided jumping off spots to help cross the rest of the way. It looked tenuous at best and downright dangerous at worst. I didn't want to do it.

I turned around. Finn had joined us.

"It's a mess in the jungle," Finn said. "I have no idea what happened here, but it would take considerable effort to go around. I recommend crossing the stream."

Basia pointed to a potential path. "What do you think about crossing here?"

Finn studied it. "I don't see a better way to go. Good plan. I'll go first."

"Whoa. Wait." I held up a hand. "How about a discussion on this? This is *not* a good plan. We could fall in and drown or be eaten alive by any number of creatures that might be lurking beneath the surface. Can we explore another possibility?"

Finn met my gaze. "There is no other possibility, and we don't have a lot of time for discussion. We can't go around the debris without wasting considerable effort and time and running the risk of losing sight of the stream. The risk of crossing the stream here is significantly less."

"Since when is drowning a significantly less risk?"

He frowned. "You're overreacting, Lexi. The water might not even be deep."

Panic welled in my throat. I didn't want to cross that stream, but I didn't think I could outmuscle Finn. The stream was looking bigger and deeper by the minute.

"I'm not doing this, Finn." It came out as more of a challenge than I'd intended, but I was scared.

Finn put a hand on my shoulder. "Oh, yes, you will. Right, Basia?"

Basia looked between Finn and me. Finally she sighed. "I'm sorry, Lexi, but Finn is right. This will be the fastest way. I know you don't like the water, but we'll be here to help you."

"How could you?" I threw up my hands. "You're siding with him? I thought you were my best friend."

"I *am* your best friend, but it's the right thing to do."

"You're going to cross this stream, so get with the program." Finn took off his pack. "I'll take you across this stream on my back if I have to."

"You wouldn't dare."

"Don't dare me, Lexi. Trust me. You won't win this argument." He stood in front of me, his green eyes narrowed to slits, his nose nearly touching mine.

Basia came between us, putting a hand on each of our chests. "Stop it right now. You're both being idiots. We're completely exhausted and stressed. No one is thinking clearly. Finn, stop threatening her. Lexi, listen to him, he's making sense."

Finn stepped away first, running his fingers through his hair and softening his voice. "Look, Lexi, I'll show you how easy it is. I'll go first."

He climbed on the log, holding his hands out for balance. "It's simple when you just think of the log as a bridge."

I held my breath as he took each step, finally reaching the end of the log. He then hopped from the log to the first stone. I resisted the urge to cover my eyes. Moving across the remaining rocks, he jumped to shore.

"See? Just a walk in the proverbial park."

My stomach knotted. "Easy for you to say. You know how to swim, you're athletic and you're large enough to wrestle a crocodile if one snaps at you."

"Do you see any crocodiles?"

I glanced up and down the stream. "No, but that's the idea. They're likely lurking beneath the surface ready to snap at me as soon as I step onto that log."

That elicited a small smile from him. "Get your arse on that log and get over here."

"Hey, who died and made you king of this expedition?" I glared at him.

"Lexi…" Finn's voice held a warning.

"Fine." I closed my eyes. "I'll do it. But if I die, it's on you."

I swallowed my fear and took my first tentative step out onto the log. I held my hands out on either side, trying not to look at the water. It was hard because I was looking at my feet and the water was swirling past. It was moving a lot faster when I looked at it from this angle.

"Just one step at a time," Finn said encouragingly. "We've got your back."

I took one step and then another. My balance was crappy and my bag was heavy so I kept listing to the right. Somehow I got to the end of the log without falling off, but my legs were shaking. Carefully I lifted the bag off over my shoulder.

"Finn, I'm going to toss my bag to you. It's throwing me off balance and I'm afraid I'll slip on the rocks. Catch, okay?"

Before he could answer, I swung it a couple of times to give it more height and velocity. As I released it, an edge of the strap caught on my index finger, yanking me forward. My feet scrambled for purchase. For an agonizingly long moment, I wavered back and forth on the log.

Then I fell forward into the stream with a single yelp.

# THIRTY-FOUR

"Lexi!" Finn and Basia shouted as I went under.

I bobbed up, flailing around, coughing and sputtering and trying to grab onto the log. I couldn't touch. The water was deep and moving a lot faster than I'd expected. I slammed more than once into the log. Finn charged into the water, swimming to me as I flailed around. He put one arm around my waist and held us against the log with the other.

"I told you I was a klutz," I said, sputtering.

"The bag," Basia shouted, pointing. "There it goes."

I peered over the log and watched in horror as it bobbed and spun around a few times before moving down the stream and disappearing around the bend.

"Go get it, Finn," I said. "That one has the briefcase and most of our water supply. Just pull me to the rocks. I'll be okay."

Finn pulled me down the log and dragged me onto the first rock. "Can you make it from here? Are you sure?"

"Yes. Go get the damn bag."

"Basia, talk her the rest of the way across the stream," Finn shouted before swimming the rest of the way to the shore and pulling himself out. He dashed out of sight along the shore, still dripping water.

I pulled myself up to stand on the first rock, shivering. I wasn't cold, but I was scared to death. On the bright side, I'd fallen into the water and hadn't drowned or been eaten by a crocodile. Yet.

"Hurry up and cross, Lexi," Basia shouted. "Finn may need your help."

I closed my eyes. My pulse was going crazy. I waited a moment until my heartbeat slowed before opening my eyes. There was no time to waste. Without thinking too hard about it, I hopped from rock to rock until somehow I was across. I jumped onto the dirt shore, water dripping off me. Mosquitoes swarmed around because my mud barrier had been washed off.

"Wait there," I yelled to her. "I'll go help Finn."

I darted downstream in the direction he'd gone, my shoes squishing water with every step.

Before long I spotted Finn and ran up to him, panting. "Why did you stop?"

He pointed to the water. "There's our bag."

I followed his finger and saw the bag had got hooked on a low-lying tree branch on the other side of the stream.

"Where's Basia?" he asked.

"I told her to wait for us. If she fell in while crossing, there's no way I could save her alone."

"Good thinking."

I studied the location of the bag. "Okay. Now what, Your Majesty?"

"Shut up. Now, we go get that bag. At the very least, we need the water bottles. I assume the water will have ruined the GPS."

"No. We're good on that. The case is waterproof."

Relief crossed his face. "Well, that's a bloody good break for us."

"Yes it is. But how do we get the briefcase? We don't have those convenient stepping stones here."

Finn looked at me. "We'll have to wade out in the water and get it."

"*What?* That's a freaking terrible idea, Finn. The water is moving way too fast. You felt that, right? We'll get swept away."

"We don't have a choice. That briefcase holds our lives. We have to get it or sit here and wait until someone finds us in time, hoping it's the good guys."

I wiped my hands against my wet, filthy jeans. "Not that I'm worried or anything, but you're using the word *we* a lot when discussing going into the water again to get the bag."

He wasn't looking at me. Instead he glanced between the bag, the shore and me. Finally he went to his bag and pulled out the rope. Uncoiling it, he held it out to me.

"You're going to have to go in the water and get it," he said briskly. "I'll be the anchor."

*"What?"*

"I'm too heavy to do it. In order for you to hold me in that current, you'd have to wrap it around the tree or I'd drag you in if I got pulled away. We don't have enough length on the rope to do that."

I saw the wisdom in his thinking, but I didn't like it. Still, it wasn't like we had a lot of choices, so I sucked it up. "Okay."

He stopped, lifted an eyebrow. "Okay? That's it?"

"Do you want me to argue? Because there are a million reasons I could list as to why I shouldn't go back in there. But none of them matter. So, tie the rope around me and let's do this."

He leaned over and kissed the top of my wet head. I closed my eyes as he tied the rope around my waist.

"Wait here," he said. He went into the jungle and returned carrying a long stick with a forked branch on the end. "Use this to pull the briefcase to you in case we don't have enough rope to make it."

I took the branch and tried to calm my breathing. I was headed toward full-blown panic mode.

Finn put his hands on my shoulders, looking me in the eyes. "Lexi, I've got you. I'm not going to let go or let anything happen to you, okay?"

I gulped and nodded.

"Good. Now go get that bag. You've got this and I've got you." Finn wrapped the rope around his waist and planted his feet on the shore, digging them into the soft soil.

I stepped into the water. It was cool and it felt good against my hot, clammy skin. I waded in until I was up to my waist. I could feel the pull of the water, but Finn anchored me, only giving me a little rope a step at a time. I tried not to think of what might be swimming around in the water, thinking about having me for lunch. I kept my focus on the bag and kept hoping it would get free and magically float into my waiting hands.

As I got closer, the water rose to my chest. I held the arm with the branch above my head. Panic kept bubbling, but I gritted my teeth and moved forward.

Suddenly I felt a tug on the rope.

"What happened?" I shouted.

"End of the rope. See if you can reach the case with the branch."

I leaned forward as far as the rope would permit and stretched the branch out, trying to slide it under the strap, which was swaying in the current.

I tried several times to no avail. My back and shoulders were aching and water kept splashing in my face, which I really hated.

"I've given you a little more reach, Lexi."

I assumed he'd moved a bit into the water to get me closer. I took another step and slid the branch under the strap. Holding my breath, I pulled the strap toward me, reaching out my other hand to grab it.

I almost had it when the branch snapped. I dropped the branch and threw myself forward and off my feet, grabbing for the strap of the bag with the tips of my fingers. I felt it brush my fingertips and then my hand closed over it. I went under the water face first, but when I came back up, I had the strap.

"Lexi," Finn shouted. "Are you okay?"

Water had gone up my nose. But I had it.

"Yes." I yanked hard on the strap until the bag finally popped free, then slid it over my head and shoulder and turned around. "Get me the heck out of here."

Finn stepped backward, pulling. I walked to shore, fighting against the current with every step. Finally I made it, collapsing onto the shore. I was completely spent.

Finn leaned down and untied the rope around my waist, heaving a sigh of relief. "Good work. I'm going back for Basia and the rest of our supplies."

I nodded, not able to speak yet.

After a few minutes Basia and Finn returned. She was dry, so I assumed all had gone well as she crossed the stream.

She sat down beside me, putting her head on my shoulder. "You're my hero. Finn told me what you did."

"I did what had to be done. We're all doing what has

to be done. But this survival thing is a lot harder than it looks in the movies."

Basia hugged me. "True. And they never mention the bugs in the movies. I would trade half of my shoe collection for a fourteen-ounce can of insect repellent and a banana split right now. So what now?"

I glanced up at Finn waiting for his response, but he didn't answer. I understood what he was doing. He wanted us to all share in the leadership of our survival.

I turned to Basia. "So, what do you think we should do?"

She cocked her head. "Now we move on. What other choice do we have?"

# THIRTY-FIVE

"HOLY JUMPING SPIDER!" I yelped.

I backed into Finn, almost knocking him over trying to get away from a fist-sized brown, yellow and red monster with multiple eyes that had just jumped onto a nearby vine exactly at my eye-level. My heart was pounding so hard I could hardly breathe.

Finn rolled his eyes and swept past me. He leaned in to take a closer look at it. "Fascinating. It looks like it has six eyes…no eight. Cool."

"Cool?" Basia repeated huddled behind me. "That is *not* cool. It's probably a two-stepper. You know, it bites and we get to walk two steps before we're dead. How far do you think it can jump? Do you think it can reach us from here?"

By this time Basia and I were a good eighteen feet away from it, but my brain feverishly calculated how quickly it could reach us if it were able to jump a foot every two seconds. It was too close for comfort, so I backed up, with Basia in tow, another two feet just in case.

Finn herded us around the spider and we walked for several more hours. Finn led the way with me holding up the rear. I got sort of dry before it rained twice more, soaking us to the skin and then steaming us when it stopped. We managed to refill our bottles with a little rainwater each time, but the rain was fast and we were slow to stop and get the bottles out of our pack in time. We were red-faced and sweating by the time Finn called a stop for the day.

Basia let out a sigh of relief and dropped right where she was. "Oh, my God. I think I sleepwalked those last few miles."

Finn sat beside her. He was hardly recognizable with his beard and banged-up face. I pulled out the water bottles and tossed one to each of them. We were going through water fast with all the heat and exertion, but I estimated we still had about another half's day worth of water left at the current rate.

"I'm totally starving." Basia took a drink. "It's been three years since I've had a hamburger, but I'd eat four in one sitting right now."

Finn handed her the tin of *Hawaiian Premium Shortbread and Chocolate Chip Macadamia Nut Cookies*. "Your meal is served, Madame."

She sighed and opened the tin, taking out a cookie and delicately biting a corner. "Why do you think it's taking them so long to find us?"

She offered me a cookie. I took one and passed the tin on to Finn. "The good guys or the bad guys?"

"Either."

"Well, in terms of the bad guys, we're on the move and trying to evade detection. We're amateurs, so we don't know what we're doing, which makes us predictably unpredictable. I also presume there is a learning curve for them in this terrain. For the good guys, it's probably the same. We're all over the place and hiding. We don't know who is good or bad, so we have to avoid both until we can be sure who is who. I'm hoping that the good guys know we can't distinguish between them and think to broadcast by loudspeaker that they are the good guys and for us to come out." I paused. "Of course, the bad guys could think of the same idea and use it to trick us into revealing ourselves. I guess we just have to keep moving and trust they'll find us first."

Finn handed me pretzels and I ripped open the bag and put one in my mouth. The salt tasted awesome, but I worried it would make me thirstier. Finn ate a couple of bags of peanuts and then leaned back on his hands.

"I don't want to be the one to break it to you girls, but this meal marks the end of my role as expedition chef. That was the last of our food."

Basia sighed. "Maybe we'll find a village soon that has a phone."

"I sincerely doubt that." I ate another pretzel and then smashed a mosquito that landed on the back of my mud-died hand. "Did you know Papua New Guinea is home to over three hundred different native tribes? Many of them have never had direct contact with people outside their tribe. So the odds of finding a phone or internet service is pretty small."

"God, I hate those odds." She stood, stretching her back. "You know, I could really use some good news for a change, but first I have to go to the bathroom."

"Want me to come with you?" I offered.

"No. I've got this."

"Okay, but don't go far," Finn warned.

"Don't worry. I won't. I have no intention of getting left behind." She disappeared into the trees.

She hadn't been gone for more than two minutes when I heard a scream and thrashing sounds behind a screen of nearby trees. Finn and I scrambled to our feet, picking our way through the underbrush the best we could.

We found Basia on her knees, bent over something.

"Basia?" I said.

She stood slowly. I took a step back, my mouth dropping open.

Finn gasped. "Holy Mother of God."

Lying on the ground, impaled through the head by the heel of one of her precious shoes, was a long, fat snake. Other wounds around its neck and body implied that she had stabbed it repeatedly before it expired.

My gaze shifted between her and the snake. "What happened?"

"It tried to bite my ass. I used the only weapon I had."

I stared at her in fascination. "You stabbed a snake with your shoe?"

"Well, I wasn't going to kill it with my hands."

Finn squinted at it. "Damn it, woman. Remind me to give you plenty of room at a party."

"Was it poisonous?" I asked.

"How the heck would I know? It wasn't like I was going to ask."

Basia bent down and tried to shake it off her shoe, but it wasn't budging. Neither Finn nor I moved forward to help her pull it off.

For a minute the two of us stood there staring at Basia and the snake, trying to wrap our heads around it. Finally Finn stepped forward and did the man thing. Using a stick, he stepped on the snake behind the head and pulled the heel out of the snake and then used a wide leaf to wipe the snake guts off the shoe as best as possible.

"Here," he said gallantly, handing the shoe back to her as a last couple of drops of blood trickled from the underside of the shoe and down the heel to the ground.

She stared at it, still in shock, then shook her head. "I

can't. I just can't. Damn it, I could kill that snake again for making me say this, but Lexi, can I have Wendy's shoes?"

"Of course."

We returned to our supplies, and I pulled Wendy's shoes out of my pack. They were actually a bit too big for Basia, so I cut another couple of squares from the blanket and we stuffed it in the toes. She walked around a bit and seemed satisfied. Still, I didn't want to waste anything and, given the remarkably high statistical probability we would come across more snakes, I put the heels in my bag.

Finn took out the tarp. "It's time to call it a day. Lexi, you and I have to take off our clothes. All of them. They are still damp and we need to lay them out to dry. Basia, you need to check Lexi for leeches."

My eyes widened. "Leeches? On me? You are kidding, right?"

"I never kid about leeches. There's a chance we picked some up in the river."

I started to hyperventilate and scratch at my jeans. "Okay, Basia can check me, but who's going to check you?"

He smiled. "Flip a coin, ladies. Or fight it out. No worries."

I rolled my eyes. "We'll both do it."

"Excellent suggestion." His smile widened as he pulled off his shirt. He held his arms out to each side. "Have at me, girls."

Basia and I walked around him and began pulling slimy, sucking leeches off his back, shoulders and scalp. I tried not to be grossed out, but after yanking the first three off, I wasn't feeling so good.

Basia on the other hand, was acting as if she did this all the time. "I only found nine so far," she said cheerfully.

I freaking couldn't believe this was the same Basia I'd always known. The Basia who was on a first-name basis with several French designers, drove her trash to the Dumpster at the end of her condo building because the walk was too far and never, ever wore white after Labor Day. My stomach was churning as I squeezed each little body off, especially knowing these same blood-sucking creatures were attached to me as well.

"Now take off your shoes, socks and pants, Finn." Basia marched in front of Finn with her hands on her hips. "But leave your underwear on. Lexi and I will check your bum—again—but we'll let you handle your private area yourself."

"Damn." Finn snorted. "You sure know how to take the fun out of leeching."

Doing as he was told, Finn stripped to his undies while we pulled a dozen more leeches from his legs and bum. At last he was leech-free. He was shivering and swarmed by mosquitos by the time he slid under the blankets. I hung his clothes on some tree branches and then it was my turn.

I endured the same treatment, then stood by the tarp, shivering in my underwear and covering my boobs with my hands.

"Finn, this may well be the most embarrassing moment of my life." Then I remembered the time I had knocked Father Murphy's toupee in his soup, danced on a stripper pole and tipped two beers down the back of a patron at a sushi restaurant and I amended my statement. "Well, at least it makes my top ten list. But right now I'm just too tired and miserable to be awkward about it. I'm coming in." My teeth chattered so hard I could hardly talk.

Finn patted the spot next to him under the blanket. "Shut up and get in, lass. No embarrassment necessary. I warmed a spot for you."

A shiver shook me. "Fine. But you have to swear we'll never, *ever* speak of this once we're rescued."

Finn held up a hand, his eyes dancing with amusement. "I do so solemnly swear. Is that legal enough for you?"

I scooted under the blankets and Basia joined us after laying out my wet clothes. She gave Finn the eye across the blanket. "Don't enjoy this too much, okay?"

He lifted an eyebrow. "It's all in the name of survival, I swear. Plus, I've seen you in action twice with those heels. I can assure you I will be a perfect gentleman."

Despite the awkwardness of the situation, I couldn't help but laugh.

As we lay huddled together for warmth, my stomach growled. "Does anyone know what else there is to eat in the jungle?"

"What about coconuts and mangoes?" Basia offered. "I always see survivors eating those in the movies."

I tried to think back if I'd seen anything that resembled a coconut palm during our walk. Actually the only place I had seen them were on beautiful movie beaches or along the streets of Hollywood. And I wasn't even sure if those were coconut or date palms.

"Okay, Basia, you let us know as soon as you spot one," I said. "We can use Finn's head to crack them open."

"Are you kidding?" Basia snorted. "We don't find the

coconuts. They find us. In the movies they fall down and brain someone on the head. Get serious. I wouldn't know a coconut tree unless I found coconuts on the ground underneath it."

"There's fish," Finn offered. He rested his head on his arm. "My da and I used to go fishing, but I always had bait and a pole. Don't know how well I'd do with a spear, but I could always give it a try. The water here is pretty muddy, so I'm not sure I could spot a fish. What we really need to know is what the most edible berries or plants are in the region."

Dang, he was right. Berries were easy to spot, easy to eat and could sustain us. At this moment, I would have sold all my earthly possessions for fifteen minutes on a laptop with Wi-Fi. "I really miss Google. A lot."

Everyone laughed.

I rolled to my side, propping my head on the palm of my hand. "You know, it's a good thing we're so tuned in to nature. A lawyer, a geek and a city girl. It sounds like the start to a bad joke."

"It's totally embarrassing." Basia yawned. "I'd be the first to die in a zombie apocalypse."

"Not true," Finn said. "You'd stab it in the eye with your shoe. Never knew you had it in you, lass."

Basia paused and then heard the smile in her voice. "Neither did I. But I do now."

## THIRTY-SIX

THE ODDS THAT I would trip and break my leg increased with every mile we walked. Given my klutziness combined with a head injury, dehydration and fatigue, I calculated the odds to be seven hundred and sixty-seven to one that I'd suffer a bad fall within the next few steps. The footing seemed to get more uneven, the foliage thicker and harder to traverse with every step.

Miraculously, I beat the odds and didn't fall. Yet. Meanwhile I kept my eyes open for paths that might lead to a village. We were past our physical limits and were continuing solely on a shared determination not to quit. We were out of food and nearly out of water. After a particularly rough traverse around a small waterfall that I would have described as scenic and gorgeous under other circumstances, I watched Basia and Finn lurching, holding each other up as we started to leave the pool at the base of the falls. I worried about Basia's arm and Finn's head injury. My nose, left cheek and forehead still hurt, but my brain had either turned off the pain receptors or I'd become more adept at ignoring it. Perhaps I was too exhausted to notice.

I decided we were overdue for a break and this seemed like a nice spot. It was also probably time to talk about what to do if we stumbled upon the local villagers.

Finn studied me as I mentioned the villagers. "Why do you bring that up, Lexi?"

"Before we started down from the falls, I could see smoke on the horizon through the trees. I'm unable to accurately judge the distance. So, it could be the bad guys or it could be the good guys. Or, more likely, it's just a native village. We know what to do with the good or bad guys, but we haven't formed a plan for interacting with the villagers."

"We could throw ourselves on their mercy," Basia offered.

I started to tie my shoe and a piece of the shoelace snapped in my hand. I tossed it aside and tied a lopsided bow. "The bad guys might have been there before us. If they offered the villagers a reward, we could be in real trouble."

Finn scratched his chin. "I hadn't thought of that. But I think I've seen a glimpse of a few natives slipping past us through the trees."

Basia looked at him in astonishment. "You did? Why didn't you tell us?"

"Because I wasn't sure and, so far, they've left us alone."

I wasn't surprised. Although I hadn't spotted anyone, I'd suspected we were being watched as soon as I saw the fires.

"Well, my thinking is that unless they make first contact, we should avoid them until we can observe them and determine if they're on our side."

"How can we determine that?" Basia asked.

"I don't know. But I'll figure it out somehow." I said that more confidently than I felt.

We pressed on halting more frequently to try and conserve what little strength we had left. It was late afternoon when we came to the top of a rise.

The stream dropped quickly away into a narrow valley with steep sides, cutting a ravine in the rock that would be too difficult to follow at the level of the water. The valley floor was very uneven with a rapid drop of almost fifty feet immediately below us. The valley stretched for at least a mile or so before ending abruptly in a dense green wall of what was clearly jungle. We stood silently for several minutes as our weary brains tried to process this new information.

Basia broke the silence. "So, what do we do now? Once we are in the valley, there's no cover. I have absolutely no interest in playing hide and seek again with another helicopter with one arm tied behind my back."

Finn shaded his eyes, looking in both directions. "If we want to take another route, we'll have to head back until we can climb out of this valley. Even then we may face a similar decision point. If we want to keep following the stream and moving downhill, we have to press on. I see little choice. What do you think, Lexi?"

I considered. We were truly spent. It looked like the climb down to the valley floor wouldn't be too treacherous, but we would be completely exposed the whole time until we reached the jungle. If we had to move quickly, we couldn't. If a helicopter chanced by, we would be spotted quicker than a novice at a Black Hat convention.

But there were really no alternatives. We couldn't realistically backtrack. We simply didn't have the energy for climbing. Staying here without food and water wasn't viable either. We needed the stream as our compass. I didn't like the idea of being in the open, but we hadn't heard the helicopter since yesterday and the chance for some sunshine suddenly appealed to me more than the danger.

"Let's go down. It's our best and probably only option."

I didn't have to say it twice. We paused, listening carefully for any foreign sounds, then Finn started down, walking sideways to offset the incline. Basia followed him, holding one of his hands as I took up the rear. As we descended, the wind started to blow around us. The breeze felt heavenly and it increased even more as we approached the valley floor.

Proceeding through the valley, we found ourselves squeezing through or walking around almost continual debris tossed haphazardly along the valley floor by countless floods that overflowed the narrow ravine. We were just over halfway down the valley when I heard it.

Helicopters. Holy bad luck. Couldn't we get a freaking break for once?

Basia turned to me. Terror was etched on her face. "Not again. What are we going to do?"

There was absolutely nowhere to hide. No boulders this time. Only half-buried branches and tree stumps, as well as piles of mud and small rocks. We were going to be spotted for sure.

Our best chance was to try and make it to the jungle before they could find a place to land.

"Run!" I shouted.

I hadn't taken more than a dozen steps when a helicopter flew right above me. I observed some guy hanging out the side and pointing at me. No hope for evasion this time.

Finn and Basia were ahead of me, running for dear life. Actually running was a generous description. They looked like a pair of octogenarians doing step aerobics and I wasn't doing much better.

Two armed men leaned forward out of the helicopter, preparing to jump out as it approached a small ledge. Finn and Basia saw them, too, skidding to a stop to watch the harrowing maneuver in morbid fascination. They waved for me to catch up, but I screamed for them to keep going. Finn hesitated, but Basia grabbed his hand and they started running again.

The first guy jumped onto the ledge. When he stood up and peered over the edge looking at us, I saw the gun. He lifted his eye to a scope and pointed it directly at me. I froze in indecision. Why was he going to shoot me now? Wouldn't it have been simpler to shoot at me from the air?

Since stopping to debate the merits of his strategy didn't seem like my best move at this point, I began zig-zagging as best I could, trying to make it a hard shot for him and still keep the pace. In front of me, Basia and Finn were passing almost directly below his position, but he ignored them. For some reason, the shooter had eyes only for me.

A bullet, then another, pinged off the rocks about ten feet in front of me. Oh, God. Somehow I was harder to miss than a Star Trek rerun, yet this guy wasn't even close. Unless, of course, he intended to miss. Maybe he wasn't trying to kill me, but just stop me from running. If that were the case, there was no way I was stopping. A single shot pinged a rock closer to my foot as I neared where the ledge loomed above. I stumbled, nearly fall-ing.

The wind had continued to pick up and was muffling the sound of the helicopter. I dared another peek at the ledge and saw the helicopter lowering again to drop an-other guy off. My shooter had paused to assist another guy as he jumped from the helicopter to the ledge, so at least I was safe from a bullet for the time being.

The second man landed on the ledge. As the helicopter began to rise to pull away, a gust abruptly caused it to list to the left. I paused to watch in fascination. The helicopter jerked hard to the right as if the pilot was overcompensating, coming precariously close with the rotors to the valley wall. He appeared to have stabilized the craft when a final gust nudged the helicopter into the wall.

While my mental processor wasn't operating at maximum gigahertz, I was sufficiently capable of understanding that standing below a falling helicopter wasn't an ideal position. I put on a burst of speed that actually resembled running, passing directly under the chopper. It was making lots of very unhelicopterlike sounds and groans. Basia and Finn were about one hundred yards in front of me, still running like halfbacks in the Super Bowl.

Sparks and metal started flying, accompanied by a horrific, screeching soundtrack. A quick peek indicated the helicopter seemed to be falling in slow motion, headed straight for me. It was going to be close. I summoned the rest of my energy and poured on as much speed as I could.

The explosion and sudden blast of heat knocked me off my feet and threw me forward. My last thought was that I never, in my wildest dreams, ever expected to die beneath a helicopter.

## THIRTY-SEVEN

"LEXI, WAKE UP."

A cool hand rested against my cheek. My eyes fluttered open. I blinked a few times before I could focus.

"Basia?"

"She's okay. Thank God."

I turned my head and saw Finn. His green eyes were filled with a mixture of concern and relief.

I struggled to sit up. "What happened?"

"The helicopter crashed." He helped me into a sitting position. "As far as I can tell there were no survivors."

"What about the guy on the ledge? He shot at me."

"I didn't see any guy on a ledge."

Basia shook her head. "Me neither. But I wasn't looking. I was just running for my life."

I pressed a hand to my head. I had a pounding headache and my nose and cheek hurt again. Badly. "Can I have some acetaminophen?"

Finn nodded scrounging around in the bag until he pulled out the bottle. He shook a couple into his hand and then handed me a water bottle. It was about one-third filled.

He met my questioning gaze and nodded. "It's the last of our water until it rains again."

I took a small sip—just enough to wash the pills down—then looked around. We were in the jungle near the stream. They must have carried or dragged me the rest of the way under the cover of the trees and a small ways into the jungle. I missed the fresh air of the valley, but the wind was up enough, there were still breezes here that helped to keep down the mosquitoes. The shade was a relief, too.

"We're in trouble, aren't we?" Basia said, rubbing her head. "And I mean that in addition to the boatload of trouble we're *already* in. They certainly had time to radio the others where we'd been spotted."

I didn't see the sense in lying. "Yes."

"So what do we do?"

I pressed my hand to the back of my head, which ached, too. "We have to rest and think for at least a little bit. We can't push on right now. It's a risk, but I'm too disoriented to walk and we have to give our bodies a little time to recoup before moving on."

Finn rolled his neck, his face gaunt and pale. "I agree. Let's set up the tarp and rest for an hour or so."

He opened my bag and pulled out the tarp. He gathered some fronds to place beneath it and then spread it out. As soon as it was ready, he stretched out, lying on his back, his forearm covering his eyes.

"Come on," he said, motioning to me.

I thought Basia would join him, but instead she went to the edge of the stream and sat there leaning against a large tree, tucking her legs to her chin and staring at the water.

Worried about her, I changed my mind about the tarp and joined her. "Are you okay, Basia?"

"No. Not really. I've been thinking about my life and Xavier. This whole plane crash thing has given me time to reflect. Why was I so stupid all those years with guys who didn't give a crap about me?"

"Is that an open-ended question I'm supposed to answer?"

"You can answer if you have a theory."

I considered. "Maybe you dated those guys because you weren't sure of what you were looking for or what you wanted in a partner."

"I didn't think I wanted anything. I didn't need anyone. I was perfectly fine on my own, except I wasn't. I dated a lot of men because I was lonely."

I wasn't sure what to say.

She pushed her hair off her neck and fanned the skin beneath. "I guess what I'm trying to say is I can't believe I resisted dating Xavier for so long. He's the one guy who's seen me for who I really am. He persisted even when I brushed him off."

"Xavier is a great guy. You won't get any argument from me on that front."

"I know. It's just that I think he may be the one. I think about him all the time. He treats me like a queen but he calls me out on the crap I pull. He sees the real me and he loves me anyway."

I put my hand on Basia's arm. "Why wouldn't he love you? You are beautiful, kind and smart. You swing a mean high heel. And you're happy in a way I've never seen when you're around him."

Tears swam in her eyes. "I don't want to die, Lexi. Not now. Not after finding the person I know is going to make me happy until I'm a little old lady."

Oh, jeez. If she started a full-blown cry, I might have to shoot myself. Hoping to avoid that, I pretended not to notice the tears. Instead, I washed my hands in the stream and patted water on the back of my neck, staying calm.

"First of all, Basia, it's not realistic to think Xavier is going to make you happy all of the time, especially not until you are a little old lady. The odds that he will infuriate you averages out to about three thousand, seven hundred and ninety two times based on a reasonable estimate of both of you living until the age of eighty years old. Secondly, we're not going to die. So, you can tell him that yourself."

She picked up a rock and tossed it in the stream. I watched the ripples spread out. "I know there'll be challenges. It was just a turn of phrase. I'm certain Xavier will infuriate me on occasion because, well, he's a man. I'm sure I'll do the same to him, too. But we're going to weather it, because that's what people do when they love each other."

"Exactly."

She turned her head. "Do you love Slash? I mean, is he the one?"

I considered. "I don't know how to answer that. He's a difficult man to know. But what I know of him, I love. It's just, this love thing is pretty complex. I'm not even close to figuring it out yet."

"You may never figure it out, and that's okay. As long as you value the relationship and the benefits that come from it." She threw another rock in the stream, leaned her head back against the trunk and closed her eyes. I thought she was going to doze off, but suddenly her eyes popped open. "So, what do you think we'll be having for dinner?"

I stood, brushing my hands off on my filthy jeans. "We're going to have to move to Plan B, which involves a spear and Finn fishing. But first we have to put some distance between us and the helicopter crash."

I turned around, took one step then froze.

The branches in front of me rustled and a woman with bronzed skin, naked from the waist up, emerged from behind a tree. She had a bow in her hands and an arrow cocked.

It was aimed right at Basia.

# THIRTY-EIGHT

EVERYTHING SEEMED TO happen in slow motion.

Before I could blink, the arrow left the bow, whistled past my shoulder and headed straight for Basia. I turned, flinging out my hand as if I could catch it, but it was too late. The arrow had long passed me by the time I had fully rotated.

Basia collapsed.

"No!" A scream tore from my throat as I staggered toward her and dropped to my knees.

I was reaching out a trembling hand to touch her shoulder when a huge black snake dropped out of the tree and landed directly on top of her. I yelped and fell backwards as the naked woman stepped past me and yanked the snake off Basia.

Finn gave a roar and headed toward the woman, when I stepped between them holding out a hand.

"Stand down, Finn. She didn't shoot Basia. She killed a snake."

Finn stopped in his tracks, looking in astonishment at the dead snake in her hand.

She cocked her head, studying us...no, studying me.

I stared back. She was young, maybe my age or possibly a little younger, with large brown eyes and long dark hair that had been braided and fell over her left shoulder. It was about the same length as mine. She had a curious birthmark on her left cheek in the shape of a crescent moon.

She wore some kind of cloth around her waist and a corded belt that held a knife pouch, a wooden cup and several small, cinched bags about the size of my fist. A quiver filled with arrows had been strapped to her waist and right thigh, instead of on her back in the way that Robin Hood wore. Other than the cloth around her waist and a magnificent necklace made of small red, blue, green and yellow feathers, she was naked.

Basia made a noise behind me, so I bent down, rolling her over. "Basia, are you okay?"

She sat up, rubbing the back of her head. "I think so. I fainted."

I turned back to the woman and observed her expertly laying out the snake. She pried her arrow carefully out of its neck and checked the tip for damage. Raising a large knife, she brought it down with a loud thwack and cut off the snake's head. Then she slit it up the middle, pulled out its guts and pushed what was left of the snake into a cloth sack, pulling it tight with a rope. My stomach heaved and I turned my head.

Finn helped Basia to her feet, shaking his head. "Are you saying she shot a snake in a tree from that distance? That's pretty damn good."

"I wouldn't advise making her mad. Basia, can you talk to her?"

She brushed off her pants. "I'll try to say hello in as many languages as I think she might know. We might get lucky."

Basia rattled off a dozen phrases in different languages, but none of them resulted in more than a bewildered look from the native woman.

Finally I pointed to myself. "Lexi."

She frowned and then pointed to herself. "Sorry."

I took a step back. "Whoa? You're sorry? You speak English?"

She frowned and tried again, pointing at me. "Wexi." She pointed at herself. "Sari."

"Her name is Sari," Basia explained and then pointed at herself. "Basia."

"Ba-sha."

Basia pointed to Finn. "Finn."

"Fwyin." Sari lowered her eyes and stepped away from him.

Finn chuckled. "Close enough."

Sari reached into the bag around her waist and pulled out the snake. Basia recoiled in horror as Sari thrust it at Finn, keeping her head down.

"She's offering it to you as a gift, Finn," Basia said.

After a moment Finn shook his head and bowed slightly. "No, thank you, Sari. You shot it. You earned it."

Sari put the snake back in the bag and stared at us, clearly puzzled by our behavior.

Sari moved closer to me, tentatively touching my arm. I wasn't sure what she was wanting, so I held it out. She grasped it and started wiping away some of the mud.

"What is she doing?" Finn asked.

"She's looking at my skin. I think she's curious."

Sari examined my skin and the earrings Slash had given me. Finally she inspected Elvis's locket, bringing her nose almost to my neck to study it.

"She's fascinated by the locket," Basia said. "She likes it."

"She probably hasn't seen anything like it before."

After that Sari examined my jeans, tennis shoes and

the zipper on my jeans. She did the same thing to Basia, spending extra time on the buttons on her blouse. When she came to Basia's earrings, I heard her give a sharp intake of breath and then a sigh.

"I think she *really* likes your earrings," I said.

"They're dangly and sparkly. Well at least they used to be. That's probably why."

She didn't approach or touch Finn. In fact, I noticed Sari didn't ever meet Finn's gaze directly and seemed to shrink in front of him.

"I think Sari comes from a male-centric society," Basia said. "She's acting very submissive around Finn."

"Should I change the way I act?" Finn asked.

She shrugged. "I'm not sure. I'm just throwing it out there."

"Now what?" I asked. "How do we ask her for help?"

Basia picked up a stick. "If we want to talk to her, we should draw a picture. Pictures are a universal language."

It made sense, so I cleared away some brush while Basia started drawing. After drawing three figures, she looked at Sari and said, "Lexi, Basia, Finn." She pointed to each figure as she said our names.

When Sari seemed to understand those figures represented us, Basia drew some tall buildings and then drew a line from our stick figures to the structures. "Can you take us here? To a city or town?"

Sari studied the drawing intently and then looked at Basia. I had no idea if she had the foggiest idea what Basia was trying to say.

Sari took the stick and started drawing. Huts and fires appeared.

"She's drawing a picture of a village," I said excitedly. "Maybe her village." As we watched, she drew a picture of a hut that was located away from the others.

She circled it. "Sari."

I looked at Basia." Why did she draw a picture of her hut away from the others?"

"I don't know."

I took the stick and drew a male figure and a baby next to the hut, trying to figure out if she had a family. I pointed at her and then the pictures.

Using her hand, Sari firmly wiped out the picture of the male figure and the baby. She pointed to the hut and then herself. "Sari."

"I think she lives there alone," Basia said.

Sari pointed at her birthmark and softly said a word. I didn't understand it, but I got the meaning. She *was* alone.

"I think she's an outcast, a recluse in her own village, probably because of her birthmark," Basia said.

"Why would a birthmark make her an outcast?" Finn asked.

"In some societies birthmarks are signs of evil." Basia tapped the stick in the dirt. "They are too afraid to kill babies with such birthmarks, but they are typically abandoned by their families and kept on the outskirts of the village."

I studied the birthmark. "She has no friends or family?"

"Possibly. It might also explain why she's so good at hunting. That's traditionally a male role in native societies. If she has to feed herself, it makes sense.

I looked at Sari thoughtfully. "Wow. An outcast. I totally know the feeling. I might get along with her just fine."

"How's that?" Basia asked.

"Well, apparently she's been alone most of her life and has to hunt for her own food. So do I. I just hunt a different kind of snake. Either way, we have to convince her to help us or we're doomed."

# THIRTY-NINE

"MY VOTE IS to start by telling her we're starving," Basia said. "Maybe she can get us some food."

"She just offered us food in the form of that snake," Finn said. "And we turned her down."

"That's because I'm *not* eating snake," Basia said emphatically.

Finn frowned at her. "You will if you're starving."

"That's extremely doubtful."

I held up a hand. "Look. I know we're hungry, cranky and exhausted, but we're still far too close to the helicopter crash. We need to put some more distance between the Chinese and us. *Then* we can argue about food. That's my vote."

Finn nodded and after a moment, Basia reluctantly acquiesced. Pointing into the jungle, I motioned to Sari that Basia, Finn and I had to go.

Sari considered and then motioned for us to follow her.

We gathered up our supplies and followed her. She wound through the jungle, following barely detectable paths until I was completely disoriented. Then she pointed to a spot near the stream and sat down.

We all stared at her. "Why did she stop here?" Finn asked, puzzled.

"I don't know," I said. "Maybe she wasn't sure if it was safe to take us to her village yet."

"Or maybe she's not sure the village is safe from us," Finn mused.

Basia, collapsed to the ground next to Sari. "I don't care what she's thinking. I'm not going anywhere."

"Do you think we've gone far enough?" Finn asked.

I shrugged. "Hard to say, but it's better than where we were."

"I don't care *where* we are as long as we can eat." Basia pretended to eat out of the palm of her hand.

Sari nodded and reached into her pouch, pulling out the snake again. Basia was so startled she stumbled backwards. Sari, clearly in an attempt to help us understand what she was saying, took a bite of the snake raw and chewed on it.

Basia gasped. "Oh, my God. Did she just eat that raw?

I swallowed hard. "If eating raw snake is what we have to do to survive, then we do it."

"Are *you* going to eat it raw?"

"I ate sushi once and I'm still alive to talk about it."

"We'll all eat it," Finn said firmly. "I've had snake before. It won't kill us, and in this case, it may well save us."

Sari observed us talking among ourselves and knelt down and started digging. We watched her for a minute. Then she disappeared into the jungle coming back a few minutes later with some small pieces of dry kindling. She dropped it in the hole.

"She's making a fire," Finn observed. "Can we risk it?"

I shrugged. "We have to eat. Unless we're all onboard eating raw snake, I say we risk it. But at some point we have to figure out how to tell her we're being chased by a bunch of bad guys."

Sari pulled out a flint, and after a few strikes, she had a spark. Soon we had a little fire. Since the kindling was so dry, there was hardly any smoke.

As we watched in fascination, Sari took a stick and meticulously cleaned it, leaving the forked tip. When she pulled out the snake from her bag, Basia gagged. Sari cut off a piece of the snake's body with a sharp stone, stuck it on the stick and started cooking it.

I patted Basia's arm. "Don't worry. It probably tastes like chicken."

After a few minutes, Sari brought Finn a piece of meat. She bowed her head as she offered it to him.

He grinned. "Sorry to eat first, ladies. But when in Rome…"

I rolled my eyes. "Ha, ha. Just eat it. But I'm warning you, don't enjoy this male-centric crap too much."

Finn blew on the meat and then took a bite. He closed his eyes as he chewed. "No kidding, it's the best damn snake I ever ate."

"It's only because you're starving," I said.

"Don't bloody care. I'm enjoying every bite." He smiled broadly at Sari and she seemed pleased with his acknowledgment. She cooked another piece for him, but he declined, pointing at Basia. As instructed, Sari gave Basia the piece.

To her credit, Basia took it and after a few minutes, ate it without complaint. Sari made one for me next and then made a piece for herself. We all, including Basia, had seconds until the snake was gone. I'd been ravenous.

"It does taste like chicken," I said, licking my fingers. It seemed absurd that I had once balked at sushi. I promised I'd be better at taking risks with food if I made it out of here alive.

Basia stood and did a downward sweeping motion with her arms. Sari smiled and pressed her hand to her chest.

"What are you doing?" I asked.

"I'm saying thank you. I saw her do it to Finn when you guys weren't paying attention. Pressing your hand splayed out on your chest means you're welcome."

I tried it and Sari responded by pressing her hand to her chest just as Basia had said.

It was getting dark by the time we finished eating. Sari and I sat by the fire while Basia and Finn crawled onto the tarp. We were all exhausted, but I felt reinvigorated by the food and interesting company.

Sari had the stick in her hand and she drew a male and two female figures. Then she drew a baby. She pointed to the figures. "Fwyin. Wexi. Ba-sha."

It occurred to me that she might think Basia and I were Finn's wives. I was amused in spite of myself.

"No. no. Finn is just a friend. "No Finn and Lexi. No Finn and Basia. We're all just friends...and that made absolutely no sense to you."

I drew a male figure and pointed to it. "Slash. Lexi and Slash." In a moment of inspiration, I drew a heart.

"Swash?"

I chuckled. "Yes. What about you?" I asked. I pointed to the female figure and then drew a line to the male. She'd said she was alone, but that didn't mean she didn't love someone. I, perhaps better than most, understood what that meant.

Sari made a circle around the male figure with her finger and sighed. "Tooh."

"Tooh? You love someone named Tooh?"

This time when she looked at me, tears shimmered

in her eyes. Oh, jeez. Not again. My first instinct was to bolt, but that's what had most likely happened to her all of her life. I bet she'd never had a girlfriend to talk to. Although I was not an expert on girl talk by any stretch of the imagination, I had the feeling that was exactly what she needed.

Sucking it up, I handed her the stick and motioned she should draw some more. "I don't know how long it will take and I don't know how much I'll understand, Sari, but go ahead. Tell me about Tooh. I'm willing to listen."

She took the stick and smiled. Somehow, even with the language barrier, I'd made a friend.

# FORTY

I AWOKE TO the sound of a helicopter. I bolted upright on the tarp and saw Sari kneeling next to me, her eyes worried. She motioned for me to hurry.

Finn and Basia woke, too, and looked up. We couldn't see anything through the canopy of the trees, but it was close.

"We've got to move," I said to them.

Without questioning me further, they quickly began gathering our supplies.

"Does she know about the Chinese?" Finn asked, sliding the bag over his shoulder.

"I tried my best to explain it. I'm not sure she understands exactly, but I think she got the gist of the idea. Bad people are following us."

Basia was struggling to get her pack on, so I snatched it from her and stuffed it in my bag.

"We follow Sari," I ordered. "Now."

"Are you sure we can trust her?" Finn asked.

"I don't think we have a choice. Let's go."

Sari slipped into the jungle and I followed first. I tried to step everywhere she stepped. How she managed to move so quickly in bare feet with all the rocks, sticks and snakes mystified me, but I did my best to keep up.

Suddenly she stopped and held up a hand. I froze as Basia and Finn bumped into the back of me. After a moment, she stepped out onto a path. She motioned for us to follow.

The helicopter was louder now. Searching I thought.

Basia shot me a worried glance. "How do we know she won't turn us in?"

"We don't. But I trust her."

We moved quickly down the path. It began to alarm me that Sari was leading us toward, not away, from the helicopter sound.

Sari turned around and held up a hand, stopping us. She said something and then turned and disappeared into the jungle along an almost invisible side path.

"Where's she going?" Basia asked.

"I don't know. Let's wait for her."

We waited for at least twenty minutes but Sari didn't return. We hadn't heard the helicopter in that period, so it looked like we had evaded their search once again. But where was Sari? I wished I knew her better.

Basia shifted nervously on her feet. "This isn't good."

"Maybe she went to get help," I offered hopefully.

Finn looked undecided as well. "I think it's too dangerous to remain here any longer. What if someone comes along? We need to move."

"Where?" I asked. "And what if she comes back and doesn't find us?"

Finn waved a hand impatiently. "We should go anywhere but here, where we're exposed. Maybe we can find a spot farther along the path where we can see who's coming. If she comes back, we can decide if she's bringing the good or the bad guys."

Finn looked back down the path the way we had come and then turned and strode ahead. Basia followed. After a last scan down the side path for Sari, I followed.

We were walking as stealthily as we could, moving slowly so that we could get off the path if we heard anyone coming. I imagined us moving invisibly and quietly like the breeze. The reality was, to the locals we probably sounded like a freight train sounding its horn as it passed through a busy town.

We hadn't gone more than a few minutes down the path when a native man suddenly appeared in front of us holding a bow with a nocked arrow. He spoke to us. When it was clear we didn't understand, he pointed the bow at Finn, motioning for us to turn around and head back down the path we'd just come.

"Do what he says," I advised. "We don't want to spook him into shooting us."

Basia threw up her hands. "I am so over people pointing guns, rifles, arrows, knives and helicopters in my direction. The next time I travel, I'm going someplace a city girl goes on vacations, like Paris."

Slowly and carefully we walked back up the path. As we proceeded down it a slight movement in the trees caught my eye. To my astonishment I realized it was Sari. She pressed a finger to her lips and then disappeared again.

Suddenly I heard a noise and Sari stepped onto the path behind our captor, aiming an arrow at his back. She spoke a quick command. There was a fast and furious exchange of words between the two of them before the guy set down his bow and arrow.

Finn scooped up the bow and arrow and pulled the guy's arms behind his back. "Girls, get me a couple of vines or something I can use to restrain him."

I yanked a couple of vines down and tested them for strength. They didn't even budge when I pulled hard on them. I handed them over to Finn. Sari gave him her knife and he cut them to length.

Finn tied him up and then tossed the bow and arrow in the bushes. He saw me watching and shrugged. "It's not like I can use it. No time to figure it out."

Sari motioned for us to follow and we plunged into the jungle after her. It was clear that time was of the essence. I tried to move as quietly as she did, but I found myself pushing aside the heavy vegetation to move forward while she seemed to somehow slip past it. Rushing to keep up, I stumbled forward when she abruptly stopped. Finn managed to avoid crashing into me and helped hold me up by grabbing my shoulder and pulling me back against him. Basia stood next to us, trembling. I didn't know what we were doing or why we had stopped. But since talking was out of the question, we simply stayed motionless and waited for a sign from Sari.

I heard a sound not a minute later. Someone was crashing through the jungle. Whoever was coming our way wasn't making any effort to move quietly. Men were talking and the static sound of a walkie-talkie floated on the air. The words were indistinct, but I could tell they weren't speaking in English.

Basia looked at me and mouthed, "Chinese."

I exchanged a worried glance with Finn. When the sound moved away from our path, Sari started moving again, motioning us to be as quiet as possible. We picked up the pace significantly. I had no idea where we were going, but Sari had kept us alive and safe so far, so there was no reason to doubt her yet.

At some point, Sari had seemed to decide that speed was more important than stealth, so we were practically running. We unexpectedly emerged at the edge of a river. It might have been the same stream that we had followed, but it was much wider here and appeared to be deeper, too, though it was hard to tell with the dirty water. Sari motioned to me and I followed her to some heavy brush near the water.

My mouth fell open. "Canoes."

"I'll be damned," Finn said.

I shook my head. "Oh, for crying out loud. Not the water again. Do I have to?"

"You have to." Finn was adamant. "Come on, Lexi. Let's help Sari get them into the water."

The canoes were river canoes similar in style, but without the outriggers typically seen on the big Polynesian canoes for ocean racing. They looked about as stable as Windows 98 to me. But seeing how it was either get in the boat or get left behind, I helped drag the first canoe to the edge of the water. Sari held the canoe and motioned for Basia and Finn to get in.

"Now what?" Basia said.

"Get the oars," I instructed.

"There aren't any. Just these long poles."

"Paddle, push or poke. Whatever works."

Before I could say anything else, Sari pushed them into the water with a big shove and ran back to the other canoe. I watched them head down the river with a sinking feeling.

I was running back to help Sari when I saw Basia had lost her pack again in the scramble. I snatched it and stuffed it in my bag, zipping it shut. Quickly, I pulled the other canoe into the water with Sari. She motioned for me to get in. After a moment of hesitation, I steeled my nerves and got into the front, grabbing a pole. Sari hopped in shortly after me and for a horrifying moment

I thought the canoe would capsize. But it straightened and we headed down the water at a faster speed than I expected. Basia and Finn were not too far ahead of us. Sari began to stab the pole in the water determinedly. Although unsure of the mechanics of the effort, I tried to help her so we could catch up to the others. My help mostly consisted of spearing the water, flailing with the pole and nearly knocking Sari from the canoe.

After just a few minutes, my arms ached with the effort. It seemed clear I needed to include canoeing in my Pilates program. We were abreast of the other canoe when I heard yelling behind me. I peered over my shoulder and saw four men dressed in black about one hundred yards up the river. They were shouting at us.

Basia cupped her hands and shouted. "It's the Chinese, but I don't think they want to invite us over for twice-cooked duck."

The men began running along the side of the river, but as we had found, there wasn't a clear path. We quickly lost sight of them. I sighed in relief and then nearly fell out of the canoe when Basia shrieked.

"What's wrong?" I shouted.

"Rapids ahead," Finn answered for her. He kept his pole moving back and forth on each side of the canoe. Their boat seemed to be rocking violently. "Better hold on, lassies, it's getting rough."

Our canoe started to vibrate from underneath as the water picked up speed. I looked back at Sari. Her faced was drawn tight in concentration. She was watching the patterns in the water as if it would magically tell her something. Maybe it would.

I used the pole, pushing off against an occasional rock as it came close, but I wasn't sure if I were helping or hurting the situation. Our canoe tipped perilously as the water became increasingly choppy. I reminded myself to concentrate on the moment. I had just survived a plane crash and a helicopter falling on me. I would survive this…I hoped. Perspiration beaded on my temples.

The water churned and boiled with a furious white foam. Basia's and Finn's canoe tossed in the water like a toy boat in front of us. I marveled at how well Finn was doing guiding the canoe. I'd known he liked to race boats in Ireland, but I suspected this was an entirely different sport. Still, he was a man of many talents.

The water sucked at my pole. I almost lost it and decided that I wasn't contributing and would do better just holding on. So, I slid my pole to the bottom of the boat and grabbed the sides in the death grip I normally reserve for when someone asks to borrow my laptop.

The canoe lurched sideways and I almost fell out. I swallowed a scream and gripped the sides of the canoe so tightly my fingers ached. The roar of water filled my ears.

I dared a frightened glance at Sari, but her concentration on the water was singular. Water sprayed in my face and mouth. I thought of my parents, my two brothers, Elvis, Xavier, the briefcase in the black bag slung over my body and Slash.

Mostly Slash. Funny how a near-death experience brought all my priorities suddenly into focus. And wasn't it interesting that he topped the list, even above the thought that I might not ever see my laptop again?

Sari gave a small cry and I snapped to attention. Basia and Finn's canoe was in real trouble.

"Look out," I yelled. Their canoe hit a rock and capsized, flinging both of them over the side and into the water.

*"Finn! Basia!"*

I didn't see where Finn went, but I saw Basia disappear under the water.

I searched the water frantically for them before our canoe hit something as well. I was thrown from the boat in a horrid, teeth-jarring motion.

I managed to yell once before my head slipped under the water.

# FORTY-ONE

I FLAILED AROUND in the water, blinded by terror. Water sucked at me, dragging me down as I tried to calm the screaming in my head and focus on one thing.

Air.

My lungs were burning. I kicked my legs hard, but I couldn't tell if I was moving up or down. Blackness crowded my vision. My cheeks ached from holding my breath.

If I didn't get air I was going to die.

I gave one more hard kick and my foot hit the bottom. Pushing up with all my strength, I shot to the surface. Gulping a lifesaving breath, I slid past a slippery rock and over another small drop before sinking back under again. I kicked again to get back up, missing the bottom on my first few tries. Somehow I managed to surface again and catch a breath, but the adrenaline rush was ebbing. It wasn't going to be long before I slipped under for good.

Suddenly a strong arm grabbed me under my armpits, pulling me toward safety. I gasped, trying to see through the spray of the water, but swallowed a mouthful instead.

I blinked and saw Sari.

She was pulling me to shore. I kicked my feet to try and help her but she shouted something at me. I didn't understand it, but figured she wanted me to stay still. I let her pull me, until I could feel the water calming around us. A few minutes later Sari stood me up. The water reached to my chest, but I could stand. I waded the rest of the way to land with Sari pulling me. I dragged myself onto the shore, coughing and spitting out water.

"Thank you," I panted, my voice sounding scratchy and hoarse. "Thank you, Sari." I made a V with my hands and then turned my head to the side and vomited water until I had nothing left in my stomach.

My ponytail stuck to my cheeks and my clothes clung to me. My tennis shoes squished with water as I moved. I marveled that the canvas bag had somehow miraculously stayed connected to my body. I pulled it over my head and then lay down, resting my head on it and trying to catch my breath. When I could breathe, I looked up at Sari, tears filling my eyes.

"Basia? Finn?"

She didn't answer and stood with her hand on her forehead, shading her eyes and surveying the water. Her hair had unraveled from her braid and stuck to her back. The beautiful feather necklace was badly damaged, but still hung around her neck. I could tell by the way she was intently scanning the water that she hadn't found anything…or anyone.

I staggered to my feet to help her look when I suddenly spotted something dark lying on the shore.

"Basia!" I shouted, my voice barely audible. I pointed until Sari saw.

"Basia!" I yelled again, but there was no movement.

I scanned the shore anxiously for Finn, but didn't see him anywhere.

Sari cupped her hands around her mouth and howled. The sound carried across the water and Basia sat up, turned around and finally spotted us.

She stood, lifting her arms and waving them back and forth. I jumped up and down, waving my arms like a maniac. She checked her surroundings and then turned back at us. Like me, she was looking for Finn.

My stomach twisted. I still didn't see him. Logic told me the odds of him surviving were not good, but I couldn't believe it. *Wouldn't* believe it.

I touched Sari's arm. "Finn?"

Sari looked up and down the shore and then shook her head sadly.

My eyes filled with tears. "No." My voice was little more than a whisper. "No."

Sari stiffened. I straightened, thinking she'd found Finn. Instead she pointed at Basia and my heart stopped.

A native man crept up behind her. Before I could scream a warning, he grabbed Basia and disappeared into the jungle.

# FORTY-TWO

*"Basia!"*

I cupped my hands and shouted over and over again until my voice was hoarse. Finally Sari closed her eyes and turned away from the water.

Panicked, I grabbed her arm. "Sari, we have to save Basia. How can we get across the river?"

But Sari wasn't listening to me. She seemed deep in thought.

"Sari!" My voice was sharp and panicked. "Basia. Please. Help me."

She turned to look at me, her brown eyes sympathetic. "Ba-sha."

Tears spilled down my cheeks. "Help me, please. I don't understand."

She touched my arm, motioned for me to come. Realizing there was nothing else I could do, I picked up my bag, slipped it across my body and followed her.

WE WERE MOVING away from where we'd last seen Basia. Finn was gone. My wet clothes weren't drying and my tennis shoes squished with every sluggish step I took. Since the water had rinsed off my mud protection, mosquitoes and insects began to bite me. I couldn't even summon the energy to swat at them. I didn't know where Sari was taking me and I wasn't sure I even cared.

As we walked it started to rain. It fit my mood.

In my misery I lost track of where we were going or how long I had been following her. We were walking along a barely formed trail when Sari stopped abruptly in front of a curtain of vines, then reached down and pulled them aside. I saw a small opening.

She motioned for me to enter, so I bent down and scooted into a snug cave. There was no way I could stand, so I took off the bag, threw it in the cave and then crawled in on my hands and knees. There was a small pallet and some jars, as well as several piles of dried leaves. Sari crawled in behind me, having secured the vines to the side of the cave so we could have light inside.

She sat on a pallet and unfastened her belt, laying her pouches out to dry. Pointing at my feet, she motioned for me to take off my shoes and socks. I shook my head, but she insisted, so I pulled off my shoes and peeled off my filthy socks. My feet were swollen and blistered. Sari crawled to a corner of the cave and came back with a soft cloth made of animal skin. She handed it to me and I wiped my hands and face. She motioned to my feet, so I wiped those dry, too. She picked up my tennis shoes and thoroughly examined them, pulling on the laces and bending the soles.

My hand brushed my bag and I stared at it numbly. Inside it were the details of perhaps one of the most significant technological invention of our time. Yet, at this moment, it was completely meaningless.

I must have looked as miserable as I felt, because Sari put a hand on my shoulder. "Wexi?"

I was shaking and there were tears in my eyes. She didn't need a translation to know why I was hurting.

She pressed a hand to her breast. "Sari." She pressed her hand to my chest. "Wexi."

She was telling me I wasn't alone. I tried to pull myself together by swiping at my eyes. Instead, I smeared mud against my cheeks.

She leaned over and took something that had been hanging against the wall. I leaned closer and saw it was a necklace with a pendant carved in the shape of a crescent moon, almost identical to her birthmark. She slipped it over her neck.

"Tooh," she whispered.

I blinked and pointed at the necklace and then at her. "Did Tooh give that to you?"

She nodded and said something I didn't understand, then she slipped out of the cave, leaving me alone.

I had no idea where Sari went or whether she'd come back. I hugged my knees to my chest and tried to stop shaking. I leaned back against the side of the cave and closed my eyes. I bolted awake when I heard Sari returning. I must have dozed off, so I wasn't sure how long she'd been gone.

She returned with a basketful of items and a small tube about three inches in diameter and about a foot long strapped to her thigh. The tube had a much narrower and longer tube secured to it by several straps. It looked like a giant straw. From the basket she removed several red fruits shaped kind of like an oversized mango. She banged one against a rock and split it open, offering me half. The inside was white with tiny black seeds. Sari took a bite of her half and urged me to do the same.

I sampled it. It tasted a bit like kiwi, but not as sweet. The juice was welcome and I realized I was thirsty. I devoured it and then eyed the next fruit. Sari split that one open, too, and we each ate another half. I felt oddly satiated. My stomach had either shrunk from deprivation or decided that it was going on vacation until this nightmare was over and I started eating properly again.

After that she opened a small clay jar that had a carved wooden top. She scooped out a glob of a gooey substance, rubbed her hands together and smeared the sap on my face and neck. It was sticky and smelled like an herb garden. She put the sap over every inch of my uncovered skin, including my eyelids and scalp. I had to resist the urge to scratch it off, but after a few minutes, my skin seemed to adapt to it. Then, she did the same to herself.

It took me a minute to figure out what she'd done. I sniffed at it. "Homemade bug spray. That's why you never seemed to be bothered by mosquitoes."

Curious, I pointed at the tube on her hip and looked at her quizzically. Sari grinned and said a word.

"What? Did you just say necktie?" I tried to copy her pronunciation.

She repeated it slowly and this time it sounded like *muktai*.

*"Muktai?"*

She nodded, then took a long tube from her supplies and strapped it to her hip. Carefully she opened the top of the bigger tube and carefully pulled out a pointed dart. The dart did not have any feathers, but it had hard, raised ridges. I understood at once what the purpose of the tube and dart was, but Sari pantomimed using it to make sure I understood. When she pretended to get hit by the dart, she clapped her hand to the imaginary dart, took several staggering steps and then collapsed.

I dipped my head to show her I understood. "Excellent. A great weapon."

Then she smiled like she knew something I didn't.

Picking up a stick, she drew a female figure and said, "Ba-sha."

Holy cow. Had she found Basia? "Sari, do you know where Basia is?"

She started carefully drawing a much more detailed image. I moved next to her to get a clearer look. She'd drawn a number of huts in what looked like a village. Except two of the huts were farther away from the others.

She pointed at the isolated huts, frowned and said, "Moro."

"Moro?" I looked at her puzzled.

She tapped more emphatically on the second hut. "Moro. Ba-sha."

I got it. "Wait. Moro is a guy? This Moro thug has Basia in that hut?"

She drew four more men and what looked like a giant bird. Then she tapped the other hut.

I studied her drawing until I figured it out. "That's not a bird. It's a helicopter. So, what I think you're saying is that some of the men in the first hut are Chinese from the helicopter and Basia is a prisoner in the other one."

She couldn't confirm, obviously, but I think we had an understanding. I wanted to ask her about guards, but realized that was more complex than our limited communication skills would support. While I was pondering what other questions I might ask and have a shot at getting answered, she started drawing again.

Sari sketched two more stick figures—a tall male with some kind of headdress and another male. She pointed at the male with the headdress and said, "Tisa."

I studied it. "I'm guessing Tisa is a village chief or elder."

The stick landed on the next male. "Tooh."

I looked at Sari in surprise. "Wait." I pointed at her necklace. "*That* Tooh?"

She nodded and looked at me expectantly.

My brain raced and I talked aloud to myself to help me sort it out. "So, Tooh and Tisa live in the same hut? Okay, I'm guessing Tooh is the son of the chief. That does complicate things. Sari is an outcast because of her birthmark. But Tooh loves Sari and she loves him except apparently they can't have each other. Oh, jeez. It's like a Pacific version of Romeo and Juliet."

Sari drew a female child holding hands with Tisa and Tooh. "Kala."

I frowned. "Kala is Tooh's child or maybe a younger sister?"

Sari dragged the stick from Kala to the second hut where she had drawn Basia. "Basia. Kala."

I stared at the drawing to make sure I understood. "Whoa. Are you saying Moro and the Chinese are holding Kala prisoner too? But why? Unless…" It took me a minute to get there. "Unless Moro and his buddies took Kala to ensure the cooperation of the village. What better way than holding hostage the daughter or granddaughter of the chief?"

Sari pressed her hand to her breast and then pointed at the prisoner hut. "Sari. Tooh."

I knew what she was getting at. "Oh, no." I shook my head vigorously. "It's going to be *Lexi*, Sari and Tooh. I'm in on this rescue, too. We'll get both Basia *and* Kala free."

Energized, I grabbed my bag and dumped the contents on the ground. "Let's see what I have to contribute."

My meager supplies consisted of the titanium briefcase, an empty water bottle, Basia's shoes, a roll of duct tape and her garbage bag backpack that I'd grabbed before we got into the canoes. I ripped open the garbage bag and Basia's purse fell out unscathed from the water.

I emptied the contents of her purse. Water, hand sanitizer, lipstick, compact, mascara, a cell phone, which was still turned off, a charger, two tampons, a wallet with three hundred dollars, a comb, keys and breath mints.

Sari watched me with interest, but did not interfere. After I was done, I sat back on my heels, looking and thinking.

How was I going to mount a rescue with this?

Logically. Creatively. It's what I did best.

I picked up Basia's cell phone and turned it on. After what seemed like a minute of holding my breath, it came on.

I pumped my fist in the air. "Yes."

Then, I had an awful thought. What if Basia had password protected her phone? I had been nagging her for months to take that simple security precaution. If she did, I had to hope she would use her birthday, the way she did for her email.

Sari gasped as she saw the phone light up and Basia's home page displayed. I was never so glad that she hadn't got around to taking my advice. But once we got home, she and I were going to have a serious security discussion. Again.

The phone's soft white glow entranced Sari and she nearly sat on me as she put her nose up to the screen, trying to figure it out.

I laughed. "Just a minute, Sari. Let me check something."

No surprise that there weren't any bars, but I flipped through the apps trying to see what I might be able to use. I sorted through Basia's music selection. Smiling, I pushed the play button and the sound of Michael Jackson singing about being bad came from the speaker. Sari was so startled by the sound that she yelped and fell backwards, scooting away.

I turned it off and motioned to her. "It's okay. Sari. It's safe. It's just Michael Jackson. He's not *that* scary. Come back over here."

She hesitated and then warily returned, looking at the phone with distrust.

I thrust it at her. "Here. Check it out."

She refused at first, but curiosity won out over fear. She turned the phone over and over in her hand and put her eyeball up to the screen as if trying to figure out how the person who was singing was trapped behind the glass.

"Meekal." She pushed the stop button and then play again, dropping it when Michael started singing where he had left off.

I picked up the phone, wiping it off. "Careful. We need this."

I turned the phone completely off and put it in the back pocket of my jeans. The time had come to explain the game plan and hope against all hope that Sari would understand what I had in mind. Evening was fast approaching and we were running out of daylight and options.

I motioned her over. "Okay, Sari. Time to get this plan going."

Technically, I didn't have a complete plan yet. I needed more information, a lot more. But this would be a start.

She seemed to share my urgency and knelt beside me.

Taking a deep breath, I picked up her stick and started to draw.

# FORTY-THREE

WE HAD TO wait for dusk to execute our plan. I needed to be able to see the village to plan our final approach, but we couldn't afford to be seen. Luckily I had my own personal guide who could see in the dark, or at least it seemed that way. I followed Sari through the jungle, keeping a hand on her arm because she seemed to know every twist and turn.

As we walked, she became impatient, motioning for me to hurry as I struggled to keep up. I was doing my best, tiptoeing stealthily but still sounding like an elephant. I tripped constantly over roots, sticks, vines and branches. Somehow the vines grabbed only me as we passed by them. As we ducked under a badly listing, vine-covered tree, an unseen tendril snagged my face just under my eyes. I only partially muffled a shriek that, to my ears, sounded close on the decibel scale to a Michael Jackson concert. Oddly Sari didn't seem to mind, which I presumed to mean she wasn't worried anyone could hear me…yet.

Twice Sari led me down a slick slope, using vines as leverage. During those forays I welcomed the vanishing shafts of daylight that penetrated the jungle canopy. Still our progress was much slower than we had planned and it was dark by the time we approached the village.

Sari called a halt at a small rise. I stood next to her, panting. Sweat dribbled down my temples and neck.

She pointed and I could see a cleared area across what must be the same stream we'd followed for days. It was much wider here and the water seemed to be moving more slowly. Even though it was night, my eyes had adjusted to the darker gloom under the trees and a nearly full moon could be seen rising just below the treetops above the village. Sari pointed and I tracked her finger to a small bridge that forded the stream.

I squinted at the bridge and changed my mind about what to call it. Bridges had substance. They were sturdy structures used to safely travel above hazardous water. This bridge looked as substantial as a teenager's party outfit, but with a few more straps. It was more like twisted rope with some wooden slats, and it sagged in the middle way more than I was comfortable with. I swallowed hard. I was supposed to cross that?

I could hear the soft bubbling sound of the water rushing past as it bounced off a few isolated rocks. The only other night sounds were the legions of mosquitoes watching for a meal. Swimming lessons were definitely in my future. If I *had* a future that didn't involve drowning, getting malaria or going to China.

Sari held up a hand and motioned for me to wait. She had to do some reconnaissance, contact Tooh, arrange our escape and confirm exactly where Basia and Kala were being held. She disappeared across the bridge, navigating it without problem.

Show-off.

I took off the bag with the briefcase and sat on it. Figuring I had a while to wait, I mentally recited the one hundred most commonly used passwords. I was on the eighty-seventh when Sari finally returned. She'd approached so quietly I hadn't even heard her coming.

Good thing my skills were breaking into secure cyber places and not physically guarding anything.

She coaxed me out from the trees and into the rising moonlight so she could draw something in the dirt for me. She sketched and pointed at several huts that I considered to be the main part of village and the two huts somewhat separate from the village. She added the river and the bridge, which looked much studier in the dirt than on the river. She circled the first hut and pointed off to the left across the stream.

"Ba-sha. Kala."

Yes, we'd definitely found them. "Wow. That's really great, Sari." I pointed to the second hut. "Who is in here?"

Sari drew four male figures inside the hut with another male outside the hut where Basia was being held.

"A guard, I suppose."

She was still drawing, so I leaned over her shoulder to see what she was doing. She'd drawn a male face with elongated eyes. The Chinese.

I pointed at the hut with the four male figures and then pointed to the face. "How many, Sari?" I held up my fingers. "How many Chinese?"

She took my fingers and made it so two fingers were left.

Two Chinese with more likely expected in the morning. She hadn't mentioned the helicopter, so it was probably gone, but I needed to be sure. I drew a helicopter in the dirt next to the hut, but she wiped it out and shook her head no.

I still wasn't sure whether or not there were guards inside the hut with Basia and Kala. While I had to consider that possibility, there weren't really any options.

We were going to go in and get her and there wasn't much we could do about unknown guards until we found them.

I glanced up at the sky. The moon was nearly above the trees and the full array of stars was breathtaking. I'd walked for so long beneath the dense canopy of the jungle trees, I'd almost forgotten there was a sky.

She tapped my shoulder and pointed at the drawing at one of the huts in the village. "Tooh."

"There?" I pointed to the hut. "That's where Tooh lives?"

"Tooh. Tisa. Kala."

I nodded. "Got it. That's the chief's hut. I sure hope Tooh and Tisa will be on board with this plan."

I couldn't see how they wouldn't be if Kala were a hostage. But it was an unknown variable that I had to trust would work in my favor. I had no room for error.

Finally at the opposite end of the village, away from the huts and adjacent to the river, Sari drew several boats. She pointed at the boats and repeated "Tooh."

I understood that to mean she was able to contact him and that he would arrange the escape boats we would need. Hopefully, he would also convince the villagers we were friends if things didn't go as planned.

I drew a counterclockwise path around the village coming to the two huts from behind so that the jungle would conceal us.

Sari nodded, so I straightened.

"Ready, Sari?"

She knew what I was asking, because she tapped her blow dart and the little quiver that held the barbed tips. In turn, I tapped the strap of my bag that I wore sideways across my body. The titanium case was safe, as were the rest of my possessions. I took a minute to get my head in the game. I had to do this just right or Basia was dead.

I took a step forward. "Let's go."

Sari crossed the bridge first, checking quickly to see if there was any reaction from the outlying huts. She nimbly stepped from slat to slat, steadying herself with the rope. The bridge hardly swayed and it looked easy. I knew it wasn't.

I stood at the first slat and froze. I wasn't sure exactly of what I was most afraid, there were too many multiple unfortunate outcomes. I first coaxed and then pleaded with my feet and hands to cross the bridge. In the games I played, it was so easy to leap and or move my character forward by just pushing command and Z. Why wouldn't that work here?

"Wexi." Sari's voice was urgent and broke through my mental paralysis.

We were visible in the moonlight. I couldn't stand here forever. It was dangerous being so exposed. Swallowing my misgivings, I stepped onto the first slat and almost fell off. The bridge swayed like a swing at a carnival. I clutched the rope handrails fiercely. Holding my breath and tensing my whole body, I forced myself forward step by step. By the time I made it to other side, my T-shirt was completely soaked with sweat and I was trembling.

But holy shaking bridge, I was alive.

Sari motioned for me to follow her. She led us off to the right, to where Tooh materialized out of the dark, startling me. They held an energetic, if whispered conversation. It was clear that Tooh wanted to come with us and Sari felt it was her mission. Neither appeared willing to back down. Finally, they came to some compromise. Tooh took her hands gently, bent down, kissed her on the forehead and then faded back into the darkness.

Sari motioned, so I followed her into the trees and walked along a shadowy path, which led around the right side of the village. The trees thinned and I could see the two huts in a small clearing framed by the light of the moon. The angle of the moon was a break for us. There was a native man with a gun standing in front of one of the huts. Basia and Kala had to be inside.

I stopped and Sari did, too. We both surveyed the layout of the huts, the location of the entrances and the guard and the nearest foliage to the huts. We then sat down to wait. We wanted to begin our attack after everyone had time to go to sleep and the guard to become complacent. I positioned myself with my back to a tree so that I could watch the huts.

I must have dozed off, because I startled awake when Sari squatted in front of me and pointed to the huts. I nodded. It was time.

We conferred silently by hand signals and when we both were confident of our intended positioning, Sari took my hand. We continued through the jungle until we reached the point nearest the hut. Finally it was time to part. I squeezed Sari's hand and she squeezed back.

Sari slipped back into the trees and backtracked slightly so that she could get into position. I crawled behind some trees and got as close to the guard as I could, hidden only by a thin screen of vegetation. I carefully took Basia's cell phone out of my pocket and waited until it turned on, praying it wouldn't make any sounds. Blocking the light with my body, I flipped through the apps until I found the one I wanted. I palmed it, creeping farther on my belly until I had a clear view of the hut door. I could see the guard through the bush hiding me, so he would be able to see me if the phone was lit. He was in partial shadow from the hut so I couldn't see if he was a native or one of the Chinese. I suspected it was the former, which would make our next move more likely to succeed.

I drew in a breath and steadied myself.

It was game time.

# FORTY-FOUR

I WAITED UNTIL the guard looked in my general direction before I stretched to hold up the phone as high as I could while lying prone. I turned on the flashlight app with my finger. I had put it on strobe, so it flashed. To my dark-adapted eyes, it was painfully bright.

It caught the guard's attention at once. I'm sure he had no idea what to make of it. He took a few cautious steps my way, stopped, then looked at the other hut. I could see he thought about calling for help. But considering the late hour, and after nothing happened, he became bolder. He strode toward my position, moving slowly and on alert.

I held my breath. Five more steps and he'd trip over me.

*Any time now, Sari.*

He was nearly upon me when he simply keeled over without a word, the gun falling from his nerveless hands and landing next to me. I turned off the phone, slipping it in my back pocket. I cautiously leaned over him. He was face-first on the ground, the gun next to his open hand. As I retrieved the gun, I saw the dart in his neck.

"Good shot, Sari," I murmured.

I tucked the gun in the back of my jeans and grabbed both of his arms, dragging him deeper into the trees.

Standing at the edge of the trees, I surveyed the area. I saw no movement. Whereas minutes earlier I'd been grateful for the moonlight so I could clearly see the guard, now I wished it would slip behind a cloud. I'd be completely exposed in the few seconds it would take me to run to the hut. But there was no time to waste. I had no idea how long it had been since they'd last changed the guard.

I darted from behind the tree to the side of the shack. I didn't know if there were any other guards in the hut, so things were about to get really exciting in a hurry. I hoped Sari was in position to watch my back in case things went badly inside.

I slipped the gun out of my jeans and held it in front of me like the actors I had seen on a hundred bad TV shows. Quietly I pushed open the door and peered inside.

There appeared to be one large room only. A small lantern had been lit and placed in the corner of the shack. The lamp cast the hut in shadows more than illuminated it. The unexpected glow caused me to blink a couple of times.

After a moment, I could make out two small forms huddled on the floor. Basia and Kala? I didn't see anyone else in my quick survey, but at least half the hut was shrouded in darkness.

I slipped inside quietly, staying away from the light and keeping my back against the wall. I closed the door quietly, alert for any movement or response. Despite having the gun, I felt way out of my element.

Then I heard it.

Breathing.

It wasn't coming from either of the two forms on the floor, which meant there was at least one other person in the hut. I strained to hear and determined it came from the rear right corner of the hut.

Friend or foe?

I didn't have time to wait around to find out.

My hand tightened on the gun as my pulse pounded. I forced myself to breathe only through my nose. Moving along the wall, I inched my way toward the corner, hoping I wouldn't stumble over something in the dark and give away my location.

I took two more steps and paused. The breathing was louder now, but it seemed as if it came from only one person.

Swallowing my fear, I held the gun steady. Better to be bold than hesitate. I jumped forward, stretching out a hand and feeling cloth and skin beneath my fingers. I grabbed hard and pressed the gun about where I guessed the upper chest or neck would be.

"If you shout, I'll shoot," I hissed. "I'm desperate and have nothing to lose."

I heard a garbled noise, as if someone was trying to talk but was gagged, so I loosened my hold on the arm and felt around until I realized that whomever I'd just come across was tied to a chair. It was time to take a chance. I reached into my back pocket and pulled out the cell phone, turning on the flashlight app.

As I shined the light, my mouth dropped open.

*Finn!*

# FORTY-FIVE

FOR A MOMENT, I could only stare at him dumbfounded while he squinted against the bright light in the dark hut. I was hidden behind the light and unless he recognized my voice, he had no reason to suspect that I would be here. Then, remembering our precarious situation, I quickly shone the flashlight around the rest of the hut.

Basia and a young girl were the only other people in the hut besides Finn. They were huddled on the floor on woven pallets. Neither was tied up. As the light passed over them, they sat up, looking at me in astonishment. I shone the light on my face with my finger pressed to my lips. Basia hugged the girl happily while trying to keep her calm and quiet.

Turning my attention back to Finn, I threw my arms around him, hugging him hard. Tears filled my eyes. Jeez, I was crying again, but I didn't care.

Finn was alive.

Basia was alive.

"I can't believe it," I whispered to him. "I thought you were dead." A million questions hovered on my tongue, but they would have to wait. I quickly unfastened the gag from his mouth.

Finn licked his lips and then whispered back, his voice raspy. "Not dead yet. I'm a good swimmer, but lousy at jungle evasion. Hurry, Lexi. Untie me."

I struggled with the knots that bound him. When he

was free, he stood, flexing his arms. After that he took the gun, which I happily relinquished.

Finn ejected the magazine to check how many bullets were left, and then pushed it back in. "Where's Sari?" he whispered.

"She's out there watching the entrance to the other hut with her poisoned blow dart."

"Damn, that girl is something else." He lowered his mouth to my ear. "As far as I can tell, there are only five of them. Two Chinese and three natives. There might be more men, but that's all I saw."

"Good, that jives with the info Sari got from Tooh. Five men. So that makes four men in the hut and one guard. Sari already took out the guard."

"It looks like the Chinese are apparently paying the thugs to keep us under wraps until the helicopter arrives in the morning to pick us up. I couldn't follow what they were saying, but the Chinese were very unhappy that you were still free. What's the plan?"

"Well, it starts with this." I bent down next to Basia and the young girl.

Basia immediately gave me a hug and whispered, "Look at you, slipping in here with a gun, ready to shoot the place up. And you were afraid you were nothing more than a geek girl who couldn't do squat without her technology. A fish out of water, my ass. You are totally kicking it."

I smiled and held out a hand to the little girl. She looked ready to cry. I murmured, "Kala. Go to Tisa."

She looked at me in surprise. I pressed my finger gently to her chest. "Kala. Go home to Tisa." Then I put a finger to my lips indicating she should be quiet and pointed to the door of the hut.

Kala was frightened, but sharp. She nodded, then without any hesitation, she slipped out the door and disappeared.

"What are you doing?" Basia whispered.

"I'm sending her home to her family so the chief knows we're on his side. I'm not sure how much Tooh can tell him, seeing as how he is cooperating with the village outcast. Come on, we have to get out of here, too. But we can't leave these guys to track us down or terrorize the village. If they wake up and find you guys missing, they might take retribution on the villagers. The Chinese have guns and have given some to these guys. We can't just run and risk the villagers' lives. I want to put a stop to it here and now if we can."

Finn nodded grimly. "Agreed. So, what do we do?"

I looked around. "Where are your supplies?"

Basia shook her head. "We lost them when we went overboard." She saw my bag. "But you still have the briefcase."

I patted the bag. "Yes. Look, we have an ally in the village who has arranged a boat for us to escape in and replacement supplies. We have the bad guys bottled up in the other hut that has only one exit. We have surprise, a gun and a blowgun on our side. So, the plan is I draw the bad guys out and let you and Sari take care of them from there. We don't want to turn this into a firefight. It needs to be as one-sided as possible. You also need to protect Sari, because she has to get close to be effective. Finn, find a good position that will give you a good view of the hut door without becoming an obvious target. Basia, you go with Finn."

"What are you going to do?"

"Give them a reason to come out. Just wait for my signal."

Finn put a hand under Basia's elbow to steady her. "Understood. What's the signal, Lexi?"

I smiled. "Michael Jackson."

As SOON AS we crept out of the hut, we parted ways. Finn and Basia headed for the trees while I snuck toward the other hut with Basia's cell phone in my hand. I couldn't see Sari, but I knew she was out there.

When I figured I'd given Finn enough time to get in position, I set the phone down close to the hut's door and pushed play with the volume set as loud as it would go. When Michael Jackson started singing about being thrilled, I dashed for the trees. Luckily the full moon illuminated the clearing and guided my feet to keep me from stumbling.

Nothing happened right away. The first sign of life was the light seeping through cracks in the huts, followed seconds later by men yelling. In short order, three men came outside and stopped just beyond the door. We'd taken them totally by surprise. They were half-dressed, with pants on, but no shirts or shoes. The first two had guns out, and they were pivoting slowly, trying to find the source of the sounds.

As Michael's falsetto reached a crescendo, one of the two guys with a gun suddenly spun and fired a burst of shots off into the dark. I prayed no one on our side was hit. Moments later he tottered and pitched forward. Apparently Sari was alive and well—and even more important, clearly at work.

The others looked around in disbelief for the source of the threat. Another armed thug took a wobbly step and fell. The remaining guy, realizing he was the only target left, scrambled for the door. He crashed face-first to the ground as a single gunshot split the air.

Finn and Sari had impeccable aim. Thank goodness they were on our side.

No one else exited the hut. From our count, there was at least one more guy in there, but we couldn't stick around much longer to find out for sure. The village was coming alive and heading our way. Sari suddenly appeared from behind the hut. She carefully grabbed one of the guns without exposing herself to anyone still inside and disappeared behind the hut again.

After several minutes passed with no evidence of action from inside the hut and villagers approaching the scene, I stood at the jungle's edge and whispered loudly.

"Sari?"

She materialized beside me so quietly I jumped.

"Jeez. How do you do that? Where are Finn and Basia?"

She motioned, so I followed her. She had the gun slung over her shoulder like a bow. We almost tripped over Finn, who was still covering the hut door with his gun.

Finn stood. "Thank you, Sari," he whispered.

She inclined her head at him, clearly pleased by his praise.

I helped Basia up from her crouch and urged everyone forward. "Guys, we've got to go."

Basia grabbed my arm. "Wait. There's at least one more bad guy in that hut. Possibly more."

The noise from the villagers was getting louder.

"The villagers have the upper hand now," Finn said. "We can leave them our two guns and they can retrieve the other weapon outside the hut. We have other responsibilities and should leave it to them to distribute justice according to their rules."

It was sound advice, but I still had a question. "What if the guy in the hut escapes before the villagers get here?"

"Then I guess he would find himself running from a bunch of motivated, expert trackers."

"You've got a point."

"So now what?" Basia asked.

I pointed to Sari. "Follow her."

Sari darted into the trees. I followed as closely as I could, my bag bumping my thigh with every step. She headed around the back of the huts. By this time, the whole village was awake. As we burst out into the clearing by the river, a man stepped out of the shadows and into the moonlight.

Finn maneuvered in front of us, holding out the gun.

I put a hand on his arm. "It's okay, Finn. He's with us. It's Sari's boyfriend, Tooh."

Sari ran toward Tooh and he pulled her into a long hug before turning to us. They started talking, their heads bent into each other, their silhouettes intertwined in the moonlight. He had a hand on her shoulder and she had one on his hip. The affection was obvious.

Then Tooh stepped forward and said something to us, pointing toward a black shape on the shore.

A boat.

# FORTY-SIX

As MUCH AS I loathed the thought of going on the water again, it had to be done.

Finn glanced at me and read the expression on my face. "Look at the bright side, Lexi," he said. "There are fewer spiders and snakes in a boat."

"But how will we know where we're going?" Basia looked out over the dark river. Moonlight shimmered on the water, making it look both lovely and eerie.

"Sari is coming with us," I said.

Finn stopped, turned to me. "Really? She'd do that for us? After all she's already done?"

"Yes. Because we're friends now, and that's what friends do. Let's go."

We scampered toward the boat and were preparing to climb in when several natives appeared on the path from the village. Some of them held torches. All carried knives and some had bows. They weren't necessarily aiming them at us, but they didn't look particularly friendly either. I guess getting woken in the middle of the night by gunfire would do that to you.

Tooh stepped forward, intercepting them on our behalf. He was talking rapidly when a large man with a tuft of gray hair and significant wrinkles on his face stepped forward. Everyone around him moved aside quickly.

Despite his age, the man had a powerful and toned body. He carried a wicked-looking steel knife in his hand

and was naked except for a simple loincloth, a belt with several pouches similar to Sari's and a necklace made of feathers, bones and crystals. Even in the moonlight I could see the jagged diagonal scar that stretched the length of his right shoulder to his left hip. Judging from reactions of the villagers, I presumed this was Tisa, the village chief—and Tooh and Kala's father.

I stood transfixed until I realized Sari was bowing, too. I bent over, nudging Finn and Basia, so we all showed respect.

The chief made some guttural noises at Tooh and he answered back. Sari finally straightened, so the rest straightened, too.

Sari stepped forward next to Tooh. She spoke for a minute and I presumed she was telling him her side of the story. Then she suddenly turned to me and held out a hand, motioning us all forward. We approached Tisa and stood directly in front of the elder man. I kept my gaze on him. I didn't intend it to be a challenge, but I sensed it was important to look at him as someone worthy of his respect and a strong person in my own right.

It was the right choice and I saw the approval in his eyes as his gaze met mine. Tisa spoke briefly. Although I didn't understand a word, I figured the speech was made on behalf of the villagers, not us. I heard the word Kala every now and again and assumed he was thanking us for our role in rescuing her.

He finally fell silent and waited. Oddly he stared at me, not Finn, maybe waiting for me to say or do something.

In a moment of inspiration, I turned to Sari, pointed to her blowgun and pantomimed how she had shot the bad guys. I then swept my hands down in a grandiose thank-you sign to her.

Sari looked at me shyly, appreciation in her eyes. Then, Tooh spoke for some time to his father. Given the way he pointed and gestured toward Sari, it occurred to me that she might have underplayed her role and Tooh was making it clear how instrumental *she'd* been in saving Kala and ridding the village of the thugs. I felt a swell of affection for him and how he stood up for the woman he loved in front of his father and the entire village.

Tisa walked to her, putting a hand on Sari's shoulder and saying something softly. The gesture clearly startled her. For a moment she was completely overcome and then she bowed to him. When she raised her head, I saw tears glittering in her eyes.

Whatever had just happened, I'm pretty sure it was good because Tooh beamed. To my astonishment, Tooh turned to me and swept his hands down in the motion of thanks. When he did that, I noticed he wore an exact replica of the necklace with the crescent moon.

Two hearts, one love. And maybe now, that love would no longer be unrequited.

I pressed my hand against my chest with my fingers spread wide. "You're very welcome, Tooh."

Pride crossed his face as he watched Sari, before ushering us toward the boat. I'm sure he would have joined us if there were room for a fifth person.

Several locals steadied the boat for us as we climbed in. An animal hide covered something at the bottom.

Finn climbed on first and then helped Basia board. Once she was secured, I quelled my resistance and got on, too. I felt the familiar dread in my stomach. I was going to be a bonafide sailor after this. *If* I survived.

The insides of the boat were wooden, sloped to a large rectangular area in the middle. Finn was checking out what was under the animal hide and I peeked over his shoulder. Fishing nets, hooks, spears, a couple of jars, a large stick and a few cloth drawstring bags.

Tooh helped Sari get into the boat and whispered something to her before she got on. She smiled.

Tooh and the village men pushed us in the water as Sari picked up a pole, helping push us off. Finn grabbed the other pole and soon we were far enough away from the shore to float down the river. Sari gazed back at the villagers. Tooh raised his hand in farewell, but he had only eyes for Sari.

I watched the shore as we drifted with the gentle current and the torchlight faded, then disappeared. The trees lining the stream cast dark shadows across the waters. But even my imaginary scenarios of crocodiles or other man-eating fish capsizing the boat and eating me alive could not begin to diminish my relief at that we were all alive and together again.

Sari was poling leisurely, keeping us in the center of the current. The stream turned and she was backlit suddenly by the moon over the mountains and the trees. It was a picture-worthy moment. I wished I still had Basia's phone so I could take a photo. I still didn't know how I would break the news to Basia that her cell phone was a lost cause. On the bright side, maybe the fact that an entire village would now be able to browse her cell phone pictures would inspire her to finally create a password for her next phone.

I heard rustling at the bottom of the boat and some scraping noise. Sari had stopped poling and pulled out a couple of the jars from the supplies Tooh had left for us. She passed one to Finn, urging him to drink.

He peered inside the jar, waved away the bugs and then sniffed. "It's some kind of drink. Do we risk it?"

My throat was parched. "Tooh stocked the boat for us, so we have to trust that we can eat and drink it. We can deal with any consequences later."

Finn set down his pole and lifted the jar to his lips. He drank, then after wiping his mouth with the back of his hand, passed it to me.

"It's good. A bit sweet. You know, I'm really beginning to like that guy."

The drink smelled pungent, like a strong herbal tea. I sincerely hoped it had been boiled so that most of the bacteria and microbes had been removed, but either way, I was drinking it. I took several large gulps, unable to stop myself. The liquid was thick like a cider, but with a heavier herbal taste. It tasted really good.

I passed it to Basia, who drank and then burped loudly. "Oops."

Laughing, she handed the jar to Sari, who took a drink and then replaced it under the hide. She pulled out the drawstring cloth and handed each of us chunks of meat that had been smoked and skewered like shish kabob.

I took a bite. It was tough and hard to chew, but surprisingly tasty. There was a spicy aftertaste from something I couldn't name. I chewed until my jaws ached, but it was worth it.

As we drifted through the night, the moon slowly sank and we huddled at the bottom of the boat, passing around the jar and talking. Sari was a statue of concentration in the stern of the boat. For longer stretches now, she brought the pole into the boat and we rode the currents. At times I could almost feel the jungle pressing in against the raft.

Basia began to doze, leaning against Finn's shoulder. Finn, apparently observing how tense I remained, coaxed me into looking at the stars to soothe my nerves.

I leaned back against the side of the boat and focused on the majestic theater of the night. With the bright moon setting, I could see most of the constellations clearly, spread out in all of their glory. My view was completely undiluted by lights or evidence of human existence.

"It's stunning," I murmured.

Finn traced one of the constellations with his finger. "When he shall die, take him and cut him out in little stars, and he will make the face of heaven so fine that all the world will be in love with night and pay no worship to the garish sun."

I turned my head sideways. "William Shakespeare. Romeo and Juliet."

"It seemed fitting."

"It is." I leaned my head on his other shoulder. "Finn, I'm really, *really* glad you're okay. When I thought you were gone…" I cleared my throat. "Well, I just couldn't imagine my life without you in it. I know the boyfriend-girlfriend thing didn't work out between us, but I never realized how important you've become to me as a friend and especially a mentor."

He took my hand, squeezed it. "It was my lucky day when our paths crossed. I can't think of another friendship I treasure more. Slash is bloody lucky to have you."

"You know about me and Slash?"

"I'm not an idiot. Just so we're clear, if he hurts you in any way, I'll kill him."

"You mean that figuratively, right?"

"No, I mean it. If he hurts you or makes you cry, he's going to have to answer to me."

"Wow. That's really sweet in a weird, macho sort of way. You shouldn't have come on this trip, though. Everyone around me keeps getting hurt."

"Och, now you insult my manhood. I'm glad I came, Lexi. I mean that. No worries about me. We Irish are a hardy lot."

"Maybe. But it scared me, Finn. A lot."

He sighed. "Me, too. But we'll get through this."

"I hope so."

"I *know* so. After all, we have to get back to X-Corp so I can give my two best employees a raise for saving the CEO's life."

I smiled and we talked for a while more. I must have dozed off at some point, because I awoke with a start when I heard a familiar sound.

The second helicopter had found us.

# FORTY-SEVEN

SARI WAS DOZING on the other side of the boat, but she opened her eyes a split second after I did.

At some point during the night she'd pulled us under the cover of trees in a small inlet. I could see the morning sky through gaps in the foliage, but it wasn't a clear view. She'd been smart. At our current location, it would have been hard, though not impossible, to spot us from the air.

"Is it them?" Finn was peering up at the sky as well.

"It's hard to say." I still couldn't see it, but it sounded like it was getting louder. After a minute the noise was right above us and headed upstream toward Sari's village. We shrank down in the boat, but it passed over us without slowing. They weren't looking for anyone on the river, anyway, as they would assume we were still captives.

"I hope the villagers have some kind of plan in mind to welcome those guys on the helicopter," Basia said.

Finn shaded his eyes, still watching the sky. "Well, the villagers have guns now. They can elect to fight if they want. But a better option, in my opinion, is to melt into the jungle. That way, when the helicopter arrives, they'll simply find the village empty. As the Chinese helicopter crew will be small, I can't see the benefit of them leaving the helicopter and trying to track down the natives in their own jungle. My best guess is that the crew will land, see the huts empty and get out of there.

But they'll be looking for us. Make no mistake, the river will be one of the first places they'll check."

"So, are we going to move on or stay here?" Basia asked.

Finn answered. "We have to keep going."

I peered downriver. "He's right. We have no choice. When we planned our rescue, Sari drew me a picture of a big village, maybe a town. It's possible we might find a phone there."

"What about my cell phone?" Basia said. "We can check to see if I get any bars."

"I'm sorry, Basia, I was trying to figure out how to tell you this, but I left it at the hut during our escape."

I expected a bit of an explosion, but instead she sighed. "It's okay. I was thinking about upgrading anyway."

"And when you do, we need to have a little discussion about password protection."

"Again?"

"Again."

Sari listened to us talk and then looked like she wanted to tell us something. She glanced around and I realized she was looking for a way to draw a picture to explain her plan to us. I looked around the boat, and suddenly it occurred to me. I unzipped my bag, pulled out Basia's purse and extracted her lipstick.

Basia's face brightened. "Hey, my lipstick. You still have it?"

"Yep."

She reached for her lipstick, but I shook my head. "Sorry, we need it to draw."

I drew a line on the side of the boat and then handed the lipstick to Sari. "Go for it. What's your plan?"

Sari curiously examined the lipstick before starting to draw. Twenty minutes later we were mostly up to speed. We were definitely getting better at communicating.

Finn leaned back against the boat. "So, according to Sari, we're headed for a town called Wasu. Tooh apparently gave her the name and instructions of where to meet his friend. That friend is supposed to help us with whatever we need to get home."

"That's my understanding." I rubbed my eyes. They felt gritty and tired.

"All we need to do is get to a phone or somewhere where there is an internet connection."

"Exactly. Except I don't think Sari has ever been to a town before. But Tooh trusts her to take care of us and so do I."

Basia leaned back, closing her eyes. "I am so looking forward to getting off this godforsaken island."

While we were talking, Sari pulled a loincloth out from underneath the tarp. She handed it to Finn.

Finn blinked in astonishment. "Why is she giving this to me?"

Puzzled I looked at her. Sari pointed to the animal skin at the bottom of the boat, motioning that Basia and I were to get under it. Then she pointed to herself, Finn and the loincloth.

I couldn't keep the grin off my face. "Ah, I get it. This is Tooh and Sari's plan to get us down the river safely. They're going to be looking for two women and a man. A native male and female in a boat, fishing, are not going to attract attention."

"Whoa. She wants *me* to wear that?"

"Well, if she asked one of us to wear *her* outfit, I'm pretty sure I wouldn't see you complaining."

"That's different."

"It's a good plan. Put it on, Finn."

"Are you bleeding nuts? They'll know it's me immediately. Even from a helicopter, my skin will be a bloody white beacon. I'm Irish. We hold our sun worshipping festivals in winter so we don't burn."

I tried hard not to laugh, but I couldn't help myself. "We'll cover you with mud."

He frowned. "Fine." He unzipped his pants and the three of us turned our heads away.

After a few minutes that involved more swearing than I'd ever heard come out of his mouth, Finn had donned the loincloth.

We turned around as he held up a hand. "Don't say a bloody word. I mean it."

He was completely naked except for the tiny cloth, and he cut a buff figure despite the bumps, bruises and beard. I worried about the beard, but figured that wouldn't be visible from the helicopter as long as Finn didn't look up as it passed over. Sari scooped up mud with her pole and all of us mashed it over his body the best we could.

Finn tried to stand still while we administered the mud. "You know, under different circumstances, I might actually have enjoyed this."

I smashed some mud on the back of his knee. "So, how does it feel to wear a loincloth?"

"A little breezy. Probably a lot like you girls when you wear a thong and not much else."

Both Basia and I erupted into giggles.

He pursed his lips. "Just so you know, there is something liberating about going the full monty."

"I bet," Basia said, finishing off his feet.

We leaned back and surveyed our handiwork. It looked good to me, but Sari wasn't satisfied. She scooped up more mud and slapped it onto his head.

"What the hell?" Finn roared.

Sari leaned back alarmed.

I stepped between them. "Are you always so difficult a patient?"

"I'm a man, aren't I?"

I rolled my eyes. "Even dirty, your hair is too light. We have to darken it."

Finn frowned. "I just wanted a little warning, that's all. Okay, tell her to do it and get it over with."

I motioned for Sari to continue and she added more mud to his hair. When she was done he looked like something between a camouflaged Navy SEAL and a mud wrestler. Another giggle escaped my lips, but I swallowed it when he glared at me.

"We've got an even harder part," I said to Basia. "We're going to cook under that animal hide. But at least we only have to go under there when we hear a helicopter or a lot of people start showing up on the river."

Basia sighed. "Fine."

Finn and Sari pushed off. Basia and I stayed hunkered down at the bottom of the boat as we headed down the river, keeping as close as possible to the shore.

The stream had widened overnight. Though the water was smooth and appeared lazy, the speed at which we were riding the currents suggested a much stronger flow than it appeared. Around midday we came to a point where the two rivers joined and became wider and slower. I hoped that meant we were approaching a river's mouth, meaning we were nearing the coast. We had two flyovers, probably from the same helicopter, and plenty of notice for each.

During the flyovers, Basia and I hid under the animal hide. Both times the helicopters hovered low to check us out, then flew away. Finn kept his head down and bent over the side of the boat as if fishing. Sari looked up and waved. The helicopters didn't stay long, so I hoped that meant they weren't interested in us. It was hard to say.

The day dragged on and we were all hot and exhausted. More settlements came into view along the banks, so Basia and I stayed low and as out of sight as possible. We were confident the increasing settlements meant we were getting closer to the town. In the late afternoon, a large island in the middle of the river came into view, with three tall palms standing in a riot of river vegetation. Sari trilled and pointed at it, steering the boat to a small inlet on the island. When we beached there, Sari indicated that we should rest. She stepped over the side of the boat and vanished among the tall reeds.

Sari had yet to return when dusk started to fall. I tried not to be worried, but I could tell Finn and Basia were getting nervous. Looking out at the river, I saw a bare-chested man standing on a boat and holding a net, his body outlined by the glowing sunset. More boats and rafts came into view, moving down the river for the night.

It was late when Sari returned, and she wasn't alone. A man holding a flashlight accompanied her. We were hunkered down in the boat, swatting mosquitoes and passing the time by talking about all the things we'd eat when we got home. We stood as they got closer and stepped out of the boat. The man was dark-skinned like Sari and wore a white polo shirt, khaki shorts and sandals.

Finn, who had changed back into his own clothes, kept his hand near the gun he'd tucked into his waistband just in case.

Sari approached us and swept out her hand toward the man. "Amborn."

The man strode right up to Finn and pumped his hand. "G'day, mate. Nice to make your acquaintance."

Finn blinked in astonishment. "Whoa. You speak English?"

"Yes, I taught myself. Australians come here to Wasu sometimes. I guide them for fishing. Big river, excellent fishing if you know where to look. Make good money."

"Get out." Finn pumped his hand enthusiastically. "That's the bloody best news I've heard in a week."

Amborn shone the flashlight in my face. "You're Lexi Carmichael?"

I gaped at him. "How did you know my name?"

"Photos in town. Everywhere. They look for you, Lexi Carmichael."

"They? Who is they?"

"China men. They give money to everyone to find for you. Big reward."

Finn swore, pushing his fingers through his hair. "They've planted people in town looking for you. For all of us probably. They figured, accurately, if we got off the mountain, this would be the first place we would come. They are most likely doubly alert since we gave them the slip at the village."

Basia frowned. "So, what the hell do we do now?"

I considered our options. "Can you get us to a phone or bring us one?"

"I don't have a phone. Phones no good up here." He looked at me. "But I'll tell you this. Wasu is not safe for you. They are watching every place. They pay lot of money to anyone who sees you. You wouldn't get far because they'd find you, and fast."

Sari said something to Amborn. He answered her and then turned to us.

"Sari says you are very brave woman and are not afraid of anything."

I smiled at her. "Tell Sari I'm the bravest when I have my friends around to help me."

Amborn translated and Sari pressed her hand to her chest as a gesture of thanks.

Finn began pacing. "Well, if we can't stay in Wasu, where's the nearest place we can get to a phone or an airport? Where do the Australians fly into?"

"Lae would be where you want to go. It's a big city." Amborn crossed his arms against his chest, the flashlight casting odd shadows on his face. "It would be much harder for them to find you there. I know a boat captain who goes from Wasu to Lae and back. He brings me all my fishing tourists. I could ask if he would carry my latest tourists back to Lae."

I looked at Finn and Basia, "What do you guys think?"

Finn lifted his shoulders. "I'm not seeing a lot of options here. I think we see if he can get us passage and then we go for it."

Basia sighed. "Thank God. If we can get to a city, any city, I am so in favor of that option."

"It won't be the kind of city you might expect," I warned her.

Basia ran her fingers through her hair. "I don't care. I really don't. There's no way you can dampen my mood.

Anything is better than the jungle. I'm never going camping again."

"We weren't camping. We were surviving."

"Whatever. I've had enough of the outdoors for a lifetime. God, what I wouldn't do for an actual toilet."

I grinned like an idiot despite the danger that might be waiting for us in the town or even in Lae."

I turned back to Amborn. "We'd be most appreciative if you could get us on board that boat."

# FORTY-EIGHT

"Okay, mates, I've got a plan," Amborn said. "I take you in your boat to Wasu tonight. Sari stays here since there's no room in the boat for all of us and she has no experience in town. There are empty fishing shacks near the dock, so you wait there while I arrange passage for you to Lae. Once you are gone, I'll come back and return the boat to Sari. If we can't get you on the next ship, we try again tomorrow or the next day until you go."

It sounded like a good plan to me. "Thanks, Amborn. We really appreciate it."

"Then we don't have time to waste." He dipped his head toward Sari. "It's time to say goodbye."

We stood awkwardly in front of Sari, not having the slightest clue how we could possibly thank her for everything she'd done for us.

Finn acted first, reaching out and taking her hands in his. "Thank you, Sari. I can't thank you enough for all you have done. Tooh is a damn lucky guy to have you."

Amborn translated for Finn and Sari smiled at him, pressing her hand to her chest.

Basia was next. She stood on tiptoe and kissed Sari's cheek before removing her sparkly earrings and pressing them into Sari's hands. "For you. Thank you for saving my life."

Sari's eyes widened as she looked at the earrings. She looked up at Basia, not understanding. Basia closed

Sari's fingers around the earrings, hugged her and stood next to Finn.

Now it was time for me to say goodbye to Sari. A lump formed in my throat and I shifted on my feet. I'd never been good at this kind of thing. How did a person adequately thank someone for saving their life and the lives of their friends?

To my surprise, Sari made the first move. She lifted my hand and pressed it against her heart, pressing hers against mine. "Sari. Wexi. *Oltaim.*"

*"Oltaim?"* I said.

"Always," Amborn said. "She said you'll be friends for always."

Her words touched me more than she would ever know. I put my hand on top of hers and held it against my heart. "I'll never forget you, Sari."

I unfastened Elvis's locket and hung it around her neck. "Amborn, please tell her that locket belongs to one of my very best friends. He gave it to me to thank me for saving his life. Now I want to pay it forward and thank Sari for saving me…us. Hopefully, someday when someone does something extraordinary for her, she'll pass it on, as a way of extending that kindness. I'll be back someday to visit her again. This isn't goodbye for good."

Amborn translated. Sari touched the locket at her throat and smiled. Without reservation, I threw my arms around her. She hugged me back hard and we stayed there for a moment, letting emotion speak the words we could not.

Finally, I released her. "I'm really going to miss you, Sari. I hope you'll be happy with Tooh."

She smiled and held up a hand in farewell. Taking a deep breath, I turned away from her and climbed onto the boat with the others.

IT WAS WELL after dark when Amborn decided where to dock. He and Finn jumped into the water, pulling the boat ashore, securing it. When Amborn gave us the all-clear, Basia and I climbed out and joined them. A rickety boardwalk led to an old fishing shack, apparently closed since it was after hours for fishing.

Basia pushed the damp hair off her forehead and fanned herself. "I think I've been cooked in every way known to man. How much hotter can it possibly get?"

"Don't ask that," I warned. "I really don't want to find out."

Amborn walked the length of the dock and motioned for us to wait while he checked out the shack. He came back and told us it was safe to wait here while he went into town to check with his captain friend.

I'm not sure how long we waited, but we leaped to our feet eagerly when he returned.

"Captain Zico says he can take you." Amborn fiddled with his flashlight. "He's already got passengers booked, but he said he can make room for you. For a price."

"How much?" Finn asked.

"How much do you have?"

I looked at Basia. "How much money do you have in your wallet right now?"

"About three hundred dollars."

"Will that work?" I asked.

Amborn hesitated. "I'm not sure."

Finn leaned forward. "Tell him I'll give him another five thousand after we get to Lae and a phone."

Amborn's eyes widened. "That should do it."

"Wait." I studied Amborn's face. "Why are you doing this? Why are you helping us?"

Amborn grinned. "Because Sari asked nicely and I

like her." His grin stretched wider. "And also because you helped save my little sister, Kala."

When my eyes widened, he added, "Yes. Tooh is my brother."

# FORTY-NINE

WE FOLLOWED AMBORN through the darkened streets of Wasu toward the town's main dock. Smells of fish, unusual spices and burning garbage from the town assaulted us as we passed through the buildings in the shadows. Twice Basia gagged and I had to breathe through my mouth to avoid the same fate.

At last we reached the port. It was mostly silent, but I saw lights on some of the boats. There were a few people milling about.

"Wait here." Amborn motioned for us to stop in the shadows of a building. "I'll check with the captain."

He left us and strolled down the dock, crossing the ramp onto a ship and disappearing below.

"Wow. That's not a boat," Basia said, sounding excited. "That's a yacht. It's going to be a significant upgrade from our last mode of transportation."

I swatted at a fly. "As long as it has a real bathroom, I'm good."

About ten minutes later, Amborn returned with a tall black man in a short-sleeved, white dress shirt, dark slacks and a captain's hat.

"This is Captain Zico. He'll take you to Lae."

Finn held out a hand and the two men shook. "Thank you, Captain. We appreciate your assistance."

"Of course. There are three of you?"

"Yes."

"You must stay below so as not to disturb my other guests."

"Not a problem."

"You have any luggage?"

Finn pointed to my black bag. "Just this."

He nodded. "Okay. You've got the money?"

Basia reached into her purse and pulled out her wallet, handing him three one hundred dollar bills.

Zico flipped through them.

"Five thousand more to follow as soon as we get into Lae and I get to a phone," Finn said.

"I understand. Come on then."

We followed him onto the boat and down a narrow set of stairs.

"How long will it take us to get to Lae?" I asked him.

"About eight hours, depending on the weather. We have to travel through the Vitiaz Straight and into the Houn Gulf."

"When we get to port will you take us to a phone?"

"Of course."

We walked down a tight corridor before stopping at the door of a cabin.

"It's small, but it should serve you for the trip," Zico said opening the door. "I'll bring you food and water shortly and let you know when you may come above for some fresh air. The loo is at the end of the corridor."

"Do you think you can get me a razor?" Finn scratched his beard. "I'd really appreciate it."

Zico nodded. "I'll see what I can do."

Zico ushered us into the tiny cabin. It had one bunk bed, a wooden wardrobe and a chair. There was no porthole of any kind. It was a tight fit with the three of us, but after where we'd just slept for the past few days, we weren't complaining.

After Zico left, Basia darted out of the cabin. "First dibs on the bathroom," she called over her shoulder.

I took off the bag with the briefcase and put it on the floor next to me, sinking down onto the chair.

Finn pounded a fist into the mattress of the lower bunk. His fist sunk into it. "There are only two beds, if you can call them that."

"No worries. Basia and I can share.

"Fine." He stretched back on the bed, putting an arm over his eyes.

After several minutes Basia came back. She'd washed her face and neck the best she could with one arm. Her face had been mostly covered with mud for the past few days, so it seemed odd to see pink skin.

Finn and I each took turns in the bathroom, as well, washing ourselves in the sink until we felt quasi-human again. It was the first time since the plane crash I saw myself in a mirror. I was barely recognizable, even with the mud removed. I still had two shiners and my nose was crooked and dotted with purple and red bruises. The knot on the right side of my forehead had turned a yellowish green.

Jeez.

Finn looked significantly better, having shaved with the razor Zico had provided. He'd nicked himself in a couple of places, but at least we could see his face.

I heard noises in the corridor outside our door and on the deck above. I assumed the passengers were boarding. Minutes later the whine of the motor started and the boat swayed as we pushed off.

I began to feel nauseated. "I think I might have liked the canoe better. It's claustrophobic down here."

"Zico said he'd bring us food soon, so maybe we can ask him when we can go on deck," Basia said.

She couldn't get up to the top bunk with her injured arm, so she scooted next to Finn on the bed and the two of them napped. I didn't feel like climbing to the top bunk either so I dozed off, sleeping in the chair.

A soft knock woke us up and Finn rose, opening the door. Zico stood there with a bag of food and some water bottles.

Finn took the offering gratefully. "Thanks. Appreciate it."

"You may come up one at a time for some air if you'd like." He pointed at me. "You first."

I figured out of the three of us, I looked like I needed it the most.

I followed him out of the cabin and climbed the steps behind him. When we got to the upper deck, I squinted in the morning sun and took a moment to breathe the fresh air. A glance at our surroundings indicated we were on the open sea. After travelling so long by pole, being on a boat with an actual engine made it seem as if we were flying across the water at warp speed.

Zico moved toward the front of the boat. I saw a table with benches on either side. A solitary man sat at one of the tables with his back to me. To my surprise, Zico waved me forward.

I hesitated, but he motioned to me again.

"Come sit, please," he insisted.

"I thought you didn't want us to mingle with your passengers."

Zico smiled. "I changed my mind."

I approached the table slowly. As I reached the table, the man turned his head to me.

"Hello, Lexi Carmichael. I've been looking forward to meeting you for a long time."

# FIFTY

I BACKED UP so fast I nearly fell overboard. The man was Asian, with short dark hair and a neatly trimmed beard.

*Zico sold us out!*

I glared across the boat at Zico. The man sitting on the bench seemed amused by my alarm.

"I suggest you sit down," the man said. "There's no place for you to go anyway. We might as well talk."

I looked out at the water and watched as the hull cut through the waves. My mind sorted through options until I realized I didn't have any. Turning around, I slid onto the bench, facing him. He had a plate of food in front of him. My stomach growled.

"Okay, apparently, I'm at a disadvantage." I leaned back on the bench. "You know my name. What's yours?"

"You may call me Quon."

I studied him. My guess was that this was Jiang Quon, the younger brother of Jiang Shi, leader of the hacking group Red Guest. Apparently they'd been up to their neck in whatever was going down for some time.

"You're a long way from China," I said. "You came all this way just to see me?"

"As a matter of fact, yes. When I heard you'd been spotted just north of Wasu, it was logical to assume you'd head to the town and seek passage to Lae. I wanted to make sure I was the first to greet you. I'd originally hoped to make your acquaintance under much more civilized conditions in Port Moresby. But after the unfortunate incidence on the plane, we had a change of plans."

"That unfortunate incident killed several people."

"A pity. Lucky for me, it didn't kill you."

"You bribed Captain Zico."

"Of course. Whatever you offered to pay him, we paid him three times more."

Quon picked up a knife and spread a white sauce on a piece of bread. He took a bite. I kept my gaze averted from the food for fear I'd leap across the table and snatch it from his mouth.

I needed to focus and figure out what to do. In order for that to occur, I needed more information. No better time than the present to ask. "So, Quon, how do I know you are who you say you are?"

He chuckled. "You may not know me by face, Miss Carmichael, but you would know me if you came across my code."

"Prove it. Where have you been?"

"The American Embassy in Belgrade, two years ago—the virus called Strangelove. Eighteen months ago, the Department of Homeland Security in the Cybersecurity Division—a worm called Uptempo. Six weeks ago, in the NSA, Operation Discord. I could name a lot more, but I'm afraid some operations are still in progress."

"Okay, at the very least I believe you're a member of Red Guest."

"Not a member. The leader."

"You sure Shi would agree with you?"

He frowned. "What do you know of my brother?"

"Enough to say that if I told him you were posing as the leader, he might be pretty pissed off."

I saw an angry flash in his eyes and then he smiled. "Ah, very good. You pass the first test."

"Oh, you're testing me now?"

"Yes." Quon lifted a napkin to his lips, dabbing at his mouth. "The captain is bringing you a plate. Please, I hope you'll join me in a drink while we wait for your food."

"It's morning."

"Ah, but as you Americans say, it's five o'clock somewhere."

As if on cue, a young man appeared holding two glasses. He placed one in front of me and one in front of Quon. The glasses were cold. Despite myself, I licked my lips.

"Mimosas," Quon said. "Drink up, please."

I resisted with supreme effort. "Sorry, it's a personal policy of mine not to drink with people who are trying to kill me."

"You couldn't be more misguided. I have no intention of harming you. I need you."

Quon took a long drink of his mimosa. I didn't touch mine.

As if testing my resolve, the young man who had just brought my drink returned again, this time carrying a plate of food. It was some kind of fish, sweet potatoes with a brown glaze, and what appeared to be a thick, delicious-looking pudding. It was the most food I'd seen in days. It took all my willpower not to attack it face first.

"Please eat," Quon said, clearly amused. "I insist."

"No, thanks. I'm good."

He shrugged and took another bite of his bread. "You know, I admit I'm quite surprised by your resourcefulness. You've been very lucky, Miss Carmichael. It took us much longer than expected to find you. In fact, I expected to find you dead. Who knew a computer hacker could survive so long in the jungle?"

"I'm not just a computer hacker."

"Indeed, I see you are much more. I should have known better after you outwitted Johannes Broodryk. Luck favors you, Lexi Carmichael, which we Chinese consider quite a meaningful omen."

"I don't believe in luck. I just happen to choose my friends very carefully."

Quon set his glass down and leaned back in his chair. He picked up a silver coin about the size of a half dollar and held it between his fingers. While I watched in fascination, he started rolling it back and forth with perfect execution over his knuckles. I was intrigued in spite of myself.

"How do you do that?" I asked.

"Practice." He paused, rolling the coin into his palm and closing his fingers over it. "Have you ever been to China?"

"No."

"You'll like it."

"Maybe. But if you're the intended guide, I won't."

"China has a lot to offer someone like you." He picked up his fork and knife and cut a piece of his food. "Everything you could ever want or imagine. It's a beautiful country with some of the world's most exotic and breathtaking locations. Our people are friendly and welcoming."

"A lot like you?" I pursed my lips.

"I can be very friendly once you get to know me."

"No thanks, and I'll pass on a trip to China this time around."

He laughed. "You know, I like you."

"And I like being an American."

He tossed the coin, catching it in his palm. "I think I can change your mind about that, which—by the way—is why we've kept your two friends alive this long."

I paused, considered. "That's a pretty ugly statement."

"Not ugly. Truthful. I sense you are not one for games."

"Not this kind."

"Then at last we agree on something." He began rolling the coin again. Despite my best effort, I couldn't stop watching.

He snapped his fingers and the coin disappeared between his knuckles. "I will be the first to say I admire your artistry at the keyboard. You would be a worthy addition to the Red Guest."

"I'm afraid you're going to have to rethink your recruiting pitch."

He chuckled. "Oh, we're not so different, you know. We're both pioneers and innovators in our field."

I pushed my plate aside. "Let me see, Quon. You're a cracker who orchestrated a hijacking that killed several people. Now you're threatening my friends and me and trying to steal someone else's invention. In my opinion, that makes you little more than a boastful bully and a murderous thief. You lost me on the pioneer and innovator part."

He didn't seem offended by my assessment. He pressed his fingers together in a steeple. "Therein lies the flaws of Americans. A narrow-minded focus. It's the end goal that matters, not the method."

"Now you sound like Karl Marx or, should I say, Mao Zedong." I made a sound of disgust. "Spare me the propaganda. What do you want? I'm not going to help you. Despite your fancy promises, you'll never let us go. We're all dead anyway."

He banged his fist on the table, startling me. "Wrong. All three of you can live very long and successful lives in China. You will be well pampered beyond your wildest dreams."

"This is a complete waste of time." I pushed to my feet. "I don't know the code to the briefcase. The twins didn't tell me. They decided to wait until I arrived in Jakarta as an extra security measure. You can torture me or my friends to kingdom come and it won't get you the code."

He folded his hands on the table and the silver coin seemed to magically appear on his knuckles. "Sit down, Miss Carmichael. Why do I care about some stupid code? It doesn't matter what it is. We'll break it eventually. What's of more interest to the Red Guest and me is that we have some very important and specific cyber questions we'd like to ask. Starting with the NSA."

I watched the coin roll back and forth across his hand and shook my head. "You didn't do your homework very well. I don't work for the NSA anymore. Besides, I was just a junior techhead there. Trust me, I wouldn't know anything of value to you anyway."

"True. You may not. But your boyfriend would."

I froze, my breath catching in my throat. Fear—cold, dark tendrils of it—snaked through my heart.

I sat down.

His eyes assessed me coldly. "Ah, now you're getting it."

I swallowed hard, trying to compose myself. "This

isn't about me, is it? It's not even about the Zimmermans' invention."

Quon's expression was hard. "I won't lie to you. Those are bonuses beyond our wildest dreams. But, no. This isn't about you or the microchip. It never was. We have bigger needs at the moment."

I felt as if I were drowning. Panic like I'd never known before welled inside me.

*Slash.*

*They wanted Slash.*

The hijacking, the men chasing us outside my apartment, the reason the Chinese hadn't shot me outright… It had never been about the microchip, the design, or me. They took the microchip because it was theirs for the taking, but it was Slash they were after all along. Once they had me, they *knew* he'd come to them. And then they had a way to make him cooperate.

*Me.*

They would use me to get Slash and get inside his head. I felt like throwing up, but I was frozen to my chair.

Quon leaned forward. "Now, Miss Carmichael, you will do exactly as I say."

# FIFTY-ONE

I KNEW IT was coming—it was only a matter of when. I wouldn't get a warning.

There was a reason they'd put me below deck in a totally dark room. Deprivation of sight would heighten all the other senses, including touch and hearing. Quon didn't want me to know when he would strike, which I presumed was his plan for keeping me off-balance and scared. He didn't have to go to all the trouble. I was already a quivering wreck.

It felt like he'd been asking me questions for hours, but the logical part of my brain told me it was certainly far less than that. Despite the dark room, I could still see the glint of his eyes and an occasional gleam of teeth when he spoke or smiled. He was enjoying himself and that alone made me sicker than his twisted techniques and repeated questions.

My face was in agony. He'd studied me when we'd been talking above board. I now understood why. Quon knew just where to hit and press to maximize the pain. Still, I wasn't going to tell him anything he didn't already know about Slash. Not that I knew all that much anyway. The irony of the situation was that no matter how much I loved Slash, and despite what I would do to protect him, I didn't really know him. He had yet to truly let me all the way into his life and permit me to know him for who he was, not just the mysterious persona he showed to everyone else.

Quon's thumb pressing into my injured cheek jerked me back to reality. I couldn't help it, I screamed like a girl.

"Since we don't seem to be getting anywhere, let's start over," he said calmly. "What's his real name?"

I gasped for breath. I was one of the few who knew Slash's real name, which ironically enough was Romeo. And boy, oh, boy, did I need my Romeo right now.

I rolled my tongue inside my mouth, feeling the swell of my upper lip. I steeled myself for the lie. "I already told you, Quon, I don't know. He's known as Slash to me and all of our acquaintants. He keeps his real identity secret even from me."

"What's his exact position at the NSA?"

"I don't know."

He pressed harder with his thumb. Tears leaked from my eyes.

"Try again, Miss Carmichael. You worked there together."

I tried to pull away, but Quon and his henchmen had tied me to a chair and one of them stood behind me, holding my head. It didn't escape my notice that with one well-placed twist it would all be over.

"Yes we did, but we're supercompartmentalized at the NSA. All I know is that he didn't work directly in my department—cybersecurity."

"What is his official title?"

"I have no idea. We aren't allowed to talk about our work outside of the office."

He dug his thumb in my cheek again. Stars of pain

flashed in the corner of my vision as I whimpered in agony.

"I urge you to think harder."

He was taking it easy on me for the time being, but all bets would be off when they had Slash. They would do worse—a heck of a lot worse—to me in order to get him to cooperate.

My entire body started shaking. I couldn't let myself go there now or I'd completely fall apart.

Quon released the pressure on my cheek and I almost wept in relief, even with renewed ache. His footsteps moved back and forth across the room. The ship was rocking pretty badly and my stomach heaved. I wondered what would happen if I threw up. I almost smiled. It would serve Quon right if I hurled all over him.

I realized he had stopped moving and I didn't know where he stood. I listened hard for any sound of him, but the goon behind me was breathing hard. He was probably getting off on my discomfort and pain. I tried to brace myself for a hit from any angle.

"You are his lover," Quon suddenly said, his voice coming from my right.

I kept my voice light, unconcerned. "One of many. You may be sorry you put all your eggs in one basket."

"Liar."

I tensed for the hit, but it didn't come. My legs were shaking uncontrollably, but I tried to sound calm. "Actually, I'm not. In case you didn't know, Slash is a really good-looking guy. And, well, you've seen me in daylight. Granted, I may not be at my best at the moment, but if you think a guy like him is exclusive with me, you'd be sorely mistaken. Think about it. You're a man. I'm sure you see my point."

"Wrong answer." He hit me hard across the face and nose, and agony exploded behind my eyes. I tasted blood. In a moment of inspiration, I let my head loll forward as if he'd knocked me out.

He shook me a couple of times, but I didn't respond.

He released me with a hard jerk, then said something in Chinese, clearly in disgust. His footsteps slapped angrily across the room before the door opened and then slammed shut. The light flicked on.

I kept my eyes closed and breathed through a tiny part in my lips. It wasn't much of a reprieve, but at this point, I'd take whatever I could get.

QUON HADN'T RETURNED for more torture. Apparently he was too busy plotting our getaway to China. At some point, he and an armed guard escorted me back to the cabin with Finn and Basia as we were nearing Lae, threw me inside and locked the door.

Finn caught me before I collapsed. "What the hell?" he roared.

Basia supported me from my other side and they helped me to the bed. "Oh, Lexi, are you okay? What's happening?"

I gingerly touched my cheek and winced. "Zico betrayed us. He turned us over to the Chinese."

"I figured as much," Finn said, kneeling beside the bed, trying to examine me for any new injuries. "Shortly after you left, some goons came in holding guns and took the briefcase and my gun. What did they do to you?"

I told them everything as quickly as I could, but we didn't have much time. The boat had come to a stop and I presumed we were docking.

When I finished, Finn stood, frowning. "Wait. Just wait. This is about Slash? The whole hijacking?"

"Yes. The acquisition of the microchip is a major bonus, of course, but ultimately they wanted me so Slash would come to them and cooperate."

Finn shoved his fingers in his hair. "We can't let you get on that plane to China."

"If you've got a plan to prevent that, I'm listening."

Heavy steps sounded outside our cabin and the door suddenly swung open. Two guys with guns motioned to us to leave the cabin. We filed out—Finn first, followed by Basia and then me.

We climbed in single file up the ladder to where Quon was waiting for us. He wore the bag with the briefcase. The dock was nearly empty with just a few people milling about and was flanked by a row of trees and a small stretch of white beach. A white bus sat just beyond the boardwalk, engine running.

We headed toward the bus with the guys with guns flanking us. Quon was in the back with me. I'd just calculated the odds of the three of us managing to overpower the five guys with guns at sixty-two million four hundred and forty-nine to one, when one of the guys suddenly went down.

"Sniper!" someone shouted and all hell broke loose.

My brain instantly recalculated the odds—factoring one bad guy down and someone shooting at the rest. The odds became *much* better at four hundred and ninety-seven to one.

I had no more time for calculations, because Quon dragged me behind a wooden crate, pressing a gun against my side while his men fanned out trying to find where the shots were coming from.

Finn and Basia were across from me, huddled behind another crate and under the control of another armed minion. Finn and I looked at each other across the dock and he suddenly nodded at me. I had no idea what he was thinking, until the guy who was guarding them came up from a crouch, aiming his gun at the tree line. Finn gave him a hard shove and the guy stumbled out from behind the crate. Seconds later he went down, caught in the sniper's view.

Quon saw what happened and aimed his gun at Finn, but I grabbed his arm, so the shot went wide. Looping an arm around Basia, Finn swept them both off the deck and into the water below.

Quon uttered a cry of frustration and yanked hard on my ponytail, pulling my head back. "You do something stupid like that again and I'll kill you."

"No you won't, Quon. You need me, remember?"

Quon shouted something in Chinese and two of his guys returned to us. Quon dragged me to my feet, using me as a shield in the front with two of them in the back.

He shouted to the tree line. "I don't know who you are or why you're shooting at us, but if even one more shot is fired, I'll kill her. Now we are going to head for that bus. If you try to stop us or interfere with us or the bus in any way, I will blow her away."

We waddled toward the bus. I held my breath, but no one shot at us. I tried to put myself in the mind of the sniper and calculate the odds of knocking off everyone around me and still leaving me alive.

When we got to the bus, Quon got in backward, still holding me in front of him. The other guys jumped on and we peeled out of the parking lot in a screech of tires.

The Chinese guys were talking rapidly among themselves and one spoke into a walkie-talkie. He shifted in his seat and said something to Quon, who nodded. He was sweating profusely and looked shaken.

He glared at me. "I may not kill you outright, but if you ever try anything like that again, I will hurt you in ways you can't possibly imagine. Do we have an understanding?"

I met his stare evenly. "I thought we weren't playing games, Quon. I think it's perfectly clear I will do everything in my power to undermine you, now and for the rest of my life, no matter what you threaten to do to me. Do we have an understanding?"

His glare intensified. "When we get to that airplane, you'd better be a good girl and follow my directions exactly or that pain will start sooner than you think."

Quon barked an order to the guy in the front passenger seat and he spoke into the walkie-talkie. I presumed they were making takeoff arrangements with the pilot and crew.

I stared out the window as the bus careened along the road. I thought of Finn and Basia and hoped they were okay. I had to believe that whoever had been shooting at the Chinese in that tree line would help them get to safety.

We passed a couple of buildings before the bus finally screeched to a halt on a tarmac next to an airplane with the movable stairs already attached. The armed guys jumped out and surrounded the plane, keeping their guns aimed out.

Quon pulled me toward him, keeping the gun pressed against my neck as we climbed off the bus. He held me as a human shield as we went up the stairs. No one shot at us.

Quon gave an audible sigh of relief when we stepped into the cockpit. He lowered the gun, pushing me into a seat.

"Get us the hell out of here now," he snapped to the figure standing in the cockpit.

The man turned around, and I cried out.

Quon took a step back, surprise crossing his face.

"Hello, Quon," Slash said. "I've been looking forward to meeting you for a very long time."

# FIFTY-TWO

SLASH LAUNCHED HIMSELF at Quon. The momentum drove them both to the floor with a hard thud. He chopped at Quon's hand, forcing him to release the gun. I considered trying to get it, but they were rolling around so much I worried about getting in the way.

Although he was a hacker, Quon apparently knew how to fight, too, because he was having some success in defending himself from Slash's blows. Quon nearly choked Slash as he brought his ankles up around Slash's neck. Slash got his hands inside at the last moment and forced Quon's legs open. Once free, Slash rolled and smashed his fist into Quon's jaw several times, until Quon went limp.

His face dark, Slash stood, dragging Quon up by his armpits. He yanked on the strap of the bag with the briefcase, pulling it over Quon's head and tossing it at my feet.

I shook my head. "Wow. You could have just shot him, you know."

Slash assessed me, relief apparent in his eyes. "I know. But it wouldn't have been nearly as satisfying. I can't tell you how good it is to see you, *cara*. How badly are you injured?"

"Despite my hideous appearance, I'm fine."

"He hurt you."

He looked so furious and terrified, I tried to keep

my voice light. "Honestly, the conversation with Quon wasn't much fun, but I don't think he broke anything that wasn't already broken."

Nope. That hadn't helped. I saw murder in his expression. I put a hand on Slash's bicep. "I'm okay, really. Some of these injuries are from the plane crash. I'm not exactly looking my best."

His expression softened as he leaned over and gently kissed my cheek. "I've never seen a more beautiful sight. Thank God you're alive."

I wished I could throw my arms around his neck and hold on to him, but we still weren't out of danger. For now it had to be enough to just stand near him.

There was a cry from the bathroom. "Hey, is everything okay out there?"

"Stand by, please," Slash said.

I gave Slash a confused look. "Who the heck is that?"

"That's a couple of FBI agents in the bathroom."

"You locked the FBI in the bathroom?" My mouth dropped open.

"I didn't lock them in. They agreed to remain there, as a personal favor to me, so I could have a private welcome meeting with Quon."

"*That* was a private meeting?"

"*That* was the best kind of meeting and one that was in their best interest not to see."

The coldness of his expression chilled me as he stared at Quon. "Well, you'd better tell the agents to come out," I said. "There are more armed Chinese guys outside."

"It's okay, *cara*." Slash shifted his hold on Quon. "The rest of the security team should have secured them by now."

I went to the window and peered out. Sure enough

the Chinese were already on the ground being cuffed by several men in dark jackets. Hooray for the FBI.

I looked over my shoulder at Slash. "What took you so long to find us?"

"Would you believe me if I told you technological problems?"

"Seriously?" My eyes widened in disbelief.

"Seriously."

"I can't wait to hear all about it, but Finn and Basia are still at the dock. We have to make sure they're okay."

"They're safe."

Relief swept through me. "Oh, thank goodness. Who was that at the dock? The FBI?"

"No. I only had a small security detail with me and they are all here. The dock encounter was not an official part of the plan. I had a couple of friends helping me out there."

I lifted an eyebrow. "Friends?"

A smile touched his lips.

Quon moaned as he came around. Blood pooled at the corner of his mouth where it had made contact on several occasions with Slash's fist.

Slash looked down at him. "Let's go, Quon."

A dazed and frightened expression crossed Quon's face. "Where are we going?"

"Outside. It's time for more of our professional discussion in private."

"No. Don't kill me."

Slash ignored his protests and wrangled Quon out of the airplane hatch to the top of the staircase. Before descending, Slash glanced over his shoulder at me. "Tell the agents they can come out of the bathroom now. I'll be right back."

I didn't know where he was going and what exactly the "discussion" would entail, but it was out of my hands now.

I headed toward the bathroom. "Don't worry, Slash. I'm not going anywhere."

SLASH TOLD ME the FBI had arranged for a pilot to fly the plane with us in it to Port Moresby where the plane would be confiscated by authorities. ComQuest had been notified of our rescue, as had Elvis and Xavier. Basia and Finn were reunited with us on the plane before take-off, along with Slash's two friends.

I recognized the first friend the moment he stepped onto the plane.

"Tito!"

I stood there gaping at him until he crossed the distance between us and crushed me in a big hug. "Hey, Lexi. How are you? I haven't seen you since Rome."

Tito was here all the way from Europe. My mind worked to process that. "What are you doing here?"

Tito jerked his thumb toward Slash, who leaned against the hull, arms crossed watching us. "Well, Nico invited me to an all-expense-paid holiday in Jakarta to hang out with him while his girlfriend was busy working. Sounds good, yah?"

Tito had called Slash "Nico" since the two of them had worked together at the Vatican. I looked over at Slash, who grinned and shrugged.

"Except there was no holiday," Tito continued. "Instead the minute we arrived, it was a security operation all the way. He had me and Giorgio on sniper duty."

I shook my head, confused. "Who's Giorgio?"

As if I'd summoned him, a dark-haired man stepped

into the cabin. He looked like a male model with wavy, dark hair, a broad chest, blue eyes and a square, unshaven jaw. Dressed in a tight white T-shirt and jeans, he headed straight for me. He took my hand and pressed a lingering kiss on it.

"I am honored to finally meet you," he said in accented English, looking deeply into my eyes. "The beautiful, enigmatic Lexi Carmichael."

His white teeth sparkled and his face was so perfect that I could only stare in wonder.

"Ah, ah..." I stuttered, my train of thought completely leaving the station without me in it.

"Careful, Gio," Slash murmured.

Giorgio laughed and, to my astonishment, pulled me in for a hug. "Ah, I've long wondered about the woman who has stolen my brother's heart so completely. And now I finally get to meet her."

I pulled back, snapping my fingers. "Giorgio. Wait. You're Slash's younger brother."

He released me and gave a small bow. "The one and only."

Basia fanned herself. "Oh, my. Do you have any more brothers, Slash? Because I'm not sure my heart can take it without advance notice."

I struggled to get my mind around it. "Wait. Slash invited you to Jakarta, too?"

Giorgio nodded. "Who can say no to a weeklong stay in Jakarta? I came because I always do what my older brother tells me to do. Except when it involves women. Then I have my own methods."

Tito clapped Giorgio on the back. "Gio is a member of the Italian special ops. He's a much better shot than me, so a lot of that fancy shooting at the dock was mostly his."

"Well, I certainly appreciate the effort." I said. "Thanks for not shooting me."

Giorgio laughed and shot a glance at his brother. "I like her."

Slash walked over to me, slid an arm around my waist and kissed the top of my head. "Good. Just as long as you remember whose girl she is."

I leaned my head against Slash's shoulder. "All yours," I said.

## FIFTY-THREE

SLASH SAT NEXT to me on the airplane, his hand on my leg, as we took off for Port Moresby. Before takeoff, we'd been interviewed by the FBI and plied with food and drink. Despite my certain dehydration and hunger, I was only able to manage a little food and water. But I kept the water bottle in my lap taking sips as often as I could.

Slash wouldn't leave my side. He kept touching me, as if to remind himself I was really there. He'd been somewhat quiet since he'd returned from his "discussion" with Quon.

When I asked about Quon's fate, Slash said it had been taken care of and I shouldn't worry any longer. His frown indicated the subject was closed and off-limits.

"What's important is that we'll have an ambulance standing by to take you, Basia and Finn to the hospital when we land," he said.

I wasn't going to have any part of that. "You can take me to the hospital for observation, Slash, but I'm not staying there for any extended period of time. I need to get to Jakarta. I have to finish this for Elvis and Xavier. It's that important."

"Your life is important."

"I know, and you just helped save it. But I'm *not* going to let the Red Guest stop this process. I'm serious."

Slash stared at me as if figuring a way to argue and then kissed my forehead. "Okay, but if you're going, then *we're* going. ComQuest is just going to have to bring me up to speed. But an initial trip to the hospital is non-negotiable. Otherwise, it's no deal."

"Deal, but then we're heading on."

"I'm going to Jakarta, too," Finn leaned forward, apparently listening to our conversation. "If she's finishing it, so am I."

"Me, too." Basia leaned over Finn's shoulder. "We're a team. No way you guys are leaving me behind now. I can translate just fine with one arm."

"*Si*, I'm in, too," Giorgio said, flashing white teeth. "I'm with you, brother."

"Yah. All for one," Tito added. "Let's get this done."

A lump formed in my throat. I looked around at them and wondered how I ever imagined I could live my life without friends and family. I could see Slash was touched, too, even if no one but me noticed.

"Okay," I said. "We'll all go. I'll see what I can do. Given the circumstances, I think I can convince ComQuest to permit all of us to provide an assist."

Once that was decided, I leaned back in my seat. Slash bent over, rummaging around in a dark green duffle bag at his feet. He pulled something out, handing it to me.

I stared at it in surprise. "A laptop? Slash, you brought me a laptop?" I clutched it reverently to my chest.

"Brand new and loaded with all the bells and whistles."

I turned and cupped his cheek. "Thank you so much. I don't know what to say. I've missed mine so much."

"I know."

"But not as much as I missed you." I looked into his eyes. "I mean it. When I was about to drown, I wasn't thinking of my computer, cyberspace or gaming, Slash. I was thinking of you and how much you mean to me."

He closed his eyes for a moment. "*Mio Dio*, I almost lost you. Again." He slid his hand around the back of my neck and pulled me in for a kiss. His lips moved across mine gently and with care not to aggravate my injuries. His thoughtfulness and tenderness undid me.

I touched his scratchy cheeks and smiled. "Guess you were right about that little black cloud following me around like a stalker. But, you know what? I'm finding I'm pretty resistant to rain...as long as I have a little help from my friends, that is."

As he kissed me again, I could feel his lips curve into a smile of his own.

After he released me, I rested my head against the seat, finally able to relax. I stroked the cover of the laptop with my fingers.

"Open it," he urged.

"No." I folded my hands on top of it. "Not yet. We still have to talk. You do know Quon and the Chinese were after you the whole time, right?"

"*Si.*" His entire posture stiffened, his hands curling into fists.

"When did you find out?"

"Shortly before you arrived at the plane with Quon. We had a little talk with one of the crew. They said their orders were to bring you alive so they could lure the real prize to them. It didn't take me long to figure out what they had in mind. Tell me the truth. How badly did he hurt you?"

"Not as badly as he could have. I suspect he didn't want to damage me too badly."

Slash's jaw was clenched so tightly, I put a hand on his arm to calm him.

"I'm okay. I promise," I said softly. "I knew you'd come for me, so it made everything bearable. How did you finally find us, Slash? Were you able to pick up the GPS locator on the briefcase?"

He closed his eyes. "It didn't work."

*"What?"* I shifted sideways in my seat, staring at him in astonishment. "You have got to be joking."

"I'm not. The GPS must have been damaged in the crash. It stopped working shortly after you went down."

"That's impossible. I thought the briefcase was indestructible."

"Whatever is in it, yes. But, according to Xavier, the GPS locator was positioned on the inside frame. It must have been knocked so hard it stopped working."

I remembered how we'd clung to the briefcase as if it were our lives. I'd almost drowned trying to retrieve it. And the whole time the GPS locator wasn't even working.

I pressed a hand to my forehead. "Wow. That's just shocking." I paused and then looked at Slash. He was waiting for my question. "Wait. If the GPS locator wasn't working, how did you find us?"

He hesitated. "You're not going to like it."

"I'm not?"

"No, you're not. But I'm not sorry. You're alive and that's all that matters."

Puzzled, I cocked my head. "Slash?"

He removed his hand from my leg. "No easy way to say it. I put GPS locators in your earrings."

*"You did what?"*

"Your earrings are mini transmitters." His expression was pained. "The locator works flawlessly in most locations on earth that have access to Wi-Fi or a cellular network. Which means, of course, you ended up in the uncharted jungle of Papua New Guinea where they were completely useless. I've got to work that kink out next. I have to either give them enough power to reach a satellite...or not let you get out of range of cell towers ever again."

I was confused. "Wait. So, did you or didn't you track me with the earrings?"

"Not until you reached an area with Wi-Fi."

It took me a minute to catch up. "Wasu. You picked up my signal in Wasu."

"*Si*. We were already in Papua New Guinea doing flybys on helicopters because that was the last known signal from the briefcase. But we didn't dare ask for direct assistance from the local authorities because we were afraid of tipping off Quon. So, my own small FBI security detail, Tito and Giorgio took matters into our own hands."

I studied him. "Once the earrings activated, how did you track me, Slash? I'm pretty sure you didn't bring that kind of monitoring equipment with you."

He smiled. "I had three pretty sharp interns back in DC assisting me."

"Piper, Wally and Brandon?"

"Exactly."

I reached up and touched the earring in my left ear. "So, you hid locators in my earrings?"

"I gave you fresh batteries just before you left. I'm sorry, *cara*. I kept waiting for a good time to tell you. But every time I imagined how the conversation would go, it didn't end well. In the end, my concern for your safety outweighed the risk that you would refuse to wear them. Given your proclivity to wind up in dangerous situations I thought it the best way to protect you. Not that you can't protect yourself, it's just I thought—"

I interrupted him mid-sentence by grabbing a fistful of his T-shirt with one hand and yanking him to me. I kissed him hard. When I pulled away, he looked at me in surprise.

"You're not angry?"

"No. I'm grateful. However, had it been anyone else or had I been suspect of your motives, it would have been another story. But we're talking about you, Slash. I trust you with my life. I love you. The earrings were a pretty good idea. Knowing my location in this case saved all of our lives and I really appreciate that." I took his hand. "Now, that being said, I ask only that from now on you tell me these kinds of things in advance. If we love each other, then we shouldn't be afraid to tell each other important things, especially when it involves our physical safety. Either we take the next step together or we don't. Someone I love once told me that relationships either evolve or they wither and die. This is a good example of how we have to share things with each other, okay?"

He lifted my hand to his lips murmuring. *"Nessuno può prendere quella destinata per te."*

I smiled against his chest. "What did you say this time?"

"I said, *'No one can take the one that is destined for you.'* We Italians like our proverbs."

"You think I'm destined for you?"

"I do not think it, *cara*. I *know* it. The biggest challenge was figuring out what to do about it."

"Oh. So, you've figured it all out?"

A smile touched his lips. "Actually, I think I have." He pressed his lips to my forehead and wrapped his arms around my waist.

I clung to him, closing my eyes. We'd been through so much together and we'd likely go through a lot more. It amazed me that I still looked forward to it—to being with him. Love was certainly an illogical thing. It baffled me still that I could so willingly accept my life would be intertwined with his needs and struggles—just as he was by me. Love wasn't a burden. It was an honor.

I tightened my arms around him. "So, Slash, when are you going to share this newfound wisdom with me?"

"Soon," he promised. "Very soon."

## FIFTY-FOUR

THE PARTY LASTED into the wee hours of the night. Avanti's pizza, beer, champagne and chocolate cake. The Zimmerman home was full of friends and littered with beer bottles and empty pizza boxes.

Xavier, who had drunk perhaps a few too many beers, stood on a chair in the middle of the room waving a champagne flute.

"I'd like to offer a toast. Here's to the future of technology and to my friends who helped make it happen. We couldn't have done it without you. Mass production of the chip begins in two months. We're a go."

We cheered wildly and Elvis reached up to slap his brother a high-five, sloshing champagne over his hand and laughing.

Grinning, I lifted my glass to Xavier and drained the rest of my champagne. I was feeling pretty tipsy, my stomach was full and my heart was happy.

I glanced around the room. Slash was talking to Basia, who lounged in a chair, sipping champagne with one hand, her other arm in a sling. Finn held court with Piper and Brandon about something, possibly soccer. He was pretending to kick something and my two interns were laughing wildly. Bonnie, Elvis's apparently on-again girlfriend, was perched on the corner of Xavier's desk, eating a piece of pizza and chatting with Xavier.

Wally, my other intern, stood to my right looking at my champagne glass with envy.

"Come on, Lexi. I'm almost twenty-one." Wally leaned over and took a sniff of my empty glass. "Can't I have just one drink?"

I moved my glass away from his nose. "You're eighteen. That's not almost twenty-one."

"I'm not going to get drunk."

"Not on my watch, you won't."

Sighing, he walked away, most likely to try and persuade someone else to pour him a glass.

Elvis spotted me alone, so he came over, his blue eyes alight and happy. Dressed in blue jeans and a dark green T-shirt, he seemed relaxed and poised. A quiet confidence seemed to surround him. He was healing from his encounter with Broodryk, just as I would come to terms with what Quon had done to me.

"I can't believe you did it, Lexi," he said. "You saved not only the microchip and the microfluid, but Basia and Finn, as well. Then you successfully executed the manufacturing process."

"I didn't do *any* of that alone. It was a true team effort. To be perfectly honest, it was Sari, not me, who saved us and salvaged the future of the microchip. Who would have guessed that the advancement of such an important technological invention would hinge on the kindness of a stranger who had never even seen a computer before?"

Elvis grinned. "True. It's both ironic and ultimately satisfying, the way of the universe. Still, I don't know how to thank you for your part."

"Yes, you do. Like this." I set my champagne glass on the table and gave him a hug.

He hugged me back and whispered in my ear. "I never

wanted you to risk your life for that chip. You knew that, right?"

"I knew. But sometimes we take all kinds of risks for our friends and the people we love. And, in this case, for the future of technology. What you and Xavier have accomplished—it's amazing and worth defending."

I paused, keeping my gaze on his as he pulled back. "Elvis, I hope you don't mind that I gave Sari your grandmother's locket as a way to pay it forward."

"I don't mind at all, Lexi." His blue eyes filled with emotion. "I'm sure my grandmother is smiling down at us right now. You passed it on and for exactly the right reason. It's the true purpose of the locket and you used it as she did. She'd be proud of you—just as I am. I'm so very thankful to Sari for your life and theirs." He dipped his head toward Finn and Basia. "It's a new start and a new direction for all of us."

I heard a laugh and realized it was Bonnie. She was chatting with Xavier, looking pretty in jeans and a fuzzy blue sweater. I turned to Elvis with a question in my eyes.

Elvis followed my gaze and understood what I was thinking. "Yeah, we're good, Bonnie and me."

"I figured." I leaned back, put my hands in my pockets. "So, what happened with Ginger?"

"Ginger and I parted ways. Seems we couldn't see eye to eye on anything."

"Wow. That's a total surprise. Are you going to tell me what was up with that?"

His cheeks reddened. "It was stupid. No, *I* was stupid." He looked down, scuffed his shoe on the carpet. "I decided I needed to catch up to where I thought a man my age should be…you know, with women."

"You thought you had to define yourself by your sexual experience?"

"Why not?" He lifted his eyes to meet mine. "It was as good a way as any. Broodryk almost killed me, and I realized then that I hadn't even lived yet. I didn't know who I was or what I wanted out of life. So, I decided to face my biggest fear first. Thought I might as well go for it."

"Are we still talking about sex?"

He laughed. "No, we're talking about women. Look, Bonnie and I are working on things. It's totally new and scary territory for me. But I'm hopeful, especially since I have my best friend as a wingman for advice if I need it."

"Wing *woman*."

His grin widened. "I stand corrected."

"I'm glad for you, Elvis. Really."

"I know. That means a lot."

Suddenly Basia climbed onto the chair Xavier had recently exited. Xavier held her champagne glass and she clinked it with a spoon to get everyone's attention. Elvis slung an arm around me as we watched her in amusement.

"Excuse me, excuse me. I'd like to have everyone's attention." Basia swayed on the chair, so Xavier put a hand on her leg to steady her. "I have a very important announcement to make."

She took a deep breath, grabbed her champagne flute from Xavier and drained it. She wiped her mouth with the back of her hand and handed it, and the spoon, back to him.

"Okay, I know this may run counter to a time-honored tradition, but I'd like to take the opportunity to do this in front of everyone I love." She looked down at Xavier. "Xavier Zimmerman, will you marry me?"

Xavier was so shocked the champagne flute slipped from his fingers and shattered to the floor.

For the longest moment of my life, time seemed suspended as Xavier stared at Basia. Then he scooped her off the chair and into his arms. "Hell yes, I will. I will! Oh, God, please tell me I'm not dreaming."

The entire room erupted into cheers. Elvis and I hugged each other again, laughing.

I'd never seen the smile that lit Basia's face as she turned to me, still safely held in Xavier's embrace.

"And Lexi, I want you to be my maid of honor."

Now everyone in the room turned toward me. I should have been thrilled, honored and excited. Instead, I could feel the color draining from my face.

"What? Me? A maid of honor?"

"Will you, Lexi?" she asked. "Will you stand next to me on the happiest day of my life?"

I swallowed hard. "Of course, I will, Basia. I wouldn't miss it for the world."

Everyone surrounded the happy couple, congratulating and hugging them while I stood there paralyzed, one thought running through my head.

Holy wedding cake. Did that mean I had to plan a bachelorette party?

# FIFTY-FIVE

I SHIFTED THE overnight bag on my shoulder as we walked through the garage to Slash's apartment. "I'm glad we're spending the night at your place, Slash. I like it here."

He stopped, staring at me. "Are you wearing leather boots?"

I looked down at my feet, most of the boots hidden by my raincoat. "Yes. Yes, I am."

"With red soles?"

I shrugged. "They go with my outfit."

He took two steps and put his fingers on the top button of my raincoat. "What outfit?"

I swatted at his hand. "Hands off. Let's get inside first."

We rode the elevator to his apartment, but he didn't take his eyes off me. He unlocked the door and ushered me in. Tapping out the code on his alarm, he flipped on the lights, letting the door close behind him.

"Home, sweet home," he said. "At least for a little while longer."

"Why only a little while?"

"The FBI believes my location has been compromised. I'm going to have to move again."

"Oh, I'm sorry, Slash." I set my bag down and fiddled with the belt on my raincoat. "It's my fault. I made you bring me here. That's how this all started."

He cupped the back of my neck, pulling me in to him.

His dark eyes were serious. "Don't be sorry. I'm not. It was worth it if it means being close to you. But now you understand the risk of being with me."

I smiled and said nothing.

"What?" He narrowed his eyes. "Why are you smiling?"

"Well, all this time I was thinking my involvement with you put you in danger. Every time we go into the police station or get interviewed by the FBI, CIA or NSA, I worry it's only a matter of time before they put out a hit on me themselves in order to protect you from me. At the same time, you've been worried your involvement with me puts me in danger."

"I am. Look at what just happened and tell me I'm wrong."

I touched his cheek with my hand, felt the stubble of his beard beneath the pads of my fingers. "It turns out we're both right. This is just the nature of our work. National security is no longer being fought only on the battlefield. We're on the front lines of world security now—people like you and me. *That's* who we are, and *that's* what we do. You've been saying it all along. I understand now why you're so guarded, Slash. Our jobs put not only us in danger, but the people we love. So to keep them safe, we stay alone. I'm sorry it took me so long to understand that's a big part of the reason why you've hesitated to share parts of your life with me."

Slash placed his forehead against mine and we stood there for a moment in silence. "I'm not alone with you," he finally murmured. "Never."

"No, you're not." I took a deep breath. "I want you to know I understand and accept the risks of being with you. I'm with you because I want to be—danger and all.

But it goes both ways, okay? Little black cloud and me, remember? I'm no walk in the park to be with either."

He laughed softly. "Ah, *cara*, how I adore you."

I took his hand. "Come on. I have a surprise for you."

He lifted an eyebrow. "For me?"

"Yes. Would you mind taking my bag back to the bedroom?"

"Of course." Holding my bag, he headed down the hall. I followed him. He set my bag on the bed and when he turned around, I unbuttoned my raincoat and let it slip to the floor.

Slash took a step backward, his expression a mix of shock and surprise. His lips wavered as though collecting his thoughts, but all that slipped out was *"Cara?"*

I glanced down to make sure I hadn't dislodged any part of the black leather dominatrix mini-dress I'd ordered off the internet. The front V, barely held together with black leather strings, plunged to my navel. Everything looked good, so I shifted to display the leather back, which barely fit over my butt and had the same plunging V.

Slash's expression shifted from surprise to, well, confusion. Not at all what I'd expected.

I tried not to let it unnerve me. I stood confidently, dominantly, and pretended not to be worried I wasn't meeting his expectations. Instead I stretched out my arms to accentuate the black leather bindings from my elbows to my wrists, and casually shifted my legs farther apart so the dark fishnet stockings attached to a pair of barely-there underwear stood out. Leaning forward, I slowly stroked the riding crop in my hand up the side of one leather stiletto boot that reached just over my kneecap and pursed my lips at him in what I hoped was the same sexy, sultry expression the online model had worn.

Now his brows raised and he gave me something akin to a wicked smile…at least I hoped it was that and not a stomachache from our spicy dinner or the little show I was putting on for him.

I cracked the riding crop. The sound was overly loud in the room. "Are you ready for this, Slash?" I put one hand on my hip and lowered my voice. "Lick my toes. Now."

I was beyond nervous by this point, but I knew the most important part of the roleplaying was confidence, so I kept my gaze steely and my mouth set in a firm line.

Slash opened his mouth, shut it, and then tried to say something again without success. My confidence began to flag.

Finally he held up a time-out signal with his hands. "Okay, I'm not sure what precipitated this, and honestly I'm *beyond* intrigued at this development, but why? I know this has to be way out of your comfort zone."

Sighing, I strode over to the bed and sat down. He sat down next to me. I put the riding crop across my lap and fiddled with the lash.

"I just wanted you to know I'm ready for the Red Room. I know I'm not the most experienced woman in terms of sexual experimentation and exploring my femininity and all of that, but if you want to try it, I'm all for it. If it's important to you, it's important to me."

Slash picked up the crop and studied it. "Exactly what Red Room are you talking about?"

I pointed toward his hallway. "That one."

"You thought I had a Red Room in there?"

"You don't?"

His lips twitched and then he started to laugh. He laughed so hard tears leaked from his eyes.

I rose from the bed. "Fine. I take it all of this means that is *not* a Red Room."

He tried to say something and then erupted into more laughter. I watched in astonishment. Finally he managed to gain control of himself and wiped at the tears at his eyes.

I crossed my arms against my chest. "Okay, fine. You can stop laughing now. I'll just take this off."

I turned away, but his hand snaked out, his fingers circling around my leather glove. His expression was still amused, but now I saw something glittering in his eyes.

"You certainly will not." He paused to catch his breath. "I'm not laughing at you, *cara*. I'm laughing at how my stubbornness caused this misunderstanding. Trust me, I've a lot more to say on this subject. But first I want you to know how touched I am you love me enough to do this. Since I know you, I'm certain this involved a lot of research—including buying the outfit and equipment—and practicing. That alone pleases me more than I can adequately express and is perhaps the most thoughtful thing anyone has ever done for me."

I studied him. "Really? Because in all honesty, Slash, I'm not sure about this BDSM roleplaying thing. I'm okay with bossing you around. I think I could be good at that. But I'm pretty certain I'm going to come out of the role or forget all the lines I memorized. I'm more nervous than expected. Not to mention the pain thing. I did create a proper spreadsheet containing the velocity for the whip and the potential pain thresholds, depending on the activity, and committed them to memory." I pulled out a tiny folded piece of paper I'd tucked between my breasts and handed it to him. "I'm just not sure I could trust myself to do it correctly, you know, in the heat of the moment. Sometimes my brain doesn't work properly when you do…well, what you do. I don't want you to get injured because I'm clumsy."

He looked like he might start laughing again, but instead he ran a finger down the V of my dress letting it rest just above my navel. "There's one thing you should know. I would never hurt you. Never. And despite this misunderstanding, I'm finding this entire situation quite stimulating." He slid his hand over my arm and down to my hip where he let it rest. "But first I want to show you what's in that room."

I took a step back. "No, Slash, you don't have to. This wasn't meant to force you into revealing what's in that room. I sincerely thought it was a sex room. I'm serious. If I'm not ready for whatever is in there, then I respect your judgment."

He shook his head. "I'm sorry I ever gave you the impression that you weren't ready. That's on me. What's in that room is not about you and your readiness. It's about mine. It's my reluctance, until now, to let my guard down even with you—the person I love."

"I don't understand."

"You will. The time is finally right for me. This is what I've wanted to share with you. Come with me. Please."

I hesitated and then followed. There was something in his expression—an openness I hadn't seen before. I wasn't sure what to make of it, but I trusted him.

Slash reached into his pocket and pulled out his keys. After selecting one, he put it in the lock and turned the doorknob. To my surprise, the door opened outward instead of inward. Behind the first door was another door, a steel door with a biometric pad, a numeric password and what looked like a retinal scan.

I looked at him in surprise. "Wow. I totally didn't see that coming. A safe room?"

He endured the dual retinal scan before he spoke. "Yes." He tapped in a code and said something in Italian. I presumed it was a voice imprint. We waited until there was a quiet click.

The door opened.

Slash paused, taking my hand and looking into my eyes.

"Are you ready?"

I squeezed his hand. "As long as you are."

# FIFTY-SIX

THE ROOM WAS DARK, but Slash bypassed the light switch
and tapped out a code on another pad. This one turned
on a set of dim lighting on the floor. It was just enough
to let us see where we were going without tripping over
anything.

He led me to an armchair. "Sit, please."

Curious, I sat, not making a sound. I tried to make
out the shapes and shadows in the room without much
success. Slash walked around the room and little lights
sprang up. He was lighting candles.

Giving up on trying to figure out what he was doing,
I tried to relax and sat back in the chair, waiting. My
pulse skittered, but it wasn't with fear or anxiety. It was
anticipation. Slash was going to show me a part of himself that he'd never shared before and I had no idea what
to expect.

The candles flickered as he sat down.

The first bars of music drifted through the room. Astonishment swept through me. Slash was playing the
piano. Given the dark room, he wasn't reading music
either. He played from his heart.

The first notes were soft and tender, exquisitely emotional. I sat transfixed as the music filled the room. The
melody was at once sweet and uplifting until it changed
into fiery and fervent chords and rifts. A dichotomy

of poetry and passion—discordance and peace. As the first song ended and the last note faded away, he finally spoke.

"*Cara*, come here."

I rose from my chair and walked toward him. Candles flickered on the piano as I approached. He patted the bench next to him.

I sat down, our shoulders and thighs touching. As I suspected, there was no sheet music, just an empty stand. His eyes closed as he began playing another song, this one surprisingly sensual. His elegant hacker hands moved across the piano keys much like I'd seen them work a computer keyboard. His fingers stroked and caressed. The flickering lights of the candle cast shadows on his cheeks framed by the dark strands of his hair that slipped across his shoulders.

It took me a minute to understand. He was making love to me with the music. The sensations flowing through my body were strikingly similar to those I felt when he touched and kissed me. I watched him mesmerized. The music soared, softened and descended into erotic whispers. He built so masterfully to the climatic finish that when we reached it, I could hardly breathe. I was awash in an erotic, sensual cocoon fashioned by the man I loved. When the last note faded away I was so overcome, I couldn't say a word.

Slash put his hands on his lap, looked straight ahead. "I came into this world through music."

I studied his face, high cheekbones, square jaw and firm, sensual lips—a man with a passionate beauty and inherent strength.

"Father Armando found me inside the church, beneath the piano and wrapped in a blue blanket. He was playing the music of his favorite pianist, Hai Tsang, when he heard the crying. He thinks I was just a few days old."

I didn't know what to say, what I *could* say. So I said nothing.

"It was a rural province and the weather was foul, so it took two days for a social worker to come for me. Father cared for me with some infant formula from the church pantry, soothing me with the sounds of Tsang's music. When they came to get me, the bond had already been formed."

I wasn't sure if he referred to a bond between he and Tsang or he and Father Armando, but I wasn't sure it mattered.

"They placed me with a foster family, and I dropped off the radar for seven years. Father Armando tried to find me for those seven years, but I'd disappeared along with the family who'd agreed to foster me. Father never gave up. Through his persistence, the police finally found me in a hospital in Sperlonga. I didn't speak and I had no idea who I was or where I came from. To this day I have not a single memory of my life before age seven."

My heart broke into tiny pieces for him. I had no idea of the pain he'd been through.

"The nurses in the hospital were kind to me. One particular nurse was so beautiful I was convinced she was an angel. Her hands were soft and her eyes held a kindness I'd never seen before. I responded to her like I'd never responded to anyone else. When it came time for me to be discharged from the hospital and taken to the orphanage, she offered to take me in. She was a widow with a nine-year-old son of her own, barely making ends meet, but from that moment on I belonged to her. Her name was Juliette and she is my mother."

I reached over, took his hand and squeezed it, still not trusting myself to speak. I needed to let him get through this, but I wanted him to know I was with him every step of the way.

"It took me two more years before I spoke my first word," he continued. "I was extremely guarded and resistant to touch, so the schools didn't know what to do with me. They placed me in a classroom for autistic children. It was the perfect educational setting for me at the time because it was a safe environment. No one pressured me to talk, the students were disarmingly innocent, and the teachers were kind and supportive. I could excel at my own pace. I became fascinated with the minds of the autistic children. In many ways, I had a lot in common with them—excellent memory and retrieval skills, a fascination with numbers and code, and an analytical mind. My label as autistic opened me up to bullying, but I learned how to use my smarts to outwit them. It also helped that I wasn't one to shy away from a fight. I spent more time than I should have studying and mastering techniques in that area. After a couple of fights, I didn't have any more problems. I also became the self-appointed protector for anyone bullying the special kids at my school."

I finally found my voice. "I'm so sorry, Slash."

"I'm not complaining. I know I'm one of the lucky ones. My mother eventually found a new and decent man to love. That man became my father and they gave me my younger brother Giorgio. I'm close to my brothers, but not as close as I should be. My relationship with you has taught me many things, but perhaps among the most important is that in order to let people in, I have to let my guard down. Even with members of my own family. Otherwise I will always be alone."

I leaned my head against his shoulder. "You've excelled at everything in your life. I see why. You are driven."

"Perhaps. Meeting you has changed my life. You've helped me to see what I want from this life and what I have to risk to get it."

I understood where he was coming from even if I hadn't really grasped that at the beginning of our relationship. "Likewise, Slash. What I learned from my experience in the jungle is that life is not just *who* we are, but the relationships we have. This relationship has become that important to me, more than I ever thought possible. *You* are important."

"Thank you," he murmured, sliding his arm around me and pulling me close.

"What about Father Armando?" I tipped my face toward him. "Are you still in touch with him?"

"Of course. He's now the Archbishop of Genoa."

I paused, my fingers touching the cool wood of the piano. There was still something I didn't quite understand. "So, why do you keep your piano behind a steel reinforced door? You play so beautifully."

He shifted on the bench and took both of my hands in his. The candlelight illuminated the curve of his cheek while casting the rest of his face in shadow. "This room is soundproof. The truth is I didn't want to share my music with anyone…until I met you."

Tears pricked my eyes and I swallowed hard. "I'm… honored."

He cupped my chin and kissed me. It was a kiss that held a promise of a lot more to come.

When he lifted his mouth from mine, he smiled. "However, in the spirit of full disclosure, this room also holds all of my disguises, false papers and passports, as well as unregistered computers and equipment."

"Ha. Good thinking."

We both laughed and in that moment of release I looked at him hopefully. "So, Slash, I've been meaning to ask you a favor."

"No." He said it without hesitation.

"What?" I stared at him in shock. "Wait. You don't even know what I'm going to ask!"

"I'm afraid I do." I could hear the amusement in his voice.

"Then what?" I challenged. "Seriously, now you have to guess."

He stood, offering a hand and helping me off the bench. In the dim light, I could see he was still smiling. "You want me to help with the bachelorette party."

Okay, that level of accuracy was frightening. "How did you know?"

"You've been worried sick about it ever since Basia asked you to be her maid of honor." He kissed me on the nose.

"You won't help?" I pouted. "Just a little?"

"Not even a little." He chuckled. "If you can survive a plane crash and several days in the jungle without technology, surely you can plan a girl party on your own. I have the utmost faith in you."

"Shoot. I was afraid you'd say that." I sighed. "I've never planned a party before, let alone a bachelorette party. This is going to be a lot harder than I thought."

Slash lifted my chin up and stared into my eyes. "I'm certain about one thing, *cara*. Whatever you do, you'll be just fine."

# EPILOGUE

JIANG SHI WAS neck deep in a complex crack against the US's Transportation Security Administration's internal network when he heard a soft knock on the door. Irritated, he tore his gaze away from the data scrolling across his screen. How many times had he told them not to disturb him when he was engaged in a delicate operation?

"Enter," he barked.

One of his male assistants entered, bowing and looking extremely nervous. Good. They obeyed him better when they were afraid. He held a small package in his hands and thrust it out toward Shi.

"I'm sorry to interrupt you, sir. This just came for you. I thought you should see it right away."

Shi took the package. It was just bigger than his fist and quite light. It had been wrapped in brown paper, sealed with clear strapping tape and addressed to him at this address in clear block letters. There was no return address.

A twinge of concern shot through him. No one knew this address was associated with him except for those at the highest echelons of the Chinese government. Who would send a package to him here?

He took a pair of scissors from his desk and cut through the tape, unwrapping the outer paper. Inside was a small, white cardboard box. Carefully, he lifted the lid and reached in to pull out something wrapped in a tissue.

Shi unwound the tissue and then sat perfectly still, staring in shock at the contents of the package.

A silver coin.

His fingers trembling, Shi picked it up. Folded into a square beneath the coin was a small piece of paper. His hand shook as he unfolded it.

Printed by hand and in clear, neat block letters was written:

YOU'RE NEXT.

\* \* \* \* \*

# ABOUT THE AUTHOR

JULIE MOFFETT IS a bestselling author and writes in the genres of mystery, historical romance and paranormal romance. She has won numerous awards, including the 2014 Mystery & Mayhem Award for Best YA/New Adult Mystery, the prestigious 2014 HOLT Award for Best Novel with Romantic Elements, a HOLT Merit Award for Best Novel by a Virginia Author, a PRISM Award for Best Romantic Time-Travel and Best of the Best Paranormal Books of 2002, and the 2011 EPIC Award for Best Action/Adventure Novel. She has also garnered additional nominations for the Daphne du Maurier Award and the Gayle Wilson Award of Excellence.

Julie is a military brat (air force) and has traveled extensively. Her more exciting exploits include attending high school in Okinawa, Japan; backpacking around Europe and Scandinavia for several months; a year-long college graduate study in Warsaw, Poland; and a wonderful trip to Scotland and Ireland where she fell in love with castles, kilts and brogues.

Julie has a BA in political science and Russian language from Colorado College, an MA in international affairs from the George Washington University in Washington, DC, and an MEd from Liberty University. She has worked as a proposal writer, journalist, teacher, librarian and researcher. Julie speaks Russian and Polish and has two sons.

Visit Julie's website: www.juliemoffett.com

Follow Julie on social media:

Facebook: facebook.com/JulieMoffettAuthor
Twitter: @JMoffettAuthor
Instagram: instagram.com/julie_moffett/

# Get 2 Free Books,
## Plus 2 Free Gifts—
### just for trying the Reader Service!

# Get 2 Free Books,

## Plus 2 Free Gifts—

### just for trying the Reader Service!

# Get 2 Free Books,
## Plus 2 Free Gifts –

just for trying the *Reader Service!*

# READERSERVICE.COM

## Manage your account online!

- Review your order history
- Manage your payments
- Update your address

*We've designed the Reader Service website just for you.*

## Enjoy all the features!

- Discover new series available to you, and read excerpts from any series.
- Respond to mailings and special monthly offers.
- Browse the Bonus Bucks catalog and online-only exculsives.
- Share your feedback.

*Visit us at:*

## ReaderService.com

RS16R

# Get 2 Free Books,
## Plus 2 Free Gifts—
### just for trying the Reader Service!

WORLDWIDE LIBRARY®

# Get 2 Free Books,
## Plus 2 Free Gifts—
### just for trying the Reader Service!

LIS17R